This was crazy.

She'd just met the man, yet he did something to her that she couldn't quite put into words. Granted right now she was having a difficult time with any coherent thought other than "take your shirt off, cowboy."

He took a step closer, never looking away from her eyes, her mouth. "Your clothes are all wet again."

"They're your clothes," she countered.

The corner of his mouth tipped up. "Yours are dry now if you want to change."

She pulled in a deep breath, her breasts brushing against his chest. Had he closed the distance so tight or had she stepped forward? She'd been so mesmerized by his voice, his predatory gaze.

"Are you changing?" she asked.

Hayes reached behind his back and jerked the wet shirt up and over his head, tossing it onto the wood porch with a heavy smack. Ink covered his chest and up one shoulder. Dark hair glistened all over his pecs.

"You're not playing fair," she told him.

"Who said I was playing?"

He thrust his hands into her hair and covered her mouth before she could take a breath.

TAMING
THE TEXAN

BY
JULES BENNETT

First Published in Great Britain 2018
By Mills & Boon, an imprint of HarperCollins*Publishers*
1 London Bridge Street, London, SE1 9GF

© 2018 Jules Bennett

ISBN: 978-0-263-93585-1

51-0118

MIX
Paper from
responsible sources
FSC™ C007454
www.fsc.org

This book is produced from independently certified FSC™ paper to ensure responsible forest management.

For more information visit: www.harpercollins.co.uk/green

Printed and bound in Spain
by CPI, Barcelona

National bestselling author **Jules Bennett** has penned over forty contemporary romance novels. She lives in the Midwest with her high-school-sweetheart husband and their two kids. Jules can often be found on Twitter chatting with readers, and you can also connect with her via her website, www.julesbennett.com.

This book is for anyone who suffers from PTSD, depression, anxiety...please know you're not alone.

One

"What are you doing here, Ma'am?"

Alexa Rodriguez spun around, her hand to her heart. The low, gravelly voice had shocked her, but not as much as seeing the man strut toward her.

Well, he had a cowboy swagger with a slight limp, so she wouldn't quite call it a strut. Regardless of the label, the man held her attention and there was nowhere to go...not when she was pinned in place by that dark-as-night stare.

When she first stepped into the impressive stables on Pebblebrook Ranch, she hadn't seen a soul. And now this sexy cowboy stood only feet away, staring at her from beneath the wide brim of his black hat. Her heart shouldn't be beating so fast, so hard. But...yeah, he was one sexy stable hand.

Was she trespassing? The owner of the bed-and-breakfast next door had told Alexa the stables were open to B and B guests, but maybe there was some disconnect because this man did not look happy to have a visitor.

"I'm a guest next door," she explained as she tried to keep eye contact and not fidget. "I was told I could come ride and that someone would be here to assist me."

The stable hand grunted, but never took his eyes off her. Well, this was awkward.

Stepping out of her comfort zone was the theme of the weekend. Her meddling yet well-meaning best friend had bought Alexa a package for a three-night stay at the B and B, stating Alexa was an overworked single mom who deserved some alone time.

Alexa had just registered next door and put her bag in her room when she decided to check out the outdoor amenities before the predicted storm moved in. She hadn't been on a horse since she was five. Yeah, she was so far outside her comfort zone she didn't even know where comfort was anymore.

But if the horse came equipped with a captivating cowboy, maybe doing something different wouldn't be such a bad thing. Her best friend would definitely be thrilled Alexa was showing signs of life in the lust department, that was for sure.

This stable hand had sultry written all over him, from the dusty boots to the fitted denim over narrow hips to the black hat. And the way he drawled out the word *ma'am* had her stomach tingling.

Clearly, it had been too long since she'd had interaction with someone outside her preschool special education classroom and her fourteen-month-old son.

"You ever ridden before?" he finally asked.

"Once," she admitted, shoving her hands into the pockets of her jeans. "I was five and at a cousin's birthday party."

He took a step closer, minimizing the gap between them, and all the breath in Alexa's lungs seemed to vanish. How could one man be so striking, so bold? The deep eyes with long, dark lashes and a stubbled jaw outlining the most perfectly shaped lips...and that was all just his face.

Broad shoulders stretched his button-up black shirt in the most glorious way, one that had her imagining what excellent muscle tone he must have beneath the fabric. Those lean hips covered with well-worn denim could make any woman beg...but not her. She'd sworn off men who made her tingle—they were nothing but a hindrance in the life she'd carved out for her and her son.

And this man? He looked like pure trouble. The kind of trouble that could make a woman forget all common sense, the kind that would have a woman crying out his name over and over, the kind—

No. Her days of flirting or dating or anything else with a man were over—at least until her son got older and she could focus on her own life. For now, Mason was her everything and all that mattered.

Still, that didn't mean she couldn't look and appreciate...and there was so much to appreciate with this cowboy.

"Do you work here?" She had to assume so, but now she wondered if he was a guest, too.

He held out his hand. "Hayes Elliott."

Elliott. She wasn't just ogling any stable hand or random guest. Hayes was the elusive, mysterious war-veteran Elliott brother. Living in Stone River, she'd heard rumors about how he never left the ranch and the term PTSD had circulated nearly every time she'd heard his name.

Also what had cropped up along with his name was how he'd saved several children in a small village overseas and then been left severely injured, and how some of his friends had died in the same battle.

Something like that alone would make waves across a small town like Stone River, but couple the rumors with the fact that Hayes was a member of the prestigious Elliott family, well…it was difficult not to have gossip.

So where were his employees? A spread this large surely had several workers so the owners didn't have to lift a finger. She knew the Elliott brothers were gearing up to open a dude ranch on their five-thousand-acre spread. What she didn't know was why this brother, the sibling scarcely seen since he'd returned home, was the only one around.

"Alexa Rodriguez."

She gripped his hand and, though it was cliché, she felt… Well, she felt legitimate sparks. Sparks she hadn't experienced for years, and never at just the simple touch of a man's hand. How did that even happen?

"You're staying at my sister-in-law's bed-and-breakfast?" he asked, still holding on to her hand and looking her over.

Alexa nodded, impressed that he knew the goings-on of the B and B—but even more impressed at how her entire body responded to a handshake and a heavy-lidded stare. "I arrived this morning and thought I'd venture out before the storm."

And because she missed Mason. Alexa had already texted Sadie three times and requested a picture of him.

"My sister-in-law has the best B and B in Texas."

The low tone combined with a dimple that appeared when he spoke drew her attention to his mouth…a place she should not be looking. Granted, the rest of him was just as impressive. So where was a girl supposed to look when presented with such an intriguing man? Even his dusty boots were intriguing. They instantly sparked fantasies of him doing manual labor around the ranch... shirtless, to show off those sweaty, tanned muscles.

"The stable hands are all gone for the day. How long will you be staying next door?"

Well, that pulled her right from her glorious daydream.

"I'm here through the weekend," she replied, nerves swirling through her belly. "I, um... I didn't know they were gone, and I wanted to check things out before the weather turned. Sorry if I disturbed you."

The horse behind her stomped its foot as if protesting. She sort of felt like doing the same. She'd talked herself into taking a ride even though she wasn't completely comfortable, because she wanted to do something for herself and she didn't want to feel guilty about her friend paying for this getaway.

When Hayes continued to stare at her without a word, she got the impression he didn't want to be having this conversation any more than she did at this point. He obviously hadn't expected to find someone in his stable, especially when he thought his workers were gone.

The awkward silence had her offering a feeble smile before she turned. No need to stay where she obviously wasn't wanted.

"Wait." Hayes muttered a curse beneath his breath that had her cringing. "I'll take you out if you really want to go."

Alexa fisted her hands at her sides and pulled in a deep breath. Hayes's boots shuffled behind her as the horses shifted in their stalls. It was almost as if they were waiting for her answer.

"Listen." She turned, but stopped short when she realized he'd moved in closer than she expected. "I don't want to put you out."

There went that stare again, the one that held her in place and made her wonder what he was thinking... because the way he looked at her seemed an awful lot like— No, it couldn't be.

Why would someone like Hayes Elliott look at her with desire? He was a sexy cowboy, a war hero, a wealthy rancher and she was, well...just a single mom and schoolteacher.

"I came to take a ride now that everyone is gone," he explained. "Might as well take you."

Didn't that sound like a lovely invitation? All warm and sincere and wrapped in Southern hospitality.

"That's okay," she replied. "It's obvious you want to be alone."

She turned to go again, more than ready to get out of here. So far her vacation consisted of irritating a grouchy cowboy. The weekend could only get better from here...right?

"Damn it. Don't go."

Alexa laughed and spun back around. "It's fine. Really."

"No. I'm just not used to dealing with guests. It's supposed to rain later and over the next two days." He shrugged and shoved his hands in his pockets. "You're here now. Let's do this."

Let's get this over with.

The unspoken words hovered in the air between them. Fine. She wanted to ride and he was here. It wasn't her fault he was the only one left or that he was angry.

The sulking, sultry cowboy continued to stare at her

from beneath that Stetson and another jolt of lust shot through her.

Who knew a cranky rancher would be the one to get her heart beating again? She'd been pretty emotionally stagnant since becoming a widow two years ago, just before discovering she was pregnant. Grief and motherhood could do that.

"You'll ride Jumper."

Hayes's words pulled her to the present before she could dive too far into the dark time of her life. Alexa took a step back and held up her hands.

"Maybe you missed the part where I hadn't ridden since I was five. I think I'd rather have a horse with a name like Buttercup or Princess."

Hayes reached just past her, causing Alexa to freeze in place. His arm brushed against her shoulder and Alexa attempted to act calm. But that smell, that purely masculine aftershave, enveloped her. For a half second she breathed in deep and cursed herself for the instant carnal thoughts that flooded her mind.

"Jumper is our newest mare and she's a sweetheart," Hayes explained, oblivious to Alexa's inner turmoil. "We're getting her used to riding long distances and she'll be perfect for you. Don't be fooled by her name."

Alexa took a step to the side to get away from his casual touch. When she focused on the horse instead of the man, Alexa noticed a gorgeous chestnut mare with a white star on her nose.

"She's my favorite girl." He rubbed the side of her face and murmured something to her. "I got her specifically for new riders and children at the dude ranch because she's so gentle."

"You'll stick close?" she asked as she came to stand beside him. "I mean, I literally have no experience."

Hayes eyed her from beneath the large black rim of his hat. "No experience, huh?"

He raked that heavy-lidded gaze over her and he might as well have touched her bare skin. There wasn't a place on her that wasn't tingling. She'd met the man only five minutes ago and he'd managed to awaken something in her that had been dead for two years.

"You're in luck." He brought those dark eyes back up to hers. "I'm very…experienced."

Okay, they were definitely not talking horses anymore. There wasn't a doubt in her mind this man was much more worldly than she'd ever thought of being. If she had to guess, she'd put him in his midthirties, nearly a decade older than her own twenty-five.

"And I'll definitely stick close," he promised.

The ride hadn't even started and Alexa was already wondering if she was getting in over her head.

What the hell was he thinking?

He shouldn't be offering rides to or flirting with a total stranger. He'd come down to the stables to be alone, to ride his brother's stallion. Being back on the ranch was supposed to help him return to some semblance of the life he'd had before he'd been gutted by experiencing things no one should ever be subjected to.

But the second he'd hinted that she'd have to come back later for a stable hand to take her on a trail ride, a burst of jealousy speared him. The feeling had caught him off guard. He didn't want to feel, didn't want to allow himself any happiness. He'd been through hell and was just trying to survive each day and uphold his promise to his brothers and his ailing father. They had a dude ranch to get up and running and Hayes had a home to renovate.

Hayes had been back home a few months and he was not looking forward to getting involved with anyone right now…if ever. So no matter how mesmerizing Alexa's brown eyes were, no matter how she seemed to be a little sad and vulnerable, sparking that fierce protective instinct inside of him…he simply couldn't act on this unwanted chemistry.

He saw how she looked at him; he wasn't a fool. She was young; she was attracted. He was only going to show her a portion of the ranch, bring her back, and send her on her way. That would be the end of things. Her attraction had no place here…and neither did his.

He carried too much baggage, had too much to sort through within himself before he could think of trying anything with a woman again. Hell, he barely left the ranch, let alone attempted to be social and date.

Taking a beautiful woman out for a ride didn't have to be anything more than just that. Once she was gone, he could ride alone like he'd originally intended. Adjusting to civilian life was more difficult than he'd believed possible and riding alone was the only thing that cleared his mind.

PTSD was nothing to mess with, and he needed space. Perhaps a little one-on-one time with a total stranger wouldn't be such a bad thing. With Alexa, there would be no need for him to talk about himself. He didn't have to put on a front like he often did with his brothers. He could talk up the dude ranch with Alexa, which was a welcome distraction in his life. This family project might be the only thing keeping him from going out of his mind and giving in to the demons that had followed him home.

"I'll get her ready and we'll go," he told Alexa.

Alexa. Such a beautiful name for a woman with such

striking features. He'd only heard the name one other time, long ago. His high school buddy had dated and married someone named Alexa. Hayes had to force himself to stop staring because she was the type of woman a man could get lost in.

All that long midnight hair, her dark skin tone and those wide, chocolate eyes. Her curves were damn near hypnotic in those jeans and fitted tank. Yeah, she would turn any man's head and he was no exception.

Years of military training had enabled him to mask his emotions—something that would come in handy on a trail ride with this beauty. The sooner he could get this ride over with, the better.

Hayes saddled up Jumper and Doc, his brother's stallion. Nolan had been working overtime at the hospital, so Hayes had offered to get Nolan's horse out for exercise.

"Right this way, Ma'am."

If he didn't refer to her by her name, maybe he could keep this little escapade impersonal…exactly the way he wanted to live his life. Detached.

Hayes took the reins and led the horses from the stable. Alexa fell in step beside him. The subtle aroma of jasmine tickled his senses. His instincts hadn't failed him in all his years overseas, and he was positive he had Alexa pegged as someone who wasn't taking time away because she necessarily wanted to. Something about her reserved nature and an underlying hint of fear made him all the more determined to make this ride to be enjoyable and memorable for her.

After all, wasn't Pebblebrook using Annabelle's B and B as a way to spread the word for the dude ranch? By the time they were ready to open, they would not only have her guests already talking, they'd also have hired the best PR firm in the country. This dude ranch was a goal of their father's and Hayes wasn't about to let that man down.

"You live on the ranch?" she asked as they stepped out into the bright June sunshine.

"I do." That was the easy answer. The ranch was now in its third generation of Elliotts, and Hayes wouldn't want to be anywhere else. He owned two other homes: one in the mountains of Montana and a tropical getaway in the secluded part of the main island of Hawaii. He had options, but the ranch was where he'd come to heal, to find that piece of himself that had been damaged... possibly destroyed for good.

"There are several homes on the ranch," he continued. "My brother Colt and his wife, Annabelle, live in the first house you see as you come up the drive. Nolan and his wife live in the back on the east side, and I live in the original Elliott homestead back on the west corner. It's set between the river and the brook running through the ranch."

He loved not only owning that piece of history from his family, but having the privacy he so desperately craved right now. His brothers respected the fact that he needed his space.

"Sounds like quite a family," she stated. She wrung her hands as she glanced back to Jumper. "Are you sure the horse is safe for me? Does she know I'm nervous?"

Hayes looped Doc's reins around the post and moved to Jumper's side, right by Alexa. "You're not nervous. You're anxious. There's a difference."

Alexa smiled, a simple gesture that packed a punch of lust straight to his gut. Damn it, he didn't want a punch of any kind. Couldn't he just enjoy the company of a beautiful woman without lust entering into the pic-

ture? He wanted this ride to be simple, but the stirring
in his body was anything but.

Someone should've notified Annabelle not to send
any guests up today because the stable hands had all
gone with Colt to the auction for more steers, leaving
Hayes in charge. Not a position he'd wanted to be in.

Despite all the pain and anguish and betrayal he'd
been through, something about Alexa made him want
to get closer. Perhaps it was all those curves packed
into such a petite frame, maybe it was those striking
eyes that seemed to look deeper than just the surface, or
perhaps it was that underlying vulnerability that made
his inner protector surge to the forefront. Regardless,
he knew this ride wasn't going to be quick and painless
like he'd first intended.

"At any time, we can turn back," he stated, hoping
that would give him the out he desperately wanted.

Alexa nodded. "I'm ready. Just tell me what to do so
I don't hurt or scare her."

"Grab the pommel and hook your left foot into the
stirrup."

She followed his command and, before he even realized what he was doing, he'd stepped in behind her
and circled her waist with his hands. Alexa stilled beneath his touch. Throwing a glance over her shoulder,
her eyes met his.

"I'm helping you up." He left no room for argument
because, while he might not have thought about his actions at first, now that he had his hands on her, he was
in no hurry to let go. "Relax," he murmured.

Her eyes darted to his mouth—as if he needed another reason to feel that pull of sexual tension. Those
dark lashes framed striking eyes and all of that rich
black hair slid over her shoulders, the tips brushing

against the backs of his hands. An image of all of that hair sliding over his body came to mind and Hayes knew in that instant he was fighting a losing battle.

He wanted this woman, the first woman he'd wanted since his return. And he planned to have her… To hell with all the reasons this ride was a bad idea. He'd just figured out the reason this was the best idea he'd had in months.

Two

This was not a good idea. Nope, nope, nope. As if the horse agreed with her, each nope in her mind fell in tandem with each stomp of a hoof.

Alexa wished she could just ignore the zing shooting through her, but how could she? This man was the first to strike any type of spark or interest in so long… There was no ignoring the emotions.

She'd done well to mask her feelings for years, but there was no way she could lie to herself right now. Hayes Elliott was one sexy cowboy, and he had the brooding, broad-shoulder thing down to perfection. And those jeans? Yeah, they fit gloriously over lean hips that produced the sexiest swagger she'd ever seen. Even with the minor limp, Hayes was intriguing and every part of her wanted to know more.

Down, girl. Alexa hadn't come on this little getaway to find some cowboy. Though Hayes Elliott would no doubt fuel her fantasies for a good long time.

Alexa's horse stayed alongside his. Clearly, this wasn't the first time they'd been out together. Her hips rocked back and forth in the saddle with the motion of Jumper's easy gait. Alexa didn't even want to glance over to see what Hayes's hips were doing. Her eyes needed to stay straight ahead.

The picturesque ranch was breathtaking. White fencing ran as far as the eye could see. The rolling hills were dotted with cattle in the distance. With the bright sun beating down on the land, Alexa found it hard to believe a storm would be rolling in soon.

She wanted to focus on enjoying the ride, but on occasion Hayes's thigh would brush against hers and those tingles would start up all over again.

Good grief. She'd met the man only moments ago and already he held such power over her... How was that even possible?

Maybe she'd been too enveloped in her classroom and her son. Alexa needed to venture out more, as Sadie had said when she'd insisted Alexa take this vacation, but in her normal life...well, where would she go? It wasn't as if she had guys asking her out or a large group of friends she went out with. She had Sadie, who taught in the class next to hers. They'd met in college and had been friends since. And she had Mason.

Alexa was fine being a single mother with not much of a social life. Her job right now was to be both mother and father to Mason, so anything else would have to wait. And that was more than okay. She had one guy in her life and he was more than enough.

"How long has this land been in your family?" she asked, desperate for a topic that would get her mind off the rugged, moody man and slice through the tension between them.

"My brothers and I are third-generation ranchers at Pebblebrook. My grandfather built the house that I live in."

So he had mentioned before. "How many acres are there?"

"Over five thousand."

Alexa had read that in the pamphlet for the B and B, which advertised the upcoming dude ranch. She'd asked because the last thing she wanted was silence. That would only be awkward and cause her daydreaming to start all over again.

Alexa couldn't even imagine trying to keep up with all this land and the livestock, but of course the Elliotts had the funds to hire people to do all the maintenance and grunt work.

Her world consisted of wrangling four-year-olds all day and coming home to a rambunctious baby boy. Her life was quite different from the Elliotts' ranch lifestyle. Part of her was proud of herself for taking this break Sadie had insisted and paid for. The other part of her wondered if Mason had enjoyed his morning snack of blueberries and bananas.

Maybe she should stop to call and check in.

"That's the first barn my grandfather built on this land."

Hayes cut into her thoughts with the history of the ranch. Up ahead, Alexa spotted a small barn, definitely old in comparison to the massive stone-and-metal structure at the beginning of the property. The Elliotts might be billionaires, but she could see the way they'd grown this estate from something small into something grand.

"You doin' all right?" Even with the concerned question, Hayes had that low, gruff tone.

"Fine," she replied.

"Want to explore more?"

Or turn back.

Alexa wasn't quite ready to head back, but at the same time she knew he didn't want to be out here with her. He probably preferred privacy.

"I could stay out here forever," she replied, finding it to be true. "But I don't want to keep you."

He grunted, whatever that meant.

"Was that a reply?" she asked as she glanced over to him. It was nearly impossible to see his face in the shadow from his hat's wide brim.

"I've got nothing," he replied, sounding way too lost, too broken.

Alexa glanced at his hands on the reins. Scars randomly crossed over his taut knuckles. Those large, tanned hands no doubt had done so much. He was a soldier, a rancher. Everything about him screamed alpha and loner. For some insane reason, she found that attractive. She chalked it up to the fact that she always looked out for those in need, not that she found him irresistibly sexy.

Hayes was the exact opposite of her late husband. Before Scott had passed away, they'd been so in love and ready to spend the rest of their lives together. He was safe, made her *feel* safe. She hadn't felt that way since he'd died of heart disease. The doctors had tried to comfort her by telling her there was no way they could have known he'd been born with the defect that had ultimately taken his life.

She hadn't been able to save him. Not that she was a medical professional, but she had survivor's guilt. There was no way to dodge it. And finding out she was pregnant only a week after she'd lost him had only added to the guilt.

Alexa was familiar with the emotion, even before Scott died. She had been only eight when her sister drowned while they were swimming. On their family vacation to the beach, they'd both gone out too far. A riptide pulled her sister out and it was all her father could do to save Alexa from being swept under as well. Years of remorse and counseling had held her family together.

So Alexa recognized the brokenness Hayes displayed.

Alexa gripped her reins and enjoyed the steady trot. They were going a bit faster than before and she figured Hayes had urged his horse to speed up and hers had followed suit. Someone like Hayes wouldn't ask permission first, but he kept glancing her way to check on her.

"So you're the only one around today?" she asked, needing to break up the thoughts swirling around in her head about the sexy man brushing his thigh against hers.

"There are a few workers milling about," he replied. "I just happened to be the only one in the stables."

"But you weren't working."

He threw her a glance and adjusted his hat. "I'd just gotten done at my house and decided to take a break and ride."

So he *had* been planning on going out alone. "You could've told me to come back later."

"I could've, but as you said, there's a storm coming in later. You would've thought I was a jerk."

Alexa couldn't help but laugh. "You wouldn't have felt bad for sending me away?"

Hayes shrugged and turned his horse slightly. Alexa followed. "I don't have feelings anymore, but this is my family's ranch and I know how hard they've worked."

"So it's about respect, then." When he remained silent, she went on. "Whatever it is, I apologize for taking you away from your personal time and I appreciate you showing me the grounds."

As they continued toward the back of the property, the sky darkened slightly and thick clouds rolled in. Texas weather was crazy; pop up showers and storms were the norm. She didn't think it was supposed to do much until later this afternoon.

If it was stormy over the next few days, as predicted, she could lounge in that oversize garden tub in her suite back at the B and B. The moment she'd stepped foot in the house she could tell no expense had been spared. The beauty of the house and her bathroom—hello, heated floors—made her want to move in and bring Mason with her.

The first fat raindrop landed on her nose. Then, before they could find shelter, the skies opened up and Hayes cursed. The next thing she knew, he'd plunked his cowboy hat on top of her head. The gesture shouldn't have touched her, but beneath his gruff exterior and grunting dialogue, he had a big heart. The fact that he was a true gentleman warmed something deep inside her, something that hadn't warmed in quite a while.

"Storm came sooner than I thought," he called over the sound of the pouring rain. "Follow me."

He and Doc took the lead and started trotting faster. Alexa gripped her reins tighter and kept up, her bottom bouncing in the saddle as the rain continued to soak through her clothes. She wasn't comfortable with the faster speed, but all she could do was hold on for the ride and pray they weren't going far.

They rode another few minutes and Alexa was starting to wonder where they were heading. Then, up ahead, she saw an old two-story farmhouse. Hayes's house. She didn't have to ask—she knew. It was just as she'd imagined an old farmhouse should look.

The white home with black shutters had a first and second-story porch and a pitched gable right in the center of the roofline. So adorable, and much different from the grand home his brother lived in on the other side of the property. This house seemed simpler, tucked in the back of the ranch as if protected.

Is that why Hayes chose to live here? So he could be away from everything and remain safe? The man might scream badass, but even after their short acquaintance she could tell he was on guard at all times. Just how deep did his pain run?

Beneath the brim of the borrowed hat, Alexa took in the beauty of the house...even through the raindrops. The brook ran alongside the home and the river flowed behind it. The house and a barn were nestled up on the hilly part of the land.

Hayes rode straight to the small barn at the side of the house. As the showers continued to pummel them, she followed and before she could hop down, he was at her side. His hand landed on her thigh, doing nothing to help with those tremors she'd been experiencing since meeting Mr. Elliott.

That hand slid up to her waist as she swung one leg over and dismounted. The brim of the hat bumped against him and fell off her head to land at her feet. His hands remained on her hips to steady her and Alexa gripped his biceps...and those muscles were just as impressive as she'd thought they'd be.

His eyes darted to her lips and Alexa didn't care about the rain anymore. She didn't care if snowflakes started falling from the sky or a tornado ripped through.

She wanted to stay just like this—it wasn't like she could get any more soaked—and have Hayes look at her like he desired her.

Oh, this was lust at its finest, but it had been so long since anyone had looked at her lips, she didn't care. Lust was a welcome emotion at this point. After two years of nothing, the idea that someone might find her attractive was quite the turn-on. The defined, taut body beneath her fingertips didn't hurt, either.

The muscle clenched in his jaw beneath that dark stubble. "Get up on the porch."

The angry tone left her wondering just what, or who, he was upset with. The fact they got caught in the rain or the fact that he clearly wanted to kiss her and opted to have restraint?

"Tell me what to do." She reached for the horse's reins. "In the barn?"

He shook his head and swiped his hat off the ground before striding back to his horse. Hayes led them into the barn and secured each horse in their own stall.

"Hopefully the rain will pass soon." He didn't even look at her as he closed the stall doors. "The bigger storm wasn't forecast until much later. You can wait here or go onto the porch."

A rumble of thunder had her wondering just how quickly this would pass.

Hayes jerked his gaze toward the opening of the stable at the storm's approach. She hadn't taken him for someone who was afraid of storms. Pop-ups weren't uncommon in Stone River, but since it was supposed to rain all weekend, she wondered if the storm had already begun. They might just have to ride back in the rain.

"We can go back," she told him. "I mean, it's not like

I'm going to get any wetter. Or I can ride back alone.
I know the way."

Hayes turned to focus on her now, and man did those
dark eyes focus. He raked his gaze over her like he was
one leap away from pouncing. Alexa's skin heated just
the same as if he'd touched her with his hands.

Mercy sakes, she'd known the man maybe an hour.
Clearly, she needed to get out more if the first good-
looking rancher made her want to sit up and beg.

"When you go back, you won't be going alone," he
told her. "We'll wait. It's a downpour and a long ride
back."

The showers beat down on the old metal roof and
there was something calming, refreshing about being
out here without a care in the—

"Oh no." Alexa cringed. "My cell phone."

She patted the pocket where she'd stored it, but her
pants were wet. She only hoped her cell had survived.
She couldn't be cut off from contact with her son. This
was her first trip away. She needed to cling to texts
and video chats.

"Texts to your boyfriend can wait."

Alexa squared her shoulders and swiped her damp
hair away from her face. "That wasn't subtle, if you
were asking if I was single."

"I wasn't asking."

Yet that gaze never wavered from hers and those
heavy lids said otherwise. Hayes might not want to be
attracted to her, but he was and he was none too happy
about it.

"Sure you were," she countered. "You keep looking at my mouth and wondering what it would be like
to kiss me, so don't pretend you didn't want to know
if I'm taken."

There went the old Alexa again. Scott had always told her she was bold. She'd always said what was on her mind, because...why play games? But since his death, she'd been quieter, more reserved.

Apparently the moody cowboy brought out the best in her.

"You're an attractive woman," he replied. It shocked her that he was just as blunt. "I'm a guy. But don't worry, sweetheart. Your lips are safe from mine."

Cocky *cabron*. Like she'd asked for a kiss?

Alexa spun away and jogged through the rain to the safety of the back porch. The old swing swayed in the wind as another rumble of thunder rolled through. She crossed the porch and took a seat. Pulling her hair over her shoulder, she squeezed out the excess water.

Glancing back to the barn, Alexa saw Hayes standing in the opening, hands on his hips, black hair plastered to his head from the rain. He stared across the yard at her as if trying to decipher his next move.

Well, he could think all he wanted, but she was staying right here until it was time to roll out...or whatever lingo ranchers used. Wagons ho?

As if she didn't have a care in the world, Alexa used the toe of her boot to push off the concrete. Even though she was completely soaked through, she sat on Hayes's porch swaying back and forth as if this were a sunny summer day and she was sipping a cold glass of Southern sweet tea. As if this were her own home... If she really stretched her imagination, she could picture Mason toddling around in the grass, splashing in the puddles.

Wait. She needn't get swept away in her own dreams. Fantasizing about a sexy cowboy was one thing, but imagining herself here with her son was flat-out dangerous.

Just because she'd been saving for a home of her own with a yard for Mason didn't mean she should picture him here. This was Elliott property. This was *Hayes*'s property. To be here with Mason would mean an emotional investment she wasn't ready to make.

Hayes started across the yard, favoring his left side, walking as casually as you please, as if he weren't getting pelted by rain. Oh, that control he managed to cling to was so maddening, even more so because she didn't seem to have any of her own at the moment.

The entire time he closed the distance between them, he had those dark eyes fixed on her.

Alexa swallowed and attempted to give herself a mental pep talk on not getting tangled up with this frustrating, captivating cowboy. But the closer he got, the more her nerves danced around in her belly.

She had a feeling her interesting day had just gotten started.

Three

Being drenched did absolutely nothing to get his mind back on track. Granted, his life in general hadn't been in the right place since he'd signed up for the Army at eighteen.

How the hell had this simple trail ride turned into Miss Alexa, of the swinging hips and sultry midnight eyes, nestled on his porch swing? Since when did he ever let anyone else take control of his life?

Oh, yeah. Ever since his former fiancée betrayed him with their commanding officer while he was fighting for his country, seeing things no man or woman should ever have to see. Clearly, he hadn't had control over that situation.

Hayes stepped up onto the porch and leaned against the post. "You might as well come inside," he told her. "This doesn't look like it will pass anytime soon, after all."

She braced her feet to stop the swaying swing. "I'm

soaking wet. I don't need to go in. I'm quite happy swinging and watching the storm. With those dark clouds, I bet it will be a doozy."

Hayes sighed. "Don't be ridiculous. You're drenched and I can at least offer dry clothes and put yours in the dryer."

"Oh, don't be so cliché," she told him as she came to her feet. "Wearing your clothes during a storm? Next, you'll find some way that we need to share body heat by wearing nothing."

Hayes had actually thought of that, but he wasn't about to mention it now. She clearly had a low opinion of his intentions.

He forced himself not to stare at the way her jeans and her tank molded to every single dip and flare of her curves. A gorgeous woman with a killer body…it was like fate was seriously testing him. He wasn't in the mood to be tempted and he sure as hell wasn't in the mood for games.

"I'm going inside to change, you can come or you can stay out here and be wet. I don't give a damn." He crossed to the screen door and jerked on the handle. "And offering you clothes in a storm isn't cliché. It's called manners."

He stepped inside and eased the squeaking screen door shut without slamming it. The old linoleum in the entry hadn't been replaced in decades, so he wasn't too concerned about dripping in here.

Hayes headed toward the utility room off the kitchen. There was laundry in there he needed to put away, so he knew he'd find something for himself and he could throw his things in the dryer.

The loud bang behind him had Hayes crouched down in an instant, his hands coming up to shield his head.

But within two seconds he realized he was home, not in battle, and the slam came from the back door.

Slowly rising to his feet, he glanced over his shoulder to find Alexa staring down at him, her eyes wide with worry.

Damn it. He didn't want pity or empathy. Hell, he didn't want company, but that wasn't an option right now. Couldn't he ever fight these demons alone without witnesses? His brothers knew to keep their distance, and he'd come out of his house when he was having a good day…which happened to be earlier today, but now he was ready for privacy.

His heart still beat rapidly in his chest, he continued to stare at Alexa, silently daring her to apologize.

"I—I didn't know that would trigger something," she murmured. "What can I do?"

Clenching his fists at his sides, he willed his mind to chill out and stay focused on the fact that he was safe here on Pebblebrook.

Well, as safe as he could be with a soaking wet woman standing in his kitchen. She'd asked what she could do. That in and of itself was rather amazing.

He was so tired of everyone asking if he was okay. Hell no, he wasn't okay. Jumping at a door was not normal. Flipping out at the roll of thunder was damn embarrassing. He never knew what would set him off until it happened, so there was no way to prepare.

Well, except the screen door. He'd let it go once and it had slammed at his back and he'd flattened himself on the floor for several minutes before he came back to reality. He'd only made that mistake once, but he hadn't thought it would be an issue again because it wasn't like he had regular visitors.

"You want a change of clothes or not?" Hayes asked, ignoring her question.

He tugged at the hem of his soaked shirt and peeled it up and over his head. Clutching the wet material in his hand, he turned his attention back to Alexa.

Her eyes were fixed on his chest, no doubt zeroing in on the scars. Definitely not a story he wanted to get in to, but he wasn't ashamed of fighting for his country. He was only ashamed he'd been fool enough not to see the betrayal going on behind his back. But even that pain paled in comparison to the horrific scene in that tiny village where he'd been able to save the women and children, but not his brothers-in-arms.

"If you have a spare shirt, that would be great," she finally told him.

"What about your jeans?" He knew his were irritating him already.

"I don't wear your size."

Her instant sarcasm had him almost ready to crack a smile. Snarky comments were a staple in the lives of the Elliott brothers, so it was nice to talk to someone who wasn't coddling him. She'd asked what she could do to help, and not pushing the issue was going a long way.

"I'm a foot taller than you," he agreed. "But I'm sure I have sweats that you could fold up while you're waiting on your jeans to dry. Your call."

She propped her hands on her hips and tilted her head. "Do I get privacy or are we both changing in the middle of your kitchen?"

"Are you always so blunt?"

She shrugged, dropping her hands to her sides. "You bring out my sunny side."

Hayes shook his head and moved into the laundry room. He quickly found a gray T-shirt and a pair of navy sweatpants. Clutching the clothes, he came back into the kitchen.

"There's a half bath right through there," he said, pointing to the hallway that led to the front of the house. "You can change and bring me your wet things after."

As she stepped forward and closed the space between them, he couldn't ignore the stir of arousal. Why? Really, why did he have to be attracted to someone? One would think after what he'd been through he would be immune to women, but apparently that was not the case.

Maybe it was that initial vulnerability he'd seen in her at the stables. Perhaps it was all of that silken raven hair. Or maybe it was how she was clearly a strong woman who wasn't afraid to speak her mind.

Regardless, the sooner this storm passed, the sooner he could get her back where she belonged. Between his jumpiness and the unwanted attraction, this was going to be a hell of a storm...both inside and out.

The bathroom was just as dated and neglected as the kitchen. Which was rather surprising, considering the Elliotts had more money than she'd ever see in a lifetime.

But finances were the least of her concerns right now. For one thing, the shirt smelled amazing. So amazing, in fact, that she might have taken her time in sliding it down over her face so she could inhale that woodsy, masculine scent.

Her other concern was really the reason she hadn't stepped from the bathroom just yet. Where was she supposed to put her bra? It was soaked, so she wasn't going to keep it on. But it wasn't like she wanted to walk out and hand him her pink lacy demi. She'd only met the man a few hours ago. Him handling her unmentionables seemed a bit too intimate.

Grabbing her wet jeans, socks and tank, she wrapped the bra inside the wad of clothes and stepped barefoot from the bathroom.

Thankfully, her phone was okay. No messages from Sadie, so Alexa would check in later. She'd only been gone a few hours, so checking in now would seem overbearing...though she probably would've already done so had this little predicament with Hayes not presented itself.

Hayes stood in the kitchen with his back to her, the coffeepot in the corner brewing to life. The sight of that broad back had her clutching her wet clothes and willing herself to calm down. He was just a man. A really sexy, intriguing, frustrating man who'd stared at her lips and stripped his shirt off in front of her.

"Can I throw these in?" she asked.

He glanced over his shoulder, his eyes flared slightly when he raked his gaze over her body. Yeah, his 2X shirt was nearly to her knees. Apparently he needed this size to accommodate those muscles, but she was neither muscular nor tall, so she looked utterly ridiculous. But she was dry and that's what mattered.

"I'll take them."

When he started toward her, she shook her head. "I can do it."

"Have a seat and give me the clothes. I've seen women's underwear before."

Of course he'd know why she was clutching her things like a lifeline. "Well, you haven't seen mine."

Not a smile or a comment from him as he took her things and disappeared into the utility room. Alexa crossed to the coffeepot and nearly groaned at the glorious smell. She glanced at the bag on the counter and didn't recognize the brand. Probably something she couldn't just pick up in the corner market. The Elliotts probably had minions to handpick their coffee beans and make a special roast just for them.

She glanced around, surprised she'd missed the French press on the counter. This kitchen had an expensive coffee maker and a French press? Well, he apparently had his priorities in order.

"They should be done in about forty minutes," he told her as he came back in.

"The rain hasn't let up," she commented as she stared out the large window over the sink. "The sky is getting darker, too."

Not a good sign. Not good at all.

"I drove my truck down to the stables before riding the horses here with you and most everyone else on the ranch is gone for the day," he muttered, as if wondering how the hell to get her back to the other side of the property in the middle of this storm.

A bolt of lightning flashed through the sky. Now she was being mocked by Mother Nature. Apparently there was no good way to get back to a vehicle that could take her to the B and B.

Alexa wrapped her arms around her waist and glanced around the room. This was all so...awkward for her. She had a small town house in Stone River and lived with an infant. But here she was thrust into the country, into an old family home with a sexy man and wearing his clothes, which smelled far too fabulous. Part of her couldn't help but think back to another man and another T-shirt she used to wear.

But that was a lifetime ago and she was in a whole new world. Everything here was so foreign, yet so familiar. From the masculine scent to the intimacy of the moment to the rush of adrenaline when Hayes had been staring at her lips out in the rain.

"You're not afraid of storms are you?"

Hayes's question pulled her from her thoughts. The way he studied her from across the room had her wondering if he always stared with such intensity.

"No, no."

Silence settled heavy between them and Alexa didn't know how to keep this situation from getting more uncomfortable.

Smoothing her damp hair away from her face, Alexa met Hayes's steady stare. "Don't let me get in your way," she told him. "I can sit here and drink coffee and you can do...whatever it is that you do."

He continued to stare, not showing an ounce of emotion. "I don't do much other than renovate this place when I'm not working on the ranch."

He worked? Like, manual labor? Alexa knew the Elliotts were well-known ranchers, but she figured they handled the glamorous side of things and hired out all the work.

"Well, point me toward the coffee mugs and I can take it from there. I'll just wait for the storm to pass."

Hayes stared another minute, then turned to the cabinet to pull her down a navy mug. He set it on the counter and walked out of the room.

Alexa simply stood there, staring at the now empty hallway. Apparently Hayes wasn't in the hosting mood. Oh well, she'd told him to go about his business and clearly that's what he intended to do.

Fine by her. She didn't want to annoy him any more than she apparently already had.

Four

Hayes flattened his palms on his desk and blew out a sigh. What the hell was he doing?

Not that he had much choice in what to do next with his unexpected guest. He might want to be left alone to battle his demons and renovate his home, but he couldn't be a jerk. That's not how he'd been raised. The Elliott boys had been taught how to treat people, and women were always treated with the utmost respect. His father had handled his marriage as if Hayes's mother was royalty.

Which was why Hayes had had to walk out of the kitchen. Because Alexa standing there in his clothes was too damn tempting. He respected her, even though she was driving him insane. Walking away was his only option.

While he wouldn't mind a little stress reliever in the most primal, old-fashioned way, something about her screamed innocence and vulnerability. He could find a better use for that sassy mouth of hers, but yet again, that desire waved every red flag inside his mind.

Yes, he wanted the hell out of her, but that was just lust. Alexa didn't seem like the type to give in to lustful feelings.

Unless properly persuaded.

He deliberately turned his thoughts to the storm. The rain pounded against the windows and the thunder continued to roll every few minutes. Thankfully, it wasn't booming. An occasional streak of lightning flashed across the sky. No, this storm wasn't letting up anytime soon. He'd thought for sure it wasn't going to do anything until tomorrow.

His eyes landed on the piece of mail he'd attempted to ignore. The governor had chosen the wrong recipient for the Man of Honor award.

This was a new award and apparently Hayes had been the first choice. When they'd called him last week to inform him, he'd been numb, shocked, then angry. Hayes didn't want a damn award for serving his country. He didn't want to be recognized because he'd been the only one in his platoon to survive. His busted-up knee was nothing compared to what his brothers had gone through.

Pushing away from his desk, he turned and headed out of his office and down the hall to the kitchen. The last thing he wanted was to see that damn gold-embossed invitation.

Initially, he'd thought working in his office would allow him to ignore Alexa. He figured he'd look over some of the dude ranch plans, but then the invitation mocked him. And now he felt guilty for walking out on her without saying a word.

His brothers, Nolan and Colt, were moving forward

with the transformation of a portion of the ranch property. It wouldn't be long before Pebblebrook's dude ranch would be up and running and pulling in tourists just like their father had always wanted. Even though he was in a nursing facility and not in his right mind, his sons planned to push through and keep the patriarch informed each step of the way. He might not recall his plans, but the boys needed the communication with their dad.

Well, three of the four boys. Colt's twin, Beau, wasn't part of the process. He was too busy out in LA, making movies and being Hollywood's playboy to worry with the ranch. Or at least that's the way it seemed. The media loved any scoop they could get on the so-called "it" actor and, as of late, Beau had been seen in some compromising pictures with an up-and-coming actress.

Beau would occasionally call or text one of his brothers, but more often than not, he couldn't be reached because he was off in some remote location working... and whatever else he did.

Hayes kept his true feelings for Beau's choices to himself. He and Beau didn't mesh well on a good day, so it was probably best Colt's twin wasn't around. It was crazy how Colt and Beau were identical twins, but Colt worked his ass off at the ranch while Beau would rather smile pretty for the camera. Definitely night-and-day brothers.

Hayes entered the kitchen and came up short. Alexa had the back door propped open while she examined the screen door. She muttered under her breath and Hayes couldn't make out quite what she was saying, but she seemed extremely determined in whatever it was she was doing.

Intrigued about what she was attempting, Hayes

crossed his arms and leaned against the door frame leading from the hall to the kitchen. Alexa opened the screen wider, then eased it back. She fiddled with the spring at the top and slid the stopper along the bar in the middle. Then she eased the door back and forth again.

Hayes chewed on the inside of his lip and tried not to focus on how slender her shoulders were beneath his T-shirt, or how she'd had to fold the waistband and the cuffs of the pants just so they'd somewhat fit. The stirring of normal emotions felt so foreign, he was starting to wonder if she'd put a spell on him. How could one voluptuous woman with eyes dark as night be so enthralling?

Her long black hair had started to dry and hung in ropelike waves down her back. He clenched his fists against his chest and ignored the fantasy of how silky all that hair would feel sliding between his fingertips... because he'd never know. Letting his mind wander was a moot point.

Alexa shifted slightly and met his eyes. Her hands stilled on the door as she slowly brought it to a close. The pounding rain blew in on his back porch and the porch swing tapped a rhythm against the side of the house.

"Sorry. I just... I thought maybe I could fix the door and keep it from slamming so hard."

Even though her eyes never wavered from his, the rest of her body language showed she was completely nervous. She wrapped her arms around her waist, pulling the material tighter and showcasing the fact that she wore nothing beneath his shirt.

His body betrayed him and stirred with arousal.

"Do you often go around fixing stranger's doors?"

She tipped her head and offered a slight grin. "I'm

wearing your clothes, so I'm not sure how much of a stranger you are. Besides, I fixed my own door at home, so I thought I could work on yours."

He could fix the damn thing himself, but he'd just gotten used to closing it softly, and not fixing it was more about the principle now. He wasn't about to let that door win. It was a damn door and he refused to be intimidated by it.

Besides, it wasn't like anyone ever stopped by. Occasionally his brothers would drop in, but usually they were in the old barn or Hayes saw them down at the main stables. With his house tucked away on the farthest corner of the property, there wasn't much use for anyone to come back here. All the livestock were kept on the west side more toward Nolan's home.

"Are you that bored?" he asked.

She stepped further into the kitchen, shutting the oak door at her back and drowning out the sound of the rain pelting the back porch. "I didn't want to get in your way. When you left a while ago, it seemed like you were angry that I was here."

Angry? No. Frustrated, sexually charged and confused as hell? Absolutely.

"I'm not angry with you."

He needed her to know that. It wasn't her fault she was stuck here with a guy who couldn't handle a door closing and who had the social skills of a wooden spoon.

Hayes remained in the doorway as she crossed the room. The way those curves moved beneath his clothes was so ridiculously hot. He hadn't been with a woman since his ex, but he hadn't been looking, either.

Yet here Alexa stood, all barefoot in his kitchen with her black hair down and those dark eyes showing way too much.

The woman couldn't hide her emotions and she wavered from vulnerable to turned on to unsure. And damn if all of those crystal clear emotions didn't make him want to pick her up and drag her to his room. He wanted to protect her, to figure out why she went from sassy to insecure in the span of seconds, and he wanted to kiss the hell out of those unpainted lips.

Damn her for calling him on that earlier. She'd pegged him...which only made him want her all the more.

"What are your plans for the kitchen?" she asked, stopping just in front of him.

Her random question threw him off. "My plans?"

"You said you're renovating," she reminded him. "And someone with that coffee setup surely has a grand idea of what he wants done in here."

Hayes pushed off the door and eased around her. How pathetic to be running from a curvaceous woman who was utterly harmless. Well, she wasn't exactly harmless or he wouldn't be so anxious. She made him achy and needy and he sure as hell did not like this unfamiliar emotional place he was in. Not one bit.

Hayes went to the coffee station he'd temporarily set up and poured himself a steaming mug. "I have plenty of plans, but everything takes time."

"What have you done so far in the rest of the house?" she asked as she turned to face him.

"Master bedroom and bath."

He was pretty proud of how the work had turned out. He'd done everything himself, often at night when he couldn't sleep.

"What are you working on next?" she asked.

Hayes shrugged. "You planning on pitching in?"

A ghost of a smile danced around her lips. "If that

rain doesn't let up, it could be a long night. Might as well find something to occupy our time."

The words were completely true, but now that she said them and they were hovering in the air between them, Hayes was having a hard time remembering why he was keeping his hands to himself.

If Alexa ended up being an overnight guest, he better find a project real soon to get started on or he'd have those clothes stripped off her before midnight.

"I plan on doing every room and then starting on the outside," he told her. "I have no timeline."

It wasn't like he was going anywhere. He'd come back to heal, in his own time, and to assist with the dude ranch. Renovating was simply a much needed distraction.

He'd had surgery on his leg in Germany before he came back to the States. Since then he'd done some in-home therapy, but he was stuck with this damn limp, a physical reminder of that horrendous day. So that portion of his healing had gone as far as possible. He wasn't too sure if the mental healing would make any better progress.

"You're doing all the work yourself?" she asked, tipping her head to the side.

"Why would I hire for it when I'm perfectly capable?"

Alexa shrugged and crossed to the kitchen table. She took a seat and rested her elbows on the scarred wooden top. "Because you're loaded."

Hayes stared for another minute before he let out a bark of laughter. He didn't remember the last time he'd actually laughed, but his temporary roommate was seriously getting through the wall he'd been hiding behind.

Maybe that was most of her appeal. She clearly knew

about the PTSD, she hadn't offered apologies and she didn't back down from what she wanted to say. All of that added up to one sexy package.

"There goes that honest mouth again."

One dainty fingertip traced a scarred pattern over the tabletop. "I mean, I love manual labor, but most people would rather just have someone else do the grunt work. Especially when they could afford to just tear this place down and build from scratch and make it five times the size."

He met her gaze. "I'm not like anyone you've ever met."

Dark eyes widened at his declaration. The whisky color called to him, but he knew that was just hormones talking. The electricity flickered, pulling him from the trance.

"Are you kidding me?" she muttered beneath her breath, her eyes rolling up to the ceiling.

"Eager to leave?"

Her eyes snapped back to his. "Aren't you just as eager to see me go?"

There were two ways he could answer that and both of them were honest. Yes, he wanted her to go because he hated visitors.

On the other hand, no. He wanted her to stay so he could watch her body move beneath his clothes a little longer. Masochism clearly had settled in deep here because at this point he'd rather be tormented by her snarky comments and her tempting curves than to see her walk away.

"No," he said, earning him another surprised face.

Her mouth dropped open and he was moving before he even realized it. Hayes came to stand beside her chair. With one hand on the back of the chair, and one hand on the table, he caged her in and leaned down slightly. "I like how you tried to protect me from the big bad slamming door."

"If you're just going to mock me—"

"I'm not," he clarified. "I haven't been attracted to a woman in a long time."

She blinked, those long, dark lashes briefly shaded her doe eyes. "And what do you expect me to do with that information?"

Damn she had a mouth on her. He liked it.

"I don't expect anything, but just as you are up-front and honest, so am I."

Her eyes studied him, more his mouth than anything. She was tempted, that much was obvious. She'd been tempted the moment she'd turned to greet him in the stables, but she'd been too ladylike to not keep her thoughts to herself.

Hayes was excellent at reading people. Well, not his ex-fiancée. He hadn't seen that coming.

"Well, Hayes," she drawled out and made every nerve ending in his body stand up and beg for attention. "As much as I'd love for you to rip your clothes off me and have your wicked way, I'm afraid I live in the real world and that's just not something I do."

Even though she delivered an impressive verbal punch, he had to give her credit. She managed to say that and sound sexy at the same time.

"I don't either, darlin', but there's always a first time for everything. Isn't that the old saying?"

Alexa pushed to her feet, forcing him to step back slightly. But he didn't move too far. Her body slid against his. He fisted his hands and willed all of his control to step up and assist a brother out. He couldn't resist this woman and her sarcasm and the way she called him on everything.

"I recognize PTSD."

And there went the arousal he'd had since meeting her.

Hayes turned away and headed to the kitchen window above the sink. He'd rather watch the rain come down in sheets than address the proverbial elephant in the room that his brothers had badgered him about for weeks.

"My grandfather had—"

"Enough."

He hadn't meant to yell, but damn it, he wasn't going to be analyzed. Not by his brothers and sure as hell not by this stranger he was more attracted to than he should be.

Hayes was well aware what he suffered from and giving it a label wasn't going to fix the issue. At some point, he'd have to go talk to someone, to bare his soul and give up all the demons in his mind that he'd lived with for years.

The electricity flickered once more, but remained on. Hayes continued to stare out into the yard where it stretched to the river. Puddles were forming in the grass and the waters in the river rolled quicker than usual. They were in for a hell of a storm and Alexa wasn't going anywhere anytime soon.

"Why don't you get flashlights," she suggested. "We better be prepared for the worst."

Prepared? He nearly laughed. He knew full well that there was no preparation for Alexa of the raven hair and mouthy chatter. She'd hit the nail on the head when she'd thrown out PTSD. Little did she know, others had tried to heal him and had failed.

What made her think she could come in here after knowing him only hours when his brothers who'd known him his entire life hadn't been able to get anywhere? Alexa might be the sexiest woman he'd ever seen, she might have a smart mouth, but she wasn't going to do any psychoanalyzing. If she wanted to do anything regarding this sexual tension, he'd be totally on board with that.

This was going to be a long, long night.

Five

Well, clearly the topic of PTSD was off the table. Alexa wouldn't make the mistake of bringing that up again. The man knew he had it—just as she knew. What level of hell did he live in on a daily basis? Did he just battle all of this on his own?

Alexa didn't know his brothers. Well, she'd seen Beau Elliott in movies, but that didn't necessarily count. From the way Hayes spoke about the others, he had a support system right here. Was he not ready to reach out? Perhaps he was too proud?

When her sister had passed, Alexa's father had a difficult time accepting help from others. But then he'd realized that was the only way he'd be able to move on and heal not only himself, but also his family.

"Tell me about your movie-star brother," she tossed out.

Hayes let out a humorless laugh. "You really know which subjects to hone in on to get on my bad side."

"Then maybe you should get me a list of safe things to discuss because I've yet to see a good side."

The glare he shot her suggested she should keep quiet, and that grouchy demeanor might work on some, but not her. She wasn't worried.

"Maybe we should try to get along during this storm and skip the getting-to-know-you portion of the night," he growled.

She thought about that for a second, but opted to ignore his request.

"I'd rather play the game," she countered. "I mean, I am wearing your clothes and it doesn't look like I'm going anywhere anytime soon."

Hayes shook his head, clearly not on board. "How about we get flashlights and candles? Then maybe I'll tell you about my renovations."

She pursed her lips and tipped her head to the side. "Sounds like a good idea to me. I can give you some tips."

"Did I ask for tips?" he countered.

Alexa crossed the room and patted his cheek. "Consider it my payment for your Southern hospitality."

"I didn't have a choice," he muttered beneath his breath.

"Sure you did, but you chose to push your moodiness aside and step up as a gentleman."

Those dark eyes traveled over her. "I'm always a gentleman, Lex."

Something shifted inside her. "Don't call me that."

Scott had always used that as his nickname for her and no one had called her Lex in two years.

Hayes's dark eyes landed on hers. "Fine. Alexa."

The way her name slid through his lips as he drawled it out made her think of skin to skin and promising nights. However, there would be neither skin on skin nor a passion-filled night.

"Let's start in the bedroom."

She blinked, then smiled. "Lead the way, cowboy."

Hayes did move, but not to lead the way. He leaned in and came within an inch of her. So close, his warm breath tickled the side of her face.

"And for the record, don't pat me like a little boy again."

Swallowing hard, she eased her face back just slightly to look him dead in the eyes. "Believe me, Hayes, I definitely don't see you as a little boy."

He wasn't sure what was more nerve-wracking, the fact she followed so close behind as he led the way up to the second floor, or the way she'd volleyed that sexual tension back in his face.

"Do we need to do anything for your horses?"

Hayes reached the landing and turned to face her. "They're all right. I have hay and feed in the barn. They're just as comfortable as they'd be down in Colt's stable."

Alexa glanced around the second story and then down over the first floor. The balcony-style hallway allowed for a beautiful view with the window behind overlooking the property and the family room below.

"This is such a gorgeous house," she muttered as she crossed to the window. "I can't imagine ever wanting to leave if I had somewhere like this to call home."

She'd mentioned that before, but he wondered why she didn't just buy a place in the country. Unless she was one of those picky people who had vast dreams and a meager budget.

"It never gets old," he admitted. "This land means

more than money. There's loyalty, family, protection. Everything is wrapped up in Pebblebrook."

Alexa turned her attention back to him. "That's the most I've heard you say at one time."

"Maybe I only talk when I'm passionate about something."

The corners of her lips twitched. One of these times when she mouthed off or gave that mocking grin, he was going to put that mouth to better use. There was only so long a man could hold out. Besides, the sexual attraction wasn't going away. If anything, the tension grew stronger the longer she was here.

Maybe a little seduction would take the edge off. Perhaps kissing her and seeing where that led would have them both putting this time to better use.

"What else are you passionate about?" she asked.

"Bourbon, fighting for what I believe in, good sex." Her eyes widened and Hayes nearly smiled. "Oh, come on. You can't be surprised by my answer, darlin'. I'm a guy."

"I guess I didn't expect you to throw the word *sex* down so easily."

With a shrug, he started down the hall that led to his master bedroom. "Sex has to be easy. Anything else implies commitment and that is impossible."

Alexa tipped her head and studied him. "Who hurt you?"

She just had to keep pressing. He'd almost rather have her pity than for her to dig deeper into his scarred heart. "My fiancée and my CO were having an affair behind my back."

Alexa gasped. Clearly, she wasn't expecting such honesty, but he wasn't sugar coating. Perhaps the bold statement would get her to back off and stop trying to pick his mind. If she persisted, he'd have to pull out the nightmare. Bringing it into the open would surely get her to back the hell out of his personal space.

"Trust doesn't come easily," he added. "Which is why sex is sex and anything more is meaningless."

"That's pretty cold," she told him.

"If you didn't want the truth, you shouldn't have asked."

There was no point in discussing this. They were completely different people and he wasn't here to make friends or make her feel good by opening up and spilling his emotions about the big, bad, scary things he carried in his mind.

The house tour was a safe subject, though he was a fool for starting in the bedroom. Unfortunately, that was the only area he'd completed.

He'd taken part of the wall in the hallway out to make room for the double doors leading to the suite. This house would be revamped from top to bottom, inside and out, but he still wanted to keep the charm of the '40s, when it had been built. No expense would be spared and he would put in high-end everything, but doing it himself was imperative. Hayes needed to stay busy, needed to be working with his hands. Idle time would only feed the devil that threatened him daily.

Hayes reached for the doorknobs and eased the doors wide open. Alexa's gasp behind him was all the validation he needed. Even his brothers hadn't seen the completed room yet.

"This is…" Alexa moved past him, her gaze traveling all around the room. "It's breathtaking and so perfect for an old farmhouse."

She crossed the wide-planked wood floor and stopped at the edge of the gray rug. Hayes moved on into the room, shoving his hands in his pockets and waiting for her to finish assessing.

Her bare feet padded over the rug and to the end of his king-size bed. "That wall of old boards is amazing."

"Those are from the original flooring that was in here. I'm reusing as much as I can to keep the place authentic, but still adding in the best fixtures and modern amenities like heated floors, lights and blinds on timers, security with motion cameras. There's so much to do in each room, it will definitely take some time."

Family and heritage meant something to him. Actually, it meant everything because at the end of the day, that was the only thing keeping him sane. After what happened overseas, if he hadn't had a sanctuary like Pebblebrook to come home to, Hayes knew he would've lost his mind.

Alexa took her time going between the built-ins he'd refinished, to the fireplace with original detailing and scrollwork extending up to the ceiling, and the wide window with custom-built seating and storage beneath. The crown molding had been refinished and he'd also kept the ceiling medallion and painted it white to match the rest of the clean lines.

After several moments in silence, Alexa turned to face him. "This is so impressive. All the detail, all the original touches that make this still feel like a farmhouse, but more up-to-date. The colors aren't what I'd have expected you to choose."

Intrigued that she'd given this any thought, Hayes hooked his thumbs through his belt loops. "And what did you think I'd do in here? Black like my soul?"

She tipped up a corner of her mouth and lifted her brows in silent agreement. "Or maybe a little happier, like charcoal to match your eyes."

Before he could question her on her reasoning, Alexa spun in another circle. She froze when she spotted the pocket door across the room. "The bathroom is in here?"

Taking off without waiting for his answer, Alexa slid the door open and gasped another surprise. "Hayes, oh my word. It's gorgeous."

He stayed back, though he knew she found the soaker tub on the far wall when he heard her delight. He'd purposely placed it right in front of the wide window. Not that he took baths, but it would make for a relaxing spot at the end of the day.

The oversize shower, big enough for four people, at least, caught her eye next. There was the pale gray tile on the floor, the original sinks he'd revamped by putting them in the old dressers from the spare bedrooms. They were mismatched, but painted the same crisp white. Still the farmhouse vibe with a touch of flair.

"Expecting company?" she asked, pointing to the shower.

He met her sly grin with a shrug. "You never know."

"I'd probably never get out of that tub if this were my bedroom."

"I'm not much of a bath taker unless I need to work out my muscles after a hard day, but a bathroom like this calls for a giant tub."

Her smile transformed into something soft, sweet. "Mason loves baths."

Mason? Hayes crossed his arms over his chest.

"Your boyfriend takes baths?"

Alexa's soft laugh filled the spacious room. "Mason is my son. He's fourteen months old."

She pulled her cell from her pocket and swiped the screen. "He's all boy," she beamed, showing him an image of a little guy with her dark eyes and olive skin tone. He sat in the middle of a pile of dirt wearing nothing but a diaper and boots. "He loves playing outside and getting messy, so bath time is just another adventure."

Alexa went on and on, flipping from one image to another. Her entire demeanor had changed and she was positively beaming as she talked about her son.

Her son.

Hayes hadn't seen that coming. That would explain her questions and trying to dig into his world. She was a nurturer by default and thought she could legitimately help him.

That was a big hell no and now that he knew the status of her personal life, that definitely changed the dynamic. This was the first he'd heard mention of a child…and most likely why she'd worried about her cell phone earlier.

Alexa being a single mother was a complete game-changer. That was reason alone for him to keep his hands to himself, but add her motherhood to his screwed-up life… Yeah. He needed to run fast and far, but he was stuck right here with temptation personified for the time being.

The last thing he needed was to get involved, on any level, with a woman with a child. He was messed up enough as it was, but to put any of his darkness onto an innocent child? No. Hell no.

"You're holding up remarkably well for someone who is stranded away from her son."

Moisture gathered in her eyes as she dropped the phone to her side. Apparently he'd said the wrong thing. He wasn't exactly known for his people skills. Which was just one of the many reasons he kept to himself.

"This is my first time away from him," she admitted, tipping her chin up and blinking back tears. "My friend

Sadie forced me to take a solitary vacation. She's the one who booked my long weekend at the B and B and she's babysitting. I don't know what I'd do without her."

Hayes didn't have friends like that. He had his brothers. That was all the support he needed. Friends, and fiancées, weren't reliable. At one time, he'd believed those in his inner circle were everything to him, but now he knew better. His eyes had definitely been opened, his heart hardened.

Maybe he shouldn't have been so gruff with Alexa earlier. She obviously missed her child and now she was trapped with a virtual stranger.

"Two of my brothers have kids," he found himself saying. "They're interesting. I don't know much about them other than they play and make a mess."

Alexa smiled. "That sums it up. Being a mother is the most important job I've ever had."

Hayes nodded. What could he say? Being a parent was never going to be a job for him. Good for those people who wanted children and took the time to nurture them, but Hayes could barely care for his own peace of mind, let alone a child's.

And he knew now that "Uncle Hayes" was around, Colt and Nolan would want him to be involved. Family was important to the Elliotts, but Hayes wasn't so sure he was the best role model for his twin nieces and nephew. Dealing with babies wasn't exactly something he was taught while he'd been jumping out of planes.

The rain continued to pelt down hard on the tin roof, which should have made for good sleeping weather. But if his demons didn't keep him awake, then Alexa being there would.

The flash of lightning and a hard clap of thunder put a viselike grip around his throat and squeezed. Hayes flung himself across the room and tackled her to the floor, sending her phone sliding across the tile. Instinct had him shielding her and taking the brunt of the fall. Pain shot through his leg.

He opened his eyes, focusing on how close Alexa's face was to his. There wasn't pity in her dark gaze, but understanding staring back at him. He didn't want to know what had occurred in her life that she could comprehend this level of hell.

"So doors and thunder." She shifted her weight off him, but put her hands on his cheeks. "What else do I need to look out for while I'm here? I don't want to trigger anything."

She wanted to cure him—those motherly instincts obviously kicking in. He didn't want to be mothered. He lived in the real world where he was permanently broken.

Sex was fine. But she was easing her way into his mind with expert grace.

Damn it. She was getting to him. The way she'd spoken about her son with obvious love had him admiring her even more than before, but that wasn't a mental green light to act on his attraction. Loyalty and family were so engrained in his life, how could he not appreciate a mother's love for her young son?

But she was here. Right here, touching him. Damn it. Resisting her was damn near impossible, no matter what common sense kept telling him.

Hayes's hands slid down her sides to rest on her flared hips. Silence settled heavily between them, but she continued to stare, waiting on him to reply. He could think of so much more to do than get into this discussion.

"Tell me," she urged, smoothing his hair away from

his forehead before sitting up. She sat next to him on the bathroom floor as if this were the most normal way to converse. Reaching for her phone, she clutched it like a lifeline…which it actually was. "I'm not judging, Hayes. I'm not mocking you or anything else. I care."

He snorted and came to his feet. "You just met me. You don't care."

Carly had cared. His CO had cared. Look where that had gotten him.

"You think because we just met today that I can't care?" She jumped up and blocked his path out of the room. Those dark eyes searched his face. "I make a living caring, wondering how I can make people's lives easier. I don't have to know you to question how I can help. It's human decency."

Needing to get away from her expressive eyes and delicate touch, Hayes eased around her, not at all surprised when she sidestepped to block him once again. This woman could drive him absolutely mad in so many different ways.

"Nothing you can do."

Crossing her arms over her chest, she gave a curt nod. "Fine. Then I'll just go out on the porch and watch the storm. I always loved a good storm anyway. It's relaxing."

When she spun around with that chin tipped up and those shoulders back, Hayes reached for her arm. Alexa stilled, but didn't look back.

"Civilian life is still an adjustment," he admitted. "Believe me, if I thought you had some magical way to help, I'd let you. But in reality, you're just here because you're stranded and probably in a few hours, you'll be back next door at my sister-in-law's B and B. Our paths won't cross again."

Alexa glanced back, her now dry hair shielded half her face. "I may not be magical, but that doesn't mean I can't help. You shut me down before giving me a chance."

Sliding loose from his hold, she left him standing alone in the bathroom. That woman was something. No, she was more. She was intriguing, sexy, compassionate…a mother. That last trait was something he had to keep reminding himself about. It made her even more off-limits. Hadn't he just seen at least ten pictures of her posing with her son? She had a normal life to get back to and he was just a blip on her radar.

There was so much that made up this intriguing woman. He found each layer appealing, even her being a mother. Because being a single mother could be difficult. She had to be strong and courageous.

Damn it all. He didn't want to discover any more layers to Alexa. He needed to stick with sexy and curvaceous. Physical traits were all he should focus on. There was room for nothing else. If she thought she could help him, she'd try again before she left. He had no idea what she did for a living, but from the way she touched him, the way she'd looked into his eyes just now, and the hurt in her tone before she left, Alexa truly believed she could do something for him. His brothers thought so, too. But they were living their own lives with their own families.

Raking a hand down his face, Hayes decided to see if Alexa's clothes were dry. Much more of seeing her parade around in his shirt was certainly going to cause him to reach his breaking point.

Six

"I'm not going anywhere anytime soon."

Alexa came into the laundry room doorway and watched as Hayes folded clothes in a precise manner. She'd gotten a text from Sadie just a moment ago with a picture of a very happy Mason hugging his stuffed horse. That horse never left his side. Even though Alexa knew he was fine, seeing a picture eased her mind.

"Texas storms can turn nasty fast," he stated as he creased another basic white tee.

"The river is up quite a bit," she told him. "If it doesn't stop raining soon, nobody will be going anywhere."

He froze. "It's not that bad already, is it?"

Easing back, she glanced to the clock on the kitchen wall. "It's already late afternoon. It's been raining for several hours and with the rain we had the other day, that river is really flowing and rising fast. When I checked the weather on my phone, it said the storm isn't going to be passing quickly."

Hayes muttered a curse under his breath. Alexa shifted out of the way when he pushed forward. Taking long, quick strides, Hayes went to the back door and headed out. Even in his panic, he closed the screen door with ease. He'd clearly trained himself, making his actions second nature.

Alexa went out to the porch as well, wondering where he'd gone. Since she hadn't put shoes on, she didn't want to go far. Stepping onto the wet stones leading to the barn, she raced toward the opening to see the barn empty, save for Doc and Jumper. They were staring at her without a care in the world. Where had Hayes gone?

Now soaked once again, she turned to the wide doorway and spotted Hayes at the edge of the river, hands on his hips, clearly not caring he was utterly soaked. The rain continued to come down in sheets and Alexa had no idea why he just stood there as if waiting for some divine intervention to solve their problem.

Unfortunately, there was no solution to Mother Nature's wrath. They were at the mercy of the elements… and this sexual charge that continued to surround them.

Finally, he turned, head down against the wind and rain as he marched back to the house. Alexa raced ahead and met him on the porch. Hayes raked a hand over his glistening black hair and flung the water aside, then he lifted that dark gaze to hers. And that's when he gave her a visual lick worthy of curling her toes.

The electrical current that had enveloped them since early this morning continued to sizzle and grow. She was powerless, captivated by a man she'd just met, yet she felt as if she knew him on some deeper level.

Hayes's eyes seemed to take her in all at once and Alexa knew exactly how she looked. Drenched, with his clothes plastered to her body, nothing beneath to hide the fact she was both chilled and aroused. She'd never been a fan of her curves, she definitely had her mother's build, but the way he was eyeing her—like she was the most desirable woman he'd ever seen—well, that made her not want to cover up and hide.

What would be the point? He'd already seen and she wasn't going to play the game of pretending to be shy. She was taking in her fill as well because Hayes had a body that would make any woman drop her panties and beg. Alexa wasn't most women and she was still determined to hold on to this thread of control and pray she wasn't here long enough for it to snap…because it wouldn't take much. His clothes were just as molded to his body as hers were to hers and he had some impressive muscle tone, glistening from the rain beading up on his skin.

"You should've stayed inside," he growled, remaining on the other end of the porch.

"I didn't know if you would need help with anything."

Those eyes ran over her again as he slowly closed the gap between them. "What did you think you could do?"

That question, delivered in such a low, gravelly tone did nothing to squelch her desire. This was crazy. She'd just met the man, yet he did something to her that she couldn't quite put into words. Granted, right now, she was having a difficult time with any coherent thought other than *take your shirt off, cowboy*.

"I have no idea," she admitted. "But I don't want you to think I can't help."

He took a step closer, never looking away from her eyes, her mouth. "Your clothes are all wet again."

"They're your clothes," she countered. Why did her voice come out so breathy?

The corner of his mouth tipped up. "Yours are dry now if you want to change."

She pulled in a deep breath, her breasts brushing against his chest. Had he closed the distance so tight or had she stepped forward? She'd been so mesmerized by his voice, his predatory gaze.

"Are you changing?" she asked.

Hayes reached behind his back and jerked the wet shirt up and over his head, tossing it onto the wood porch with a heavy smack. Tattoos covered his chest and up one shoulder. Dark hair glistened all over his pecs.

"You're not playing fair," she told him.

"Who said I was playing?"

He thrust his hands into her hair and covered her mouth before she could take a breath. Hayes's body leaned over hers, tipping her back slightly, but one large hand came around and flattened against her back, pushing her further into his strong build.

Alexa had never been so turned on and caught off guard at the same time. She gripped his bare shoulders and opened to him. There was no gentleness, nothing delicate in the way he kissed her. This was full-blown hunger and held so much promise of a stepping stone to something more.

"You're driving me out of my damn mind," he muttered against her lips. "My shirt molded to you is killing me."

"Take it off."

Where had that come from? It was one thing for him to take his shirt off, but she'd just ordered him to remove hers. What on earth was she thinking? This wasn't like her. Well, the blunt honesty was, but to be so brazen about her wants with a virtual stranger was completely out of the norm.

Those dark eyes seemed to go even darker. "Don't say things you don't mean."

Squaring her shoulders and taking a step back, Alexa found a boost of confidence and bravery as she reached for the hem and eased the shirt up and off. She threw it on the porch next to his.

"I never say something if I don't mean it."

And then he was on her. Strong hands gripped her waist and lifted her up. Her back hit the side of the house. Her breasts smashed against his chest. Locking her legs around his waist, Alexa ached in places she hadn't thought even worked anymore. It had been so long since she'd felt any desire, let alone given in to it. But Hayes sure as hell knew exactly how to make her feel, make her want and ache and tingle and all of the fantastic things that came with being aroused and out of control.

Whatever this temporary situation was, count her in. It wasn't like she'd see him again after she went back home and for once in her life she was going to be completely selfish and live in the moment.

Alexa arched against him as his lips found her neck and traveled down to her chest. Thrusting her fingers through his hair, she ignored all the reasons why this was not a smart idea that were swirling around in her head.

They'd been dancing around the tension for hours. So what if she wanted him? She was human, she had needs, and damn it, she'd never needed like this before.

Hayes shoved a hand between them and slid it into the oversize waistband of her pants. With no panties on, the access was easy as his fingertips found her most sensitive area.

Crying out, Alexa clung to him even tighter. His

hand moved over her, in her, and there was no way she could prevent the onslaught of ecstasy that overcame her. He muttered something in her ear a second before he nibbled on the sensitive spot on her neck.

Alexa's entire body tightened as she bowed, closing her eyes and letting the wave of ecstasy consume her. Hayes moved right along with her, slowing as she began to still. He didn't let up until the final tremor ceased. When he eased back, Alexa instantly felt cold and reality came crashing back. The rain, the storm…she was half naked on the back porch of a brooding billionaire's house and she'd just had the orgasm of her life.

Hayes continued to stare at her as he eased away. That hard stare, the heavy breathing and his chest rising and falling all indicated he'd not been unaffected by her pleasure.

He took an uneven step back.

"We should get inside."

From the tone and the slight gap between them, she knew he didn't mean taking things inside to finish where he'd left off.

What had happened in the last few moments? Whatever battle he faced internally had settled itself right between them.

He'd come at her like a man on a mission and she'd been the only one satisfied. Was he just going to go on like he wasn't miserable and aroused? Because she could see for herself he was both.

"That's it?" she asked, bringing her arms up to shield her bare chest. "What was that?"

"If you have to ask, I did things wrong."

Alexa continued to stare before she marched around him and grabbed their discarded shirts. She tossed his at

his chest with a wet slap, cursing him in Spanish words
her mother would've never allowed.

"Oh, you did things wrong," she agreed as she went
inside, still careful of the door. "You claimed you
weren't playing games, but you sure as hell just did."

Hayes remained on the porch for a few minutes after
Alexa had gone inside. Somewhere between seeing her
with his shirt molded to every wet curve and having her
come apart in his arms, he'd had realized he was going
about this all wrong.

And he spoke fluent Spanish, so he knew exactly
what she thought of him at the moment. He wasn't too
pleased with how he'd handled things either, but lust
had overridden common sense and he'd been selfish.
He'd needed to see her come apart; he'd wanted to be
the one to make that happen.

From the moment he'd seen her in the stables, Hayes
had imagined her writhing beneath him. He'd been set
on seducing her. But the more time he spent with her,
the more he learned about her, the more he wanted her
and the more he knew he shouldn't have her…which
meant his thoughts became even more jumbled.

She was a single mother. He might not know Alexa
well, but he already knew enough to realize she wasn't
the fling type. She had her life together and certainly
hadn't taken a getaway to have some heated affair with
a broken cowboy.

Hayes had vowed to get his act together. Of course
that mental declaration came just as he was giving an
orgasm to his temporary roommate.

Just because he was a mess didn't mean he had to
make his unexpected guest miserable. It wasn't Alexa's
fault he wanted her, but had issues of epic proportions.

It wasn't her fault the mere mention of kids put fear in him because he didn't want to get involved on any level with a woman with a child. Hell, he shouldn't be getting involved with a woman at all until he got his life together...if that ever happened.

The betrayal he'd experienced had scarred him, probably more than the hell he'd lived through during his tour of duty. Not that he was looking for a relationship or anything with Alexa. He had a need, a craving he hadn't experienced in so long, so he thought he'd act on it.

But she was a mother. A single mother. She was worried about being away from her son and here Hayes was worried about his hormones. They couldn't be more opposite. Sexual attraction was a fickle battle to fight.

And right now, he was a jerk. He'd nearly consumed her on the porch, taking what he wanted and leaving her little room to argue. Oh, he could tell she enjoyed his touch, but now what? He'd pushed her away because he had no clue what to do next, but she was stuck here, so he would have to face her at some point.

He was about as personable as that damn screen door he wanted to scrap.

Drawing in a deep breath, Hayes stepped inside the kitchen. Alexa wasn't around, which wasn't shocking. He'd be surprised if he saw her again while they were stuck here together. Most likely, she'd retreated to text her sitter or scroll through images of her son to keep her grounded and away from the big bad wolf.

Damn if he couldn't still feel her against him, though. He wanted her more than ever, but there was a line he shouldn't cross... Not until or unless he was certain she wanted...what?

There was a term for what he wanted and it was hot sex, no-strings, a one-night stand. But approaching Alexa with such crass words really didn't fit. There was something special, innocent about her and he shouldn't be trying to taint her.

Right now, the only thing he knew was that they were stranded together and the emotions were getting the best of them—or of him, at least.

He sure as hell had more than hormones to worry about. This water was rising. Their only saving grace, for now, was that the house and barn were up on a knoll that sloped down to the river and creek. But being surrounded on most sides was going to be a major problem if the rain didn't stop soon.

Since Alexa was not in sight, he shoved on the old work boots by the back door and headed out, sans shirt. He marched straight to the barn to check on the horses. If anything happened to Doc, Nolan would never forgive him.

His doctor brother had recently found his high-school sweetheart and had reunited. She'd been expecting another man's baby, which was a level of baggage Hayes never wanted to deal with. Between Nolan and Colt, both with their ready-made families, Hayes was starting to wonder what the hell was in the water around here.

The irony was not lost on him that he was now stranded with a single mom. Fate was tempting him or mocking, he wasn't sure which. Either way, he was getting damn uncomfortable.

Hayes checked the feed, refilled the water and decided to refresh the hay. Maybe something normal, some sort of manual labor would keep his mind off the fact Alexa had been panting in his ear and shattering against him only moments ago. He wanted to go straight into the house and finish what they'd started. His ache hadn't dissolved; if anything he wanted her even more than he had before he touched her. The way she'd come apart with such freedom and fire... He wanted more. If she was that open with her passion, how would she be once he got her into bed?

Her body hadn't been perfectly toned. Rather, her full hips, her soft abs were so damn sexy. She had the body of a woman with confidence and that was sexier than anything he'd ever experienced. Hayes wished like hell he could take his time and explore every dip and curve.

Again, though, they were total opposites and she wasn't looking for an affair with a stranger.

After staying in the barn for as long as possible, Hayes resigned himself to the fact that he was going to have to go inside and find her. Alexa deserved an apology.

Cursing on his way back to the house, Hayes had no idea how to go about this, but he knew no matter what he decided, he'd find some way to botch it up.

After stepping back into the house and closing both doors, he headed to the laundry room to change once again. He stopped short when he saw the clothes Alexa had been wearing. She'd taken her own things and left his draped over the drying rack.

Obviously she wanted to get out of the wet things, but all Hayes could think was that she'd wanted to be rid of him. The battle he waged with himself had slid between them and he didn't intend for her to be a target.

Already the darkness that plagued him was affecting others, and not just his immediate family. This should be reason enough for him to keep his distance from her, but he had to say something.

Now he had to figure out how the hell to make this up to her because neither of them were going anywhere anytime soon.

Seven

Given the fact Hayes had been a bastard, Alexa took it upon herself to explore the rest of the house. She'd texted to check on Mason again and got a picture back of him napping cuddled on the sofa with the infamous horse. At least one aspect of her life was normal.

Wandering around with her thoughts in a stranger's house wasn't helping her get over what happened on the porch.

If her body would stop tingling, that would be great. She was having a difficult time being so angry with Hayes when every part of her was still extremely revved up and ready to go. She didn't even have to concentrate to be able to feel him against her.

Alexa stepped into what appeared to be an office, but the cover on the couch and the stale scent told her this room had been neglected for some time. She wondered how long he'd been in the military and how long this house had sat empty. A room like this would have a story to tell and be rich with history.

The wall of shelves drew her in even farther. She adored reading, though lately it was more books about the ABCs or colors and shapes than anything. Which was fine, she loved snuggling with Mason after he'd had a bath and just before bed. They would settle in his room in the corner rocker and read and sing. It was actually the most relaxing part of her day. She wanted traditions and routines for her son, so he always felt safe, protected, loved.

Alexa blew out a breath and tried not to get too upset about being stranded here, away from Mason. She would've been away this weekend anyway, but now there was a real threat she'd be away even longer than the weekend.

The far wall of windows reaffirmed her fears as the rain beat against the side of the house. Alexa chose to keep her eyes on the books and something that would take her mind off her current situation. Surely there was one title in all of those she would find interesting.

The dust on the shelves was thick enough she doodled a heart. Wait. What? No, no hearts. She swiped her fingertips over the juvenile design and focused on reading the spines.

"Hope you like history."

Alexa cringed as Hayes's voice washed over her, but she didn't turn to face him. "Better than any other way to occupy my time," she muttered.

"I deserve that."

Alexa laughed, still staring at the titles as if some self-help book on dealing with cranky, sexy cowboys would jump out at her. "Oh, you deserve more, but I'm holding it in."

"Why? You've been brutally honest up until now."

True, but just because he'd been less than hospitable didn't mean she needed to be rude. Besides, she truly didn't know what to say. This situation was so far out of her comfort zone, she didn't even know what zone she was in. She was well aware that anything that happened here was temporary because she wasn't about to get involved with anyone and take them home to her son, but she'd never done temporary before.

"Are you going to look at me?"

Of all the times she'd wished for a snarky comment, now Alexa's mind came up blank. She blamed the intense encounter on the back porch for her momentary lapse.

"You don't use this room much," she commented casually as she shifted to examine more titles. "This is every reader's dream. A wall of books, a view out the window, a couch to curl up on. Not that I have downtime, but if I did, this place would be perfect."

"This was my grandfather's study. It hasn't been used since he passed."

Alexa turned now, crossing her arms over her chest. He'd changed his clothes, and thankfully put a shirt on. His hair was still damp, as was hers, but he looked… exhausted. Not merely tired, but absolutely worn down, almost beaten and defeated.

A piece of her softened because she truly had no idea what Hayes had gone through. If he'd open up just a little, maybe she could help. Then again, they'd just met and someone like Hayes wasn't about to bare his soul. She'd bet her entire year's salary that he'd been appointed a counselor through the military and had balked at talking to a professional. Someone like Hayes would think he could get through the difficult times on his own, or maybe he'd enlist the help of his brothers. But he was strong and determined, and not about to admit any type of weakness.

Hayes took a step inside the room. "What happened earlier—"

"Won't happen again."

He stopped a few feet from her and lifted one dark brow. "Is that right?"

"I'm pretty positive, considering the way you backed away from me."

Not to mention the fact that she hadn't missed how he'd closed up when she'd flashed images of Mason. Some men just weren't interested in children. Which was fine, it wasn't like she was about to take Hayes home or anything.

Hayes's lips quirked into a grin. Damn that man for being sexy and for making her want him. He'd touched her, kissed her, teased the hell out of her, and that orgasm hadn't done a thing to rid her of this desire. Now she wasn't just fighting attraction—she was trying to fend off the memories of how amazing he'd made her feel.

"Darlin'." He took another step closer "I set out to seduce you."

"Really? You have a terrible way of going about that."

He stopped just beside the cloth-covered sofa and leaned a hip against the arm. "You threw me for a loop when I saw you down in the stables and then to have you stranded here didn't help. But seeing you in my clothes, the way they plastered all over your curves, made me snap."

"How is that a problem?" she asked, her heart revving up all over again at his bold declarations. "I thought we were both on the same page."

He shook his head and glanced down to his hands. "We were until my mind started lying to me again and I went to war with myself."

Alexa padded across the hardwood toward him. "Don't be so cliché to say 'it's not you, it's me.'"

"My entire life is a damn cliché," he snorted. "You recall my fiancée and my CO, but I'll save you the sob story. In this instance, though, it was me. Damn it, I still want you, but…"

He shook his head and glanced toward the windows, where the rain skewed the view.

"You can't leave that sentence hanging."

Those dark eyes came back to hold her. "You don't seem like you'd be happy with a fling and I would honestly be using you to fill a void."

He'd be using her? Did he know how long it had been since a man looked at her the way he did? Did he realize that in the past two years she hadn't taken an interest in anyone at all and everything about him had her practically begging? She'd been turned on well before he made her come apart, and now that she knew what he was capable of…well…

"You don't know what type of girl I am," she countered. "No, I don't do flings, which should tell you something, considering I want you, too. But standing around chatting about it isn't helping either one of us. We're stuck here, we're attracted to each other and we're adults with our eyes wide open."

"What do you suggest?"

Alexa knew it was a risk, but she kept her eyes locked with his as she pulled her tank over her head and clutched it at her side.

"I suggest you finish what you started and quit worrying. Do you want me or not, cowboy?"

* * *

Holy—

Was she really doing this? After the way he'd treated her and acted like a complete jerk, Alexa stood before him wearing her lacy bra and hip-hugging jeans. With that midnight-black hair flowing around her shoulders, framing her mesmerizing face, she held all the power. His resolve had evaporated…if he'd truly ever had it to begin with where this vixen was concerned.

What was it about her? Her looks were definitely striking, but there was so much more. Her no-nonsense attitude, the vulnerability she tried to hide, her compassion he kept pushing away while she thrust it in his face anyway.

"Alexa."

She raised a brow and propped her hands on her hips. "I've seen the way you look at me, Hayes. I know this isn't some fairy tale or promise of commitment. We're adults, we're stranded, we're attracted. It's like the trifecta for a fling."

He laughed. Damn if this woman wasn't saying everything a man would want to hear. No-strings sex? What the hell was he waiting on? She'd already come apart in his arms, so he knew the desire was there.

Just because he was ready to rip the rest of their clothes off didn't mean he could stop worrying. She wasn't like other women who threw themselves into meaningless sex. He might have just met her, but that was one thing he knew for certain. So why him? Why now?

The Southern gentleman in him made him pause to assess the situation, but the Alpha male inside him was roaring to life and pumping with anticipation.

"Unless you've changed your mind—"

Hayes took one step to close the gap between them. Snaking his arms around her waist, he pulled her flush against him. "What do you think?"

"I think you better not go inside your head again and start thinking of all the reasons this isn't a good idea."

"It's not a good idea."

She trembled against him and threaded her fingers through his hair. "Do you really care?"

"Hell no."

He crushed his lips to hers, his need growing even more when she moaned and arched herself against him. Just one touch and the woman damn near exploded. He'd never been a one-night stand type of guy; he left that to his brother Beau. But if Hayes was going to have one, Alexa was perfect. She knew full well going in exactly what this was…and what it wasn't.

Hayes shifted his hands and gripped her backside, needing to feel her hips against his. She opened her mouth wider, taking more and giving just as much. Her fingertips trailed down and found the hem of his shirt. She tugged until he eased back just enough to be free of the unwanted garment.

When her hands went to the waistband of his jeans, Hayes gripped her wrists. "Protection."

Her lids lowered, her shoulders sagged as she blew out a frustrated sigh. "Obviously that's not something I carry with me, especially when I go out of town alone."

Disappointment rolled off her, but Hayes nipped at her lips. "My bedroom."

He might not have planned to be intimate since returning home, but that didn't mean he was a fool, either. And right now, he was beyond thankful he'd grabbed a box of condoms when he'd gone out for other necessities at the drug store.

A naughty smile spread across her face. "Then it looks like we're in the wrong room."

Hayes lifted her against him, forcing her to wrap her arms around his neck and legs around his waist. "Don't worry. I'll make sure you get where you need to go."

Those expressive eyes darkened at his veiled promise. Hayes flattened his palms against her backside as he left the study and turned down the hall to head toward the steps.

"You can't possibly carry me up there."

He nuzzled the side of her neck. The scent of something floral combined with fresh rain drove him out of his mind. Everything about this woman got under his skin.

"I can and I will."

"What about your leg?"

He gritted his teeth, hating there was any flaw to consider. "It's fine."

Alexa jerked her face back. "I'm not a lightweight."

"Neither am I," he countered as he reached the base of the steps.

"Put me down."

His firm hold on her tightened. "I'll not only carry you up, my knee will hold, I won't be winded and I'll still have plenty of stamina for other activities. You're welcome."

"I've had a baby," she continued to argue. "I'm seriously not as light as I used to be."

Hayes started up the steps, his eyes never leaving hers. "I don't know what you felt like before, but right now you feel pretty damn perfect."

Alexa pursed her lips as if she were biting back another argument. There was no way he was going to let her think for one second that she was less than perfect. Alexa fascinated the hell out of him.

Once he reached the top landing, he smacked his lips to hers. "You're still a lightweight," he informed her.

"How did you climb those stairs that fast carrying me?"

She sure knew how to stroke his ego. "I'm a former paratrooper. We're strong by default."

"A paratrooper? What exactly—"

"Is this something you really want to get into now?" he asked, taking long strides toward those double doors leading to his massive bedroom.

"No." She framed his face with her hands and slid her mouth over his. "I'm not really interested in talking at all."

He kicked the doors open with his foot and crossed the space. Right now he didn't care about the rising waters, the flickering electricity, the fact that they might be stranded for a while. He wouldn't mind being holed up with Alexa. Being alone would give him the opportunity he'd been waiting for to finally get her in his bed and take advantage of her lush body.

Hayes had even managed to block out the thunder that coupled with his PTSD to threaten his sanity. All he cared about was Alexa, about seeing her come apart in his arms again, because the sampling he'd had was not near enough.

Maybe she was the drug that could help him…temporarily of course.

Hayes stood at the end of the king-size bed and eased her down. When she lay back, he took a good, long look at the woman spread out before him. He'd never had a woman in this bed, hadn't given it much thought. He'd been so consumed with occupying his time and his thoughts with the ranch, but having her here was definitely helping him stay distracted. Who knew a perfect stranger would be the one to start healing his brokenness?

Alexa watched as he unfastened her jeans and tugged them down her legs. The plain white panties were more of a turn-on than any lingerie. The flare of her hips, the softness of her rounded belly and the fullness of her breasts straining against her lacy pink bra had Hayes rushing. He could do slow later...because there would be a later.

Alexa sat up and reached around to unfasten her bra. There was no way he would stop now. The sultry temptress displayed on his bed was more than enough motivation to ignore all the reasons why this was not his smartest idea.

All of this was temporary. The housing situation, the feelings...his lover.

While Hayes kept his eyes locked on Alexa, he stripped out of his clothes. In seconds, he retrieved protection from the nightstand and had it in place. The urgency spiraling around them had him rushing...but later, he vowed. Later he would explore that body because he already knew once would not be enough to exorcise her out of his system.

Alexa met his eyes with her heavy-lidded gaze as he came to stand between her spread thighs. Taking control, she reached up to grip his shoulders as she pulled him down on top of her.

"I think you need to take charge," she whispered. "I don't want any setbacks right now."

Damn. His heart clenched and that was the dead last thing he wanted. She got him. She understood the beast he lived with in his own mind. But he wasn't about to get too attached or emotionally wrapped up in how perfectly she understood his demons. There was no space for anything other than physical.

But taking the lead now that he'd finally gotten her where he wanted her was exactly what he'd been hoping for.

"That makes two of us, darlin'."

Alexa shifted her knees up by his hips and wiggled to get closer. "Don't make me wait."

Bracing his hands on either side of her face, Hayes joined their bodies, earning him a low groan and the sexiest arch from that sweet, luscious body beneath his. He might be physically in control, but right now she was getting into his head, overriding all the ugly to give him something akin to hope.

This was just sex, he reminded himself as he closed his eyes. He was taking every bit of this opportunity to use her sweetness to drive out his pain. No matter how temporary, he would welcome it.

Alexa framed his face, forcing him to look at her. "Stay here," she commanded. "Don't look away."

Yeah, she definitely held all the power here and he wasn't going to complain. Not one bit.

Their hips moved in perfect sync and she never let her eyes waver from his. There was a level of comfort with her he'd never found before. Finding something so rare had him drawing from her, using her in this moment.

When Alexa's knees clenched tighter against him, Hayes leaned down and covered her mouth with his. He wanted them joined in every way possible. There wasn't enough—he needed more.

Hayes reached down, slapped a hand over her hip and surged forward harder, faster. Alexa cried out, breaking their kiss and squeezing her eyes shut.

"Look at me," he demanded, echoing her words. He wanted to see and feel every bit of her release. They were both drawing from each other and he didn't want that bond severed...at least not yet.

Swollen lips, heavy lids, Alexa came apart all around him, which was all it took for Hayes to follow. His body tightened, he clenched his teeth, gripped that hip and lifted her leg even higher. Alexa's fingertips trailed up his arms and over his shoulders. She threaded her fingers through his hair as his body slowly started to come back down.

After his tremors ceased, Hayes started to shift to the side, but Alexa locked her ankles behind his back.

"Wait," she murmured. "One more minute. I'm not ready for reality just yet."

Reality was a bitter bitch. He wasn't ready to face it, either. But getting too cozy with this lush, passionate woman wasn't the smartest idea. Forget the fact that she matched him perfectly in bed, but she'd also honed in on his deepest fears and still managed to calm him with little effort.

Hayes ultimately gave in to her request to stay just a little longer. When he rolled to the side, he pulled her with him and cradled her head in the crook of his arm. He'd never admit that his knee hurt like hell. This was worth the pain. *She* was worth the pain.

He wasn't getting comfortable all nestled here with her in his bed, his home. He *wasn't*. He was simply coming down from great sex. That's all. This wasn't snuggling or cuddling or post-coital bonding. Their bond had come and gone during their intense intimacy.

But when her hand slid over his chest, Hayes had to close his eyes, because the warmth and tenderness from this woman was climbing over that wall he'd erected.

What happened to the quickie he'd set out to have? The seduction he'd wanted since he saw her in the stables had somehow turned into lying in bed together in each other's arms. How had they gotten to this point?

The second he'd discovered she was a mother, he'd vowed to keep his distance emotionally. Unfortunately, his emotions were scraped raw, exposed and easily accessible. And Alexa knew exactly how to make him feel, how to make him think about all the things he didn't want rolling over in his mind.

She felt too damn good.

Just another minute. He'd hold her one more minute and lie to himself about how he didn't enjoy this precious moment with this precious woman... Because right now, he truly didn't want to be anywhere else.

Eight

Alexa grabbed Hayes's T-shirt and slid it over her head. She'd apparently fallen asleep in his bed, but when she woke up, he was missing…and the bed was cool. Had he waited until she'd passed out and slipped away?

Regrets already?

Her tank top was still down in the study, so she pulled her jeans on to go with the shirt he had folded on his dresser. The sky outside the window had darkened and the rain continued to pour down. Alexa's stomach growled as she padded through the room and into the hall. A light shone from the first-floor family room as she glanced over the balcony railing. Still no Hayes in sight.

Surely he wouldn't mind if she went to the kitchen to find something to eat. Other than coffee, she hadn't had a thing since she'd grabbed a granola bar on her way out to the B and B this morning.

Alexa gripped the handrail and froze. Had it only been this morning that she'd left her house?

This morning she hadn't even known Hayes Elliott and she'd already been in his bed.

The woman she was here at Pebblebrook Ranch was not the single mother, teacher of special needs preschoolers. It was like she'd completely transformed into someone else the moment she got here.

Never in her life had she thought of having a temporary fling. She'd been married, then once widowed she'd focused solely on her son and providing for him. Dating hadn't even been a priority, let alone sex.

Something about Hayes brought out a side of her she hadn't even known existed. She'd only been with two people in her life before today, and one of those people had been her husband.

Pulling in a deep breath, Alexa descended the stairs. Some yeast-like aroma hit her as she got about halfway down. Pans clanging echoed through the house. Hopefully whatever he was making had enough for two.

Nerves curled in her belly. She truly hoped this wasn't about to get awkward. As confident as she'd been before, well…that had all stemmed from desire.

Right now, she was back to boring Alexa. She could turn snarky at a moment's notice if she started to get too overwhelmed by the intensity—and Hayes was definitely one intense man, in bed and out.

The second Alexa stepped into the kitchen, all her nerves were gone, quickly replaced by another rush of arousal. Hayes stood at the stove wearing only denim on the bottom half and ink on the top. Mercy, who knew a half-dressed man at the stove could be so sexy?

Her bare feet slid over the old linoleum, landing on

a squeaky spot in the floor. Hayes jolted and focused his attention over his shoulder, eyes alert.

"Sorry," she told him. "I didn't mean to startle you."

His shoulders relaxed as he raked his gaze over her and she was instantly aware of how potent those dark eyes could be. Almost as potent as his hands.

"You like wearing my clothes."

Maybe she did. Or maybe she liked the way they smelled, like a rugged man. "My shirt wasn't upstairs."

His mouth quirked. "You could've come down without a shirt. I did."

Great. He wasn't in a funk brooding about regrets and being noble or some other nonsense that would make this situation extremely uncomfortable. She was already feeling nervous again because she'd stepped so far out of her element.

At least he was talking like this situation was no big deal. Because it wasn't…right? Just because her body still tingled, she wore his shirt and she wanted to do it all over again didn't mean anything. It *couldn't* mean anything.

"If I'd come down without a shirt, you'd ravage me again and then we'd never eat," she replied as she crossed to the stove to see what he was making. "I'm starving, by the way."

"Who said I wasn't going to ravage you again?"

Standing right next to him, her wearing his shirt and him with no shirt, seemed far too intimate. Much more than the act of sex. Add in the fact that he was cooking and this whole scenario took on a domesticity she definitely wasn't comfortable with.

She'd done family before…then her husband died and she was left raising a baby alone and trying to piece together her shattered heart. She wasn't looking for someone to fill the void. One day, she would put herself first and find a man who loved her. She wasn't afraid of marriage, but she certainly wasn't looking right now.

Then again, she hadn't been looking for a fling either, but here she was with her breasts brushing against the shirt of a man she'd only met hours ago.

"Calm down, cowboy."

She patted his cheek. The bristles along his jaw tickled her palm and reminded her of how glorious he felt tracing his lips all over her.

In a swift move, Hayes grabbed her hand. Then he took it and flattened it against his chest. "That's the second time you've patted me like a child. I wouldn't do it again."

She shivered because, as he left the veiled threat dangling, there was so much heat in his tone, in his eyes, she wanted to pat him again just to see what would happen. She had no doubt it would be glorious.

And mercy, those muscles beneath her hand had her wanting to curl her fingers in to get a better feel.

"What are you cooking?" she asked, sliding her hand from beneath his. Alexa leaned over and spotted a pot with noodles. "You cook something like that?"

With a grunt, Hayes turned back and picked up the spoon from the counter. "I'm thirty-four years old, Alexa. I'm a single man. I either needed to learn to cook or starve."

"Aren't you supposed to live on bacon and beer?"

He threw her a sideways glance. "Those are definitely staples in a single man's diet. Hell, any man's diet. But I also appreciate real food and my mother was the best at homemade chicken and noodles."

Surprised, Alexa stepped back. "You make homemade noodles? Like, with a rolling pin and everything?"

"I'm wounded you think I can't." He continued to

stir as she stared, until he finally said, "Okay, fine. I didn't make these noodles, but I can."

Alexa crossed her arms and leaned against the wall next to the stove. "Is that right?"

"I swear, ask my brothers," he exclaimed. "We all can. My mother insisted we know our way around the kitchen, because she wasn't raising men and future husbands who couldn't help in every room of the house."

"Sounds like a smart woman."

A faint smile danced around his lips. "She was the best. My dad never was the same after she passed. Hell, he's really not the same now."

"Does your dad live on the estate, as well?"

Hayes shook his head and dropped the spoon back into the pot. "No," he replied, turning to face her. "He's in an assisted living facility not far from here. He doesn't know who we are most days."

She hadn't expected that. She knew Pebblebrook Ranch was the biggest in the state. It was the pride of the area, and now that rumors were swirling about the dude ranch extension, she would've never guessed there was heartache beneath all of that wealth and power. The dynamic family that seemed to have it all suffered brokenness just like anyone else. Money couldn't buy everything.

"I hate to hear that," she told him. "Has he been suffering long?"

Hayes leaned back against the corner of the L-shaped counter. Resting his hands on either side of his hips, he gave her a tantalizing view of...well, his amazing self.

"When I came home last year for a brief visit, I could tell he was much worse, but this time..."

Hayes shook his head and didn't finish. Alexa couldn't imagine having either of her parents not know who she was. How crushing and life-altering that must be. Hayes truly battled quite a bit between the PTSD and his father's mental state. So tragic.

"I'm sure he'd be proud of what you all are doing here," she replied. "Clearly, your parents raised some powerful children. Tell me more about your brothers."

Hayes pushed off the counter and went to the cabinet to grab a couple of bowls. "Not much to tell. Nolan and Colt are in love and married with kids. The only time I see Beau is when his face is on the screen. That's all."

Okay. Clearly, he loved his family, but he had some hang-ups. Not territory she wanted to venture into, and he'd made it crystal clear she wasn't welcome into the personal side of his life. Probably best all the way around if they kept their emotions out of the mix.

She didn't think that would be much of a struggle for Hayes, but she was one to get attached. Between her job and raising a toddler, her emotions were always getting involved in the lives around her. Simply because she and Hayes had just met didn't make her any less compassionate toward him, his burdens and the family who no doubt loved him and wanted to help him heal.

Alexa had to keep reminding herself this was simple. Adults did flings all the time. Not her, but other adults.

"I wasn't trying to make this any more than what it is," she informed him. "I'm not asking to meet them, just figuring out a way to pass the time."

What time was it anyway? This had been the strangest day and she couldn't keep track between the storm making the sky dark, the midafternoon romp and nap session, and then not eating.

Hayes scooped out hearty portions and sat the bowls on the table. Then he grabbed a loaf of bread and started slicing it.

"If you tell me you made that bread, I'm going to force you to come home with me and cook because I burn microwave noodles."

"Hell no, I didn't make this." He laughed. "Nolan brought this to me the other day. It's from our favorite bakery in town."

"Sweet Buns?" she asked.

"The very one."

After he got everything on the table, including sweet tea, she held on to the back of her chair and stared at the intimate dinner. It was simple, yet…still intimate and so like when she and Scott first got married.

"You all right?" he asked, taking a seat.

Blinking back the burn in her eyes, Alexa kept her gaze on the intimate setting. It didn't seem all that long ago she'd set the table for her husband. They'd share a meal and conversation, taking for granted how simple and perfect their life had been.

Alexa swallowed the lump in her throat. She'd not mentioned anything about Scott. Bringing him out into this temporary fling would make all of this seem more real, or like she was fully ready to move on. She hadn't quite gotten there yet.

"We all have our demons to face, don't we?"

Hayes fisted his hands on the table and pulled in a deep breath. "Let's take our dinner elsewhere."

She tipped her head, clutching her hands in her lap. She was a guest in his house and she didn't want him to make adjustments simply because her own issues snuck up and had her in a chokehold.

"Where do you suggest we go?"

Hayes came to his feet, grabbed his bowl and drink and jerked his head toward the front of the house. "Follow me."

* * *

Hayes had no clue what he was doing, but he'd seen Alexa's white knuckles as she'd stared at the dinner on the table. He hadn't even asked what she'd been through in the past, but obviously something spooked her when it came to…what? Eating with him? Sitting down to a kitchen table?

She'd asked about his family a few times, so if he were to add the pieces together, he'd guess whatever plagued her had to do with her own family.

Regardless, Hayes was glad to get out of there as well because eating together in his kitchen was a different level of intimacy. Sex was one thing, but settling down to a dinner he'd made? Yeah, that seemed to be sliding right into that relationship territory he'd vowed to stay far away from.

And a relationship with a woman and a child? No. Because if he got involved with a mother, then he'd be involved with a kid. He just couldn't do that, not to an innocent baby.

Years and years ago, before he went into the Army, he'd thought of having a family of his own. He saw his wife here at the estate helping to raise their children. He imagined teaching them about ranching. Then reality and war and all the ugliness crept in and corrupted every pure thought he'd had about the picture-perfect family.

"In here?" she asked, standing in the door to the study.

Hayes pulled himself from his thoughts and gestured her in ahead of him. "You seemed pretty happy in here earlier. And that was even before you started stripping for me."

Alexa laughed as she crossed the open space. "It's a room full of books with a large window, and if it weren't raining I'm sure there would be a killer view. All I need is a chaise and I'd be set. There's nothing to be unhappy about in here."

She went to the large window that stretched across the exterior wall. The padded seating area beneath the window was where she curled up with her dinner, obviously more relaxed and comfortable than in his kitchen.

Hayes stood a good distance away, taking her in with her legs crossed, holding a dinner he'd made, wearing his shirt... Perhaps the kitchen table would've been a better choice. He'd thought a dining table seemed intimate, but that was nothing compared to having her curled up in the room where his father had spent so much time. This room held so much history and now Alexa had wedged herself inside like she belonged here.

She took a bite and groaned. Well, hell. No matter where they ended up, his body would stir at the low grumble of her approval. That was the same groan she'd delivered in his ear as he'd slid into her earlier. Was he seriously considering another round?

Hell yes, he was. Who was he kidding? He'd had a sampling of Alexa's sweetness and her passion and he wanted more. They were stuck here and keeping his distance from her at this point was pretty much impossible. Night was fast approaching and at some point they'd have to discuss sleeping arrangements.

He just had to get her on the same page as his plan. An affair for the duration of her stay? He didn't think she'd be too opposed. A woman who bantered as easily as she did, who paraded around in his clothes... Yeah, he could get her back into his bed.

"Are you going to join me?" she asked, glancing over.

Hayes crossed the room and sat on the window seat, but left a good amount of space between them. Their dinner and glasses sat in the middle, providing a flimsy barrier.

"Tell me you're not going to change this room."

He forked up a hearty bite. "I haven't thought about this one to be honest. This was my grandfather's office, then my dad's. I don't really have much use for it."

Alexa's eyes widened. "You don't have use for a room where you can read and relax? Do you even know how lucky you are to have something like this?"

"Believe me, I know exactly how lucky I am to have everything I do." Flashes of another life he'd led for years boomed through his mind. "Just because I have money doesn't mean I'm not grateful."

"Do you have a panel that slides open and reveals a secret room?" she asked, picking up her tea. "Because I have to tell you, if you don't, then I highly recommend putting that on your renovation list."

"Is that right? And what else would you do?"

Alexa took a drink, then set her glass down as she drew her brows in as if trying to come up with some ideas. "Are we talking what I would do or what you should do? Because one of us has a ton of money and the other doesn't and lives in a town house about an eighth of this size."

Hayes shifted back and brought his knee up onto the window set. "Pretend this is your house and money isn't an issue. What do you see?"

Her brows lifted as those dark eyes widened. A breathtaking smile spread across her face and for a second, his heart clenched.

"This is fun," she stated. "Okay, well I'd definitely have a tire swing and a tree house out in that large oak by the creek for Mason. I'd want his bedroom to be the one facing that same tree so he could see his play area."

Of course she put her son's needs first. Someone like Alexa wasn't going to instantly go for the glam. Her son was her life. A fact Hayes would do his best to remember.

"You've nailed the master suite," she went on. "I think for the kitchen I'd keep it separate from the living area. That gives it the farmhouse feel. But I'm different in that I don't like the open concept everyone else wants. Personally, I don't want to see the dirty dishes from my living room."

Hayes shrugged. "When you live alone, there aren't many dirty dishes."

Alexa eased back and rested her shoulder against the window as she brought both of her legs up and crossed them. "But we're pretending this is my place and I don't live alone. Believe me, we have dishes. And the laundry. I never knew such a little person could have so much laundry."

Everything in her life circled back to Mason. He admired her for her strength and independence. Clearly, she was a wonderful mother. There was something special about the bond between a mother and her son. Hayes would always carry the memories of his mother in a special place in his heart.

"So you'd want a nice utility room?" he asked, trying to focus on their conversation and not the parallels between Alexa and his mother.

"Definitely," she said with a firm nod. "I'd want the laundry close to the bedrooms so I didn't have to haul it all over the place. I think for the living room I'd want soft, peaceful colors. I'd want sheers on the windows that stayed open so I could see the land. I'd have windows that opened easily because there's nothing like an evening breeze."

As she spoke, she looked outside, but the rain continued to beat the house. Alexa seemed lost in her own fantasy, as if she saw beyond the rain. Was life that simple? Could he look beyond the storm and see the other side?

"I think the house calls for an old farm table in the kitchen," she went on. "Or at least a long bar where friends or family can gather and eat in one room. My parents don't live around here, so I wouldn't have many visitors."

She stared down at her plate as she continued. "Growing up, we were constantly hosting family for dinner. Not only on holidays, but just because. That's part of my heritage. My father's family came from Puerto Rico. We gather together and fix an insane amount of food. I miss having a big house that I can fill with my family and friends. Sometimes I like to get together with my friends from work."

"What is it that you do?"

The question slipped past before his common sense could stop it. He shouldn't ask such things. He worried she'd get the impression he wanted more.

But he hated that longing in her tone. Hated that she was missing her family and the bond that obviously ran deep. He understood that all too well.

"I'm a special education preschool teacher."

Of all the things she could've said, he didn't expect that, but on the other hand he wasn't surprised. Alexa was a giver, so a teacher of children with special needs definitely made sense. He hadn't known her long at all, but he knew those kids were damn lucky to have a teacher like her.

"Sounds like a rewarding job."

A soft smile slid over her perfect mouth. "I love what I do."

And it showed in the way her eyes lit up and love laced her tone. There were certain things Alexa was extremely passionate about: her family, her son and her work. The similarities between them were starting to hit too close to home and he had to keep reminding himself they were stuck here and making the most of the situation. This wasn't some get-to-know-you start of a relationship.

"Working with children sounds terrifying."

"Says the man who served overseas," she retorted with a wide grin. "What did you do? Or can you tell me?"

"I was a paratrooper in the US Army."

When her brows rose, his ego volleyed up a notch. "You jumped out of planes and you think a room full of children are scary?"

With a shrug, he came to his feet and closed the space between them. "We all have our talents," he said, taking her hands and pulling her to stand before him.

"What are you doing?"

Hell if he knew, but he was going with his gut. Okay, he might be leading into this with another body part, but he wanted this woman and why should they deny it?

"Figured I'd show you more of my talents."

Her lips quirked up as she looped her arms around his neck. "Lead the way, soldier."

He reached to his back pocket and pulled out protection. "I grabbed it when I left the bedroom earlier. I wasn't sure where I'd want to ravage you again."

Dark eyes went from the foil wrapper in his hand back to his face. "Sure of yourself?"

Hayes lifted her off her feet and headed to the covered sofa. "Hell yeah, I am."

Nine

Alexa toweled off and slid into another of Hayes's shirts. She found herself becoming more comfortable in his clothes than her own. He'd definitely delivered on those promised talents, both in the study and in the shower.

Now he was outside assessing the rising water and checking on the horses. He'd made her promise she wouldn't come out because there was no sense in both of them getting soaked again.

She made him promise that if he needed help he'd come back and tell her and not be so hardheaded. Alexa worried with the storm still raging that the thunder would thrust him back to the darkness inside his mind, but she had to let him go on his own. She wasn't his keeper. She wasn't even his girlfriend, so hovering was not going to fly with this sexy cowboy. Besides, once she left he'd be on his own to handle matters his way.

Two stubborn souls trapped together proved to be quite the tug-of-war.

Yet they matched each other in bed and out. She shouldn't be thinking of all the ways they blended and complemented each other, but she couldn't help herself.

Alexa padded barefoot back into the bedroom and started adjusting the covers. Her body heated all over again as she recalled exactly what they'd done here hours ago.

But her heart clenched as night fell and she worried about Mason. Even if she'd been next door at the B and B, nighttime would still be difficult. She'd laid out his favorite book for Sadie to read him after his bath, but Alexa just wanted to hear his voice.

More than likely this separation was more difficult for her than for Mason. He was probably playing, watching his favorite cartoons and keeping Sadie on her feet.

What she and Hayes had going on was as simple as it was complicated. Bringing her son into the mix, other than just speaking of him and showing off pictures, was just another layer of intimacy that probably wasn't a smart idea.

This was all so temporary. She definitely wasn't ready to bring anyone home to meet her son or step up to play Daddy.

"The rain has slowed."

Alexa glanced over her shoulder. Hayes came into the room wearing nothing but his boxer briefs. "You lose your clothes in the rain?"

He hooked his thumbs in his briefs and stripped them off as well. Oh, mercy. That man had some serious confidence, and for good reason. All of those well-defined muscles, lean hips, broad shoulders, the smattering of hair across his chest, and that ink she'd all too happily traced with her tongue earlier… Honestly, if she looked half as sexy as he did, she'd parade around naked, as well. Alas, she had dips and curves and dimples in places that were not attractive. Yet Hayes made her feel exactly the opposite. And desired.

The man definitely made her feel desired.

"I put my clothes in the utility room since they were soaked. Figured you wouldn't mind."

"Not a bit." She crossed her arms over her chest and tried to calm her heart. "What are we doing, though?"

He continued coming toward her. "I plan on messing up that bed you just straightened."

Those big firm hands slid around her waist. Every time her body lined up with his, she couldn't help but think how perfectly they felt together. Why did something so temporary feel so right, so comfortable?

Were her mind and her hormones playing tricks on her? Even though it had been a couple of years since she'd become a widow, was Hayes the rebound guy?

"I'm not asking for more, but this is all we are, right?" she asked. "After I leave, we're done."

The muscle clenched in his jaw as he lined their hips up and palmed her backside. "But you're not leaving yet."

If he was trying to throw her off by dodging her question, it was working. "Do you ever get tired?" she joked.

He nipped her lips. "Oh, I'm tired. I plan on crawling into this bed and holding you until I get my stamina back."

Her heart ached. She hadn't slept in a bed with a man other than her husband. "Um…maybe I should sleep in the spare room."

And that was really saying something about her fear

of becoming too attached or pretending to play house. The man was wearing nothing and she had on only his shirt as he ground against her…and she was making plans to sleep elsewhere.

"Is that what you want?" he asked, easing back to look her in the eye.

Alexa swallowed. "I have no clue, to be honest. I haven't slept in the same bed with a man since my husband died."

Something dark slid across his eyes. "I wouldn't make you do anything. You want to sleep somewhere else, then I'll get the bed ready. You're in control here."

Was she? Because this all felt eerily out of control and spiraling into something she was neither ready for nor could wrap her mind around. Since meeting him in the stables, everything had snowballed. It was almost like she was watching this all happen to someone else.

Placing her hands on his shoulders, Alexa stared at the difference between their skin tones, hers dusky and his lighter. They might be completely opposite in their lifestyles, their upbringings, pretty much everything. But Hayes seemed to get her, to understand her need for space, and how could she not find that even more attractive than just the physical package?

"Why don't we watch a movie? Could we do something simple like that?"

Raking his hands up her sides, pulling the shirt with them, he let out a soft laugh before stepping back and dropping the material back in place.

"Sure, on two conditions."

"What's that?"

He nodded toward the bed. "We lie right there and you wear nothing."

Alexa opened her mouth, but Hayes held his hands

up, palms out. "That's all. Anything that happens beyond that is your call."

"You think we're going to lie there naked and nothing will happen?"

Hayes leaned forward enough to brush his lips against hers. "I said you were in charge. I never said nothing wouldn't happen."

Yeah, well, there was only so much a woman could take and Hayes had already proven he was well beyond her breaking point.

"You fight dirty," she muttered as she turned toward the bed and jerked the T-shirt over her head.

She was treated with a smack on her bare backside and a deep laugh.

One hour later, the movie still hadn't captured her interest. How could it? The man was not playing fair. Oh, he hadn't so much as touched her. He remained across the king-size bed with the sheet draped over his hips, just low enough to torment her. He'd propped pillows up and crossed his arms behind his head, showcasing ripped arms and a mouth-watering chest.

But even when the oversize footboard procured a gigantic flat screen at just the touch of a button, she still hadn't been able to concentrate on anything other than the dangerous game they were playing.

At the time, she wondered if he was just going to lie there, but he'd put on some new movie she'd never seen and hadn't said one word. Not one. He hadn't looked her way or "accidentally" brushed a hand in her direction.

For the past hour, Alexa had lain on the other side of the bed with an ache. Her bare skin slid over his sheets each time she shifted. She was seriously trying to hold still. The last thing he needed was to realize just how much this little cat and mouse game affected her.

Fine. If he wanted to play, then she was about to bring her A game.

Alexa pushed the sheet aside and eased from the bed. As she crossed the room toward the bathroom, she didn't so much as look his way, but she most definitely sucked her belly in and attempted to look somewhat fit and sexy. Not an easy feat when the only workout she received was chasing her kids in the classroom and giving Mason piggyback rides.

From the corner of her eye, she noted Hayes's attention following her as she entered the master bath. Once inside, she stood there for just a moment and simply stared straight ahead at the large soaker tub on the far wall. She had nothing to do in here, but she wasn't going to just lie in that damn bed and let him drive her out of her ever-loving mind.

Bare feet slid over the tile floor behind her. Before she could turn, strong arms banded around her midsection. Alexa found herself hauled back against a very chiseled, very firm chest. She couldn't suppress the smile that spread across her face.

"I thought I was in control and calling the shots," she reminded him.

Hayes's lips nuzzled her neck, causing goose bumps to race over her skin.

"Oh, you did call the shots when you strutted by me," he murmured in her ear. "You lay beside me shifting those legs, trying to ignore that ache. So here I am."

She should've known he'd see through her. Still, if this was her punishment, she welcomed the discipline… she was on borrowed time, after all.

Hayes's hand splayed across her stomach. His other slid up to cup her chin and turn her head just enough to look at him. But she didn't get a chance before his mouth crashed down onto hers. That hand on her belly went lower and Alexa whimpered.

The moment he touched her where she'd been aching for the last hour, Alexa nearly slid to the floor. Her knees weakened as every one of her senses was assaulted in the most glorious of ways.

Hayes continued to stroke her, kiss her, drive her completely insane until her body tingled more as it climbed higher and higher. Finally, she jerked from the kiss and cried out. He murmured something as he continued to pleasure her and Alexa reached to the side to grip the edge of the counter.

Moments later, her body settled, but she wanted more. Damn him for touching her exactly the way she needed to take the edge off but still leave her craving more.

"We should be ready to finish that movie now."

Alexa spun around, ready to tear into him for such an asinine statement when she realized he'd been joking. The gleam in his eyes was part amusement, part arousal.

"You better finish what you started, cowboy."

Those rough hands came to her waist and lifted her up onto the cool vanity. "We both know who started this, darlin'."

She locked her ankles behind his back and he reached into a drawer to pull out protection. Clearly, as long as she was here, they were going to have to keep those packets in every room.

In no time, he was sheathed and joining their bodies. Alexa knew this was absolute insanity to be this attracted to a man she'd just met. Still, there was nothing that could stop her from taking all the passion he gave. It had been so long… Didn't she deserve a little selfish happiness?

"Stop thinking," he whispered against her mouth. "Just feel. Relax."

Their bodies moved together as if they'd been together for years as opposed to less than twenty-four hours. Hayes's hands roamed all over her, his lips made their own path over her heated skin. The pleasure he gave was all-consuming. Alexa had never felt so needy and fulfilled at the same time. The way Hayes continued to explore her as if he couldn't get enough wasn't something she was used to…and she was quickly slipping into something deeper than just a heated affair.

Hayes slid those talented lips up the column of her throat as her body tightened all around him. He nipped at her ear before jerking his hips faster and capturing her lips. Alexa held on to him as she let the euphoria sweep over her.

Beneath her hands, Hayes's shoulders tightened as he continued to assault her mouth. For a long time, they clung to each other and she wondered when they'd be finished with each other. Would it be when she left? Would she be out of his system before then?

She'd never favored one-night stands, but she had to admit this was a memorable experience. Life-altering, actually. Because she knew for certain the next time she took a partner to bed, she would demand more than she'd ever realized she'd wanted.

Hayes rested his forehead against hers and let out a low grumble of laughter. "You ready for that movie now? Because I sure as hell couldn't concentrate earlier."

Alexa eased back as much as she could to look him in the eye. "You're such a liar. You lay there like you were so enthralled without a care in the world."

That naughty grin she'd come to appreciate spread across his face. "I knew you'd cave."

Swatting at his chest, Alexa uncrossed her legs. "You came after me."

"After you paraded in front of the screen. I wouldn't be much of a gentleman if I ignored your invitation."

When he stepped back, Alexa rolled her eyes, hating the instant chill that fell over her bare skin. "I'm picking the next movie and you're going to watch it."

With a shrug, he replied, "Fine by me."

Alexa named a title, something old that was ridiculously unpopular and very rare. Hayes lifted his brows in surprise.

"There's only one other person I've ever heard mention that film," he told her.

She hopped off the counter. "Really? Who else?"

"My best buddy from high school. We remained pretty close even during my first deployment, but then we lost touch and he passed away recently."

Unease curled through her. There was no way. Absolutely not.

"What was his name?" she asked, almost afraid of the answer.

"Scott Parsons."

Alexa's stomach dropped, her heart twisted, all the moisture in her mouth dried up the second her late husband's name landed right between her and Hayes.

Now what the hell did she do? She'd slept with her husband's best friend and Hayes already had issues with trust.

Tonight was about to get even more interesting.

Ten

Somewhere between the bathroom and the movie, Alexa had mentally and physically checked out. She'd slept in the spare bedroom, claiming she wasn't comfortable sleeping with a man since her husband.

That was understandable. Hell, he wasn't looking for snuggles and whispered promises in the dark so he should be relieved at her decision. But he wasn't.

Hayes wanted her beside him so he could roll over and touch her, pleasure her when he wanted. He'd never been this way with another woman—not even his fiancée.

So why Alexa? What was it about this affair that had him craving even more?

When he'd been with Carly they just fell into everything because of timing, something he could see clearly after the fact. Hindsight and all that. They'd been stationed together, had fallen into an easy pattern of friendship, which led them straight to bed. Of course they'd snuck around, but once their relationship turned serious, with an engagement, they went to their CO and explained things.

Hayes hated how he must've looked like a fool from the start. All of those inclinations of marriage, family and settling down here at Pebblebrook were naive goals he'd once held close.

Between the war zones he'd jumped into and the shock from the betrayal, it was a wonder Alexa had even made it into his bed. He'd been the poster child for needing a distraction and the perfect storm literally landed her on his doorstep.

So what the hell had happened last night that had spooked her? They'd both agreed this was only temporary. She'd been even more adamant than he had.

On the flip side, Hayes should be relieved she wasn't in his bed when the nightmares hit. She'd already witnessed his waking demons—there was no sense in her experiencing them while sleeping, as well.

The next morning, Hayes stood at the kitchen sink sipping his black coffee and staring out at the riverbank. Well, where the bank used to be. The usual cut-off from the land to the water had shifted somewhat as the flooding came up to nearly the slope that led to his porch. The rain had stopped. The storm had eased sometime during the night.

Actually, it had come to a head at eight minutes after two. He knew because he'd lain awake staring at the ceiling. After another nightmare and a clap of thunder, his sleep had been nonexistent. More than likely he'd never get a good night's rest again, not with the demons constantly chasing him away from any type of normalcy.

The crashing overhead jerked him from his thoughts.

His eyes went to the ceiling as he set his mug on the counter. Whatever Alexa had done, it sounded as though something had broke and his gut tightened at the thought of her being hurt.

Hayes raced up the stairs and down the hall leading to the room she'd chosen on the opposite end from his.

When he turned the corner, Alexa sat on the floor, his T-shirt bunched around her hips, and one of his grandmother's antique pitchers, which had sat on the dresser, was in the floor in shards.

"Don't come in," she told him as she reached for the larger pieces. "Go get me something I can put all these broken pieces in. I just… I wasn't paying attention and bumped the dresser. I'm so sorry."

Her hands shook as she lifted another piece. Hayes carefully watched where he stepped and crossed the room.

"Put those down," he ordered. "You're going to cut yourself."

She sniffed and glanced up to him, unshed tears swimming in her eyes. "Just get me the trash so I can throw these pieces away."

Hayes took the three large chunks from her hand and set them back on the floor. Without warning, he lifted her from the floor and adjusted until one arm was beneath her knees and the other behind her back. He left the room with threatening protests from his houseguest.

"We'll clean it up later," he informed her as he went to his room. "Are you upset because you broke that piece? Because I don't even go in that room and my mother wouldn't want you to cry over broken porcelain."

Alexa swiped a hand over her face. "I'm not crying, though I am sorry I broke that."

"Your eyes are pretty watery. Must be allergies." He sat her on the end of his bed and picked up one foot to assess for any cuts. Satisfied there were none, he checked her other foot. "You're not cut anywhere. Let me see your hands."

Like the hardheaded woman he'd come to know, she put her hands behind her back and tipped her chin. "My hands are fine. I'm going to get dressed and ride Jumper back to the main house."

Hayes shook his head. "Not a good idea, darlin'. That low area on the property is swimming in water. Remember the spot I showed you when we rode through?"

Her chin quivered, but he had to hand it to her, she didn't give in to the emotion. "I want to get back to my son."

"How long were you staying at the B and B?"

"Two more days." She narrowed her eyes. "I can't be here that long."

Hayes crouched down in front of her. "Listen, I don't know what's got you so spooked since last night, but there's no pressure from me. If you're worried about my expectations, I have none. Do I want you in my bed while you're here? Hell yes, but I won't push you."

"That's not..." She shook her head and looked away.

Whatever she was dealing with was none of his concern. He didn't want to take on any more baggage from anyone. He could barely carry his own mess.

Hayes came to his feet and backed up. "Why don't you get your clothes on, or stay in mine, I don't care. Then meet me in the kitchen."

She brought her focus back to him, drawing her brows in and narrowing her eyes. "Why?"

"I've got something planned for both of us to take our minds off everything else going on."

When her eyes trailed over his body, he had to laugh. "As much as I'm tempted to give in to that silent invitation, I have something else in mind."

"I wasn't inviting," she stated.

"You said the same thing last night after you paraded naked in front of me. We know how that ended." He sauntered from the room and called over his shoulder, "You'll want pants and shoes on for this. Meet me downstairs in five."

Well, ten minutes later and she was in the kitchen, where Hayes was absent. What on earth was he doing?

Alexa went to the French press and figured she'd fire it up and have a good cup of coffee. It was so rare she managed to grab a cup at home. Mornings were usually rushed getting Mason ready for the sitter and her trying to get to school on time to be the smiling teacher ready to go when her students arrived.

"Taking your coffee break already?"

As the drip started, Alexa turned her attention from the much needed morning fuel to the man behind her clutching a sledgehammer.

"Um, what are you doing?"

"We're going to take down the cabinets."

Stunned at his bold statement, she leaned against the counter and crossed her arms. "Why are we busting them out? I didn't think you'd decided what to do in here, yet."

With a shrug, Hayes eased the sledgehammer on the floor and propped the handle against the door frame. "I know these need to come out before I can do anything else. So the first thing I'll do is empty them. Considering nearly every room in this house is bare, it shouldn't be difficult to find a home for the few dishes and pans

I have. And my microwave can go anywhere for the time being."

Alexa figured she had two options: she could drink her coffee and get going on this demolition or she could drink her coffee and spend the rest of the day worried about things she had no control over.

Either way, she was getting her liquid jump-start.

"Let's get these cleaned out then," she told him.

An hour later they had everything out of the kitchen and eating area. The counters were cleared off and Alexa was caffeinated and ready to go.

"Do you want to hit them first or should I?" he asked.

"I'll do it."

Hayes crossed the room and grabbed the sledgehammer. Before he handed it over, he pulled a pair of work gloves from his back pocket.

"Put these on."

She eyed the well-worn leather. "Where are yours?"

"I have one pair and you're wearing them. Not up for discussion."

She wondered if he ever wore gloves. Those strong hands of his were rough, but they slid over her skin easily and sent shock waves all through her.

If she didn't focus on the sledgehammer instead of those masterful hands, she'd knock herself out while doing this demo work. Without arguing, she slid the gloves on and adjusted the wrist strap. When she picked up the sledgehammer, she was a little surprised how heavy it was. She didn't do too many teardowns. While she had lived alone for some time now and did most repairs herself, she'd had no reason to own such a tool.

Though she did re-screen her back door and change out the leaky pipe in her bathroom faucet. She was rather proud of herself when she managed things on her own. Considering everything was on the Internet, she would at least try once before calling in reinforcements. She didn't always have the funds to pay someone to ride to her rescue when things went wrong.

"You got it?" Hayes asked.

Alexa nodded. "Where should I start?"

"Anywhere. As long as you don't bust the window, feel free to smack anything. I want it all gone."

She went to the side of the base cabinet and gave a swing. Well, in her mind it was a hefty swing, but it barely made a hole in the side of the old wood. How embarrassing considering Mr. Muscles behind her could probably take it out with one whack.

"Harder," he demanded. "Whatever you were upset about this morning, whatever came between us last night, use that emotion and smack the hell out of that cabinet."

Thoughts about how life wasn't fair ought to do it. The fact her husband had been taken, her child robbed of a father, then to find the one guy she was interested in had been her husband's friend...

The sledgehammer came around, her grip tightened as it made contact with the cabinet and busted right through.

Apparently channeling heart-clenching emotions was the perfect solution for demo work. She needed something to demo at home on those days that she struggled to get through.

"At this rate I won't have to do anything but haul everything away," Hayes joked. "Swing at it again."

Alexa banged over and over. The muscles in her shoulders and arms burned, but this was the greatest therapy she'd ever had. Even if she could get over that hurdle of Hayes's insistence about being alone, now she had the barrier of her late husband. How had she never known about Hayes?

Obviously, they'd lost touch after school when Hayes went overseas, but Alexa had never heard his name and—

Oh, no. She had. She'd heard his name several times. Well, she'd heard Scott talk about his friend "Cowboy." Ironically the same name she'd called Hayes right before they...

"Okay," Hayes called over the crashing sound.

Alexa took a step back. Sweat dampened her skin, causing her tank to cling. She eased the head of the sledgehammer down to the ground and rested the handle against her thigh. She was definitely going to feel that workout in the morning, or quite possibly tonight.

"Feel better?"

Alexa glanced over to see a very smiley Hayes. She hadn't seen that much emotion from him other than when they were naked.

"I'm sweating and sore," she told him. "That was amazing."

Hayes chuckled and stepped forward. "Maybe I should exorcise some demons, as well."

Alexa stepped far enough back to not get hit by the debris, but still close enough to admire that very masculine form in action. Muscles clenched and bulged as he took his own frustrations out. Before long, the entire wall with the sink was done.

Hayes stepped back and pulled in a deep breath. "Well, that didn't take as long as I thought."

"What about the other wall?" she asked.

"That's a gas stove, so I'll wait to pull that out. I think we've done enough for the day."

Alexa took in the carnage and propped her hands on her hips. "So how are we going to cook?"

Hayes propped the sledgehammer against the new-found wall. "I have plenty of things. We won't need to cook."

Alexa narrowed her eyes. "Like what?"

"Ice cream, cereal, bread from Sweet Buns."

"I'm here for two days and I'm going to leave fat if all you have is carbs."

Hayes's gaze raked over her entire body. "You're perfect now and you'll be just as perfect when you leave even with a buffet of carbs."

Words every woman wanted to hear. If she was ready for something more, maybe he'd be the one who helped her get back into life as a couple, the man who fed her every fantasy, the one she told her every secret...

Except, oh, that's right. She was now the one keeping a secret from him.

She couldn't tell him about Scott. Something about the admission felt too emotional, too raw. She'd be gone soon and Hayes would never have to know who she was. That was for the best, considering both of them had determined this to be physical only and nothing personal.

Bringing Scott into the mix now would only make it seem like she'd been keeping something from him all along. And considering they weren't going to see each other again, it was best she just kept her late husband to herself.

"I say we have ice cream for dinner," he told her as he closed the distance between them.

"You don't have to talk me into that if that's what you're thinking."

A corner of his mouth tipped up as he reached her

and banded his arms around her waist. "Oh, that's not what I'm thinking."

Alexa flattened her palms against his chest. "We're filthy, Hayes. And I know I smell."

His lips trailed over her jawline. "We're definitely on the same page. You do stink."

She swatted his shoulder with a laugh.

"Which is why I'm about to go scrub you from head to toe and work out those sore muscles in the shower."

She squealed as he scooped her up. She started to say something about his knee, but he wouldn't care. He'd ignore the pain and push through because once Hayes had his mind set on something, he followed through.

And apparently he had his mind set on making sure she was thoroughly clean.

Eleven

By the time Sunday rolled around, it was like the sky opened up and poured down some much needed sunshine. Alexa was sore in places she hadn't even known muscles existed—from the sex and the demolition. She'd ended up staying in Hayes's bed last night, though she'd vowed to herself not to. Things just progressed and that was where she stayed.

The man had a power over her she couldn't comprehend. It was as if the word *no* didn't exist where he was concerned.

And her time there had come to an end. She'd been in contact with Sadie, never once admitting where she'd truly been. They were expecting her home this afternoon and Alexa knew the water had gone down and she'd be able to deliver on that promise.

Alexa adjusted her tank over the top of her jeans. She was most excited about putting on different clothes.

Even though Hayes had washed her things while she'd worn his shirts, she still wanted something else.

But part of her hated to be leaving. The house was amazing and she wanted to see more of what would be done, but she'd never be back. She'd never see what happened with the kitchen they'd torn up and she'd never know if he put that long farmhouse table in for guests or if he'd keep it simple so he didn't have to invite people over.

So much about this house, and this man, she would miss.

Being in bed with him last night, not just the sex but the actual intimacy, had sparked something deeper inside her. After sleeping alone for two years, having someone right beside her had been…perfect. She'd slept so well, all cradled in Hayes's arms. When morning had come, she didn't want to get up, but she knew this fairytale couldn't last forever. The real world waited on both of them.

As Alexa came down the steps and headed toward the kitchen, she heard Hayes cursing.

"Something wrong?"

Her question had him jerking around, eyes wide. His hair was all a mess, from sleeping or running his fingers through it. "Just a minor electrical issue."

"Do you want to ride back with me?" she asked, knowing full well he would.

He pulled in a deep breath and met her gaze from across the space. "Stay."

That one word held so much power as it settled between them.

"You don't mean that."

Those dark eyes that held so much pain never wavered from hers. "You know I never say something I don't mean."

That was true. She'd come to know him pretty well over the past couple of days. "You'll be glad to see me go," she informed him, remaining where she was in the doorway.

"I slept better last night than I have in years."

She didn't want to hear that. She didn't want to know that she had an impact on him because last night had been a turning point for her, too. She was having a difficult time gearing herself up to leave. And if he were being honest, he wouldn't want her to stay. This euphoric state would wear off and he'd want his privacy once again. It was best for everyone if she left as planned and they forgot about each other.

In theory, that's exactly what should happen, but Alexa wasn't so quick to believe that she could just let all of this go.

"You'll do fine once I'm gone," she assured him, and tried to take the advice herself. "You only slept so well because of the sex."

Hayes shrugged. "Maybe so. I wouldn't turn down sex or a good night's sleep if you stayed."

"We both know that's not a good idea and I have a son and reality to get back to."

Now he did cross the room, and her heart kicked up. Maybe it was the whirlwind weekend or perhaps it was just the man himself, but every time he looked at her she couldn't help the fire that continued to blaze within her.

"Maybe I don't want reality," he told her as he nipped her lips. "One more day. Stay one more day."

The man could tempt a saint, and she was surely no saint. Alexa slid her hands over his arms and tipped her head back.

"You make me want to forget responsibilities."

That naughty grin from his lips had her biting back her own. "Don't look at me like that," she scolded. "I'll never leave here."

Hayes slid his hands under her tank as his lips captured hers. Easing her back, he completely covered her, but held her all at the same time. The man's strength never failed to impress her, which was just another reason she found him so intriguing.

Her time was up, but she desperately wanted to stay. She wanted to get Mason here to play in the yard and ride the horses. But that was all fantasy because the reality was Hayes was a billionaire living in a far different world.

As his lips pressed deeper into hers, Alexa clutched at his shoulders. Those fingertips brushed the underside of her breasts.

"Looks like everything is fine here."

Alexa jerked, but to Hayes's credit, he only cringed. He kept his hold on her, tipped back and all, and merely turned his head to the back door where a tall, broad man stood. He had to be an Elliott. He had the same dark hair, dark eyes and naughty grin.

"Get out, Colt."

Annabelle's husband. No doubt Annabelle wondered what had happened to her B and B guest.

"Is that any way to treat your brother who came all the way back here to check on you?" Colt asked, stepping farther into the room. He eyed Alexa. "Colt Elliott. You must be Alexa. My wife has been worried, but I told her if you were with Hayes, you'd be in good hands."

Pushing against Hayes, Alexa stood upright. "I was definitely in good hands, as you can tell."

Colt's brows rose as he let out a bark of laughter. "I didn't mean to interrupt."

"Yes, you did," Hayes growled. "Now leave."

"Actually, I was on my way out." Alexa turned her attention to Hayes for the briefest of moments before looking back to Colt. "I need to get to the B and B and settle my bill and gather my things."

"There's no bill."

Alexa spun around. "There is a bill. Just because I didn't stay there doesn't mean I don't owe."

"It's taken care of," he insisted.

Narrowing her eyes, she crossed her arms. "You're not paying my bill."

"It's taken care of," Colt repeated.

Turning back to the other brother, Alexa sighed. "Is this how it's going down? I'm getting overruled? I can pay my own way."

"I thought your friend was paying," Hayes asked as he came to stand beside Colt. She could definitely see the similarities now. "Why are you settling up?"

"She gave me the money to put on my card for the room, but I'm giving it back. She watched my son all weekend. That was enough of a favor."

"Well, consider your stay free and clear," Colt declared. "Annabelle was so worried, though we figured you'd gone out with the horses and since Doc was missing, we knew Hayes had taken him."

"Nolan's always too busy at the hospital or with his new wife and baby to get Doc out that often," Hayes added.

This familial moment was not helping her get out unscathed. She'd already fallen in love with this house; she'd partly fallen for the man, though she chalked the unwanted emotions up to the whirlwind affair. If she stayed much longer and heard more about their brotherly bond and witnessed their banter firsthand, she wasn't sure she could push aside what she was feeling for Hayes.

Oh, yes, he'd asked her to stay, but he meant in his bed. And, tempted as she was, she had to leave. Now.

"I can ride Jumper back," she suggested.

"Nonsense," Colt replied. "Why don't you take my truck? Hayes and I will get the horses back to the stables."

"Take your truck?" she asked.

"I'll drive her," Hayes stated. "In your truck. You can stay here until I get back or you can ride Doc. Leave Jumper for me."

"I can send a stable hand," Colt suggested.

"Jumper is fine here and I'll take—"

"I'll drive myself."

Both sets of eyes turned to her. Alexa cleared her throat and squared her shoulders. "That is, if you don't mind," she said to Colt.

"Not at all. Keys are in it. Just leave it parked at the B and B."

Hayes's dark eyes held her in place for only a moment before she crossed the room. The two men parted at the back door as she passed through. With her hand on the screen, she carefully let it close softly, so as not to bang.

Her heart clenched as she froze on the porch. She risked a glance over her shoulder where Hayes stood on the other side of the screen, his hands shoved in his pockets, the muscle in his jaw clenching.

She wanted to say something, anything, but with Colt only feet away what would she say? Even if they'd been alone, what words would fit this type of situation?

Thank you seemed a bit ridiculous, and she couldn't tell him *see you later* because they both knew that to be false.

With a brief smile, Alexa pivoted away and headed toward the shiny black truck in the drive. She didn't risk looking back again as she turned around and drove away. She didn't even glance in the rearview mirrors. She needed to make a clean break and forget how much her heart got wrapped up in this heated affair…and she needed to forget the fact she'd deceived him by not telling him the truth of her identity.

But they'd never see each other again, so she needn't worry. Right?

Twelve

"If you're going to sulk and be moody, then go home."

Hayes ignored Nolan's comment and patted Jumper's side. He hadn't ridden his horse in five days. Not since he'd brought her back after Alexa left.

Actually, he hadn't been down to the stables since then at all. He'd been doing some behind-the-scenes work for the dude ranch, contacting engineers to do some surveying since they'd decided to add another set of cabins on the west side of the property. Hayes was fine with that locale. Nolan could oversee it once it was up and running.

When he hadn't been working with the settings and contractual aspects, Hayes had spent many sweaty hours in his kitchen. But every time he'd try to demo or stand back and think exactly what he wanted, he saw Alexa in there. He heard her telling him about her family and the gatherings and how he should have a large table stretching down the length of the room.

"Go home."

Hayes glanced up at Colt's demand and found both brothers staring at him now. "I'm tending to my horse. If I'm offending you two, why don't you leave?"

Colt shifted his boots on the stone walkway between the stalls and crossed his arms over his chest. If he thought that would intimidate Hayes, that was absurd. Nothing got to him anymore.

Well, one person did. She'd gotten to him with her compassion, the way she spoke of Mason, the images he'd seen of how she held her son like he was the most precious thing on earth. There was so much love in a woman like that.

"Listen, we've given you space to deal with the hell you've endured. I know you don't want to talk about it, but since your houseguest left, you've been especially standoffish."

Hayes smoothed a hand down Jumper's mane and snorted. "How the hell would you know? This is the first time you've seen me in days."

"You ignored my texts and didn't return my call about the engineer's ideas," Colt countered.

"I've been busy."

Trying to sleep without Alexa.

How insane was that? He'd actually slept with her only the one night, but for some reason that was the best rest he'd had since he'd come home. Maybe it was the sex relaxing him, but he didn't think so. Alexa understood him. She hadn't pushed verbally, but emotionally she'd been there. They were virtual strangers, yet they knew each other in the most intimate of ways.

"What the hell happened?" Nolan asked, then held out his hands. "No, don't tell me. If you like her, why are you here?"

Hayes glanced back toward his meddling brothers. "I refuse to get into some locker room chatter. Whatever happened between Alexa and myself is between us."

"Annabelle said she was crying when she came back to get her things," Colt supplied. The concern in his eyes could barely be seen beneath the wide brim of his hat, but Hayes missed nothing. "I saw how the two of you were."

"You saw us kissing," Hayes corrected. "Don't read any further into it."

"After that." Colt uncrossed his arms and took a step forward. "I saw the way you two looked at each other, the way you stared after her when she left. Don't tell me it was all physical because I don't believe it."

Hayes stared for a second before he turned his focus back to his mare. "I don't care what you believe."

But he did care that Alexa was crying. He shouldn't care. He should just let her go. When he'd asked her to stay he'd had a moment of weakness, though he hadn't been lying when he'd told her it was only so she'd stay in his bed. That was precisely where he wanted her and five days later his need was just as strong, if not stronger.

"Have you been to see Father lately?" Nolan asked, thankfully changing the subject.

Hayes led Jumper back into her stall. "I was there yesterday. He didn't know me, but he knew my name. He kept referring to the time I fell into the river."

"You were eight," Nolan stated. "He's been in that time frame for a while now. I think that's where he wants to stay. When I'm there, he's always talking about Mom, but we're all very young."

Hayes hated seeing his father robbed of his memories, of his dignity. They'd gotten him the best care possible and kept the rumors about the Elliott patriarch at bay. Nobody outside the immediate family needed to know just how bad their father was.

As much as he hated seeing his once robust dad in such shape, Hayes made a point to visit every few days. He knew his brothers did the same and they tried not to go on the same days so as not to confuse him. The dude ranch had been his baby and no matter what happened with his health, the Elliott brothers would see this through…which was just another reason he didn't have time to get swept away in some affair.

The weekend was enough. It had to be.

"Pepper said Alexa came into the store yesterday."

Hayes shot Nolan a glare, to which Nolan merely shrugged.

"And how does she know Alexa?"

"Stone River isn't that large of a town," Nolan replied. "And nearly everyone has been in Pepper's shop."

Nolan's wife had opened a flower shop that also showcased her one-of-a-kind paintings. Apparently the store had been thriving since the grand opening last year. No doubt Nolan had a hand in helping to make sure his wife's venture was a huge success.

Hayes slid the stall door closed, then turned and hooked his thumbs through his belt loops. "Is there a point to this story?" he asked his brother.

Nolan merely smiled. "Just gauging your reaction."

Glancing from brother to brother, Hayes took his hat off and tapped it against the side of his leg. "This is why I rarely come down here. Being analyzed by you two is not my idea of work or a good time. I'm fine. Okay, I'm not, but I will be."

"Is this the war trauma or your houseguest we're

talking about now?" Colt asked, leaning against the stall on the opposite side of the walkway.

Hayes leveled his gaze. "All of it."

Colt nodded and turned away. Heading toward the open end of the stables, he called over his shoulder, "Annabelle has Alexa's address on file."

Hayes clenched his teeth as Nolan stared with that damn smirk on his face. "Shut up."

He didn't want his meddling brothers, or his sisters-in-law, getting in his personal business. Though apparently it was a little too late for that.

Without a word, Hayes spun on his booted heel and left the stables. He either needed to work on some more demo to get this frustration out of his head or he...

No. That's not what he needed to do. He'd cut ties with Alexa. He'd learned his lesson about getting tangled up with the wrong woman and Alexa being a single mother was definitely not for him. Not that he didn't love kids. He adored his brothers' children. How could he not? Two beautiful twin girls and a bouncing baby boy?

There was just so much evil Hayes had seen. All the nightmares he had, sleeping and awake, would not be a good atmosphere for a child. Being an uncle was a far cry from being hands-on with a child every day and if he and Alexa became involved, he'd want to be hands-on. That goal from when he was younger still lived deep inside him. The goal of a family, of children. But he'd had to ignore that need—he'd had to push it so far down it wouldn't creep up and make him realize he was missing everything he'd wanted for his future.

Hayes hopped into his truck and pulled up the drive leading to his house. As he passed the main house, Annabelle sat on the porch swing watching her twin girls playing at her feet.

A small tug of jealousy slithered through him, but the unwanted emotion had no place in his life. Growing up, he'd always thought he'd have a family and they'd all live here on the ranch. Then life happened and reality smacked him in the face with a sledgehammer.

He threw up a hand in greeting when Annabelle lifted her head and smiled as he drove by. His brothers may have found happiness, and he was grateful they were bringing up another generation of Elliotts for the next chapter in their lives.

But if anyone was looking to him to carry on the name, well, they were wasting their time. Hayes wasn't about to take over rearing a child.

"You are so rotten."

Alexa laughed as she settled Mason onto her lap. She sat on the stoop and held her son in one hand and the container of bubbles in the other. Well, the now empty container, since Mason had opted to dump the bottle down her legs.

Good thing she was barefoot and in shorts. Mason only wore his swim trunks and a little dirt on his feet from where he'd been running around in their meager front yard for a while. The postage-stamp-size yard was such a disappointment after seeing the spread on Pebblebrook.

Alexa groaned. That certainly wasn't the first time that ranch, or the sexy rancher, had flooded her mind over the past week. It had been seven days since she'd left and there wasn't a day that went by where she didn't wonder what he was doing, how he was doing. Was he sleeping? Was he still tearing out the kitchen?

"Play." Mason clapped his hands, then smacked her legs. "Play."

Alexa sat the bottle next to her thigh and wrapped her arms around his slender little frame. "You silly boy. You dumped all the bubbles on Mommy. They're all gone."

"No."

"Yes," she countered. "They're all gone."

Mason reached over her hold and picked up the bottle. Turning it upside down, he shook it. A few random drops filtered out, onto her leg once again, and his lip started quivering.

"More," he cried.

"How about we clean up and go to the park?" she suggested.

The park was about a twenty-minute drive, but it had a fabulous play area and a nice walking path where she could take him for a stroll once he tired of playing. That way he got a nap and she got a little workout.

Granted the best workout she'd had in ages was the sledgehammer to the cabinets.

And once again her thoughts circled back to Hayes. Why couldn't that man just leave her head? In such a short time, he'd embedded himself so deeply into her life she worried what would've happened had she stayed longer.

Alexa shifted Mason and came to her feet, holding him against her hip. "Want to go swing and slide?"

He nodded, despite the tears in his eyes. "Swing."

"Let's go get some shoes and a shirt for you," she told him. "Then—"

The words died as a big, black truck pulled into her short drive and stopped right against her garage door. She'd seen that truck. And the man inside it had haunted her dreams for the past week.

What was he doing here?

"Truck, truck, truck," Mason chanted.

Adjusting her hold on her son, Alexa hated that her first thought was how frightening she must look. She was wearing her go-to outfit: old cutoff shorts, neon yellow to really accentuate how wide her backside was, and an old white tank with paint stains.

Oh, well. He'd come to her so he was going to have to see her in all her tacky glory. No doubt he had on another pair of those hip-hugging jeans, a T-shirt that stretched across glorious muscle tone and that familiar black hat with a brim, shielding a most impressive set of black eyes from the sun.

The man just sat there staring at her. Well, she assumed he was. That hat shadowed half his face. Was he going to get out? Had he changed his mind about visiting her? Were they in some warped staring contest?

Mason patted her cheek, pulling Alexa from her trance. She smiled at her son, though her stomach was in knots. She'd needed to break from Hayes. As amazing as their time together had been, she had to keep her distance.

He had been her husband's best friend. Hayes valued honesty and commitment and after all he'd been through, she wasn't sure he'd be too happy with sleeping with his best friend's widow.

The second his door swung open, Alexa pulled in a deep breath and stepped down onto the narrow walkway leading to her portion of the drive.

As he rounded the hood, her heart clenched and she couldn't stop herself from raking her gaze over him. Indeed, he wore exactly what she'd feared and he was absolute perfection. These seven days apart had done nothing to settle that attraction rooted deeply inside her.

"What are you doing here?" she asked as he came closer. Not the friendliest greeting, but they'd agreed to be done.

"Seeing you."

He said the words so simply as if leaving his ranch wasn't a big deal.

"You never leave home," she reminded him. "Or that's what the rumor has been."

He nodded, crossing his arms over his chest. "Some things are worth leaving for."

Now, why did he have to go and say things like that? Why did he have to make this about more than physical? Because showing up unannounced at her home was definitely taking things to another level.

"Wait. How did you know where I lived?" she asked, shifting Mason to her other hip. "Never mind. I'm sure you just asked your sister-in-law."

Mason reached out toward Hayes's hat, but Alexa eased back. "No, baby."

"He's fine."

Alexa held on to her son's hand. "He'd pull your hat off and chew on it or throw it down."

Hayes took his hat off. "And that would be just fine."

He held the hat out to Mason. Alexa did not want this little bonding moment, no matter how harmless. Nothing about Hayes Elliott was harmless.

Not only had she gotten way too attached during those few days, she now carried a secret that would no doubt anger him and make him look at her with disdain and resentment. She'd rather not have that hanging over her. Hayes had been hurt enough.

Mason grabbed the hat and sure enough, the brim went straight to his mouth.

"Oh, Mason," she cried. "Don't do that."

Hayes's mouth quirked into a grin. "He's really fine."

Yeah, but she wasn't. Watching another man interact with her son…well, that was something she hadn't prepared herself for. Mason wasn't used to being around men. Alexa never dated, certainly never brought a guy to her house, and the babysitter was a woman. Mason didn't really have an adult male in his life.

And she sure as hell couldn't let Hayes into her son's life. The fragility of her heart where this man was concerned was simply too much. And he was in such a delicate state himself. No matter how amazing they'd been together, him showing up here was a bad idea.

"Why are you here?" she murmured.

"You already asked that."

Alexa lifted her eyes to meet his. "You never answered."

"I told you I wanted to see you."

She quirked a brow.

"Fine. What do you want me to say?" He put the hat on Mason's head and lifted her son from her arms. Shocked, Alexa watched as Hayes smiled down at Mason as if this were the most normal thing in the world. "Do you want me to tell you my sleep has gone back to hell since you left? That when I walk in my kitchen I wonder if you'd like what I've done? That I put up a damn tire swing because you mentioned it?"

Oh, no. This was even worse than she'd thought.

"We agreed—"

He held up his free hand. "Yes. We agreed to be physical. I miss the hell out of you, Alexa. I'm not here to ask for a relationship or even marriage. I want you and when I want something, I make sure I have it."

Mason ran his hands over Hayes's stubbled jaw. Back and forth, his little fingers raked over the dark hair along his chin. Alexa couldn't tear her eyes away. They were literally bonding right before her eyes and she couldn't do a thing to stop it.

"You can't just come here and expect me to... What? What do you think will happen now?"

Hayes strong hands held her son so tightly. "Come back to the house with me."

"No."

Those lips twitched again as if he were trying not to smile or laugh. It was great to see that emotion from him, but at the same time, she couldn't fall into that rabbit hole.

"Bring Mason. Play in the yard. That's what you wanted, right? A yard for your son?"

Alexa narrowed her gaze. "You're not playing fair."

He eased closer, his eyes dropping to her lips. "We've already established I'm not playing and I never said I was fair."

Mason turned his head, causing the hat to bump against Hayes's face and topple to the ground. Alexa quickly scooped it up and handed it back to Hayes before reaching for her son.

"We're headed to the park," she informed him. "So, if you'll excuse us."

He remained right where he was, unmoving, barely blinking. The way he stared at her with those dark eyes made her wonder if he could see into her soul. Could one broken person actually connect so deeply with another?

Alexa shook off the haunting thought.

"You get me," he stated, taking a half step closer. "Hell, I've only known you a week and there were ways you understood me better than my own family."

Swallowing, Alexa adjusted Mason as he laid his

head on her shoulder. Apparently he was ready for a nap, so maybe the park wasn't in their immediate future.

"That's not true," she argued. There was no way.

"Do you think it was easy for me to come here?" he asked. "I battled this for a week, but damn it, I want you to come back to my house. Just come for the day and I'll drive you back."

Alexa laughed. "This is absurd, Hayes. You're getting caught up in a moment that passed."

In a lightning-flash move, he snaked an arm around her waist and hauled her free side against him. "The moment didn't pass. I still want you. I've been through hell, and when I see something or someone that will bring a semblance of happiness, I'm going to take it."

Oh, mercy, she wanted him, too. The fierce need she had a week ago had only grown and now he was here and touching her, looking at her with the same hunger as he'd had when they'd been stranded and naked.

"Bring Mason. We'll ride horses."

Alexa closed her eyes. He'd put himself out there and come to her. He'd shoved aside his fear of leaving the ranch. He was inviting her son to ride horses, which he'd never done, and he wasn't even close to backing down.

"Fine," she whispered. "We'll come. But I'm driving myself and I'm not spending the night."

Hayes ran his lips along her jawline. "We'll see."

The shiver raced through her and Alexa vowed to herself not to sleep with Hayes again. Not with the secret she carried. Maybe one day, when he healed and they were friends?

No, not even then. Someone like Hayes would see sleeping with his late buddy's wife as a betrayal. He could never know.

Thirteen

"You were pretty sure of yourself."

Hayes stepped into the stable by his house and threw a glance over his shoulder to Alexa. "I had the stable hands bring them up. If you hadn't come, the horses still could've stayed here."

He was a damn fool for bringing her back here, but it felt right. She felt right to have here. Not that he was thinking long-term or a commitment, but damn it, he was at a point in his life that if any happiness came his way, he was going to grab hold with both hands and to hell with the consequences.

He could even accept the bond he was forming with her kid.

Right now, he was going to take a ride with Alexa and Mason. The little guy was too adorable and when he'd reached out for Hayes earlier, he hadn't hesitated to take him. Children were so innocent, so loving, and that was something he'd quickly discovered when he'd gotten home. His nieces and nephew had calmed him and kept him grounded and sane at times. Having Mason here with Alexa, damn it…there was something a little too familial about it, but he hadn't been lying when he'd said he'd missed her.

And he hated that underlying vulnerability and loathed even more that she'd witnessed it.

"I'm still not comfortable around horses," Alexa commented. "So how should we do this? Maybe just set Mason on the saddle and let him pet the horse?"

Hayes slid open a stall and shook his head. "Nah. He can ride with me on Doc and you can take Jumper. We'll stay right around here so you're comfortable."

He tossed a thick blanket on Jumper's back and grabbed a saddle from the wall. Alexa's silence had him risking a glance her way. She chewed on her bottom lip as she held tight to her still-sleeping son. Apparently the kid could sleep through anything.

Hayes had held him while Alexa had changed earlier. He hadn't been opposed to the little shorts and tank she sported, but her jeans and T-shirt would be a better option for riding.

"I'll hold on to him," he assured her. "We'll go slow and he'll be just fine."

She smoothed Mason's black hair across his forehead and nodded. The kid looked exactly like her with that dark skin and coal-like hair. Even his eyes were dark as midnight. And her love for her son was so evident. Hayes knew she'd do anything to protect him. That family bond and loyalty ran deep in him too, so he knew full well how much Mason meant to Alexa. They were all each other had left.

"I want to talk to you about something."

Her eyes darted to his as she lifted her brows. Mason

stirred in her arms and she patted his back. "What's that?"

After securing the saddle, Hayes rubbed the back of his neck. "I have a thing I need to go to in a couple weeks and I need a date."

Why did he feel like a fool in high school asking out the homecoming queen? Probably because he'd never asked out the homecoming queen. He'd simply hopped in the bed of his truck after the game and flipped up her dress and lost his virginity. So...yeah, this was quite different, but he still hated the uncertainty.

No, he actually hated the whole ordeal he'd been faced with and the ceremony coming up. It was absurd, useless, and he was the least deserving person to be honored.

"I received a phone call from the governor a couple weeks ago."

"What?" Alexa stepped forward, her eyes wide. "The *governor* called you? You just throw that out like it's not a big deal."

He shrugged and eased Jumper from her stall. "It's not. I mean, they want to have a dinner and present some award for my service and sacrifice. It's completely unnecessary, but it's in two weeks and I want you to go with me."

Mason continued to stir until he popped his head up with a yawn. He glanced around, his attention landing on Jumper and the little guy immediately started clapping.

"I'd say he's ready for his first ride," Hayes stated. He lifted the rein and hung it on the hook outside the stall before moving to the next one with Doc. "Give me one second and I'll get my horse ready, then I can help you onto yours."

"I don't need help," she stated. "Can you get back to
the governor and why I need to be your date?"

He quickly blanketed and saddled Doc. "I'd rather
move on and we just agree I'll pick you up two weeks
from yesterday at six. I guess I'll wear my uniform, so
you'll probably want to wear a fancier dress."

"I don't—"

"Have one?" he asked, tossing her a glance. "I've
already called in some favors and they're being delivered. Keep whatever you want. Keep one, keep them
all. I don't care."

Hayes led Doc out and hooked his reins, as well. He
patted the side of the stallion's neck, smoothing out the
coarse mane.

"Would you slow down for a second?" she demanded.

Blowing out a sigh, he turned to face her. "Listen, I
don't want to go. The award is absurd and the last thing
I need is recognition. I didn't do anything overseas that
any of my fellow soldiers wouldn't have done. I just happened to survive. I don't want to go, but I sure as hell
don't want to go alone, because…"

Softening her facial expression, Alexa stepped forward and reached for his hand. "Because you don't like
going anywhere?"

Shame and guilt slithered through him. "So you'll
go?"

The silence settled between them. Mason lifted his
hands toward Jumper and Hayes slid the boy from Alexa's arms.

"Right here," he told Mason, taking his little hand
and laying it on the velvety part of Jumper's nose.
"Soft."

He'd much rather focus on the horses, on introducing
Mason to his first ride. There was something so magi-

cal about getting on the back of a horse and setting out for nowhere. Not a care in the world, no troubles followed him… Well, they did, but at least he was more at ease out in the pasture.

He'd also been at ease with Alexa lying next to him in bed. She might be adamant that she wasn't going to get between the sheets with him again, but he was just as adamant that she was. How could he give up on something that felt so perfect? On something that settled him in ways nothing else had in months?

Whether she liked it or not, Alexa was exactly what he needed, and wanted, right now. And he'd be damned before he let her just walk away because he knew full well she felt something, too.

"I'll go," she finally conceded. "But I'll buy my own dress."

"Already taken care of." He took her hand and led her to Jumper. "They'll be there on Wednesday evening."

Her lips thinned as she settled her free hand on the saddle horn. "You're arrogant."

"True," he agreed. "But I'll have a smokin'-hot date."

With a laugh and an eye roll, she mounted the horse. Damn if she didn't look good here.

But that was an image he'd have to get out of his head. Pebblebrook was his. At least this portion was. He wasn't looking for another woman to fill the void his fiancée had left. He sure as hell wasn't looking for a baby in his life.

He wasn't looking for anything more than what Alexa had to offer—sweaty nights and a sense of peace. He needed that, so he needed her.

Her vow to stay away and keep her feelings compartmentalized was shot all to hell. Somewhere between him showing her how perfect he was with her son and him swallowing his fear and asking her about the dinner, Alexa had slipped further into…

No. Even she couldn't say it to herself. There was no room for anything other than friendship. Okay, they'd slept together and now they were friends, but whatever. Anything more would be tragic…and simply asking for heartache. Hers and his.

Seeing Hayes with her son, riding through the fields, it had been too much so she'd kept her eyes on the horizon.

Now they were back at his house and he was making sure the horses were fed and watered. Alexa sat on the edge of the back porch and watched as Mason toddled around plucking up random grassy weeds. The tire swing swayed in the distance from a large, sturdy branch.

It was all Alexa could do not to peek inside the kitchen window. She was dying to know what stage he was in with the space they'd demolished. Knowing him, he hadn't sat around and done nothing inside there.

A large black truck moved slowly up the drive and Alexa came to her feet to gather Mason. She remained on the porch and watched as Annabelle stepped from the vehicle. Alexa didn't need to be spotted here; that would only be fodder for the family gossip mill. They all undoubtedly knew she'd spent the entire weekend here during the storm. And here she was again, this time with her son.

Annabelle hopped out of the truck, her blond hair swirling around her shoulders. She offered a big smile and a wave. Alexa returned the kind gestures, though her heart was pounding. How was she going to explain being back? It wasn't like she and Hayes were... What? Dating? Nope. They weren't even having sex anymore.

Friendship, that's all this was. And really, could their relationship even be labeled as friends? She kept an epic secret from him and he had hang-ups about life in general. She wasn't ready to have a man come into her son's life and Hayes wasn't looking for an instant family. They were going nowhere fast and there was nothing she could do but hold on.

Thankfully, Hayes stepped from the stables and crossed to Annabelle. Alexa really didn't want to have to make awkward conversation.

"What are you doing back here?" Hayes asked, a smile on his face as he accepted a hug from his sister-in-law. "Where're the girls?"

"Actually, Colt is home with them because he's been in the stable all night."

"What's wrong?" Hayes asked. "I had a couple horses sent down to me and never heard anything was wrong."

Alexa stepped off the porch and eased Mason back down into the grass. She tried not to appear that she was eavesdropping, but it was rather difficult to not overhear everything.

Annabelle waved a hand as she reached for the passenger-side door. "Oh, you know how he is. Since the vet told him that the new weanling needed extra care, he's like a worried father. But I got up this morning because I couldn't sleep without him there, so I made you some sticky buns and herb bread."

Alexa's mouth watered at the thought...and she gained five pounds just from this conversation. Carbs were not her friend. But Annabelle used her baking to her advantage and advertised that along with the B and

B. The two went hand in hand…or so Alexa assumed. It wasn't like she'd actually experienced anything the B and B had to offer.

No, Alexa had been taking advantage of what the mysterious Elliott brother had to offer instead.

"Good thing I brought extra, since you have company." Annabelle pulled the dishes from the truck and Hayes quickly took them from her. "Thanks. I can bring more later."

"No, she's not staying."

Alexa's shoulders stiffened. True, she wasn't, but he was awfully quick to dismiss her. Most likely that was for her benefit, since Alexa had been so adamant about not staying long.

But now that she was here, she wanted to. She loved watching Mason roam around the yard. She'd loved seeing him on the back of Doc and nestled against Hayes…but those were things she couldn't want and Hayes had made it abundantly clear that he wasn't looking for more.

She wasn't either, but she could see herself here. No matter how she'd fought it during their time together, she realized now that she could see herself with him— if there wasn't a secret settled between them.

Now she was going to a formal dinner with him and he'd managed to get dresses ordered for her. Did he know her size? Did he know that anything too form-fitting would only accentuate the flare of her hips and the roundness still in her belly from having a baby?

Alexa rubbed her forehead and smiled as Mason ran and toppled over. He got right back up and took off again, this time straight to Hayes.

Coming to her feet, Alexa started for Mason, but without missing a beat, Hayes scooped him up and held him in one strong arm while juggling the baked goods in the other.

"Let me take him," Alexa said as she neared. "We really should be going anyway."

Hayes shot her a look, holding tight to Mason. Instead he handed her the bread and buns. "Take these into the kitchen. I know you've been wondering what I've done in there."

Alexa narrowed her eyes, to which he merely quirked one dark brow. This was not the time for a standoff, not with his sister-in-law mere feet away, taking in the whole scene.

Taking the baked goods, Alexa turned to Annabelle. "Thanks. These smell wonderful."

"I hope you'll stick around long enough to enjoy them."

Nothing could be said to that, not without incriminating herself, so Alexa turned and headed for the house. Hayes knew exactly how to pique her interest…in more ways than one. But she wanted to see what he'd done inside. Then she would take Mason and go. The longer she stayed, the harder it would be to leave.

But the second she stepped inside, her mouth dropped. He'd not only gutted the room, he'd taken down the wall to the dining room. Dark flooring had been laid and right in the middle was an old farmhouse table that stretched so far, it could easily seat twenty people. There were no chairs or benches and the cabinets weren't installed, but there was a table.

Just like she'd suggested.

Well hell. Now what was she supposed to do? She wanted to keep her distance, but how could she? Everything he did—

The back door squeaked open and Alexa sat the

baked goods on the table before turning around. Hayes eased the door shut with one hand while holding on to Mason.

"What do you think?"

It was all she could do not to choke up at the heart-clenching emotions swirling around inside her. "I love it."

And it was all too much. The table, the tire swing, the horse riding…the man standing in the doorway holding her son. If she stayed, she'd never leave and that simply wasn't an option.

"I—I have to go."

She crossed the room, took Mason from Hayes's arms, but he didn't move out of her way to let her through.

"Why are you running?"

Keeping her eyes locked on the tire swing outside the back door, Alexa patted Mason's back and held him tight. "Because I can't do this. You don't need me to heal. You seem to be doing fine."

"I'm not," he muttered. "I want you here."

She shifted her focus to him, her eyes locking onto his. "But for how long?"

The muscle in his jaw tightened as silence settled heavy between them. His eyes darted to her mouth, but Alexa couldn't let him kiss her because she wanted so much more than a kiss.

She wanted to start thinking about a future and moving on, and no one had stirred anything within her like Hayes.

Yet she had to keep her son in the forefront of her thoughts. He needed stability in his life. Not only that, Alexa worried what would happen if Hayes decided family life wasn't for him. Sure, he was close to his own family, but she was a package deal. He had so many issues to deal with and adding that instant family to the mix hadn't been on his list.

Plus, she'd kept Scott's identity to herself. She'd thought they wouldn't see each other again so she hadn't brought it up when she'd been at Hayes's house. Now though, they were seeing each other and that secret hovered between them. Had she just told him when she realized it, maybe it wouldn't have been a big deal, but enough time had passed that he would feel betrayed by her silence once he found out.

There were just too many barriers between her and the man she wanted. But she was discovering over and over he was the one man she couldn't have.

Fourteen

Hayes's father wasn't looking any better and his mind was being flat-out cruel today. Hayes had visited earlier and was instantly confused for Nolan, but not Nolan now—the Nolan in kindergarten.

Having the most influential man in his life not even recognize him was hell on Hayes. But he couldn't stay away. No matter how far gone the patriarch was, Hayes had to see his dad, had to talk to him and use him as a sounding board. Now more than ever he wanted his father's advice, but that hadn't happened.

His dad had stared out the window and started talking about his wife in the present tense, as if she hadn't been gone for years. Then he'd turned his attention to Hayes and told him when he grew up, he should find someone to love and settle down and have babies to continue on at Pebblebrook. He went on and on about finding the love of his life, how he almost let her go once but came to his senses and put his pride aside.

Hayes knew all about how his parents had almost lost each other because of his father's pride. His mother had often reminded him in a joking manner.

Now that he was home, all he wanted to do was ride. He needed to talk to Colt, though. The engineer had been out early this morning and his survey had ended up on Hayes's property. Hell no. The dude ranch would come to fruition without infringing on his area. That was nonnegotiable.

He pulled up next to the stable and didn't see Colt, but that didn't mean anything. After several minutes of searching, Hayes gave up and started walking toward Colt's house. Finally, he found him in his study on the second floor behind a closed door.

"You hiding from the world?" Hayes asked, closing the door at his back.

Colt didn't even look up from the computer. "I'm working on this absurd marketing plan. I had it hired out and the damn thing came back looking like an amateur organized it. Annabelle gave me some ideas to fix it, but I'm actually looking for another firm. I don't want this messed up."

Hayes crossed the spacious room and took a seat in one of the leather club chairs across from his brother's desk. "I just came back from seeing Dad."

That got Colt's attention. "I was there yesterday. How was he today?"

Shaking his head, Hayes pulled off his hat and propped it on his knee. "He called me Nolan, referred to that time Nolan brought home a Mother's Day picture he'd made in kindergarten, then he fell into talking about Mom."

Colt eased back in his seat and sighed. "At least he's in a good mood when talking about Mom. I'll take that over the rage any day."

Hayes hadn't experienced those days with his father, but he'd heard that sometimes his father demanded to see his home, demanded someone take him to Pebblebrook. On those occasions, he still wasn't in his right mind. He was confused about where he was and why he wasn't home. Every day brought a different challenge.

"That's not why I came," Hayes stated. "I had a visit from the engineer. He mentioned expanding onto my property."

Colt eased forward, resting his forearms on the desk. "I never okayed that."

"Then why was he there?"

Colt shook his head. "He mentioned it to me in the beginning stages. He said there might be more revenue if we spread out over the land."

"And that was while I was away?" Hayes asked.

"Yeah. But Nolan and I had the area where we wanted the cabins marked off on the map." Colt narrowed his gaze. "What did he say to you? Because I'd hate to have to find another engineer this late in the game."

Hayes blew out a breath. "He was nosing more than anything, trying to get a feel from me what I thought. He left knowing exactly where I stand on outsiders on my part of the property."

The engineer wasn't the only reason Hayes was in a pissy mood. He was so damn confused about Alexa.

Tonight was the awards ceremony, which he hadn't mentioned to his family. He honestly didn't want this to be a big deal. If they found out later, fine. But if they knew now, they'd blow it all up and insist on attending.

He'd invited Alexa because he wanted to be with someone without feeling the pressure of being someone he wasn't. He wanted a friend.

But she was more than that, wasn't she? She was so much more and there was no denying he was in deep with her, which ultimately was going to put him in deep with Mason.

Damn it. That little boy was so sweet, so precious. He looked like Alexa and was so loving and free with his affection. When Hayes had been holding him... Even now just thinking about that weight in his arms had Hayes pausing, his heart tightening in fear...and affection.

Colt tipped his head. "Everything else okay?" he asked.

"Getting there." Hayes didn't know that he'd ever be the man he was before leaving, but he was slowly making steps to improve himself little by little. Alexa definitely had a hand in his recovery. "I need to head out."

Hayes came to his feet and slapped his hat back on his head. He had to get back to dress for the ceremony and leave with enough time to pick up Alexa and head to the governor's mansion, which was nearly two hours away.

"You know we're all here for you."

Hayes stilled in the doorway at Colt's words. He threw a glance over his shoulder. "Yeah. I know."

The look Colt gave him was that same one he'd had when Hayes had first returned. Pity. When would they stop? When would they start acting like he wasn't going to shatter?

Hayes headed back to his house. He had a date tonight. He hadn't spoken to Alexa since she'd left the ranch, but he knew she wouldn't go back on their date. Besides, he also knew she'd chosen a dress; she'd sent the others back. He'd paid for delivery of jewelry and shoes, too. Hopefully she'd found what she needed. He knew she'd be stunning in anything, but he wanted her to feel special.

There was too much going on in his mind for him to decipher the newfound emotions, but he didn't have time to figure them out. He wanted to get to Alexa and get this night over with.

As he pulled up to his house, he knew he'd be lying if he said he wasn't going to try to seduce her. He meant it when he said he wanted her still. Relationships weren't for him, but Alexa was the one bright spot in his life right now and he was damn well going to hold on to her…which meant he better wrap his mind around the fact he'd have to man up for Mason.

Hayes wasn't about to enter a child's life and not be anything less than stable.

Maybe she should've kept the classic black dress.

Alexa turned side to side in front of her floor-length mirror. The red dress draped over her shoulders and hugged her every curve…maybe a little too well. Something about the trumpet-style skirt and fitted bodice had made her feel sexy when she'd been trying on the host of dresses Hayes had sent.

But now that it was go time, she wondered if she should've ignored the sexy and kept the black with a modest scoop neck.

What did one wear to a governor's mansion?

Alexa smoothed a hand down her abdomen, hoping to rid herself of some of those nerves. Sadie had offered to take Mason for the night. All Alexa had to say was that she had a date and Sadie jumped at the opportunity to quiz Alexa. She didn't give in. What she and Hayes shared was… Honestly, she wasn't even sure, so how was she supposed to tell anyone else?

Just as she fastened the bracelet around her wrist, her doorbell rang. In that instant, her heart sped up and the chaos of jumbled nerves returned.

She headed toward the door figuring if she was nervous, she couldn't imagine what Hayes was feeling. The man didn't want to leave his ranch, let alone go to some fancy ceremony where he was going to be awarded for something he felt guilty about.

Alexa wasn't sure what had happened overseas, but those events had changed Hayes forever.

Pulling in a shaky breath, she opened her door…and was greeted with the sexiest man she'd ever seen. He'd forgone the cowboy hat and boots, the well-worn jeans and T-shirt. He stood before her wearing his uniform. The black single-breasted jacket stretched across his broad shoulders. Various pins and patches adorned the shoulders and chest. The offset beret seemed to draw even more attention to those black eyes.

The man flawlessly slid from hardworking rancher to hero in uniform.

Alexa shivered at the way he raked his eyes over her. Slowly, inch by inch, as if assessing what she wore beneath. Arousal curled through her, as she knew it would. She hadn't seen him in days and just being near him put her body on high alert. She hadn't mentally prepared herself for the uniform, though.

"We're ditching the ceremony," he growled as he stepped over the threshold. He slid his arms around her waist and aligned his body with hers. "Damn, Alexa."

She held on to his biceps to keep her balance. "We can't ditch. I'm pretty sure there's some unwritten law about snubbing the governor, especially considering you're the guest of honor."

"You smell so damn good," he murmured against her ear.

Alexa shivered against him and was having a difficult time recalling why they couldn't just stay here.

Oh, yeah. The award and the fact she'd promised herself not to get more deeply involved. Because if she took things further, then she'd have to tell him who her husband was. And because she was still unsure about bringing a man into Mason's life. She didn't want to confuse her son. She made continual efforts to make sure his life was secure.

"We're going to be late if we don't go."

Hayes eased back. "You're the perfect reason to be late and they'd all understand once they saw you in this dress."

Apparently she'd kept the right one.

"Thanks for this," she told him, stepping back and removing herself from his arms. She couldn't think when he touched her. "I would've gotten my own dress, though."

"I wanted to buy this for you."

"And the jewelry and shoes?" she questioned. "I thought I was just borrowing these things."

"They're yours," he replied, tugging at the cuffs of his jacket. "You could've kept everything I sent."

Alexa laughed. "There were nearly thirty dresses to choose from."

He stared back as if he didn't see the problem. First of all, what would a single mom and preschool teacher do with that many formal dresses? Second, she couldn't even imagine the cost. This dress alone was probably one paycheck. She'd seen the label and that wasn't even adding in the cost of her accessories.

Yeah, definitely nothing she could wear to the playground with Mason.

"Thanks for not backing out," he told her, all joking and flirting set aside.

"I wouldn't do that to you."

Hayes nodded and held her attention with those serious black eyes. "I know you wouldn't. You should have, but you didn't. Let's just put all our issues aside and enjoy our night together."

She opened her mouth, but he held up a hand. "I know it's selfish," he went on. "If you want to talk, I'll listen, but after the ceremony."

Alexa stepped forward and framed his clean-shaven face. "I know this is difficult for you, but you are deserving."

He started to turn his face away, but she pulled him back. "You are."

A corner of his mouth kicked up. "Are you wearing underwear?"

Alexa smacked his chest, getting a palm-full of medals. "We better go."

"It would help distract me from the award I don't want if you just tell me what you're wearing underneath." He snaked a hand out and ran it over her backside. Letting out a groan, he muttered, "A thong. You're killing me."

Alexa shifted away from him, knowing full well if they didn't get out that door, they'd be in her bedroom… if they even made it that far.

"Now that you have something else to concentrate on, let's go." She grabbed her clutch and placed her keys and phone inside before closing the gold clasp. "I hope they have chocolate cake at this dinner."

Hayes held the door open for her and swatted her on the butt. "Dessert isn't happening at the ceremony."

Shivers raced through her as she came to the realization that they would end up back here. And the realization that he was going to keep coming around and she was going to let him.

She was going to have to tell him the truth about Scott and then he'd have to trust that she never purposely betrayed him.

But not tonight.

Tonight was about him getting a prestigious award whether he wanted to accept it or not. Tomorrow, she would tell him everything.

Tomorrow, she would explain how she'd fallen for him and see if this could be more than just a friendship with intimacy.

For the first time in two years, Alexa was ready to move on and cling to the happiness she'd discovered. If only her lie by omission didn't stand in the way... If only Hayes wanted a family, because she and Mason were a team.

Fifteen

The handshaking, fake smiles, impromptu speech and that damn shiny award with his name engraved on the gold plate were all sickening.

Hayes drove back toward Alexa's home. It was close to midnight according to the glow from the dash clock. Alexa had slipped her shoes off onto the floorboard of his sporty car. He'd opted for something nicer than his truck, mostly for Alexa because he didn't give a damn what anyone else thought of him.

She hadn't said a word since they left. It was almost as if she knew he needed to be alone inside his mind. That was what was so great about her. She just knew what he needed.

"Seven of my best friends were killed that day." He wound through the streets leading to her town house. He didn't even realize he'd started speaking, but now that he'd started, he found he didn't want to stop. "We were sent in to rescue three women and eighteen girls at a school that had been overtaken. We had a solid plan, but nothing is foolproof."

Alexa reached across, sliding her hand over his on the console. Silence settled between them, but her act of compassion spoke volumes. Damn it. She was getting to him. He'd known she was, had known the more he was with her the more likely he was to want more of her.

"I'll spare you the details, but there was an ambush," he added, trying in vain to block the images that played like a horror movie inside his head. "The women and girls were saved, I was spared, but…"

"I won't tell you not to have survivor's guilt." Her soft words filled the cramped area. "That's human nature to wonder what if. I went through it. I'm still going through it. I wonder what would've happened had we known about my husband's condition. Could we have prevented his death? But I can't get stuck in that mindset, mostly because of Mason. He deserves to have his mother at one hundred percent."

"Mason is a lucky boy," Hayes stated. "I'm sure he'll know how loved he is."

Alexa sighed. "That's my hope. But you're doing remarkably well, considering. You only tensed a few times tonight being with all those people."

He turned his hand over, lacing his fingers with hers. "Figures you'd notice."

"I know you," she said simply.

Wasn't that the truth. After such a short time, she'd honed right in on what made him tick, what his fears were, how to handle them. He hadn't wanted to show any vulnerability, but Alexa never made him feel as if he had. She made him feel…human. Like everything he was going through was okay and he'd make it.

"I just pictured your underwear."

Her laughter warmed him, taking him to that place that was so perfect, so right. He hadn't thought such a place existed after he'd come home, but since meeting Alexa, he'd discovered maybe there was a bright spot in the world. Maybe that was the one thing he shouldn't fear.

"I could tell when you'd look at me across the room," she told him. "I knew exactly what you were thinking."

"Good. Because I'm about to show you exactly what was running through my mind."

He pulled into her drive and barely got the car in park before he reached across and cupped the back of her head, bringing her mouth to his.

Finally. He hadn't kissed her all evening, hadn't touched her in the way he'd wanted to. In short, he'd been on his best behavior.

Now, he was about to be on his worst. He reached for the zipper on the back of the dress. "How the hell did you get into this thing?" he growled against her lips.

Alexa laughed, her eyes shining bright as she stared back at him. "Side zipper, but we better get inside before my neighbors see us making out like teenagers."

"Your neighbors' lights are off."

Alexa tugged on the door handle. "I'm not taking the chance."

Hayes followed her inside. They barely made it in the door before he backed her up against it, flicked the lock and caged her head between his forearms.

"You have three seconds to get that side zipper or I'm going to rip this dress off."

Her hands were moving as she tossed her head back with a sultry laugh. "You paid for it."

"Best money I've ever spent."

As the dress peeled away and fell below her breasts,

Hayes was on her. He couldn't get enough and this entire evening of foreplay had nearly done him in. Watching her curves move beneath that red dress, the way her dark hair flowed around her shoulders, seeing her laugh across the room, then catch his eye. He knew he wasn't the only one thinking of this.

Her little striptease had him jerking his uniform off, quickly ridding himself of everything so he could be skin to skin. They still hadn't turned on lights, but he didn't need them. There wasn't a spot on her body he wasn't familiar with.

He lifted her against the door, dipping his head to capture her mouth once again. Alexa's legs locked around his waist and he wasted no time in joining their bodies. Finesse would come later—much later. Right now he had a need that had been building all night.

Her fingers dug into his shoulders as she arched that sweet body against his. Hayes slid a hand down the dip in her waist and over the flare of her hip, gripping her to hold her in place. She dug her heels into his backside and Hayes knew she was on the brink.

He tore his lips from hers and shifted just enough to see her face. The slight glow from the porch light filtered in through the window, slashing just enough of a beam across her face for him to fully appreciate her pleasure.

"Look at me," he commanded, squeezing her hip.

Those black eyes immediately locked onto his and a second later she cried out. That's exactly what he'd been waiting on. Seeing her come apart in his arms, knowing he was the one who made her lose control was all he wanted. Her hips quickened as she came apart and that's all it took to have him joining her.

Hayes's body trembled as he fisted one hand on the

door beside her head and continued to hold on to her hip. His knee was starting to shake from being too weak, but hell if he'd give in now.

Alexa ran her fingertips up and down his back, his arms, murmuring something in Spanish as he came down from the tremors. Resting his forehead against hers, he pulled in a breath of sweet jasmine...the same scent she'd tortured him with all night.

"Do you have the energy to get to the bedroom?" she asked.

Hayes laughed. "If it's not far. Or we could sleep here on the floor."

"Let me down," she told him, untangling her legs from his waist. "Your knee has to be hurting."

He stepped back and said nothing.

"Exactly," she confirmed. "You shifted too much and kept fisting your hand by my head. Get in bed and rest that."

Hayes instantly lifted her up and over his shoulder.

"Put me down," she cried, smacking his back. "Hayes, your leg is going to give out and we'll both be down."

"Like hell," he growled. "I'll rest it when we get in there. Better yet, you can give me a rubdown. Now tell me where the bedroom is."

"Last door on the right."

He palmed her backside, earning him another laugh from her. Damn, that laugh made everything seem so right, so perfect. Could such happiness be his for the taking? Alexa had lost her husband and never claimed to be looking for a relationship. Hell, he hadn't either, but the idea of letting her go, the thought of another man even touching her settled a new level of rage within him.

She also hadn't mentioned wanting or even needing a man to fill the role of daddy to her son. Maybe that's not something she wanted at all. It was one thing to be involved in an affair, but quite another to become a family.

Hayes's eyes had gotten used to the darkness and the small night-light glowing from Mason's bedroom across the hall lit up enough for him to make out the shape of her bed. Hayes dropped her on the end and instantly was on her.

"I'll take that rubdown in a bit," he told her as he covered her body with his. "First I'm going to show you exactly how thankful I am that you went with me tonight."

Alexa stretched, smiling when her body protested. She was sore in the most glorious ways. The sun shone through the sheers of her room and one thick arm draped across her midsection. How could she not wake up with a smile on her face after last night?

She was glad she'd let Mason stay over with Sadie. Alexa knew they'd get home late and didn't want to put Sadie out too much...or more than she already was. But Sadie was so happy that Alexa was going on a date, she'd eagerly volunteered to watch Mason all night.

Hayes shifted and groaned, and his heavy leg slid over hers. The coarse hairs made her shiver. Who knew all the little things she missed from a man's touch? Obviously, he was the first man in this bed since Scott... but Alexa didn't feel like this was wrong in any way.

That's how she knew it was time to come clean about who her husband was.

She flattened her hand over Hayes's arm and slid it up and over his shoulder. Keeping her eyes on his face, she watched as his lids fluttered. His hold on her tightened as he pulled her closer.

"Stop, temptress," he mumbled.

Alexa couldn't help but laugh. "You slept good."

"I'd keep sleeping if you weren't feeling me up."

Shifting in his arms, Alexa nipped at his chin. "I believe I woke with your bare arm over my midsection and then you wrapped your leg around me. You want to be felt up."

Hayes slid his hand over her bare hip and settled on the dip in her waist. Alexa's body instantly responded, but then he curled those fingers in and started tickling her.

"Hayes," she squealed. "Stop that."

A cell started ringing somewhere in the house. She didn't recognize the tone, so it must be his. She smacked at his arms as he continued to tickle her. He wrestled her beneath him as she continued to wriggle around and try to dodge the torture.

"Your cell," she panted, trying to breathe. "It's... Stop that. It's ringing."

Hayes loomed over her, the widest smile on his face. She hadn't seen him like that before. A smirk here and there, a naughty grin, sure. But a full-fledged genuine smile was staring back at her. Alexa's heart tumbled over in her chest.

"What's that look for?" he asked, resting his hands on either side of her head. "You were just laughing and now you look on the verge of tears."

The cell stopped in the other room, silence once again settling around them.

"I haven't been this happy in a long time." She reached up, framed his face and stared into his eyes. "I didn't think I could be, but you've done something to me. I wasn't expecting this."

"I—"

His cell went off again. With a sigh, he eased off her and turned to head from the room. He'd only taken two steps when he froze. His shoulders tensed and Alexa followed his line of vision.

Her heart immediately sank. How could she have forgotten about that photo? The wedding picture of her and Scott had sat so long on her dresser, and she hadn't been able to remove it after his death. Then she just...didn't.

The cell continued to ring, the only thing breaking through the heavy tension. Hayes slowly made his way to the silver frame and picked it up. Alexa sat up in the bed, pulling the comforter up and under her arms.

"Were you ever going to tell me?" he asked.

Alexa closed her eyes, not wanting to see his face when he turned around. She was a coward—clearly.

"I didn't know at first," she said. "Then I didn't think we'd see each other anymore."

When he didn't say anything, Alexa risked looking up, but wished she hadn't. Hayes stood at the end of her bed, clutching the picture in one hand and staring at her as if he hadn't just been with her all night, as if everything up until this point had been a lie.

"What's your excuse for all the times you've seen me since then?" he asked.

"I have no excuse," she muttered, picking at the thread on the comforter. "I was going to tell you, but I didn't know how. When you first mentioned his name, I was so shocked. Then I knew what we had was temporary so I figured I would keep it to myself and not make things awkward. Plus, talking about Scott with you seemed wrong, like if I started opening up about him too much it would seem like I was ready to move on and I didn't know if I was."

The muscle ticked in his jaw. The cell stopped, then started seconds later, and finally stopped again.

"Then when you showed up at my house and we

fell back into…well, us, I didn't know what to say. I hadn't expected to see you again and I was afraid if I said anything you'd see it as betrayal. There was no good time, Hayes."

She wanted him to look at her so she could see his eyes, to hopefully get a glimpse of what he was thinking, feeling.

"I didn't want you hurt any more," she whispered. "I care for you. You have to know that."

Hayes cursed and sat the picture at the end of the bed. He stared at it a moment before raking a hand through his messy hair.

He turned without looking at her and stormed from her room. Alexa climbed out of bed and quickly pulled on a T-shirt and panties. As she headed down the hall, she saw Hayes holding the cell between his ear and his shoulder. He hopped from one foot to the other pulling on his pants.

"I'll be there in five minutes."

He shoved the cell in his pants pocket, grabbed his jacket and shoes without putting them on.

"My father had a stroke," he told her without looking her way.

Alexa stepped forward. "I'll drive—"

"No." That sharp gaze of his cut to her. "You're getting your wish. We don't have to see each other anymore and then you won't have to worry about telling me any more truths you conveniently forgot."

Her heart broke, shattered. "Hayes."

He jerked on the door and stepped out, not bothering to spare her one last glance. The door didn't slam, but the final click resonated throughout the open space.

Wrapping her arms around her midsection, Alexa stared at the door. He was gone. She'd done this. Had he not seen that picture, had she told him the minute she realized who his best friend had been, she would probably be with him now.

Who would be there for him? How bad off was his father? Alexa knew how much his family meant to him and knew how fragile his father's health had been.

How would Hayes cope? With all the ugliness he'd experienced, Alexa prayed he wouldn't lose his father.

She padded back to the bedroom, stopping just inside the bedroom door to look at the messed-up bed and the image of her and Scott on their wedding day.

It didn't matter that he'd told her he didn't want to see her again; she had to explain herself. Not that she had much defense, but she had to go to him. She couldn't let him believe she'd set out on betrayal. Plus, she needed to check on him regarding his father.

Tonight, she'd go to him and pray she hadn't lost this second chance she'd been given. How often did anyone get another shot at love? She'd been so afraid before, too scared to even think about opening her heart, but not anymore. Hayes had taught her all about courage and just how strong she was.

To think she'd been worried about having a man in Mason's life. There was no better man to fill the role of father to her sweet son. Hayes might be afraid, but she wasn't going to let him hide and she wasn't going to let him think for a second that she'd hurt him on purpose.

She would make him see that she loved him, that they belonged together...that they were a family.

Sixteen

"He's going to be all right."

Hayes had barely gotten into the waiting room when Piper, Nolan's wife, delivered the news.

"The doctor said the damage is minor from what they can tell, but they are keeping him."

Hayes breathed easily for what felt like the first time in an hour. Between the news of his father and Alexa...

No. He couldn't think of her. Not here when he was surrounded by his family.

"Why are you in uniform?"

Hayes turned at Colt's voice. "I didn't go home last night," Hayes explained.

"And you were out somewhere that required a uniform?"

Colt crossed his arms over his chest as Nolan came up behind him wearing his scrubs. Most likely his brother had been on call when they'd brought their father in.

"I had a ceremony I had to attend." They didn't need to know any more. He'd tell them about the award later, but right now they had more pressing matters. "What's going on with Dad?"

"He was slurring his speech with the nurse at the assisted living facility and had some paralysis on his right side," Nolan explained. "She called the squad to bring him in and they ran some tests, did an ultrasound of his carotid. It's a minor stroke and we won't know more until the days progress, but he's going to be all right."

How was any of this all right? His father suffered from dementia and now he'd had a minor stroke? Hayes felt like the only stable world he'd known was crumbling around him.

"Can I see him?"

Nolan nodded. "He's not supposed to have visitors, but I requested an exception. Only a couple minutes. Room 108. It's at the end of the hall."

Hayes nodded and started to push past his brothers. Colt reached out and gripped Hayes's arm.

"After this, we want to know what you were doing," he murmured, probably so the ladies couldn't hear. "You wanted so far away from the Army, to forget what happened, and you show up in uniform after a ceremony? Something isn't jibing."

Hayes jerked his arm away and continued down the hall toward his father's room. He stopped just outside the door, pulling in a deep breath and trying to prepare himself for what he might see.

As he rounded the corner, Hayes zeroed in on his frail father lying in the bed, his head turned away. His thinning, silver hair had been smoothed back. There was once a time this man never went without his black hat. He'd been robust, strong, the rock of their entire family. Now that duty fell to the four boys…well, three when they removed Beau from the equation.

Hayes needed to make sure someone contacted Beau just as soon as he was done here.

As Hayes moved closer, his father shifted and turned his way. A ghost of a smile slid across his lips.

"Hey, Dad."

"Hayes."

Relief like he'd never known crashed through him. "You remember me."

"For now." His father's eyes filled with tears. "I'm sorry, son. I—I hate the b-burden I've become."

Hayes eased a hip on the edge of the bed and took his father's worn hand. "You're not a burden. You're our father and we'll do anything for you."

"I raised good b-boys," he stuttered, then narrowed his gaze. "U-uniform?"

"Long story," Hayes stated, then found that he wanted to share it. He wanted to have a moment with his father because it might be the last. "I got an award last night. I was invited to the governor's mansion to receive it."

"That's a-amazing. S-so proud…of you. Did your brothers g-go?"

Hayes shook his head and glanced to his father's frail hand in his. "No. I didn't tell them. I ended up taking a date."

"Someone serious?"

"I thought she was," Hayes admitted. "Not sure anymore."

"Since last n-night?" his father questioned. "If you think…she is, d-don't let her go."

Hayes glanced back to his father. "Neither of us were looking for a relationship."

His father attempted a smile and squeezed his hand.

"Those are the best k-kind. Your mother and I w-weren't, either. L-loved her more than anything. S-still do."

Hayes didn't want to think about this right now. He didn't want to try to deal with Alexa and her reasons for keeping something so monumental from him while he was also worried about his father's health.

He understood that she'd been stunned when he'd mentioned Scott's name. That was understandable, but she'd had ample time to come to terms with the fact. She should've trusted what they had. She should've trusted him enough to tell him the truth.

He hadn't just gotten involved with her, he'd gotten involved with Mason and thinking of both of them out of his life had a void settling deep in his heart.

"I should go and let you rest." But he didn't want to end this moment. Would his father even know who he was next time? "I love you, Dad."

"Love you, Hayes."

After placing a kiss on his father's forehead, Hayes forced himself to leave the room. If that was the last time he heard his father say he loved him and call him by name, that would be enough. Hayes honestly hadn't believed he'd get that again. Perhaps the uniform helped his father recognize him or perhaps his father just knew that at this moment Hayes needed him now more than ever.

No matter the reasons, Hayes was thankful to have had those few minutes. He needed to check to see if anyone had contacted Beau and then he wanted to head home. There was too much swirling around his mind and he just wanted to be left alone.

Alone.

Ironic that was exactly what he'd wanted when he

came home, but then he'd been enveloped by his brothers, their wives, their kids… Alexa and Mason.

The pain she'd left buried inside him wasn't going away anytime soon. He knew she'd come to him, knew she'd want to defend herself. So he needed time to prepare his heart. Because as hard as he tried, his damn heart had gone and gotten involved. Now he had to figure out how the hell he was going to move on.

Maybe he should've saved some demo work because Hayes could sure have done some damage with the sledgehammer. Unfortunately, he was on the back end of the kitchen renovation and coming close to the finish.

In the past several days he'd gotten his cabinets installed. Countertops, backsplash and new appliances were to be installed next week. Now he was working on the lighting over the giant table that mocked him. He couldn't look at the damn thing without seeing Alexa and her expression when she saw it.

For the last two nights he'd slept like hell and had pretty much kept to himself. He'd visited his father a couple times, but he'd reverted back inside his mind. Hayes knew he would, but there was still that sliver of hope each time he went that maybe there would be some remembrance.

When the back door opened, Hayes steeled himself for the slam. He turned just as the screen door hit and Nolan and Colt were standing there like a force…one he didn't want to deal with right now.

"This must be important to get you both here at the same time."

Nolan stepped in and glanced around. "You've done a lot with the place since I was here last."

Hayes went back to screwing in the base for the light over the table. "That's the goal."

"Where were you the other night?" Colt demanded.

Hayes twisted the nut around the screw and grunted. "Well, Dad, I don't have to tell you everything I do."

Glancing down onto the table, Hayes searched for the screwdriver to tighten the rest of the screws.

"We just want to help," Nolan stated, handing him the tool. "You haven't mentioned one thing about the Army in months, so you have to understand that when you show up looking like you slept in your uniform, we get a little concerned."

Concentrating on the light, Hayes let the silence stretch out. Once he was done, he climbed down and pulled in a breath.

"I was at the governor's mansion receiving an award."

"What the hell?" Colt shouted.

"And you didn't tell us before now?" Nolan demanded at the same time.

Hayes shrugged. "I didn't want you guys to make a big deal about it."

"A big deal?" Colt questioned. "You're joking, right? This is a very big deal."

"I didn't want the award." He still didn't want it. "Taking that seems so wrong, like I'm actually accepting the fact that all of those deaths happened, like I'm moving on with my life when they can't move on with theirs."

A weight settled heavy on his chest. Isn't that what happened with Alexa? She'd been afraid to mention Scott because that would've brought to life the fact that she was moving on and she hadn't been ready. His response to receiving that award was the exact same thing.

He hadn't wanted to come to grips with the fact he was moving on.

Hayes cleared his throat, pushing aside the turmoil of regret. "The award was given to the wrong man anyway."

"If the governor gave it to you, then that was the right man." Colt crossed the room and stood on the other side of the table, his hands propped on his hips. "Why the hell didn't you want us to know? Because we might care? Because we might want to go and show support?"

"Do you think Annabelle and Piper are going to enjoy hearing that you didn't want them there?" Nolan added, twisting the knife deeper.

Hayes knew this would be their reaction, but he hadn't thought about his sisters-in-law. "I'll explain the same thing to them. I didn't want a big fuss made."

"Too damn bad," Colt gritted out. "Why do you think we want to cause a fuss? Because we're damn glad you came home, Hayes. Maybe we want to celebrate the fact you're alive."

Hayes turned away. "Well, maybe I'm not quite ready for that yet."

He went to the box with the antique light fixture and stared down at it. His first thought when he'd seen it was Alexa. Would she approve? She'd had so many ideas for the house, specifically this kitchen.

"So you went to this awards ceremony alone and decided to keep everyone else at arm's length?" Nolan asked.

Hayes glanced over his shoulder. "I didn't go alone."

Colt's eyes narrowed. "Alexa."

"Where is she now?" Nolan asked. "She wasn't at the hospital with you. She's not here, but she's serious enough to take to the governor's mansion."

She had been important enough to take. She'd been… everything.

That couldn't be right, could it? Alexa had been someone he'd turned to when he needed an outsider who wasn't offering pity. Yes, his heart had gotten wrestled into the mix, but he'd been confused and beaten down. It was only natural. Right?

"We're…not together," he confirmed.

Colt let out a bark of laughter and adjusted his hat. "So you pushed her away, too?"

"No, asshole, if you have to know, I found out she'd been married to Scott."

Nolan's brows shot up. "That's Scott's widow?"

Hayes nodded. "I just found out the morning I got the call about Dad. I didn't leave her house on the best of terms."

"And you've not reached out since?" Colt guessed.

Hayes turned and sank down on the bench that ran along one side of the table. "Just leave me alone."

He was done. Exhausted. The lack of sleep, the ache in his heart, he just wanted to get through this on his own…like everything else.

"Being alone doesn't seem to be working for you." Nolan slid in next to him. "I'm not trying to get into your love life—"

"Then don't."

"But you seemed almost happy when Alexa was here," Nolan went on.

"How the hell would you know?"

Colt eased onto the bench on the other side. "Because I saw you. Annabelle saw you. You think we all don't talk? There was something so different about you. You actually smiled."

"I smile now."

Okay, that sounded like a lame argument. But he smiled...didn't he?

"Is it because she has a baby?" Nolan asked. "I know you're worried about moving on with your life, about getting involved with people again, so I'm sure kids are scary."

He didn't want to discuss Mason with his brothers. He sure as hell wasn't ready to have the family bonding talk about how to raise kids and how to form a life and step into the role of dad.

"I know your fiancée did a number on you and that was on top of whatever hell you experienced during that extraction." Nolan shifted and kept his focus on Hayes. "But are you really going to blame Alexa for being married to your friend and not telling you? Hell, you've kept nearly everything from us and we still love you."

"I don't love her."

Colt snorted. "I didn't love Annabelle, either. And then I realized I couldn't live without her or her girls."

Hayes could live without Alexa and Mason. He could, damn it.

He just didn't want to. He wanted them both, he wanted them to be his family and he wanted to provide for them, to take away their worries and fears.

"Did you tell her about what happened over there?" Nolan asked.

Hayes nodded.

"Don't you think that speaks volumes, little brother? She knows and you've yet to open up to your own family."

There was no hurt in Nolan's tone, just a matter-of-fact manner.

"Damn it," he muttered, dropping his head into his hands. "I'll talk to you guys. Just not yet, okay?"

Nolan's hand came down hard on Hayes's back. "If she was important enough to take to the ceremony and to tell your darkest secrets to, don't you think she's important enough to apologize to?"

"I didn't do anything wrong."

He glanced across to Colt who merely raised a brow.

"Fine, I left without hearing her side, but Dad was in the hospital. And since then... I just needed to get my head on straight."

"If you wait too long she might not want to explain at all," Nolan stated.

His brothers came to their feet and headed to the door.

"What? That's it?" Hayes asked. "You two have some code? When I'm emotionally beaten down you get up and leave?"

"Pretty much," Colt confirmed as he adjusted his hat again. "But we didn't discuss it."

Hayes rested his hands on the table and pushed up. "Get the hell out of here. I have more work to do."

"You also have to call Annabelle and Piper and tell them about your award," Colt stated. "And when they want to throw you a party or a dinner, or any other celebration, you'll let them and you'll be thankful."

Hayes saluted. "Yes, sir."

They left with a slam of the back door that had Hayes jumping, but at least he was still upright and not in the fetal position on the floor.

He had a few finishing touches to do before contacting Alexa. He wanted things to be perfect, but he also wanted an explanation. She'd hurt him, that he couldn't overlook. But he would give her a chance to defend herself because she deserved it...and he missed her.

Seventeen

Alexa smoothed a hand down her dress and knocked on Hayes's back door. She seriously should've called, but she didn't want him to flat-out tell her no. She figured if she was there in person, maybe he'd listen to her. She couldn't wait another day. Two had seemed like a lifetime and she was taking a risk driving here and crossing through Elliott land like she owned the place.

Shifting Mason higher on her hip, she stepped back and waited for Hayes to answer the door. Mason had fallen asleep on the way over and was still out. He rested his little head on her shoulder and she drew her strength from him.

Even when this was all said and done, even if she left here with her heart broken, she still had her amazing son and he was the greatest thing in her life.

The wood door swung open, leaving the screen separating them. Hayes had on his jeans and a large buckle with the Pebblebrook emblem, but no shirt.

When he said nothing, Alexa cleared her throat. "I hope you're not in the middle of anything. I just... I wanted to talk to you."

Hayes reached out, pushing the screen door open. Without a word, he gestured her inside. Well, at least that was something. He didn't close the door in her face and didn't tell her no.

"Oh, my word, Hayes." She glanced around the room, taking in all the clean lines, the bold splashes of color. The table now had benches, the appliances were missing, but everything else was absolutely perfect. "This is even better than I imagined it would be."

He crossed to the table and started cleaning up some tools. "I just got this light hung," he told her as he moved the large box back toward the laundry room. He sat the tools in the toolbox on the floor and turned back to her. "Say whatever it is you have to say."

Okay, so he wasn't going to make this easy. She hadn't expected him to and she probably didn't deserve the break.

"I know saying sorry now seems convenient and the easy way to start, but I am sorry."

Mason shifted in her arms, but she patted his back and he settled.

"Sit down," Hayes demanded. "You don't need to be standing and holding him. He's got to be heavy."

Alexa smiled. "I'm used to him and I doubt I'll be here long."

She'd say what she needed to say and leave. The ball would be in his court, so to speak.

"I had no clue you were Scott's friend," she started. "I knew he had a best friend in school he called Cowboy. He told me his friend went into the Army and I knew you guys texted and talked on occasion. But I swear, I never heard him say your real name. I never really asked, either."

Hayes remained across the room. He crossed his arms over that broad chest and continued to stare at her with that darkened gaze. Alexa laced her fingers beneath Mason's bottom and kept going.

"I didn't know anything until I mentioned the movie and you said his name," she admitted. "And by then we'd slept together. I figured once I left, we'd never see each other again and you wouldn't have to know. You were so angry with your fiancée and your commanding officer, I just didn't want you to see similarities. Admitting everything would've meant I was feeling something for you and that I was accepting that my original family was in the past. I realize that was a mistake, but I did what I thought was right. I was afraid.

"But then you came to my house," she went on as she paced the room. "I thought staying away from you would be best, but you came by and I had no willpower. The more time I spent with you, the more my feelings were growing and I never thought I'd have feelings for another man again."

"And what do you feel?" he asked.

Alexa stilled, then turned back around. "I fell in love with you. I'm completely in love with you, and so is Mason."

If he was shocked at her words, he didn't show it. This was one of those times she wished her blunt mouth would zip it, but she was here to tell him the whole truth so she couldn't stop now.

"I have no idea when I fell for you," she went on, ignoring her nerves. She'd come this far. "But I knew you needed to know who I was, who my husband was."

"Why the different last names?" he asked.

Alexa shrugged. "I never changed my name when we married. I just wanted to keep mine."

Hayes dropped his arms and crossed the room. Her eyes darted to that bare chest, the smattering of dark hair, the swirling ink. He was a beautiful man inside and out and it absolutely hurt to know she might have destroyed their chance.

"Do you want to say anything else?" he asked, looming over her.

Alexa swallowed. "No. I just want you to know I'm sorry I hurt you."

Damn it. Her throat was burning. Tears were on the horizon and she wanted to at least get back to her car before she lost it.

Mason stirred again, this time lifting his head and glancing around. He rubbed his eyes and dropped his head back onto her shoulder then toyed with the strands of her hair. She knew he was awake—all the more reason to leave.

When Hayes continued to stare and the silence became too much, Alexa turned and headed for the door. There was nothing else she could do.

"Stay."

His command cut through the tension. Alexa didn't turn around as she clutched Mason tighter.

"I listened to you, so now you'll listen to me."

Alexa swallowed and eased around to face him. Hayes crossed the room, his limp a little more prominent today, most likely from the renovating he'd been doing.

When he reached for Mason, Alexa started to protest, but her son instantly wrapped his arms around Hayes's neck. The sight was too much to bear. The strong cowboy she'd fallen for holding her fatherless son…she'd hit her breaking point.

The tears fell without control and Alexa covered her face—both to block the touching sight and to hide the fact she was a wreck.

"Don't cry," he told her. "I haven't even told you I love you yet."

Alexa froze, slowly dropping her hands. There was no way she'd heard him right, but when she met his gaze, he was smiling. Hayes Elliott held her son and was smiling like she'd never seen before.

"I was coming for you," he told her as he closed the narrow space between them. "I wanted to finish working in here, maybe grab a shower, but I was coming for you. I didn't give you a chance to talk before and I wanted to believe you didn't betray me."

"I did betray you by not telling you the second I knew," she whispered, swiping at her damp cheeks.

"You didn't betray me," he told her. "You guarded yourself from more hurt and you didn't want to hurt me in the process. If the roles were reversed, I can't say I wouldn't have done the same. Actually, I have done this, so I get where you're coming from."

Hope spread through her, warming her and healing her shattered heart. "Can we get back to the part where you said you love me? Because if you love me, does that mean you forgive me?"

With one strong arm around Mason, Hayes reached for her with his other and pulled her in tight. "You're everything, Alexa. When I said stay, I meant forever. And you will be taking my name. I'd like to adopt Mason as my own, but only if you want him to have the Elliott name. I understand if you—"

She placed her finger over his lips. "I want both of us to have your name."

He blew out a breath, grabbing her hand and kissing her fingertip. "It can't happen soon enough."

Unable to stop the flood of emotions, Alexa dropped her forehead to his shoulder and let the tears fall. She didn't care at this point. The relief, the happiness, the fact she was home with her son and the man she'd fallen so hard, so fast for, was just too much to take in.

"Tell me again." She lifted her head and wrapped her arms around Mason and Hayes. "Tell me you love me, because I can't get used to hearing that enough. I thought I'd leave here and never see you again."

His hand settled on her backside as he drew her closer. "This is home, Alexa. I want to build a life here, build a family."

The gasp escaped before she could stop herself. "You want more kids?"

With a slight shrug, he glanced to Mason who was wide-eyed and staring at his crying mother. "I'm not opposed to more. I love this little guy. I'm messed up, so I understand if you don't—"

Alexa put her finger over his lips. "Don't finish that sentence. If you want kids, I'll give them to you."

Hayes kissed her, hard, fast, then eased back. "What are the odds he's ready for bed? Because we could start practicing now."

"Oh, it will be a while before he goes to bed. He slept on the way over here. Maybe if we play outside or take him for a ride he can go to bed early."

Hayes curled his fingers into her rear end, pulling the fabric of the dress up. "Then you're mine," he growled against her lips.

"Yours."

"Forever."

Alexa hugged her family tighter. "Forever."

Epilogue

There was a party and he hadn't been invited.

What did Beau Elliott expect? He'd been gone from Pebblebrook for years. Busy making his life in Holly-wood and living up to all the media claimed him to be. Playboy, throwing money around, billion-dollar home, traveling with a new woman each week.

Yeah, he'd been busy according to the press. But there was so much they didn't know.

Beau sat in his car halfway up the drive on the Pebblebrook ranch. There were kids playing in the front yard of Colt's house. Kids. His brothers had married and had kids.

Glancing in the rearview mirror, Beau swallowed the lump of fear, remorse.

What was he doing back here? What the hell did he expect to accomplish? His brothers would give him hell, and he deserved nothing less.

His father had had a stroke a week ago, but Beau hadn't been able to get away. He'd called the hospital every single day asking for updates. He'd also asked for his calls to be kept from his family.

Beau was dealing with some issues that couldn't be ignored or put aside. Not even his money could get him out of this.

Squeals of laughter came through his open windows. He watched as his brothers interacted with their wives or girlfriends…whatever the status was. He saw four children and wondered just how much had changed since he'd been gone.

He wasn't naive. Beau knew his family wouldn't exactly welcome him with open arms, but he had nowhere else to go. Oh, he had a flat in London and a cottage in Versailles, but he couldn't go to either of those places.

No matter where he'd been in his life, no matter what he'd been doing, he couldn't deny that Pebblebrook was home. And now more than ever, he needed to be here.

Beau put the car in Drive and started easing toward the entry just as he heard a cry from the infant in the back seat. His heart clenched.

Yeah, now more than ever he needed his family, his home.

* * * * *

*If you liked Hayes's story, don't miss
his brothers' romances in*
THE RANCHER'S HEIRS *series from
Jules Bennett!*

*TWIN SECRETS
CLAIMED BY THE RANCHER*

And pick up these other novels from Jules Bennett

*TRAPPED WITH THE TYCOON
FROM FRIEND TO FAKE FIANCÉ
HOLIDAY BABY SCANDAL*

Available now from Mills & Boon Desire!

***

And don't miss the next
BILLIONAIRES AND BABIES *story*
FOR THE SAKE OF HIS HEIR

*By Joanne Rock
Available February 2018!*

"Tyce."

Sage called his name again. He lifted his head and looked at her with those intensely dark, pain-filled eyes.

"Take my offer to walk away. This child will be raised a Ballantyne—no one will ever have to know that he, or she, is yours. I'm giving you permission to forget about this conversation."

Something flashed in Tyce's eyes. Sage tried to ignore him as he stepped up to walk beside her, a silent, brooding, sexy mass of muscle.

"We're not done discussing this, Sage," he said, his voice a low growl.

"We really are, Tyce." Sage forced the words through her tight lips. "Don't contact me again. We are over."

"Yeah, you can think that," Tyce said, standing up. "But you'd be wrong."

* * *

Little Secrets: Unexpectedly Pregnant
is part of the Little Secrets series:
Untamed passion, unexpected pregnancy…

LITTLE SECRETS: UNEXPECTEDLY PREGNANT

BY
JOSS WOOD

First Published in Great Britain 2018
By Mills & Boon, an imprint of HarperCollins*Publishers*
1 London Bridge Street, London, SE1 9GF

© 2018 Joss Wood

ISBN: 978-0-263-93585-1

51-0118

MIX
Paper from
responsible sources
FSC™ C007454

This book is produced from independently certified FSC™ paper to ensure responsible forest management.

For more information visit: www.harpercollins.co.uk/green

Printed and bound in Spain
by CPI, Barcelona

Joss Wood loves books and traveling—especially to the wild places of southern Africa. She has the domestic skills of a potted plant and drinks far too much coffee.

Joss has written for Mills & Boon KISS, Mills & Boon Presents and, most recently, the Mills & Boon Desire line. After a career in business, she now writes full-time. Joss is a member of the Romance Writers of America and Romance Writers of South Africa.

One

"Why does this sculpture make me think of hot, amazing, fantastic sex?"

Sage Ballantyne looked at the woman she hoped would become her sister-in-law, but didn't reply to her outrageous statement. Tyce Latimore's work, whether it was an oil painting or a wood-and-steel sculpture, always elicited a strong reaction. He was one of the best artists of his generation. Of many generations.

Thank God he was also the only artist of his generation who refused to attend his opening nights. If there had been even the slightest chance he might appear, then Sage would've stayed away.

Sage flicked her eyes over the abstract six-foot-high sculpture. It was unusual and very unlike Tyce's normally fluid lines.

"There isn't a curve in sight but it screams passion and lust," Piper said.

Sage's eyebrows lifted. "I'm not seeing what you are."

Piper pulled Sage to stand next to her.

"Try this perspective," Piper suggested, her cheeks tinged with pink.

Sage laughed at Piper's embarrassment and turned back to look at the sculpture. Actually, from this angle it did look like two people bent over a desk, and Piper was right; when you made that connection you saw the passion in the piece. This sculpture would be a talking point in his reviews. The art critics would wax eloquent about Tyce's take on human sexuality.

Sage knew how he felt about sex; he liked it. Often and any way he could get it.

"But why the frog?" Piper asked before moving on to another display.

Every muscle in Sage's body stiffened. Oh, no, he hadn't. No way, no how. Not even Tyce Latimore would have the balls to...

She looked at the sculpture again and yep, there on the "desk" was a tiny, beautifully made steel frog, its surface treated so that it took on a greenish hue. In an instant Sage flashed back to three years before.

They'd arrived separately to a party, not wanting to tip off the world about their relationship—the heiress and the hot artist, professionally and personally, would be big news—and they'd spent the evening pretending not to know each other. The tension had been hot and sexy and, by the time Tyce dropped a quick suggestion in her ear that they meet in the library, she was a vibrating, hot, sticky mess of take-me-now. Within twenty seconds of slipping into the room, the door was locked, Tyce had her dress up her hips and had stripped her of her soaking thong. He'd unzipped, leaned her over the desk and he'd taken her, hard and fast, from behind.

The jade frog on her host's desk had watched them, thoroughly unamused.

Sage hauled in a breath as her heart tried to claw its way out of her chest. How dare he? What they'd done together was not for public dissemination.

Just another reason she'd been right to walk away from him three years ago.

"That sculpture was difficult." Tyce's unmistakable deep and velvety voice came from behind her. "I was constantly distracted by the memories of that night. And others."

His words were low enough for only her to hear. She didn't turn, but she felt the heat pouring off his body and she inhaled his soapy, sexy all-man smell. Lust skittered over her. As usual, Sage felt like she'd been plugged into the nearest electrical outlet. Her skin buzzed, her heart stumbled and her mind felt off-kilter.

Three years and he still had the ability to rocket her from composed to crazy. Three years and her first instinct was to beg him to take her to bed. Three years and instead of being angry with him for depicting their encounter in the library in an, admittedly, very abstract way, she wanted to kiss him.

Or slap him...

Then, like now, he pulled her in and tempted her into edging closer. Generally, Sage found it easy to step away from men she found too attractive or too interesting. They weren't worth the hurt that was the inevitable outcome of becoming entangled in someone's life.

Determined to protect herself, Sage seldom allowed relationships, especially those with men, to deepen past a week or two. With Tyce, it had taken her six weeks to convince herself to leave. He was supremely dangerous.

Tempting, addictive... All that and more.

So, obviously, kissing him was out of the question.

Sage spun around on her ice pick heels and her hand connected with his cheek. Instantly mortified and regretful, she watched that too-handsome face harden, his obsidian eyes turn, if that was at all possible, darker. He opened his mouth to say something but instead of speaking his hands gripped her hips and he yanked her into his hard, muscled chest. His temper-tinged mouth covered hers, his hot tongue slipping between her lips, and Sage was lost, swept away to a place only Tyce could take her. Sage dug her nails into his arms, feeling his bulging muscles through the thin fabric of his black dress shirt and, wanting more, her hands skated over his broad chest, danced across those washboard abs she'd loved to tickle and taste.

Tyce lifted his mouth off hers. "Come with me."

Sage looked around for Piper, caught her eye and Piper waved her away, silently giving her permission to leave without her. She shouldn't; this really wasn't a good idea. But instead of saying no, instead of dismissing him or walking away—creating distance between herself and people was, after all, what she did best—she placed her hand in his and allowed him to lead her out of the gallery.

Tyce rolled out of his king-size bed in his borrowed apartment and headed to the luxurious en suite bathroom. Three years later and sex with Sage was still fantastic. He never had better with anyone else, he thought as he tossed the condom away. Sex had never been an issue; everything else was... Had been.

Tyce leaned forward and placed his fingers on his right cheekbone, checking for but not expecting to see finger marks from the force of Sage's hand connecting with his face ten hours before. Tyce blew out a long breath. Only they could rocket from a slap to a kiss to having wild sex all within the space of an hour. He and Sage Ballantyne were, had always been, a combustible combination. There was a reason why they'd avoided each other for three years; put them in a room together and some sort of firestorm always occurred.

Tyce gripped the edge of the vanity. Judging by her deer-in-the-headlights look when she turned around, she hadn't expected to see him at his own exhibition and he couldn't blame her. His presence last night had been an aberration. He hated discussing his work, having people fawn over him and his art. To Tyce, it was a simple equation. If you liked what he did, buy it. If not, he didn't care. There was no need to endlessly discuss his influences and inspiration for every piece. Luckily for him, art lovers seemed to connect with what he produced. His taciturn attitude to publicity and art critics and his reclusive nature added, so his agent, Tom, said, to his mystique.

He'd only gone to the exhibition because Tom insisted he meet the wealthy CEO who wanted a sculpture for the lobby of her new corporate headquarters. It was a commission that would raise the levels of his depleted coffers and it wasn't an offer he could treat lightly.

All thoughts of the commission, his agent and staying at the exhibition evaporated when he laid eyes on Sage for the first time in three years. A second after noticing her, Tyce felt his head buzzing, his skin shrinking and his world tilting. Damn; she was still as enticing and compelling and make-him-crazy as she'd been before. The world faded and he'd spun away from the CEO—who happened to be very female, very into him and very willing to give him a commission—and pushed his way through the crowds to reach her.

It was easy to call her hair black but it wasn't, not re-

ally. It was the deepest, darkest brown he'd ever seen.
Her eyes were the blue of Moroccan tiles and her body
a product of a lifetime spent in ballet class. Sage, damn
her, was effortlessly graceful and knee-knocking sexy.
She was the only woman who'd ever caused his heartbeat
to spike, his lungs to contract and his brain to chant…
mine, mine, mine. He'd been thinking of cotton sheets
and a massive bed as he'd approached her and it seemed
natural to open their conversation with a sexy quip. She,
obviously, hadn't and responded with that furious slap.
But, because he'd seen the desire in her eyes and heard
her low, excited gasp as his lips met hers, he ignored
his stinging cheek and…yeah, hell then broke loose. An
hour later they were both naked and panting and pretty
much stayed that way for the rest of the night. Tyce ran
his hands over his face. Last night they'd let their bodies do their talking but the sun was up and reality was
knocking on the door.

Literally. Tyce opened the door to Sage's soft rap and
looked into her vivid eyes. Ballantyne eyes. She was
gorgeous, Tyce thought, feeling the action down below.
They'd just had rock-my-world sex for most of the night
and he wanted more.

Tyce tensed, waiting for her to ask him when they'd
see each other again, whether he'd call her later. He
couldn't do either; there were far too many secrets between them, a history that didn't make that feasible.

"I should give you hell about that sculpture," she said,
"but I don't have the energy for anything more than coffee. Too bad there isn't any. I checked. Do you actually
live here?"

She posed the question as a joke but it cut too close to
the bone for comfort. How would she react if he told her
that he only occasionally used this Chelsea apartment be-

longing to his biggest client? It was easier to meet Sage in Manhattan than to explain to her, and everybody, that he, despite his sculptures and paintings selling for up to five million each, had just enough cash to keep producing his massive abstracts, to buy steel for his sculptures and to pay the mortgage and amenities on his warehouse in Brooklyn where he worked. And actually lived.

Sage waited for him to respond but when he didn't, she shrugged. "So, since you don't have the juice of life, I'm going to take off."

He wanted to protest but knew it was for the best so Tyce just nodded. After all, nothing had changed.

Sage shimmied those slim legs into a pair of designer jeans and hooked the tabs of a lilac bra together. Tyce, comfortable in his nudity, pushed his shoulder into the doorframe and watched the tension seep into her spine, into those long, toned limbs. He knew what she was thinking: How could they be so perfectly in sync between the sheets and unable to talk to each other outside the bedroom?

They'd done this before. They'd been amazing in bed but out of the bedroom they'd been useless. Used to being on his own, he'd struggled with giving equal attention to his art and to her. Art, it had to be said, always won the battle. At that time, as always, he'd needed to sell as many of his pieces as he could. But, on a more fundamental level, he knew that he had to keep his emotional distance. Relationships, with Sage or anyone else, demanded more than he had to give. His lovers objected to his need to isolate himself, to spend hours and days in his studio only coming out for food, a shower and, yeah, sex. They wanted attention, affection and he, mostly, wanted to be left alone, content to communicate through his vivid, dark oil paintings and his steel-and-wood sculptures. He wasn't good at personal connections. He'd expended all the emotional energy he'd been given caring for a depressed mother and raising his baby sister and he never again wanted to feel like he was standing on a rickety raft in a tempestuous sea. He'd held Sage at an emotional distance, unable to let her go but knowing that she needed and deserved more from him. Her adoptive father's death had been their personal tipping point. Since he couldn't see himself in a relationship, didn't want to be tied down, he'd used Connor Ballantyne's passing to put some space between them, and Sage, surprisingly, had let that happen by not trying to reconnect.

Stepping up and helping her deal with Connor's death would've flipped their relationship from casual to serious, from skimming the surface to ducking beneath the waves and he'd been too damn scared of drowning to take that risk.

Tyce rubbed his hands over his face. The Ballantyne situation was complicated—he and his sister, Lachlyn, were the only people who knew that Lachlyn was Connor Ballantyne's illegitimate daughter—and his attraction to Sage was not, had never been, helpful. His art, the paintings and the intricate sculptures, were the one thing in his life that made complete sense. He knew exactly what he was doing with his art.

Reaching back, Tyce snagged a towel from the rail and wrapped it around his hips, keeping his eyes on Sage as she pushed her feet into spiky heels. She picked up her leather bag and pulled it over her shoulder.

She pointed a finger at him. "So, I'm going to go."

Tyce saw the shimmer in her eyes that suggested tears and his heart constricted.

Hurting Sage was never what he intended to do, not now and not three years ago.

"Sage, I—" Tyce didn't complete the sentence, not sure what he was about to say. *Don't go? Thanks for a great night? Let's try again?*

Because the second thought was trite and the last impossible, he just stepped forward and when he was close enough, dropped a kiss on her temple. "Take care," he murmured.

Sage pushed the sharp tip of her fingernail into his stomach. "If I see anything in your art that references this night, I will personally disembowel you."

Not bothering to look at him again, she glided from the room, a perfect package of class and sass, her back ramrod straight.

Turning back into the bathroom, Tyce lifted his head and looked at his reflection in the mirror, unimpressed with the man looking back at him. His sister, Lachlyn, deserved to own something of the company her father, Connor, created, and in chasing down and buying Ballantyne International shares he thought he was doing the right thing, the honorable thing, but sleeping with Sage, then and now, had never been part of the plan. Originally he'd just wanted to get to know her to find out as much as he could about the iconic Manhattan family because he'd intended to use that knowledge to his, or Lachlyn's, advantage.

He hadn't banked on their chemistry, on the desire that flared between them. He'd thought that she would be easy to walk away from once they got each other out of their systems, but that had proved to be more difficult than he thought. Last night had blown those preconceptions out of the window. For as long as he lived he'd crave Sage Ballantyne...

As fast as a snakebite, Tyce's fist slammed into the mirror above his head and glass flew from the frame and dropped into the basin, onto the floor. Tyce looked at his ultra-distorted reflection in the thin shards that remained in the frame and nodded, satisfied.

That looked far more like the person he knew himself to be.

Two

Three months later...

"Are you going to slap me again?"

"The night is still young, who knows?"

Tyce slid onto the barstool next to Sage, ordered a whiskey from the bartender and looked at his former lover. She'd pulled her long, normally curly hair into a sleek tail, allowing her eyes to dominate her face. Tonight her irises were periwinkle blue surrounded with a navy ring; they could be, depending on her mood, navy, denim or that unusual shade of Moroccan blue.

Her eyes always, every single time, had the ability to drop him to his knees. God had not been playing fair when he'd combined an amazing set of blues with a face that was near perfect—heart shaped, high cheekbones, sexy mouth, stubborn chin—and then, just for kicks, placed that head on top of a body that was naturally lean, intensely feminine, all sexy.

He loved her face, he loved her body and God knew that he loved making love to her, with her... He wanted to kiss that mouth, suck on her skin, allow his hands to stroke that endlessly creamy, warm, fragrant skin.

It had been so damn long and, after three years of sheer hell, one night with her had been like offering a dehydrated man a drop of water. He wanted her legs wrapped around his hips, to hear her soft moans in his ear, his tongue in that hot, sweet mouth.

Sage had no idea that his pants were tighter and that his lungs were battling to take in air. She just took a sip of her drink and wrinkled her nose in a way he'd always found adorable. "I suppose I should apologize for slapping you but the incident made all the social columns, creating more publicity for your already successful exhibition and sending your already overinflated prices sky-high."

Overinflated? Tyce winced and then shrugged. It wasn't like he hadn't had the same thought a time or two. The prices his art commanded were ridiculous; it wasn't like he was a modern-day Picasso or Rembrandt. He was just a guy who slapped steel and wood together, tossed paint onto a canvas in a way people seemed to like. Art critics, his agent and the gallery owners would be shocked if they ever found out how little effort went into the art they all revered.

No one knew or suspected that most of his time was spent painting intensely detailed portraits that were accurate to the last brushstroke. His portraits, intimate, honest, time and blood sucking, were where he found and lost himself. Many of those never-seen portraits were of Sage, and Tyce neither knew or cared to speculate what that meant.

Silence fell between them and Tyce looked around the

room. He'd been surprised to receive a text from Sage inviting him to attend the Ballantyne cocktail party and jewelry exhibition and there had never been any doubt that he'd go. Firstly, if one was personally invited to look at one of the best collections of fantastically rare and ridiculously expensive jewelry one took the opportunity. He also wanted to look at the new line Sage designed and it was, as he expected, fabulous. Whimsical but modern, feminine but strong…so Sage. And because he was a guy he was hoping that Sage's request to meet would lead to some head-bangin', bed-breaking sex.

There was only one way to find out. "So, is this a booty call?"

Sage blinked. "What?"

"Did you ask to meet so that we can hook up again?"

"You arrogant jerk!" Her eyes sparked with irritation and color seeped into her face. "Are you insane?"

Probably. And, if he was, then her incredible eyes and rocking body and the memories of how good they were together were to blame.

"So, you didn't call me to try and talk me into a night of hot sex?" Tyce didn't have to pretend to sound disappointed; the memories of touching, tasting, loving Sage kept him up most nights. He wished he could ring-fence his thoughts so that he only remembered her scent, her soft, creamy skin and the taste on his tongue. But, unfortunately, his mind always wandered off into dangerous territory—how it would feel to wake up to her face in the morning, to hear her soft *good night* before he slept. He only allowed himself the briefest of fantasies about what a life spent with Sage would look like before he vaporized those thoughts.

Sage was part of a dynamic, successful family and he wasn't referring to the immense Ballantyne wealth.

Sage and her brothers knew what family meant, how to be part of one.

He didn't have a cookin' clue. The Ballantyne family, from what he understood, worked as a well-oiled machine, each part of that machine different but essential to the process.

Tyce had been the engine that powered his family along—an engine constantly on the point of breaking down. He'd done his best to provide what Lachlyn needed but had been so damn busy trying to survive that he emotionally neglected his sister. Sage's life partner would be an emotionally intelligent dude, would be able to slide into the Ballantyne family and know how to be, act, respond… The man who she married would know how to deal with and contribute to the clan.

Tyce wasn't that man. He'd never be that man and it was stupid to spend more than a minute thinking that he could be.

So, when he'd seen her text message asking him to meet tonight, he'd jumped to the only conclusion that made sense, that she wanted another hookup. During his shower he'd fantasized about how he would take her… Fast or slow? Her on top or him? Either way, the only thing that was nonnegotiable was that he'd be looking in her eyes when she shattered, wanting to see if she needed him as much as he needed her.

Instead of looking soft and dreamy, her eyes blazed with pure blue anger. Right, real life…

"No, Tyce, I didn't call you because I wanted hot sex." Sage answered him in a dry, sarcastic voice.

Tyce took a sip of his whiskey, the urge to tease fleeing. Did she suddenly look nervous? He lifted his eyebrows until Sage spoke. "But I did—do—have something to tell you."

Tyce looked around the room while he rubbed his jaw, his gut screaming that whatever she had to say was going to rock his world. He didn't want his world rocked, he just wanted to either have sex with Sage or to go home and paint. Since sex wasn't happening, he itched to slap oil onto canvas, eager to work his frustration out with slashes of indigo and Indian red, manganese violet and magenta. "Just spit it out and get it done." Tyce snapped out the words, his tone harsh.

Sage blew air out over her lips and briefly closed her eyes. When they opened again, he saw her resolve. And when she finally formed the words, they shifted his world.

"I don't expect anything from you, not money or time or involvement. But you should know that I am pregnant and the baby is yours."

Tyce was still trying to make sense of her words, trying to decipher them, when Sage placed a swift, final kiss to the left of his mouth. "Goodbye, Tyce. It was... fun. Except when it wasn't."

Sage, having said what she needed to, took advantage of his astonishment and stood up. She was about to pick up her clutch and leave when his hand shot out and gripped her wrist.

When she looked at him she noticed that his eyes were pure black fire. "Sit. Stay."

Those eyes, God, they still had the power to dissolve her knees. Eyes of a warrior, Sage thought. Because he made her feel off-kilter, she handed him a cool look. "I am not a puppy you are trying to train."

Tyce gripped his nose with his thumb and forefinger. "God, Sage, just give me a sec, okay? You've just told me that you're pregnant. I need a goddamn minute! So, yeah, sit your ass down, okay?"

Hearing the note of panic in Tyce's voice, Sage slid back onto the high barstool and crossed her legs. She listened as Tyce ordered another whiskey from the bartender and watched the color seep slowly back into his face.

"We need to…" she began.

Tyce shook his head and held up his hand to stop her talking. "Another drink and some more time."

Sage nodded and leaned back in her chair, a little relieved that she'd told him, that it was finally done. It had taken every gram of courage she possessed to send that text message asking him to meet, and she'd known that he'd think she was looking for another one-night stand. Could she blame him? Their entire relationship had been based around their physical attraction and he was a guy… Of course he'd think she just wanted sex.

But their crazy chemistry had led to a very big consequence…

Sage rolled her head, trying to loosen the tension in her neck. She'd sit here, let him take the time he needed for the news to sink in and after what she hoped would be a drama-free conversation, she'd leave. Then she could put him and their brief roller coaster—What should she call it? Fling? Affair? Madness?—behind her.

God, though it had been brief, their time together had been intense. They'd met at the opening of a small gallery around the corner from her apartment and the attraction between them sizzled. Sage would like to blame that on his mixed heritage, Korean and French, on his dark Asian eyes, square chin and blinding smile, and his tall, muscled body. But she'd grown up surrounded by good-looking men and looks didn't impress her much. No, it was Tyce's stillness, his control and his aura of elusiveness, and unavailability, that attracted her.

Tyce had told her, straight up and straightaway, that he wanted to sleep with her but that he wasn't the settle-down, buy-her-flowers type. They could hang, enjoy each other, but she shouldn't expect anything more from him. She appreciated his up-front attitude and it soon dawned on her that she was drawn to a younger, darker, less chatty version of her beloved uncle Connor. Connor had been utterly devoted to his adopted kids, had looked after his employees and had been a hardworking, focused businessman, but a monogamous, committed relationship never featured on Connor's list of priorities. Trying to pin men like Connor and Tyce down was like trying to capture smoke in a sieve.

And maybe she'd found Tyce a little more attractive because she knew he would never offer her the very thing that scared her the most: an emotionally intimate relationship. She'd been the apple of her parents' eye, the baby girl who had her entire family wrapped around her finger, loved and adored until she woke up one morning and heard that the biggest part of her life was gone and wasn't ever coming back.

She'd avoided relationships outside of the people who lived in Connor's iconic brownstone fondly referred to as The Den—her brothers, Connor, and Jo, Linc's mom and the woman Connor hired to help him raise three orphans. She had girlfriends she enjoyed but whom she kept at an arm's length, and she wasn't much of a dater.

Tyce had been hard to resist. Sage had been in love with his art for years. His work was detailed and exquisite, full of angst and emotion. From their first meeting, admiration and attraction swirled and whirled and she'd quickly said yes when he suggested dinner. They didn't make it to a restaurant; instead they'd tumbled into bed and Sage finally understood the power of addiction. She craved Tyce with a ferocity that scared her.

After six weeks of fantastic sex, Sage realized she was on the brink of falling in love with Tyce and couldn't, wouldn't allow that to happen. Terrified, she did what she did best, she made plans to run and immediately booked a ticket to Hong Kong, telling her brothers that their Asian clients needed her attention. The day before her scheduled flight to Asia, Connor passed away and her entire world changed. Connor's death allowed her to put the distance between her and Tyce she'd been seeking with her trip to Hong Kong.

And Connor's death reminded her of why it was better to keep her distance from people and that she was wise to avoid emotional and intimate relationships. It hurt too damn much when the people she loved left her life.

She had enough people to love, enough people to worry about. And now—Sage placed her hand on her stomach—she had a baby on the way, a little person who would become the center of her world. Her baby, she ruefully admitted, was one person she had no choice but to love, someone she couldn't push away.

Well played, Universe.

What did having a baby mean to Tyce? Sage wanted to ask him but, judging from his give-me-space expression, he wouldn't answer her. Would he walk? Would he want to be involved? If he wanted contact with his child, how would that work? What if he wanted to co-parent? What then? When she'd texted him she'd been consumed by the idea of telling him, needing to get the dreaded deed done. She hadn't thought beyond that. Well, she had thought about how sexy he was and how much she wanted to make love to him again...

Like those thoughts were productive. Besides, them going to bed was exactly what led to their current predicament. Then again, one couldn't fall pregnant twice. *Jeez, Sage, pull yourself together, woman!*

Tyce abruptly stood up, nearly tipping his barstool with the force of his movement. "I need to get out of here."

"Okay, well…" Sage bit her bottom lip and looked around. "Give me a call if you want to chat about this some more."

Tyce looked like a hard-assed warrior about to go to battle. "Oh, hell, no, we're leaving together."

Sage frowned at his high-handed comment. She wasn't ready to leave. This cocktail party and exhibition of the Ballantyne family jewelry collection was the culmination of their latest PR campaign to attract new customers. Her family was all in attendance and she was expected to stick around. Not that anyone would notice if she left… Her brothers Jaeger and Beck were both slow dancing with their women—Piper and Cady—and she was the last thing on their minds. Her oldest brother, Linc, who'd brought Tate, his son's temporary nanny, to the party, was nowhere to be seen.

Sage was sure that she could leave and no one would be any wiser but that would mean leaving with Tyce and that wasn't an option. "I don't think so."

"Walk out with me or I swear, I'll toss you over my shoulder and walk you out that way."

His alpha bossiness only turned her on when they were naked but since they weren't—and would never be again—his terse tone ticked her off. She opened her mouth to blast him and closed it again at the determination in his eyes. She could either leave walking or over his shoulder and she didn't want a scene to ruin this

fabulous evening. Sage glared at him, picked up her designer clutch and walked with him into the foyer of the
ballroom. She collected her coat and went to stand by
the elevators.

The doors opened, Sage followed Tyce into the cube
and pushed the button for the first floor. As the doors
closed, the spacious interior shrunk with a big, broad,
freaked-out man inside.

Tyce slapped his hand against the emergency stop button.

"What the hell, Sage? You're pregnant?"

Obviously, he was taking some time to process the
news. Sage winced at his shout, his words bouncing off
the wood paneling. She lifted her hands as the elevator
shuddered to a stop.

"Okay, calm down, Tyce."

Pathetic as it was, it was all she could think of to say.
Even furious, he was ludicrously good-looking. Blue-
black hair cut stylishly with short back and sides, equally
dark eyebrows over those black sultry eyes. When he
smiled, which was, in her opinion, far too rarely, he could
charm birds down from trees, criminals into converting
and start polar caps melting. Sage wished that she could
say Tyce Latimore was just a pretty face but he was so
much more than that. He was tall, a few inches above six
foot and his body, that body she'd licked and explored
and teased and tasted, was all muscle honed from a lifetime dedicated to martial arts. Tae Kwon Do, judo, Krav
Maga…they'd all contributed to creating a body that was
spectacular and spectacularly sexy. The hair on her arms
lifted and her fingers ached to touch him. Her off-the-
shoulder silk dress felt abrasive against her sensitive skin
and want and need danced through her.

Focus, Sage. Sheesh.

Tyce pushed his jacket back to place his hands on his hips, his expression summer-storm vicious. "Are you messing with me?"

Sage just barely restrained herself from rolling her eyes at his question.

"Yeah, Tyce," she sarcastically muttered. "I crave your attention that much that I'd make up a story like this to play games with your head!" Seeing his still skeptical face, she shook her head and, needing support, she leaned her back against the wall of the elevator. "I am pregnant. Since you're the only guy I've slept with in the three months—" Three years, she mentally corrected, but she wasn't telling him that! "—I think it's safe to assume that the kid is yours."

"But we used condoms," Tyce said, pushing his shaking hands into his hair.

Sage blushed. "That first time…you did slide in without a condom. You put one on later but maybe…" Lord, this was embarrassing! "…something slipped past."

Tyce stared at her, his hands linked behind his head and his expression stricken with panic and fear. "I can't be a father, Sage. I don't want to be a father. I don't want kids!"

Sage assumed as much.

Sage reached around him to release the emergency stop button. "As I told you, that's not a problem. I don't expect anything from you. You can carry on living your life as you always have."

"You can't do this on your own!" he said and for the first time ever Sage saw Tyce a little unhinged. He banged his fist against the stop button to prevent it from going any farther and the car's shudder reverberated through her.

"I am young, healthy, have huge family support and

ample resources to hire the help I need to raise this child," Sage told him, pushing a finger into his chest. "I don't need anything from you."

A little support would be nice, a kind word, but wishing for either was futile. Tyce wasn't the kind, supportive type. Hot and hard, amazing, fantastic sex? Yes. Warm and reassuring? No. She'd only told him because he had the right to know and not because she expected anything from him. She didn't want anything from him...or from any other man.

She was fine, *safe*, on her own.

"Miss Ballantyne?" Sage jumped at the disembodied voice coming from a speaker above her head. "Is everything alright in there?"

She nodded at the camera in the top corner of the elevator. "Everything is fine, thank you. We're just having a chat."

Chat? They were having a life-changing conversation. There was nothing *chatty* about it.

"Okay then." The voice sounded dubious. "Um? Do you think you could, um, chat somewhere else? There are people waiting for the elevator."

Sage nodded, walked to stand between Tyce and the light panel and pushed the emergency stop again. She pulled in a large breath and turned to face Tyce, who was staring down at the mulberry-colored carpet. "Tyce."

He didn't lift his head, so Sage called his name again. He eventually looked at her with those intensely dark, pain-filled eyes.

"I'm letting you off the hook. Look, I'm presuming that your statement from three years ago—when you told me that you don't do commitment—still holds?"

"Yeah." It was a small word but a powerful response. Sage nodded. "I'm very okay with that—I'm not looking for someone to nest with me. Take my offer to walk away. This child will be raised a Ballantyne. No one will ever have to know that he, or she, is yours. I'm giving you permission to forget about this conversation."

Something flashed in Tyce's eyes and Sage frowned, not sure what she'd seen. Before she could say any more, the doors to the elevator opened and they faced a bank of people waiting for the tardy lift. Sage pulled on her practiced, cool smile and stepped into the throng. She swiftly walked into the lobby and she nodded when the concierge asked her whether she wanted a taxi. Sage pulled on her coat and tried to ignore Tyce as he stepped up to walk beside her, a silent, brooding sexy mass of muscle.

She'd barely stepped onto the curb when a taxi pulled up and the doorman hurried to open the door. Sage climbed inside and sighed when Tyce crouched in the space between the open car door and her seat.

"We're not done discussing this, Sage," he said, his voice a low growl.

"We really are, Tyce." Sage forced the words through her tight lips. "Don't contact me again. We are over."

"Yeah, you can think that," Tyce said, standing up. "But you'd be wrong."

The slam of the taxi door was an exclamation point at the end of his sentence.

Three

In his converted warehouse in Brooklyn, Tyce stood at the massive windows that provided perfect light for his studio, his forearm resting on the glass. He'd been home an hour and he was grateful that he'd fought the impulse to follow Sage to her apartment. Instead of acting impetuously, he'd fought his way through the shock to slow his thoughts down, to think this situation through. He needed time to let the fact that he was going to be a dad sink in, to figure this out.

Tyce walked away from the window to the far wall, to a row of canvases that were stacked against the wall. Sitting cross-legged on the paint splattered floor, he reached for the most recent canvas, a portrait of Sage at her workbench, her brow furrowed in concentration, a pencil in her hand. He'd painted the portrait from a photo published in an arts magazine and it was, he admitted, as lifelike as the photo. Bending his knees, Tyce stared at the canvas, thinking that his child was growing her belly, that his DNA was joining with hers to create a new life.

God, what an awesome, terrifying, crazy thought. What the hell did Life think it was doing, asking him—the most emotionally disconnected person on the planet—to be a father? As a child he'd been consumed by anxiety, responsibility, overwhelmed by a world that asked him to deal with far too much, far too soon. Adulthood, his and Lachlyn's, and his mother's death, allowed him some measure of relief. But, because he never wanted to feel so unbalanced—*scared*—again he deliberately distanced himself from emotionally investing in situations and people because that would make him vulnerable. To Tyce it was a simple situation, vulnerability equaled hurt and pain was to be avoided. The logical conclusion was to avoid emotion altogether, like he had with Sage three years ago, or to disconnect, like he had learned to do with his mother.

Tyce supposed that, to the world, he looked normal, content, like he had it all. Nobody knew, not even Lachlyn, that on the inside, he felt hollow and empty. Kicking the crap out of his sparring partner at the dojo and pushing his body to the limit made him feel alive but the endorphins soon wore off. Art, mostly, provided a distraction and he, occasionally, felt the hit of adrenaline when he painted his oils or constructed his sculptures. Mostly he found the process easy and intellectually undemanding.

Tyce tipped his head back. Instead of seeing paint-streaked wooden beams and the steel pipes that were a feature of his converted warehouse he saw the faded walls of the small, two-bedroom apartment he'd lived in for most of his life. He was sitting on the cold floor outside his mother's bedroom door, rocking a crying Lachlyn, wishing that his mother would unlock the door and tell him that she was okay. That they'd be okay. He'd always wondered what he was doing wrong, why his mother needed to hide from him and his sister. He remembered the hundreds of drawings he did for her, hoping that, maybe once, she'd acknowledge his effort, desperate for any attention from her.

His index finger traced the line of Sage's jaw. At one time selling portraits—quick charcoal or ink sketches— had kept the roof over their heads, food in the fridge. In his early teens he'd sold rough sketches on street corners and in Central Park and later he sold his sketches to the women attending the art classes where he posed, naked, as an artist's model.

He clearly remembered feeling anxious as his hand flew over the paper, working out how much he could charge, how many sketches he needed to do to cover the latest unexpected expense; a kid struggling to gather rent money. Eventually he managed to control the anxiety, the burning resentment, and he'd learned to do that by detaching. From things, from the need for support and affirmation and, eventually, from people. Sage was the only person who'd ever threatened his control, who tempted him to edge closer, to climb into her head and let her climb into his. He couldn't do that, wouldn't allow himself to open up again.

And her being such a temptation was exactly why he'd allowed her to walk away from him years ago, why he'd let her slip through his fingers. It had been self-preservation in action.

He'd been an adult all his life, had dealt with situations no child should have to, had raised his sister as best he could. He wasn't scared of much but, God, Sage having a baby terrified him. Tyce linked his arms around his bent knees, as fear, hot and acidic, bubbled in a space just under his heart. And, like it or not, he and Sage were now joined together in an age-old way, through the mingling of their DNA. No matter how Tyce looked at it, as the mother of his child, Sage would be a permanent fixture in his life. Sage was also the only person who'd ever come close to cracking his armor and that meant that she was desperately dangerous.

He didn't like it but the situation couldn't be changed and all he could do was manage the process. How to do that? Tyce stood up and walked over to his desk in the corner of the studio, pulling out his battered office chair and dropping into it. First things first... Since he was going to be connected to the Ballantyne family for a long time to come, he had to come clean. About everything. First to Sage, then to her brothers.

And yeah, that was going to be as much fun as running around outside, naked, on a winter's night in Siberia. But it couldn't be avoided and it had to be done, and soon.

Sage, resentful that she'd been pulled away from her workbench to attend a meeting at Ballantyne International headquarters, stepped out of the elevator and immediately turned left, waving to the staff working behind the glass walls that were a feature of the Ballantyne corporate offices. Sage deeply appreciated the people who worked for their company, each one an essential cog to keep the massive organization running smoothly. She knew enough about business to contribute to the partners' meetings but she trusted her brothers to run the company, just as they trusted her to translate their rich clients' vague desires for "something special" into works of gemstone art.

But occasionally, as a full partner of Ballantyne International, she was expected to attend the meetings Linc called. She'd reluctantly shrug out of her work clothes—comfortable jeans and loose tops—and change into something more businesslike; today's outfit was a red-and-pink geometric top and plain black wool pants worn over two-inch-heeled boots. Her makeup consisted of a swipe of nude lipstick and she'd pulled her hair into a long braid.

She had the jewelry-designer-to-Ballantyne-partner switch down to a fine art.

At the end of the hallway, Sage pushed open the glass door to Amy's office, thankful to see the PA Linc and Beck shared at her desk, laconically typing on her computer. The walls to the offices on either side of Amy's desk were opaque and Sage couldn't tell whether Linc and Beck were in their respective offices or not.

"Why is your phone off?" Amy demanded, looking at her over the frames of her trendy glasses. "FYI, smoke signals are notoriously unreliable these days."

Knowing that underneath Amy's glossy and sarcastic shell was a gooey center, Sage leaned across her desk to drop a kiss on her cheek. "Sorry I worried you."

"I nearly came to your place myself. I hate it when you don't answer your phone." Amy pushed her chair away from her desk, her eyes brightening. "So, what do you think about Linc and Tate's engagement? Isn't it fabulous?"

Sure, her life was in turmoil but Sage was genuinely happy for her brothers. Linc and Tate aside, there was more good news: Piper and Jaeger were expecting twin boys, Tate was going to adopt Linc's son, Shaw, and Linc was going to adopt Ellie, Tate's ward and niece. Beckett was going to raise Cady's still-baking baby as his own. Sage felt no surprise at Beckett's generous offer; in the Ballantyne family blood was a nebulous concept.

Love…love always trumped DNA.

"Are you okay? You seem anxious and stressed."

As she always did, Sage shook her head and, wanting to distract Amy, ran her finger over the open face of a rose, bending down to inhale the subtle scent. "A gift from Jules?" Sage asked, thinking of Julie, Amy's soon-to-be wife.

Amy smiled softly. "Yeah. She's better at romance than I am."

Between her brothers and Amy, she was the only one with no interest in the concept. Besides, she had far more pressing problems than romance—or the lack of it in her life—she was pregnant and only Tyce knew. And, speaking of her baby's daddy, she couldn't keep ignoring his calls and messages. They'd have to talk sometime soon…

When their baby was old enough for college?

Sage pulled a face at her silliness. She'd spent two weeks with her head in the sand; she couldn't keep it there much longer. When this meeting was over she'd invite Tyce to her apartment for a chat. No, not her apartment, that was too intimate a space, too revealing. And her bed was up a short flight of stairs, above her sitting area. She'd spend the entire time looking at his mouth and hoping that he'd put her out of her misery and kiss her. His mouth had always been her downfall; their lips would touch and she'd immediately feel he was stripping her soul of all its barriers.

The fantasy was both wildly exciting and intensely dangerous and that was why she should keep the man out of her private spaces—her apartment, her body, her heart—and meet him in a public venue.

After they'd thrashed out where they stood, what they wanted, what their expectations were, she'd tell her brothers and the rest of the family about the pregnancy.

It was a plan with a hundred holes in it but it was, at least, a plan.

Amy looked at the massive clock on the wall behind Sage. "You need to move or else you're going to be late for your meeting."

"What's this meeting about, by the way?"

"I don't know." Amy frowned, looking displeased. She loathed being outside the loop. "I know nothing except that the meeting is in Connor's boardroom."

Sage turned around slowly, her eyes wide. Connor's boardroom was a little-known boardroom on the top floor of the Ballantyne building. It was only accessible by an elevator within the iconic jewelry store, Ballantyne's on Fifth, on the ground floor of this building or by a non-descript steel door at the back of the building. The room was used for very high-profile clients who demanded anonymity, buyers and sellers of gems who demanded that their movements not be brought to public attention. Or any attention at all.

Sage frowned, realizing that she had to head downstairs, enter the store and then use the elevator. It was a pain in her ass and she was guaranteed to be late.

"Dammit."

Waving a quick goodbye at Amy, Sage headed back to the private elevator that would take her directly into the back rooms of Ballantyne's on Fifth. As she stepped into the hallway, Sage tossed a look over her shoulder and saw Amy standing behind her desk, still looking worried. Worried and hurt. It was an expression she'd seen on many faces over the years and she felt the familiar stab of guilt-slicked pain.

Amy hated that Sage kept her arm's length but it wasn't personal, she kept everyone there, except, possibly, Linc. At the age of six she'd experienced a double whammy, the deaths of both her parents. So, really, was it any surprise that her biggest fear was that she'd lose anyone she loved, that she would be left alone? Her rationale at six still made sense to her: the more distance she kept between her and the ones she loved, the less it would hurt when they went away.

Sage fully accepted that life was a series of changes, that people came and went and that life required a series of emotional shifts. Loved ones, sadly, died. Friends moved away. Relationships broke up. They all came with their own measure of pain but Sage was very sure that she never wanted to be left behind again and it was easier to walk away than stand still and endure the emotional fallout.

Sage hauled in a deep breath. Her childhood had shaped who she was today. She looked after, as much as she could, the relationships she couldn't walk away from—her brothers, their partners and Amy—but she didn't actively seek new people to add to the small circle of people she loved to distraction. She dated casually, not allowing herself to fall in love. If she did find herself someone she liked, really, really liked, she never allowed the relationship to dip beneath the surface because she could never be sure of who would stay or who would go so she made it easy and pushed them all away. Somewhere between her sixth and seventh birthday she'd realized that it was easier to retreat from people and situations than to give them a chance.

Pushing people away, creating distance, it was her thing.

Tyce was the easiest and most difficult person she'd ever walked away from. Easy because she knew that he didn't want anything serious from her, difficult because she'd been so very close to throwing her innate caution and self-preservation to the wind. He'd tempted her to try, to see what the hype about relationships and commitment was all about, to take a risk. Already teetering, if Tyce had given her the smallest sliver of encouragement, she might have toppled into love. But he hadn't and she did what she did best; she'd walked away.

And he'd let her.

Sage shook her head, annoyed with her thoughts. She was focusing on the past and she wasn't going in that direction. Tyce might be the father of her child and she might be crazy, fiercely attracted to him but, baby or not, she intended to keep him on the periphery of her life.

She did, however, have to find another way to interact with him because—she glanced down at the screen of her cell phone showing the number of calls she'd missed from Tyce—he wasn't going away.

Sage stepped out of the elevator into the back room of the original Ballantyne jewelry store and smiled at an employee who was on her way to the break room. Stepping across the hallway, she punched in the code to access the private elevator that would take her up to the secret room on the top floor of the building, adjacent to rooms holding the safes and hundreds of millions of dollars' worth of precious gems.

Sage bit her bottom lip, resigning herself to the inevitable. When this secretive meeting was over, she'd call Tyce and set up a time to meet, to discuss how involved he wanted to be in the baby's life, how they were going to deal with each other when the baby arrived. She would be cool, calm and collected. She wouldn't lose her temper or slap or kiss him.

Sage stepped into the small boardroom. Her stomach immediately rebelled at the smell of coffee rolling toward her and she frantically looked around for a trash can or a receptacle in case her morning sickness turned nasty.

A hand on her back steadied her. Sage slowly lifted her eyes to look into that familiar face, the high cheekbones, the stubble covering his strong jaw. Hard, black eyes. "You okay?" Tyce asked her, holding her biceps in a firm grip. He'd catch her if she fell, Sage thought, relieved. If her knees gave way she wouldn't hit the floor.

"What are you doing here?" she whispered, wondering if she'd dropped down Alice's rabbit hole.

An indefinable emotion flashed in Tyce's eyes. "Now that's a long story. Take a seat and we'll get into it."

Four

Tyce guided Sage to a chair and stepped away from the table, deliberately walking over to the far side of the room and leaning his shoulder into the wall, crossing his feet at the ankle. It was an insolent pose, a deliberate maneuver to keep the Ballantyne men off-balance. Tyce had deliberately dressed down for this meeting; he wore faded, paint-splattered jeans over flat-heeled boots and a clean black button-down shirt over a black T-shirt, cuffs rolled back. Linc and Beck were dressed in designer suits; Jaeger was a little less formal in suit pants and a pale cream sweater.

Sage, well, Sage looked stunning in the clashing colors of pink and red, most of her hair in a messy knot on top of her head, tendrils framing her face and falling down the back of her neck. She was innately stylish, yet people assumed it took her hours to look so perfectly put-together, but he'd seen Sage on the move; she could shove her hair up in thirty seconds, could dress in another minute. Sage wasn't one for spending hours in front of a mirror.

Tyce looked at her face and frowned at the blue stripes under her eyes, at the pallor in her skin. She looked like she'd dropped weight and it was weight she could ill afford. She kept sucking her bottom lip between her teeth, darting anxious looks at his face. Tyce, deliberately, kept his expression blank, his face a mask. She could've avoided this meeting, he reminded himself; she could've taken one of his many calls; they could've done this differently. But, after trying to reach her for two weeks, her refusal to see him or talk to him limited his options so he contacted Linc and convinced him that a meeting would be beneficial to all parties.

Tyce watched as Linc stepped forward and placed both his hands on Sage's shoulders, his gentle squeeze conveying his support. Jaeger and Beck flanked Sage on either side, arms folded and jaws tense. Her brothers were very protective of their sister and he hoped that this conversation wouldn't turn physical but who the hell knew? When you were dealing with family and money and business, anything could happen.

"Since you asked for this meeting, Latimore, would you like to get the party started?" Linc asked, his voice as cold as a subzero fridge.

Tyce nodded, straightened and walked to the table, pulling out a chair at the head, another deliberate gesture. It was a silent *screw you* to their pecking order, telling Linc and his brothers that he wasn't going to neatly slot into their order of command.

Tyce rested his forearms on the table. He turned his head to look at Sage and wished that they were alone, that he could kiss her luscious mouth, trace the fine line of her jaw, kiss his way down her long neck to her shoulders. Peel her clothes from her body...

Tyce sighed. He was imagining Sage naked because, yeah, *that* was helpful. He ran his hand across his face and caught Sage's eye.

"This could've gone differently, Sage. If you had taken my calls, answered my emails, had a goddamn conversation with me, I wouldn't have had to do it like this."

Ignoring her frown, Tyce reached across the table and pulled his folder toward him. He flipped open the cover and withdrew a sheaf of papers and tossed them in Linc's general direction. "Share certificates showing that Lach-Ty owns around fifteen percent of Ballantyne's."

Four backs straightened, four jaws tensed. Linc picked up the share certificates, examined them and carefully placed them facedown on the table. "Would you care to explain," he asked in a dangerous-as-hell voice, "why you own fifteen percent of our company?"

Sure, that was why he was here, after all. "Technically, I don't own the shares. I just paid for them."

Linc gripped the table, his hands and knuckles white. "Then who does own the shares and why the hell did you pay for them?"

"My sister owns those shares because I thought it was right that she owned a percentage of the company her father left to you." Tyce hesitated and thought that he might as well get it all out there so that they could move forward from a basis of truth. "I thought that, since your sister is carrying my baby, it was time to lay my cards on the table."

And that, Tyce thought, his eyes moving from one shocked Ballantyne to another, was how you dropped a bombshell.

Shock, horror, surprise, anger...all the emotions he expected were in their faces, coating their questions, their shouted demands for more information. Tyce ignored them and kept his gaze focused on Sage, who stared at him with hellfire in her eyes.

She half stood, slapped her palms on the table and leaned toward him. "How dare you tell them without my permission?"

Tyce held her gaze and lifted one shoulder in a shrug. "Because if I left it up to you, then you'd be ready to go into labor and you'd still be hemming and hawing about how to tell them, what to tell and whether you should."

"You had no right—"

Tyce pointed at her stomach. "That's my child in there too and, might I remind you, if you'd agreed to meet with me instead of ignoring me, then we could've resolved this and more."

"More? What are you talking about?" Sage demanded, her voice vibrating with fear and concern.

Linc placed a hand on Sage's shoulder and urged her back into the chair. "He's talking about the sharcs and alluding to Connor having a daughter."

"What? Connor never had any children," Sage emphatically stated. "That's crazy!"

"You're pregnant?" Jaeger yelled.

"Everyone shut up!" Linc ordered and looked at Sage. "Let's finish with Latimore first. Then he can get out of our hair and we can talk about your baby," Linc added in his CEO-everyone-must-listen-to-me voice. Yeah, well, Tyce didn't have to.

"Your optimism is amusing, Linc," Tyce drawled. "It's my baby too and, sorry to disappoint you, but I'm going to be around for a hell of a long time."

"No, you're not," Sage stated.

"Oh, honey, I so am. But we'll discuss that later," Tyce said, his voice quiet but holding no trace of doubt.

"Why would you think that your sister is Connor's daughter?" Linc asked, his jaw rock tight with annoyance.

"I don't *think* she is Connor's daughter, I know she is," Tyce replied. Tyce saw that they were going to argue and lifted his hand. "Look, let me start at the beginning and I'll talk you through it."

Where to start? As he said, at the beginning. Well, at Lachlyn's beginning, not his. They didn't need to know about his childhood, about those dark and dismal years before, and after, Lachlyn came along. As quickly and concisely as he could, Tyce recounted the facts. His mom had worked as a night cleaner at Ballantyne International, in this very building—something he had no reason to feel ashamed of; it was honest work and if the Ballantynes were too snobby to understand that, to hell with them—and, because Connor worked long hours, they struck up a friendship. His mom and stepdad separated, she and Connor started an affair and she became pregnant.

"My mom knew that she had no future with Connor so she went back to my stepfather hoping that he'd raise Lachlyn as his."

His stepdad, originally from Jamaica, took one look at Lachlyn, a blond-haired, blue-eyed baby, and lost his temper. Tyce took his disappearance that same day as a firm *no* on the raising-and-supporting-Lachlyn question. Those months following his stepfather's disappearance had been, by far, the worst of his life. His mom sunk into what he now knew to be postpartum depression, made a hundred times worse by her normal, run-of-the-mill depression. Looking after the baby had been a struggle for her. She hadn't had any energy left over for a confused eight-year-old boy.

"Did your mother ever tell Connor that he had a daughter?" Beck asked, his voice laced with skepticism.

"No," Tyce snapped back, frustrated. "Since Lachlyn's birth certificate states that my stepdad is her father, she didn't have a legal leg to stand on. She assumed that Connor would dismiss her claims."

"Which is exactly what we are going to do," Linc told him, his blue eyes hard.

Linc reacted exactly as he expected him to so Tyce wasn't particularly surprised. "You can, but it won't make any difference to my plans."

Tyce ran his hand around his neck, hoping to rub away the headache at the base of his skull. He darted a look at Sage and saw that her face was even whiter than before and her big, endlessly blue eyes were dark with pain and confusion. She looked like he'd punched her in the gut. The fight immediately went out of Tyce and he moved his hand across the table to cover hers. He desperately wanted to scoop her up, soothe away her pain, assure her that everything would be okay.

But Tyce, more than most, knew that life had a nebulous concept of fairness and had a shoddy record at doling out good luck.

Sage snatched her hand out from under his, as if he were contagious with some flesh-eating disease. She folded her arms against her chest and glared at him. He couldn't help his smile.

"You should know that your prissy, 'I'm a princess and you're a peasant' look turns me on."

His comment also had the added bonus of pissing her brothers off. Score.

Sage lifted her hand, her lips thinning. "This is business so let's keep it to that, okay? You and I have nothing to say to each other."

Oh, they so did. "We have a great deal to say to one another and we will," Tyce promised her, lowering his voice.

"In your dreams, hotshot," Sage retorted, fire in her eyes.

Tyce reached across the table and pushed a curl out of her eyes with the tip of his finger. "You can fight this, kick and claw and scratch, but you and me, and that kid, we're going to come to an understanding, Sage. I'm not crazy about this arrangement, neither are you, but we're going to have to deal. I'm not going anywhere. Start getting used to the idea."

Because he so badly wanted to frame her face with his hands, to lower his mouth to cover hers—God, it had been so long since he'd held her, tasted her, feasted on her—Tyce stood up and jammed his hands into the pockets of his jeans. Feeling wiped, he blew out a breath before locking eyes with Linc again. It was time to get this done.

"I've purchased enough shares to earn a seat on the Ballantyne board. I'm going to take that seat, I will oppose every decision and I will vote against every motion you make unless you actively try to establish whether Lachlyn is Connor's child or not. Do not underestimate how much trouble I can cause. I'll undermine your position and I'll actively campaign to have you removed as CEO."

Linc's face paled at the threat. But because he was a deal maker and a strategist, Linc then asked the question he was expecting. "So if Lachlyn is Connor's daughter, how much do you want?"

These rich people, they always thought it came down to money. "I don't want any of your money," Tyce replied, enjoying the surprised shock on their faces. "If the DNA results come back saying that Lachlyn is not Connor's daughter, then I will sell the shares."

"What's the catch?" Beck demanded.

"If Lachlyn is Connor's daughter, then I'd like you to give her a chance…to get to know you, to become part of your family. She missed out on that, having a family."

So had he but that didn't matter. Lachlyn was the one who'd spent her childhood and teenage years in a dismal house permeated with the sadness of a perpetually depressed mother and a too tense, uncommunicative brother. She deserved the chance of being part of a close, happy family. And nobody, apparently, did family better than the Ballantynes.

Tyce held the back of a chair, his hands white against the black leather. He didn't drop his eyes from Linc's face, didn't break the contact. Linc, confusion all over his face, frowned. "I don't understand any of this. You spent tens of millions buying those shares but all you want is for us to give your sister a chance to get to know us?"

Tyce nodded. "You'll be happy to hear that she's a lot nicer than I am."

Linc's mouth twitched in what Tyce suspected might hint at amusement. He leaned back in his chair and folded his big arms across his chest. "This is batcrap insane, Latimore."

"Probably," Tyce admitted, darting a look at the still-fuming Sage. Oh, that reminded him. Hardening his expression, he looked from Linc's face to Jaeger's and then to Beckett's. "I have one more demand…"

Beck groaned and Jaeger swore. Linc just waited, his eyes narrowed.

"My last demand is that you leave us, Sage and me, alone. Having a baby, becoming new parents, is something new to both of us and we don't need her three angry, protective brothers muddying the waters."

God, he was tired of this conversation, so tired of it all. All he wanted to do was to climb into bed with Sage and wrap himself around her. He would even forego sex just to hold her and sleep.

Sage held up a hand and stopped what he was sure was going to be a hot response from Jaeger. Hot seemed to be Jaeger's default setting.

"You three don't need to fight my personal battles," Sage said, her voice clear and determined. "Tyce and I will deal with our personal situation, ourselves. Not—" Sage sent him a look that was designed to shrivel his balls "—that we have much to discuss."

"Are you sure, shrimp?" Jaeger asked her, doubt in his voice.

"Very." Sage nodded. "I can handle him."

"If he lays a finger on you, we will rip him from limb to limb and bury him so deep that no one will ever find his body," Beck added, his voice so flat and so bland that Tyce had no choice but to believe him.

"Tyce is an ass but he's not violent," Sage told them.

So nice to know how she really felt about him.

"Still…" Beck's eyes connected with his and Tyce nodded, acknowledging Beck's threat. Hurt her and he'd die. Got it.

"One tear, Latimore, and all bets are off," Linc said, rising to his feet. "We'll need a week or two, and your sister's DNA, to ascertain whether she is Connor's daughter and, if she is, we'll meet again, with your sister, to determine a path forward."

It was, Tyce realized, as much of a deal as he was going to get today and it was, honestly, better than he hoped. Lachlyn would finally have, if the Ballantynes cooperated, a shot at having the large, crazy, loving family she'd always said she wanted.

"Two weeks and then we'll reevaluate?" Tyce held out his hand and wondered if Linc would shake it. "Deal?"

Linc's warm hand gripped his and their gazes clashed and held. "Deal."

Linc dropped his hand, sidestepped him and opened the door to the conference room. "I'll contact you to set up the time and place for the DNA swabs." Linc walked out of the conference room and punched a code into the pad next to the elevator opposite the conference room. The doors slid open. Right, it was official; Linc was kicking him out.

Tyce ignored Linc's impatient expression and walked past Jaeger to drop to his haunches in front of Sage, resting his forearm across his knee. He waited until Sage lifted defiant eyes to meet his. "After you've spoken to your brothers, go home and sleep. I'm going to drop in this evening and—we'll talk then."

"I won't be there."

Tyce resisted the impulse to roll his eyes. "We need to talk, Sage. We can do it this afternoon or tomorrow morning but we are going to talk."

Sage muttered a curse under her breath and Tyce swallowed his smile at her hissed profanity. "Okay, this evening. Around five."

Tyce nodded, stood up and bent down again to drop a kiss on her head. Not wanting to see her reaction, her disgust, he spun around and headed out the door and into the lift. After punching the button for the ground floor, he looked at Sage and electricity, as it always did, hummed between them. He wanted to run back into the room, scoop her up and run away with her, to hell with

Lachlyn and Sage's brothers. To hell with his art and her status as one of the wealthiest women in the world.

To hell with it all.

Unfortunately, Tyce thought as the elevator's doors closed, running away solved nothing.

The meeting had run longer than they thought and Beck and Jaeger left a few minutes after Tyce, both of them assuring her that they were in her corner, that they would help in any way they could.

"Up to and including beating the crap out of Latimore," Jaeger told her as a parting shot.

When she and Linc were alone Sage walked to the small window, laying her hand on the cool glass. Droplets of icy rain ran down the pane and the low, gray clouds outside threatened snow. Late winter in New York City, she thought; she felt cold inside and out.

"You okay, shrimp?" Linc asked her. Sage turned, put her back to the wall and looked at her brother, his chair pushed back and his long legs stretched out.

"Mentally or physically?" Sage asked.

"Either. Both," Linc answered her.

Sage lifted one shoulder and shrugged, biting her bottom lip. Linc's eyes were on her face and she knew that her brother was hoping for an answer. Unlike Jaeger and Beck, Linc didn't nag and as a result, she found herself talking to him more often than anyone else.

Still, it was easier to stick to the facts. "I'm about twelve, thirteen weeks pregnant. I'm not seeing Tyce, it just happened."

Linc's expression was sober. "Do you want to keep this child?"

Now there was a question she could answer without hesitation. "With every breath I take."

Linc relaxed and his lightened. "Okay then. If you want to keep the baby, then we'll all pitch in to help you... You know that, right?" Linc stated.

Sage nodded. "I do. So does, apparently, Tyce." She tapped her index finger against her thigh. "I'm really surprised that he wants to be involved. I thought he'd take my offer to run."

Linc scowled. "A hell of a lot surprised me today and that was only one thing of many." Linc flipped through the folder Tyce had left and pulled out a letter-sized photograph of his sister, Lachlyn. He placed it on the table so that they could both look at the photo. "I can't deny that she looks like Connor, she has his eyes."

"And his nose," Sage added. Apart from their hair color, she and Lachlyn could almost be sisters.

Linc folded his arms. "He made quite a few threats today. Do you think he'd act on them?"

Sage knew he would. Tyce never said anything he didn't mean and she told her brother so. "The media is fascinated by him and, because he's so reclusive, when he speaks the world will sit up and listen."

"Crap."

"If his sister is Connor's daughter... God," Sage said, her voice trembling. She couldn't say more, hoping that her brother would know what she was trying to say without her having to verbalize her thoughts.

"If she's his daughter she's entitled to some part of his wealth? Is that what you are trying to say?" Linc asked her, pain in his eyes.

Sage nodded. "Isn't she? We're not his biological children, Linc. Yes, he adopted us but we're not his blood," Sage muttered. "If he knew about her, he would've scooped her up and pulled her into the family, his family."

"He wouldn't have tossed us aside," Linc stated, his

voice full of conviction. "Connor had an enormous capacity for love."

"But he wouldn't have ignored her either."

Linc nodded, his face grave. "You're right. She would've been pulled into this family. And five people would've inherited his wealth and not four."

Sage traced the curve of Lachlyn's cheek with her finger.

Tyce's sister would've been hers, as well. The mind just boggled at the thought.

Linc rested his arms on the table, his brows lowered. "It's important that we take this one step at a time, that we don't get carried away. We need to do the DNA testing."

She had a sister; Connor had a child; there was a missing Ballantyne out there. Sage felt the world tilting and she leaned her back against the wall and closed her eyes. She couldn't do this; it was all too much. The pregnancy, Tyce, Lachlyn... Too much change.

And let's not forget the little detail of Tyce deliberately targeting her to gather information on her family. Their meet-cute at that art gallery had been anything but fortuitous. He'd intentionally set out to meet her with the goal of getting her to spill company information. And strangely, that hurt the most and made her doubt everything that had happened between them. Were they really that sexually compatible or had he been just pretending? Was he as attracted to her as she was to him? Had it all been one horrible, well-thought-out, excellent act on his part?

God, just the thought that the six weeks they'd spent together three years ago might be one-sided made her feel like someone was ripping out her internal organs without any pain relief.

Had he laughed at her, was he still laughing? Did he

think she was a gullible idiot? That she was easily manipulated? God, she had to know.

Right now.

Sage lunged for her phone and pulled up his number, punching the green button. Tyce answered just after the first ring.

"Yeah?"

"Where are you?"

"In the alley behind the store—I went out the back exit," Tyce replied. "Why?"

"Wait there," Sage ordered, her skin prickling with embarrassment. She disconnected the call and picked up her coat, draping it over her arm. She could cope with a baby, with being on her own, but she didn't know how she would handle the truth that she was simply a means to an end for Tyce.

And a very easy lay.

God, she'd never felt more off-balance in her life. She looked at her favorite brother. "I'm going to go. I'll talk to you later."

Linc placed a hand on her shoulder and squeezed. "Shall we all have dinner at The Den tonight and you can break the news to the rest of the family? That way you can answer all the questions that I don't have the answers to."

Sage nodded. "Sounds good."

Linc pulled her into his arms and rubbed the top of his chin across her head. When he spoke, his voice was rough with emotion. "Our baby is having a baby. How is that possible? How did it happen?"

Her eyes burning from unshed tears, Sage knew that in order to stop her tears from falling, she needed to diffuse the emotion swirling between them. "Well, Latimore and I met and then we stripped each other naked—"

Linc took a hasty step back and slapped his hands over his ears. "Shut up, shrimp. God, now I need brain bleach to get that picture out of my head."

Sage was a bundle of dread and anxiety.

She wanted to run away and hide, to do her ostrich impression—head in the sand—but at the same time she needed to know, she needed to have her worst fears confirmed.

Because when they were, she could, finally and without a smidgeon of doubt, bury those lingering doubts around whether walking away from Tyce three years ago was the right thing to do.

She'd know and she could be free of the what-ifs that occasionally plagued her. What if she was braver? What if she took a chance?

When he told her that it was all one-sided, then she could finally step away from him, physically and mentally.

At the door leading to the alley Sage punched the master code into the access panel and heard the click. She gave the heavy door a hard push and stumbled down the two steps that led into the narrow space behind the building.

"Easy there," Tyce said, grabbing her arms and keeping her from doing a face-plant.

Sage slapped his hands away and tossed him a scathing look. "Did you deliberately set out to meet me three years ago?"

Tyce frowned and his expression turned inscrutable. "Initially, yes."

"And after that?" Sage demanded, hearing the shrill note in her voice. "Did you keep sleeping with me to get information about the business and my family?"

"You didn't give any," Tyce pointed out.

"That's not the point! Did you use me for information?" Sage shouted, slapping her hands against his chest. "Did you keep sleeping with me because it was a means to an end? Were you into me, at all?"

Sage felt her ribs squeezing her heart and lungs and thought that her skin felt a size too small. She reminded herself to breathe, telling herself that she could deal with hearing that Tyce wasn't that into her, because it would give her the impetus she needed to stop thinking about him, dreaming about him, being tempted by him.

"Is that what you think?" Tyce asked, gripping her wrists and holding her hands against his broad chest. And, just like that, heat flowed into her and her fingers tingled with the need to touch and to explore. She could feel the slow, hard thump of her heart against her tight ribs and her nipples tightened, desperate for attention.

Tyce was touching her and that was all that was important...

"Are you seriously asking me whether I was pretending to be attracted to you?"

Tyce's harsh question reminded her that they were standing in an alley in the rain-tinged wind. Oh, and that she was as mad as hell with him.

"Are you insane?" Tyce demanded, his face saturated with frustration. He abruptly dropped her hands and slapped a hand on the top of her butt, jerking her into him. Sage released a surprised gasp when her stomach connected with the long, hard length of him. Holy cupcakes, he felt so good...

Tyce grabbed her elbows and lifted her off the ground, easily carrying her until her back touched the rough concrete wall. Holding both her wrists in one hand, he lifted her hands above her head, her breasts pushed into his chest. His deep, dark eyes met hers as he brushed her hair off her cheek. Sage held her breath as he slowly, so slowly dropped his head and his lips finally—God, he felt so good—covered hers.

His lips danced over hers, a soft, slow exploration, his tongue gentle as it wound around hers. She expected fire; she expected heat; she expected the maelstrom of want and need that always swirled between them but she didn't expect tenderness or reassurance. She didn't want to feel either. She wanted to be able to walk away from him, not be tempted to step closer... God, how could he make her feel like this?

Sage wrenched her mouth out from under his and glared up at him with what she hoped were stormy, accusing and not dreamy eyes.

"Did you kiss me to avoid the question?" she demanded, begging her heart to stop its relentless attempt to leave her chest. She dropped her eyes and, feeling the length of him still pressed against her, tried to pull her hands from his grip.

Tyce held her chin and forced her to look at him again. "I admit that I set out to meet you but this—" he hesitated "—crazy buzz between us had nothing to do with Lach-Ty, with the Ballantyne shares. It was, is, all you." He pushed his hard erection into her stomach and closed his eyes. "And me. You walk into the room and I immediately start thinking about how soon I can get you naked."

Dammit. His voice was deep and slow and lifted every hair on her neck. It made her want to feast on him, to gulp him up.

So much for finding some distance.

Tyce abruptly dropped her hands and stepped away from her, pushing his free hands into his hair. "It's cold and—" he nodded to the camera above their head "—not the most private place for either kissing or conversation. We'll talk more tonight."

Sage nodded, her head hurting with an overload of information and emotion.

Two thoughts ran through her head like toddlers on a sugar high: *I want him bad and it's so bad that I want him.*

Five

As an artist, Tyce immediately noticed the windows running from her floor to the ceiling, and massive skylights maximized the amount of light streaming into her loft apartment. This place was so Sage, he thought, looking around. The front door swiveled on a hinge in the middle of the frame as Sage closed the door behind him. The floor was comprised of light wooden planks holding a subtle tinge of pink. The wooden beams in the ceiling were partially stripped of their off-white cream paint, allowing the natural grain of the wood to bleed through. The entire loft was open-plan, except for a divider at the far end of the room, which suggested a bed and a bathroom hid behind. He looked up and saw the main bedroom overhead. There were two faded couches in a cream-and-nude stripe, beanbags tossed on the floor, and the back corner held her workbench and a massive corkboard containing sketches of her designs.

Tyce, because he appreciated the artist she was, immediately walked over to that wall, examining her sketches. There was an intricate diamond choker, a bracelet that reminded him of a serpent crawling up an arm and teardrop earrings. Tyce looked at her scribbled notes on each drawing where she'd detailed the stones she'd use. Four-carat emeralds here, a six-carat diamond there. Sage didn't play around.

Tyce lifted his finger up and tapped the letter-sized photograph of a ring sporting a massive red stone for its center and delicate diamond petals. Even he, stupid when it came to stones, could see that this was a serious piece of jewelry art.

"Is that a ruby?"

"It's a red diamond," Sage said, coming up to stand at his shoulder. "Ridiculously rare, practically flawless. It's—" she placed a hand on her heart and Tyce could see the emotion in her eyes "—the same chemical composition of coal but it amazes me that pressure and millions of years can turn coal into that."

"Is it really that red?" Tyce asked, intrigued.

Sage half smiled. "That photograph doesn't even begin to capture the color. It's a deep, luscious red that defies description."

"I take it that the Ballantyne family owns the ring?"
Sage nodded.

"Then why wasn't it with the rest of the collection at the cocktail-party-slash-exhibition? I thought the point of the exhibition was to display the fabulous stones your family has collected over the past hundred years. I'd say that this ring qualifies as fabulous."

Sage picked a pair of pliers, examined the handle and dropped them back onto the bench. "We decided not to show it to the world."

"Why not? Is it stolen?"

Sage glared at him. "No, it's not stolen." She sighed and Tyce noticed her eyes darkening with something akin to pain. "I asked Linc not to exhibit the ring. For personal reasons." Before he could ask what those personal reasons were Sage held up her hand and continued to speak. "Not going there, not now, not ever."

Yeah, good idea. Talking was a damn good way to crack the door allowing those pesky feelings to slide on through. They had enough to deal with as it was and they didn't need emotions muddying the water.

Bare feet peeking out from under the long hem of her jeans, Sage walked back to the center of the room and sat down on one of the two couches.

Tyce sat in the far corner on the couch opposite her, trying to put as much distance between them as possible. If she was in arms' reach, then there was a damn good chance that he'd say to hell with talking and take her to bed. As his lack of control in the alley earlier showed, resisting Sage was not something he'd ever excelled at. And, he admitted, making love to her would be like adding C-4 to a bonfire. Stupid and dumb-ass crazy.

They were adults and they had to have a mature conversation about their situation. Tyce thought that adulthood wasn't all that it was cracked up to be...

Then again, it was a damn sight better than being a child trying to operate in an adult world.

Sage pulled up her feet and tucked them beneath her bottom. She still looked a little shell-shocked and he couldn't blame her. Nothing was simple about this situation... Nothing ever would be.

While he wasn't a talker, he did concede that sometimes the only way to move forward was to communicate. Dammit, something else he wasn't great at.

"Are you still mad because I deliberately set out to meet you?" Tyce asked, keeping his voice mild.

"You used me!"

Initially he had. He'd asked her out that first night because she was Sage Ballantyne, because he'd just found out that Lachlyn was Connor's daughter and, in his anger, he'd thought that Sage was living Lachlyn's life. He'd expected to find a pampered princess, someone he would despise, but Sage had turned out to be totally different. She was funny, down-to-earth, a little crazy.

"Within an hour of meeting I established that, while you adored your family, you wouldn't talk about them. I also quickly realized that you weren't that interested in the business side of the company."

He caught the defiance in her eyes but he knew she was listening.

"If I was only interested in you for business information, I wouldn't have bothered to call you again," Tyce told her. "I paid a fair price for every share I purchased. I bought enough shares to bring Lachlyn to your attention, which was my eventual goal. Hearing that you are pregnant with my child moved my schedule up a bit. I haven't cheated anyone out of anything."

"You're blackmailing us!" Sage retorted but he saw the doubt in her expression. Tyce didn't feel offended, realizing that she was just trying to find solid ground, trying to make sense of this situation.

"I'm asking for DNA to be tested and if that DNA proves my theory, I am asking for my sister to meet you and your brothers. I am not asking for money, time or involvement." Tyce rested his forearms on his thighs, his eyes steady on her face.

Sage picked at the rip on her thigh, opening up a hole in the denim that wasn't there before.

She looked so lost and alone, out of her depth. Easily able to identify with those emotions, Tyce ignored his brain's insistence to play it cool. He moved across the bare wooden floorboards and dropped in front of her, bending his knees and linking his hands. "I wanted to tell you first, Sage, but you wouldn't take my calls."

Sage opened her mouth to argue and abruptly closed it again. Yeah, she couldn't argue that point. "You wouldn't talk to me so I went on to plan B."

Sage looked past him, to a painting on the far wall, and Tyce followed her gaze. It was the back view of a ballerina but unlike Degas's pretty, perfect renditions of the dancers, Tyce's piece was full of angst, accurately capturing the pain and persistence a dancer went through to achieve perfection. The dancer, dressed in a grubby tutu, her hair falling out of her bun, was massaging her toes, fatigue and pain radiating from her. It was one of his early pieces but emotion poured from it. It was good, he supposed. Not great, but good. Tyce idly wondered when Sage had bought it and why. He knew that she loved ballet but it wasn't, after all, a Degas, an artist whose work she could afford.

"Tell me about your sister," Sage commanded, her eyes clashing with his.

"What do you want to know and why?" Tyce asked, lifting an eyebrow at her imperious demand.

"Well, you want us to meet her. What does she do? What is she like?"

Tyce thought a moment, wondering what to say. He adored Lachlyn but he wasn't in the habit of talking about her. Or his family. "Uh…eight years younger than me. She's an archivist."

"Really? Does she enjoy her work?"

Tyce's mouth softened into a smile. "She loves it. She's history, and book, crazy."

Feeling antsy, Tyce rolled to his feet and walked across the room to look at the framed photographs on the wall. He smiled at a picture of a very young Sage in a tutu, attempting a pirouette, of Beckett on a diving board about to race, Jaeger and Linc in tuxedos at a wedding. All across the world were millions of walls like this one, holding ten billion memories.

He didn't have a wall, neither did Lachlyn.

Like most New Yorkers, he'd watched the Ballantynes grow up. The press was consistently captivated by the closest the city had to a royal family. He remembered the day their parents died, devouring the reports about their plane crash. Tyce remembered reading about Connor, a confirmed bachelor, stepping in and scooping up his orphaned nephews and niece. The Ballantynes had been, were, a constant source of fascination to the mere mortals of the city for a long time.

He had been amazed when Connor adopted Linc, his housekeeper's son, along with the three Ballantyne orphans. He'd wondered what type of man did that. Neither his own father, who'd bailed on him before he was old enough to remember him, or his stepfather ever gave a damn for anyone other than themselves. They'd both been so immature and unreliable, so it was no wonder that Connor's easy acceptance of children who weren't his made such an impression on him.

His mom just managed to keep it together enough to keep working, but navigating the world for a few hours a day sapped all her energy. She'd had nothing left to give to her son and her infant daughter. A month after he'd graduated from high school, his mom fell in on herself and refused to leave her room, to go back to work, to talk and to interact. Six weeks passed and Tyce knew that she wasn't getting better and that it was up to him to support his family. He gave up his scholarship to art school and found a job to feed, clothe and educate his ten-year-old sister. Since he worked two jobs and their mother slept as much and as often as possible, Lachlyn grew up alone. She'd craved a family, siblings, teasing, laughter and support but she got a mother who stopped speaking and a brother who retreated into an impenetrable cocoon, his thoughts consumed by how to stretch five dollars into ten, what new argument he could use to placate their landlord.

He and Sage couldn't be more different. They'd come from two situations that were polar opposites. She knew how to "do" family, to love and be loved in return. To support and be supported. He adored Lachlyn but love and support had fallen by the wayside when held up against his desire to keep them off the streets.

"What do you remember about Connor, about the time when he and your mom met?"

Tyce jammed his hands into the back pockets of his jeans. "As I said, my mom worked as a cleaner at Ballantyne International and I remember her leaving for work in the late afternoon and coming home as I got ready for school."

"Who looked after you?"

Tyce frowned at her. "What do you mean, who looked after me? I was seven, I looked after myself."

Sage's eyes widened. "She left you alone?"

"It wasn't like she had a choice, Sage," Tyce snapped back. "There wasn't money for a babysitter."

Sage laid a hand on her heart and looked horrified. God, they'd had such different childhoods. Sage probably hadn't been able to sneeze on her own at seven.

"Did she ever try to tell Connor about your sister?"

Tyce shook his head. "No. After she died, we found a letter she left for Lachlyn, telling her the truth. She said that she could see that she'd already reached the end of the road with Connor. She knew he was going to dump her."

"Connor didn't do long-term relationships," Sage said, her voice trembling. "It was just who he was... He felt trapped by people, by women. He never married or was engaged."

He could relate. He'd had the odd affair that lasted longer than a hookup but his relationships never lasted long because he always ended up feeling trapped. Funny, he'd never felt like that with Sage, possibly because they parted ways before he started to feel claustrophobic. But he had no doubt that it would've happened, that he would've eventually felt like he was running out of air.

Getting back to the subject... "When I heard that Lachlyn was Connor's daughter I tried to contact Connor but I couldn't get beyond his personal lawyers. They told me that many women have tried to scam Connor, saying that they had birthed his child. They told me to subpoena his DNA but I had no grounds to do that, especially since Lachlyn's birth certificate stated that my stepdad was her biological father. I couldn't prove jack."

"So you decided to buy Ballantyne shares." Sage bit her bottom lip, her eyebrows raised. "God, Tyce, that must have cost you a fortune."

Practically everything he had. "Yeah. But, at least, Lachlyn now owns a portion of what Connor created." Tyce rubbed the back of his neck. This was the longest conversation he'd had in a long, long time. But he still had more to say. "We both understand that Connor left his assets to his kids. He didn't know about Lachlyn and that's the card life dished out. I dished another card and she now owns shares in his company. That's enough for her, and me."

"Seriously?"

"Seriously," Tyce answered her, holding her eye. It was important that she realize he didn't want anything from her or her family. All he wanted was for Lachlyn to have a chance to meet them. Anything that happened after that was in the lap of the gods.

It was raining outside; he could hear the ping of droplets on her roof. Soft light bathed her apartment in pinks and cream and made Sage look younger and softer. They were alone; he could feel his heart pounding against his rib cage, heated blood pumping through his veins. The hair on the back of his neck and his arms stood up as all that warm blood headed south.

God, he wanted her. He always did, would... Tyce looked at her and clocked the exact time when her mind moved from Lachlyn to the attraction arcing between them. Her cheeks turned pink, her mouth softened and he could see her pulse beating in that delicate vee at the bottom of her throat. She stroked the arm of the couch, her fingers gliding over the fabric as they'd once glided over his erection. She had no idea that she'd subconsciously lifted her chest, that her nipples were pushing through the fabric of her bra and T-shirt.

One look and they were both jittery with need. He had to kiss her again, he couldn't resist...

Tyce moved across the floor quickly, stopping in front of her and placing his hands on the back of the sofa, on either side of her head.

Sage lifted her chin and shook her head. "Not happening, Latimore."

She didn't sound very convincing, Tyce thought. Besides he'd seen the flash of interest in her eyes, the smoky blues that suggested she was remembering how he made her feel. His junk immediately tightened and the hot, hard thump of his heart reminded him that it had been months since he'd had sex. Sage was the last woman he'd had in his bed and she was still, damn her, the only woman he wanted.

"I'd rather walk through cut glass without shoes than sleep with you," Sage defiantly muttered, dropping her eyes to stare at her hot-pink toes. Sexy toes with the middle toe sporting a delicate toe ring.

The saying about ladies and protesting too much dropped into his head but Tyce was smart enough not to verbalize that thought. He ran the back of his knuckles over her cheekbone and down the line of her jaw.

"You might not like me at the moment. You're angry and confused and feeling a bit overwhelmed by the fact you are pregnant and that my sister might be a Ballantyne but you still want me and I still want you."

Even though he knew it was a bad idea, Tyce leaned down. Their earlier kiss hadn't been nearly enough. He just needed to taste her again, once, maybe twice, and he'd be satisfied. He covered her mouth with his and sighed at the perfection of her silky lips. He swallowed a moan when those lips opened and his tongue slid into the hot, spicy space that was all Sage. He pulled her bottom lip between his teeth, nipped it and slid his tongue over the bite to soothe its sting. Sage's hand on the back of his neck held his head in place, her tongue dancing with his as her other hand pulled his shirt up to find his bare skin.

He had to stop this now, but he couldn't, didn't want to. He wasn't satisfied; he wanted more. When it came to Sage he always wanted more: one kiss, one bout of sex, was never enough. She was like the most addictive drug in the world. He doubted that there would ever be a time when he wouldn't want Sage Ballantyne and that complicated the hell out of this situation. He had to stop...

Tyce pulled away, lifted his mouth from hers and leaned backward, raising his hands in the air. Sage's mesmerizing eyes slowly refocused and when she was fully in the present, she shook her head and let out a whimper. "What the hell is wrong with us?" she whispered.

"An inability to talk, a desire to avoid anything that smacks of intimacy combined with white-hot heat," Tyce retorted, pushing his hands through his hair. He stood up, willed his junk to subside and walked over to the large windows, staring out at the wet street below him. Night was falling and he and Sage hadn't progressed one inch.

"We need a new way of dealing with each other," he muttered, jamming his hands into the pockets of his jeans. In the reflection of the glass he could see her pulling her long hair off her face, raising her knees to her chest and wrapping her arms around her legs. "I'd say that we should try to be friends but that's ridiculous, since we both know that friends don't generally want to rip each other's clothes off."

"I'm not very good at being a friend."

Tyce, intrigued by that odd statement, turned around to look at her. "What do you mean by that?"

Sage made a production of looking at her watch. She gasped, wrinkled her nose and jumped to her feet. "I'm so late! I have to go to The Den and break the news that I am pregnant to Jo—"

"Jo?"

"Linc's mom. Connor employed her as a housekeeper when he adopted us and she became our second mom. And my brother's wives are going to be pissed that my siblings heard the news first."

Tyce lifted his eyebrows. "You avoided my question."

Sage handed him a snotty look but her eyes begged him not to pursue the topic. "I really do need to get to The Den and I really am late," she said, walking to the door.

And you really don't want to explain why you think that you are a bad friend. Tyce walked across the room to pick up his leather jacket and scarf. Making a quick decision, based purely on the fact that he wasn't ready to walk away from Sage just yet—something he'd worry about later—he tossed the suggestion out. "What if I go with you and help you drop the news?"

Sage, holding her shoe, stared at him with panic-filled eyes. "You can't! They aren't ready for you, for us... I need to tell them on my own."

Tyce shook his head. "The sooner they get used to the idea that I am going to be hanging around, the easier this situation will become." And really, irritating her brothers would be an added bonus.

"Tyce..." Sage's eyes slammed into his. "Please, I need some time. Your revelations today, the pregnancy, my family... You've known about your sister for years and... we've only just learned about her. We need time to catch up, to process all of this."

Tyce considered her statement, impatience and a need to move forward warring with her words. She did have a point, he reluctantly conceded. They were playing catch-up and he needed to give her, and her family, time to do that.

Tyce opened her front door and held it open. "Okay, I hear you. But we still have more to discuss, a lot more."

"I know...we didn't get very far tonight," Sage said, pulling on a long navy coat and winding a cashmere scarf around her neck. "But I need some time, Tyce, and some space. I'll call you."

He wanted to argue, to have a firm date and time in mind but he also knew that, if he pushed her, she'd retreat back inside her shell. It was, after all, exactly what he would do.

"You'd better. And soon," Tyce told her, bending to drop a kiss on her temple. He stepped away and touched her stomach with the tips of his fingers. His kid, growing inside her. God, what a concept. "Take care of yourself, Sage. Call me if you need me."

Sage sent him a puzzled look, her expression stating that she couldn't imagine a situation in which she might need him. She had three brothers, three new sisters and more money than God. She didn't need him for anything except, possibly, sex and that wasn't on the table. Tyce ran his hand through his hair and followed her into the elevator opposite her front door.

He looked at their reflection in the mirror finish of the lift. Sage's hands were in her hair—where his really wanted to be—and twenty seconds later she'd, somehow, secured all those waves into a messy knot at the back of her neck. She pulled a tube of lipstick from the side pocket of her bag and swiped the color across her lips, turning her mouth from sweet to luscious. The lipstick was returned to the bag and a multicolored scarf appeared in her hand. She twisted it around her neck, tied it into a complicated knot and she was, once again, Sage Ballantyne, heiress, ready to face the world.

Tyce glanced at his outfit, old jeans, hiking boots, a black sweater over a black shirt and a leather bomber jacket that he'd had for too many years to count. Sage was an heiress from a family whose blood ran blue; he was an artist who genuinely thought that the art world would one day wake up from their stupor and realize that he wasn't half as good as they'd proclaimed him to be and definitely not worth the ridiculous money the collectors paid for his work. He plowed the bulk of the money he earned from his art into buying those Ballantyne International shares so he was, well, not broke but he wasn't flush with cash either. He didn't have a college degree and his only asset was a battered warehouse on the edge of an industrial park.

He was her former lover, the father of her child...the man who'd given her the bare bones of a very complicated story involving both their families, too scared to open up and make even the smallest emotional connection. He was also the man who wanted her more than he wanted to keep breathing, existing. His raging need to strip her naked and sink inside was part of the problem, he reluctantly admitted, but it went deeper than that.

Sage was, had always been, in a class of her own. She was funny and smart and generous and, surprisingly, she was the most down-to-earth girl he knew. She had no idea that her smile could stop traffic, that her legs could make grown men weep, that her eyes could be weaponized. She had the ability to cut him off at the knees and that was the primary reason why he needed to keep her at a distance. He could fall into something deeper with Sage. She was the one woman who could tempt him into opening up, to explore a world that went beyond some bed-based fun.

Tyce banged the back of his head on the wall of the elevator, feeling his throat constrict. His mind was all over the place, as unsettled as a raging river. She'd always had the ability to mess with his thoughts, to disturb his equilibrium.

He'd explained about the shares, about Lachlyn, and it would be at least two weeks until the DNA tests came back. Sage said that she needed space and, yeah, judging by his crawling skin and accelerated breathing, maybe he did too. He'd take some time, put some distance between them, get his head on straight, to figure out how to deal with Sage on a long-term basis.

A basis that didn't, sadly, involve getting her naked.

Six

Sage glanced at her laptop screen and frowned at the brief message from Linc that had popped into her inbox five minutes ago.

DNA testing confirms that Lachlyn Latimore is Connor's biological daughter. Family meeting?

Family meeting? What did that mean anymore? Did that mean just her and her brothers, her brothers plus their partners, Lachlyn, Tyce?

They were all now connected through DNA. She was connected to Lachlyn because their fathers were brothers, she was connected to Tyce through the DNA their baby shared. It was all crazy, too much to handle. She had a cousin. A sister, sort of. Who was also her baby's aunt.

The news that Lachlyn was Connor's daughter wasn't a surprise: from the moment she saw Lachlyn's photo she'd known who'd fathered her. How to interact with Lachlyn, what to do, how to approach her had played on an endless loop in her head over the past ten days. They were frequently joined by *How involved does Tyce want to be with the baby?* and *What would he do if I jumped him?*

The question of Tyce's role as a father was constructive thinking; the thoughts and memories of Tyce's muscled body and his skilled mouth, and rediscovering what lay under his clothes, were not.

Throwing her pencil onto her workbench, she picked up the sketch she'd been working on—resetting an eight-carat cabochon-cut diamond—scrunched it into a ball and tossed the piece of paper over her shoulder. Her concentration was shot; she couldn't draw a stick figure if someone put a gun to her head.

Sage pushed her chair back and walked across her loft to the windows to look at her city. Linc's email sealed the deal—Lachlyn was Connor's daughter and was a Ballantyne. That meant changes and Sage wasn't fond of change. In her experience change meant sadness and grief. Every time change slapped her it hurt like hell: her parent's deaths, Connor's death. Change always meant tears and she was quite convinced she'd shed enough of those.

Lachlyn's connection to her family meant that Sage had to make an effort to know her, to pull her into the family circle. It was such a big ask. God, she was still getting used to her siblings' women and she was still finding her way with them. She adored Piper, Cady and Tate but she didn't understand them. How could they be so open, so unafraid? They lived bold lives, believing, erroneously in her opinion, that their lives would only and forever be wonderful. Her parents had lived like that:

fearlessly, daringly, without worrying about the future, without worrying that life could smack them in a hundred and ten different ways. She'd experienced that intense grief when her parents died, again with Connor's death.

Nobody understood that fear kept her sane, that standing apart from people gave her some measure of control, a tiny barrier to deflect the hard wallop of people dying, leaving, moving away...*changing*.

Sage heard the first bars of her ringtone and looked at the screen of her phone and hesitated. She should answer Tyce's call but fear and frustration kept her hands firmly in the pockets of her jeans. She ran her hands over her face as a wave of guilt crashed over her. She'd promised to call him but she was still digesting him and their situation, desperately hoping that her fairy godmother would creep into her loft and wave a wand and make sense of her life. It would be easier if she knew what she wanted from Tyce, how she wanted to raise this child, how to start a conversation with him.

The problem was that every time she laid eyes on him, her brain shut down and her body started to thrum. Desire coursed through her and skin prickled and her stomach quivered. She wanted to make love to him again, to explore the angles and ridges of his muscled body and hear him moan with need for her. She imagined his fingers on her, in her, his mouth licking its way down her body, testing her, tasting her, filling her...

Sage placed the palm of her hand against her forehead. Tyce was an alpha male, possibly the most alpha male she'd ever met. He was ridiculously fit and almost overwhelmingly male and thoughts of him made her womb throb and her lady parts tingle.

Okay, this was ridiculous; she was burning up from

the inside out. There had to be an explanation for why she was feeling a hundred times hornier than usual...

Tyce was ludicrously good-looking and phenomenally talented at getting her off, but even when she was younger, she'd never felt so on edge, so aware of her libido. Usually when she was stressed—and the events of the past few weeks were enough to stress out a sloth—her libido took a dive.

Her horniness could be pregnancy hormones, she decided and, almost immediately, cursed herself for lying to herself. It was all Tyce, only Tyce. God, maybe she needed a cold shower.

Sage looked out her windows at the dingy day. Or maybe a walk in fresh air would do the trick. Although it was snowing, a brisk walk would clear her mind and work out some of the tension in her body. Making up her mind, Sage headed to her front door, pulling on flat, warm boots and a thick coat. She placed a floppy burgundy hat over her messy hair and wound a scarf around her neck. Her gloves were in her pocket and with her front door key, her phone and a little cash, she headed downstairs.

It was colder than she'd thought. Sinking her chin into her scarf, she pulled on her gloves and started to walk. In summer the trees were leafy and the cafés scattered chairs and tables on the sidewalk but on a bitter winter afternoon, with snow falling, the residents of this neighborhood were either in Florida, at work or tucked up in their apartments. Only fools and the insane walked the streets in a biting wind. She wouldn't last long, Sage thought; she'd walk a block or two to clear her head and when she returned to her apartment she could justify a decadent cup of hot chocolate. Damn, it was slippery, she thought when her feet skidded across a patch of ice. Maybe this wasn't such a great idea.

Turning back to her apartment building, Sage saw a tall figure approach her front door and frowned, thinking that his height and build reminded her of Tyce. When he walked up the steps and jabbed his finger on her button she recognized his profile, the odd snowflake settling on his black hair. Tyce was leaning on her bell, waiting for her to buzz him in. Impatient man, Sage thought, stepping from the road onto the sidewalk.

Because her eyes were on Tyce, she didn't notice the patch of ice and her right foot skidded out from under her. Her left foot followed suit and then she was freewheeling her arms, trying to keep her balance. Can't fall, she thought, she had to protect her baby. She tried to break her fall and her hand slammed down on the pavement and she heard the distinctive crack.

The pain in her coccyx hit her first, the sharp sting rocketing up her spine. Not wanting to be outdone, her wrist radiated short, sharp bursts of agony, causing dots to appear behind her eyes and her breath to catch in her throat.

Sage knew she didn't call out to Tyce—she had no breath to speak let alone to yell—but by some miracle he appeared and dropped to his knees next to her. "Crap! Sage, are you okay? What the hell happened?"

Sage, still looking for air and fighting pain, couldn't reply.

Tyce's hand on her cheek anchored her and his deep, calm voice steadied her. "Okay, honey, just breathe. Slowly. In and out."

Sage concentrated on getting air into her lungs, vaguely aware that Tyce held a phone to his ear, his eyes locked on hers. She heard something about an ambulance, that they should hurry. Sage tried to wave his concerns away; she would be okay; she just needed a minute.

And, she thought, a new coccyx and a new wrist. Then she would be fine.

"Yeah and she's pregnant, about four months," Tyce said. "Breathe, dammit."

Okay, that statement was directed at her. Sage pulled in some more air and felt the light-headedness pass and the pain increase. She was also, she realized, lying flat on her back and every inch of her body was freezing, except for her butt and her wrist, both of which were on fire.

Tyce pushed his phone back into the inside pocket of his jacket and pushed a strand of hair out of her eyes.

"I need to sit up," Sage rasped. "I'm cold."

"They said not to move you," Tyce replied, his hand covering her stomach.

"I'm freezing, Tyce." Sage heard the distant wail of ambulance sirens and wrinkled her nose. "That for me?"

Tyce looked up and nodded. "Yep."

"I'm sure that's not necessary."

"What wasn't necessary was you going out on a freezing day and endangering yourself," Tyce growled as the ambulance pulled up beside them.

"I needed air," Sage protested.

"Then open a damned window!" he retorted as EMTs approached them.

"We're going to need you to stand back, sir."

Tyce stood at the young female EMT's command and Sage noticed that his jeans were soaked from the knees down. That meant, she supposed, that she was wet from tip to toe. Wet and cold. "Any cramping? Any signs that you might be bleeding?" the EMT asked her as he pointed a penlight at her eyes.

"Nope," Sage replied. "I bounced off my butt. Look, my apartment is right over there—if someone can help me up, then I'll go on upstairs and I'll be fine."

The EMT looked up and Sage saw him exchange a look with Tyce. "I strongly suggest that, because you are pregnant and because you are cradling your hand like a baby, you go to hospital." Sage nodded, sighed and looked at her front door, so near but so far away. She really, really needed that cup of hot chocolate.

"They x-rayed my wrist and I have a greenstick fracture, which is why I have this stupid cast."

"Are you allowed to have X-rays when you're pregnant?"

Tyce heard Linc's question and quickly realized that Sage was talking to her brother via speakerphone and waited to hear her answer. Stopping, he stood to the side of the partially open door to her hospital room and put his back to the wall, holding a small bag containing dry clothes and shoes. Luckily the hospital wasn't far from her apartment and Sage had handed over the key so that he could collect clothes for her to wear home.

"I checked—they said it was completely safe," Sage said, sounding bone-deep weary. Tyce ran a hand over his eyes, the image of her feet flipping up and her butt hitting the pavement with a loud thump playing over and over in his head. Okay, she hadn't been knocked by a car but she'd landed hard and he kept expecting to see blood soaking through her jeans.

Tyce felt his stomach lurch into his throat at the thought. Up until a few hours ago he'd understood Sage's pregnancy on a purely intellectual basis: his sperm, her egg, a baby later in the year. But when she fell, he felt bombarded with fear. How badly was she hurt? How could he fix her? What could he do? What if she lost this baby? How would she feel?

How would *he* feel?

Lousy, he decided. Sage's baby, he realized, their baby, wasn't something he wanted to wish away.

When had that happened? And how?

"Are you sure you don't want me to come down? I can be there in about a half hour," Linc said.

Tyce held his breath, waiting for her answer.

"I'm sure Tyce will see me home. He was with me when I fell."

"Then he did a piss-poor job of catching you," Linc grumbled.

"He was at my door and I was stepping onto the pavement. He's not Superman, Linc."

Silence fell between the siblings and Tyce straightened, prepared to enter the room again. He stopped when Linc spoke again. "If your right wrist is in a cast and if walking causes you pain, then you can't stay on your own."

Linc was right, Tyce thought. Sage needed help for a while and maybe he should be the one to offer to stay with her. Sure, living with her and not making love to her was going to be hellfire difficult but the reality was that they couldn't keep circling round each other. At some point they had to start dealing with each other. And it would be better for the baby if they managed to establish some sort of a relationship—hopefully something that resembled a friendship—before their child dropped into the world and their lives.

Tyce fully accepted that he was a loner, that he didn't need people but he was connected to his child and through that little person to Sage. He doubted he could give the child what he or she needed but, along with offering whatever financial support he could to Sage, he was prepared to try to be a dad. That way, he could look himself in the eye and say that he'd tried to be the best

father he could. Part of this new role was looking after
his child's mother. And if that meant moving in with her
and helping out while she was injured, that was what he
intended to do.

Seven

"Let me talk to the brothers and we'll draw up a roster so that one of us will stay with you until you can manage on your own," Linc replied.

"I'm not a hundred and three, Linc! I don't need anyone to stay with me. You know I hate having people in my space."

Tough, Tyce thought, despite the little spurt of sympathy he felt for her. He didn't like people in his space either but she'd just have to suck it up and deal.

"I'll stay with you tonight—"

That was his cue, Tyce thought. Nobody was staying with her but him. He walked into the room, dumped her clothes on the foot of her bed and walked around the bed to look down at Sage's phone into Linc's worried face. Taking it from her hand, he ignored Sage's annoyed "Hey!"

"Forget the roster, Linc. I'll be staying with her."

"Latimore," Linc said, his eyes and tone cool. "Is that what Sage wants?"

Judging by her annoyed and fractious expression, Sage would rather have a mutant cockroach move in but he didn't care. He was looking after Sage so that she could look after their baby.

And maybe you're also doing this because you need to know that she is okay on a day-by-day, minute-by-minute basis? Tyce ignored the errant thought. He looked at Sage, who was squawking her displeasure.

"Pipe down, Sage. It's a done deal, Linc," Tyce said before disconnecting the call.

Her eyes hazy with pain, Sage tried to skewer him with a look. "You are not coming home with me and you are not moving in!"

Tyce jammed his hands into the back pockets of his jeans, conscious that the bottom half of his jeans was still damp from kneeling on the sidewalk beside her. He opened his mouth to argue with her and then noticed her pale face and pain-filled eyes. Dammit, he hated knowing that she was in pain and that there was nothing he could do about it.

Arguing with her was a waste of energy: he was taking her home and he was temporarily, very temporarily, moving in. As he'd told Linc, it was a done deal.

Placing both hands on the bed on either side of her hips, he looked into her face. "No BS. How, exactly, are you feeling?"

Sage opened her mouth, shut it again and the heat of her sigh caressed his chin. "The baby is fine. I'm not at risk of miscarrying if that's what you are worried about," she said in a quiet voice.

She had no idea that he wasn't half as concerned about

the baby as he was about her. The baby had its own cus-tom-made airbag; Sage hadn't had anything between her and the cold, hard sidewalk.

"Sage…" Tyce used his knuckle to lift her face up, waiting until their eyes connected again before he spoke. "I know that but I want to know how *you* are feeling."

"My wrist is sore but bearable, but my tailbone is ex-cruciating. It hurts to sit."

Tyce had to touch her so he cupped the side of her face. "Have you had some pain meds?"

"Just acetaminophen. They also gave me some cream to help with the bruising." She looked at her wrist, closed her eyes and sighed. "That's not something I'm going to able to manage myself."

Tyce laid his lips on her forehead, holding the kiss there for longer than necessary. *She's okay*, he reminded himself as panic clawed up his throat. *She's okay…and the baby is okay… Breathe.* When the unfamiliar wave of, God, *emotion* passed—yeah, Sage's superpower was to turn him to mush—Tyce pulled back and dragged a smile onto his face. "I happen to like your butt and I have no problem touching it, with cream and without."

As he hoped, Sage rolled her eyes and amusement touched her lips. She picked up her phone from the side table and sent Tyce an uncertain look. "Are you sure you want to look after me for a couple of days? Wouldn't it be easier if my family took turns to help me out?"

Tyce straightened. "Probably. The thing is, Sage, you and I need some time to talk, to get to know each other again. We didn't spend that much time talking three years ago."

She blushed and Tyce knew that she was remembering the hours, days they spent in bed…not talking. "In less than half a year," he added, "we'll have this child and it will be affected by everything we do, from how we talk to each other, treat each other, interact with each other. I genuinely believe that we have to try to find a sensible way of dealing with each other."

"And you think that way is to move in with me and rub cream on my butt?" Sage asked, skeptical.

"If I move in for a few days, we'll have time to talk, to figure out a way forward, to talk about this baby and how it will change our lives. We can discuss your expectations, my expectations, how we're going to tackle this." Tyce pushed his hands into his hair, frustrated. The adults in his life had lurched from crisis to crisis, had been reactive rather than proactive. By moving in with her, she couldn't avoid him and he'd be able to find out what type of father Sage wanted him to be and whether he could live up to her expectations.

They could build something small but meaningful between them, some type of relationship that would help them to co-parent their child effectively. Yeah, it meant him stepping out of his comfort zone, opening up a little, but his child deserved his best effort. Tyce sucked in a deep breath. They needed a plan and with one in place, there was less chance they'd go off script and venture into unknown, scary, emotional territory. "Am I making any sense?"

Sage wrinkled her nose. "Unfortunately, yes."

"Your enthusiasm is underwhelming," Tyce stated, his voice dry.

Sage tried to swing her legs off the bed and groaned. She closed her eyes and Tyce's heart contracted at her low whimper. "Dammit, that hurts."

Thinking that the easiest way to get her onto her feet was to lift her, Tyce slid one arm around her back, the other under her knees, and easily lifted her into his arms.

Backing away from the bed, he looked down into her lovely face. "Okay?"

"Yeah." Sage curled her hand around his neck and lust skittered down his spine. "I'm okay. You can put me down."

"I'll keep my hands on you so that you don't fall," Tyce told her, keeping his voice steady and calm. After Sage was on her feet, he held her elbows and checked her face for pain. Seeing that she was coping, he leaned back and snagged the bag of clothes from the bed. He'd wanted, desperately, to remove her clothes but not like this. He'd intended to kiss every inch of her skin as he undressed her, inhale her scent, drive her crazy.

Sage's eyes slammed into his and, despite her pain, he saw the flash of awareness, heard her quick intake of breath. He couldn't help noticing that the gap between her thighs widened, that she'd subconsciously arched her back, a silent signal that desire bubbled under her pain.

He had to be the better person here... Sage was injured and he was sex deprived. But it would help if she stopped looking at him like he was a piece of fine Belgian chocolate that she couldn't wait to sample.

"Stop looking at me like that," he grumbled.

"Like what?" Sage asked, her face flushing.

"Like you want me to get you naked," Tyce snapped. "You're injured and I need to get some dry clothes on you. I shouldn't be thinking about how it feels to hold you naked, up close and against me."

Sage pulled her plump bottom lip between her teeth. "Are we ever going to get past this, Tyce?"

"Me wanting you?" Tyce clarified.

"And me wanting you." Sage rubbed her eye socket with the ball of her hand. "We keep telling ourselves that we can ignore this heat between us but it's constantly there, like the proverbial elephant in the room."

Nailed it, Tyce thought. Forcing his big brain to think, he pulled out her clothes from the bag. "We have so much else to deal with that I think we should keep our lives as simple as possible. Sex always adds a layer of complication."

"I suppose you're right."

He was but this was one time when he didn't want to be. He wanted to have her, take her and damn the consequences, but he knew that those complications would come back and take a solid chunk out of his emotional ass.

Be smart, Latimore.

"Okay then. If you have a car waiting, let's not worry about my clothes. I can handle the cold for a few minutes," Sage told him, cradling her plaster-cast arm.

"Probably, but you'd be a lot more comfortable, and warmer, in yoga pants and a hoodie than in those scratchy scrubs the nurse found for you to wear."

"I refused a hospital gown."

Tyce gestured to the sterile, unattractive hospital room. There was less chance of them getting carried away here than there was at her apartment.

"Let's just get this done."

Pulling out her clothes from the bag, Tyce stopped to look at her. Her cheekbones were slightly red. They'd discussed this, discussed making love, why was she now embarrassed? Girls could be so weird about their bodies and nudity. "Honey, I have kissed, tasted and explored every inch of you. What's the problem with me seeing you in your bra and panties?"

Sage's shoulders lifted up to hover around her ears. "That was sex. This is… I don't know how to explain it…this is different."

It was more intimate, Tyce realized. And intimacy scared Sage, as it did him. She liked being in control of what she shared with him and how much of herself she gave him and she was suddenly thrust into a situation where she had to allow him control. Tyce sympathized. He didn't like losing control either. He dropped a hand onto her shoulder and squeezed before holding up a pair of soft, well-worn yoga pants.

"So, those clothes or these?" he asked in his most businesslike voice.

Sage nodded at her pants. "Those, please." She started to fiddle with the band of her scrub pants with her left hand, muttering soft curses. "God, it even hurts to stand."

Tyce dropped to his haunches, whipped her pants down and off, trying to ignore those long, gorgeous legs that had wrapped around his hips, back and neck many times in the past. Ignoring the wave of memories, he slid the yoga pants over her lifted foot and then the other. *Just get it done, Latimore.* He pulled the stretchy fabric up her legs, standing up to pull the material over her butt. He glanced down and noticed the football-size bruise starting to form on her lower back. "Holy hell, Sage, how hard did you fall?"

"What?"

"You have a hell of a bruise on your butt. That's why sitting hurts," Tyce said, reaching for her socks. He quickly put her sneakers on her feet and tied the laces. Standing, he lifted the top half of her scrubs up her torso and gently pulled the shirt over her arm, trying to keep his eyes off her round, firm breasts half covered by a dusky-pink lacy bra that matched the color of her thong. God give him strength! And please, God, make her injuries heal fast; he couldn't wait to have her under him again... No, wait, that wasn't on the agenda; that wasn't part of the plan. The mission was to find a new way of dealing with each other and not to reexplore the missionary position.

Sex, moron, he chided himself, *will only add a truckload of complicated to an already convoluted situation. Did you not say that ten minutes ago?*

"Are you okay?" Sage asked him as he dropped a long-sleeved T-shirt over her head.

"Not even close," Tyce muttered under his breath. He picked up her hoodie, threaded her injured arm through the sleeve and frowned at the blank canvas of her plaster cast. "I'm going to have to make that more gangsta."

"Huh?"

Tyce tapped her cast. "It's white and boring. We'll graffiti it up."

The corners of her mouth tipped up. "It'll be the most expensive cast in the history of the world. You'd better sign it so that when it's removed someone can sell it on the net and make a fortune."

Tyce finished dressing Sage, helped her with her sling and picked up the spare coat he'd brought with him. "Right, let's bust you out of here."

Sage took one step, yelped, took another and groaned. Not bothering to ask her, he picked her up and held her against his chest, his temple against her head. "Better?"

"Much," Sage murmured as her good arm encircled his neck. "Though they are going to insist on a wheelchair, hospital policy."

"They can insist until the air turns blue, I'm not letting you go," Tyce told her, walking in the hallway.

I'm not letting you go.

Why did that statement resonate with him? Tyce couldn't understand why that particular order of words made deep, fundamental sense. This was the problem with being around Sage, he thought, and the reason why he'd backed away all those years ago. With her, strange thoughts and concepts popped into his head.

Keeping her, he fiercely, and silently, told himself, wasn't an option, not then and not now. He liked his own company, liked the freedom of not being tied down to a woman, a place, city or town. If he wanted to he could leave New York and go to Delhi or Djibouti; he could go anywhere. Lachlyn would be fine. He would sell or rent his space and he could take off. He could only do that because he was free of commitments; he didn't have another person to consider, someone else's feelings and wishes to take into account.

He wouldn't have to explain...

Maybe when Sage was back to full strength, he'd backpack for a couple of months. He could travel, only coming home a week or two before the baby was due to be born.

But then, he thought as he lowered Sage into the back seat of the waiting taxi, he'd miss seeing Sage's tummy grow with life, would miss the ultrasound scans, the doctor's visits. Could he do that? Could he leave?

He so badly wanted to say yes, to be convinced that she would be fine, but uncertainty twisted his stomach, his gut instinct insisting that he wasn't going anywhere, that he was going to see this process through.

So no Delhi or Djibouti then. That was okay, Tyce thought as he took the seat next to Sage. He could deal.

Much later that afternoon Sage's eyes fluttered open and she pulled in the familiar scent of her apartment... She was home, in a bed. Rolling over, she yelped. Every inch of her body was sore, from the back of her head to her shoulders, her damned tailbone, her legs. Her wrist throbbed. Glancing down at her cast, she sucked in an astonished gasp. Her plaster cast was no longer white but filled with miniature portraits, all wickedly accurate. Linc, Jaeger, Beck, Jo, Connor—God, Connor's picture looked so like him, his patrician face wearing a huge smile. Tyce had sketched her nephews, her niece. Her brother's partners. She could see that they'd been drawn quickly but, quick or not, they were fantastic. It was another reminder that Tyce was phenomenally talented...

"I was bored."

Sage's eyes shot up to see Tyce leaning against the half wall that separated the spare bedroom from the rest of the apartment. Uncomfortable with Tyce carrying her up the narrow staircase to her bedroom, she'd told him she'd be fine in the spare.

She immediately noticed the smudges of charcoal on his white T-shirt and faded jeans. Sage traced the outline of Connor's face with her finger, happy to see that the lines didn't blur. "They are fantastic. How did you seal them to stop them from smudging?"

"There was a tin of clear lacquer under your workbench." Tyce shrugged. "Thanks to your obsession with framing photographs, I managed to get them all."

"They are amazing. How long did they take you to do?"

Tyce shrugged. "Not long. I would've been quicker but you kept distracting me."

She distracted him? How on earth? "I was asleep when you did this!" she protested.

"You've always been beautiful but I'd never watched you sleep before. You're simply stunning," Tyce said, sounding utterly sincere.

Sexual awareness arced between them and Sage pushed her fingers into her hair, thinking that it felt odd to wake up with someone in her home. She felt a little self-conscious, a tiny bit awkward but, mostly, having Tyce in her apartment made her feel protected, cared for. Safe.

Safe? Not possible, Sage thought. She hadn't felt safe for years, not truly safe, not since before her parents were alive. She was misreading what she was feeling; she had to be because safe wasn't something she expected to feel, would allow herself to feel, ever again.

Either way, it was time she stopped.

Sage rolled onto her back and winced, using her good arm to push up. In a flash Tyce was at her side, strong arms helping her up the bed so that she could lean against her headboard. He disappeared into the bathroom and came back with a glass of water and two pills. "Acetaminophen—they'll take the edge off."

"Thanks." Sage took the pills, threw them into her mouth and chased them down with a long pull of water. Right, it was time to take back control. She needed her home back, some distance between her and whatever she was feeling for Tyce.

"I appreciate you bringing me home from the hospital, for watching out for me, but it's time for you to go."

Tyce just lifted one dark eyebrow in response. "No."

Sage glared at him. This was her apartment; he was here only because she allowed it. "Tyce, I don't like having people in my space, in my face."

"I don't either but—" Tyce shrugged "—tough." He pointed at her stomach. "In less than six months we're both going to have a new person in our lives—a very demanding creature if I understand the process correctly. So maybe we should try to, and get used to, the notion of sharing space so that we don't die from shock."

Sage's mouth dropped open. What was happening?

She was trying to push him away but he wasn't budging. This wasn't how this was supposed to go! When she pushed people away, most people were polite enough to give her the distance she needed.

Not Tyce.

Then again, she was quite convinced that God broke the mold after Tyce was born. One of him, she was pretty sure, was all the world, and she, could handle.

What could she say to make him leave?

"I'm going to be around for a few days so…you might as well get used to it."

Crap.

Tyce continued speaking, utterly at ease. "So, while you were sleeping, I answered what felt like a million calls from your family." Tyce took her empty glass and placed it on the bedside table. He sat down on the side of the bed, lifting his knee up onto her comforter, and resting his hand on the far side of her leg. His other hand gripped her thigh. "I don't normally talk to that many people in a month, let alone in an afternoon."

She was trying to keep up with the conversation, she really was, but his hand on her leg turned her brain to mush.

Sage could feel the size and shape, the heat of it through the covers and her yoga pants. If his hand moved a little up, and a little in, he'd find her happy spot—

Aargh! Really?

Sage mentally gave herself a head punch and pulled her focus back to their conversation. "Well, that doesn't surprise me. You were never chatty."

"Oh, I can mingle and make small talk when I need to, although it's very dependent on whether I want to. I don't often want, or need, to."

"And, let's face it, people like your surly and brooding attitude. It's, apparently, sexy," Sage muttered.

"Only apparently?" Tyce murmured, leaning forward, his eyes on her mouth. Sage's breath caught and held as he moved closer and her heart rate inched upward. He hovered just above her, prolonging the anticipation, and then his mouth met hers in a kiss as seductive as it was sweet. There was passion in his kiss, but it was banked, restrained. This kiss was designed to give comfort, to rediscover, to seduce.

It wasn't a kiss she'd received from Tyce before and Sage didn't know how to respond. She wanted to urge him to deepen it, to take more, to stoke the fire but she also didn't want the sweetness of this kiss to end. It was pure seduction, totally charming. And over far too soon. Tyce lifted his mouth off hers and leaned back, his black eyes glinting in the low light of the room. Sage was surprised to see the fine tremor in the hand he put back on her thigh.

"Seeing you fall… You scared the crap out of me, Sage."

Her words had deserted her so Sage just nodded, unable to drop her eyes from the emotional thunderstorm in his eyes. It was the first time she'd seen Tyce without his reticent cloak, his barriers. There was so much emotion in those dark depths that it made her breath hitch, her heart rate accelerate.

Her hand lifted to touch his face. She longed to run her hands down his big biceps, to pull his shirt up and feel the definition in his chest. She wanted to crawl inside him, explore that steel-trap mind, his creative genius, peek into his soul. Tyce made her forget to keep her distance; he tempted her in ways that petrified her.

It was time to step back… Way back.

"So, the phone calls," she said, her voice curt.

At her prosaic words, his shields came up. "Everyone said they would come over tonight to check up on you, so instead of them arriving in dribs and drabs, I told Linc to tell them to come around after work and to stay for dinner."

Sage nodded, resigned. Sure, they were worried about her but she knew that her brothers wanted another chance to check up on Tyce, to see if he was treating her right and to, possibly, drop another threat or two in his ear.

One day they'd wake up and realize that Tyce marched to the beat of his own drum and didn't really care what they thought.

Sage ran a hand over her face, pain pounding through her head and her tailbone and her arm in symphony. "They'll want food and I don't have much in the fridge. I'll have to order in."

Tyce squeezed her thigh to get her attention. "I made a chicken casserole and there's more than enough for everybody."

Sage frowned at him. "You cook?"

"I do."

"Since when?"

"Since I was a kid and the only way to get a good meal into my stomach, and more important, into Lachlyn's, was to learn," Tyce shot back and immediately looked annoyed that he'd allowed something so personal to slip.

Sage knew that he didn't want to pursue this conversation but since he'd opened the door, she was going to walk through it. She was just…doing a background check on him, she told herself. Finding out information about her baby's father.

Pffft. Even she didn't believe the garbage she was thinking! The truth was that Tyce fascinated her. And, yet again, she was venturing where she shouldn't go.

Oh, well…

"Where was your mom? Didn't she feed you?"

"When she felt well enough to do so," Tyce replied, standing up. That action and his closed-off face was a sign—billboard high and painted in neon—that he wasn't discussing his past anymore. Or again.

"Was she sick?"

Tyce stared at the abstract painting above her head and he eventually shrugged. "She suffered from depression. There were days when she wouldn't get up off the floor, when she'd rock herself for hours. Most days, she managed to work—just—but when she got home she'd collapse into a nonresponsive heap. If I didn't look after myself, feed myself, and Lachlyn when she came along, we didn't eat. It was… Yeah, it was tough."

"Where is she now? Is she…" Sage hesitated, keeping her voice neutral, knowing that she had to be careful how she framed her questions. If she was too blasé she'd sound callous; if she came across as being too sympathetic Tyce would immediately stop talking. "…still alive?"

"She died from a bout of pneumonia a long time ago."

Sage pulled her bottom lip between her teeth. "I'm so sorry, Tyce."

Tyce shrugged. "It happened."

When he looked around the room, Sage knew that he was trying to change the subject. She wasn't surprised. Tyce had told her more in ten minutes than he'd shared the entire time they'd been together three years ago. He resumed his seat next to her on the bed and picked a curl up off her cheek and pushed it behind her ear. "I keep looking at that photo of the red diamond flower ring. It's amazing. It's your time to spill. Tell me about it and tell me why you didn't want it displayed at the exhibition."

And this was the price she had to pay: she'd peeked

under the lid of his Pandora's box and he thought he could do the same. Damn the person who'd invented the concept of tit for tat.

Sage sighed, pushed the rest of her wayward hair behind her ears and looked at a spot behind his head. She eventually looked at him again. "How much do you know about red diamonds?"

"Not much. That they are rare? That they are phenomenally expensive?"

Sage nodded. "There are only around twenty to thirty true red diamonds in the world and most are less than half a carat. My father was, like Jaeger, a gem hunter and my mom often accompanied him on his trips. He bought that diamond from a Brazilian farmer and it's, as far as we know, the largest red diamond in the world. It was his biggest find, ever, and I remember how excited they, and Connor, were. My mom assumed that the stone would be sold but my dad wanted to give it to my mom to celebrate their tenth wedding anniversary. Connor designed and made the ring. The flower petals represent each of her children."

Tyce frowned. "There are four petals but only three of you."

Sadness passed through Sage's expressive eyes. "My mom was pregnant with her fourth child when she died."

Tyce swore and rubbed a hand over his face. He then slipped his hand around the back of her neck and he rested his forehead against hers. "Now it's my turn to say I'm sorry."

Sage managed a small smile. "One of my clearest memories is of her looking at that stone, holding it up to the light, a soft smile on her face. She was utterly entranced by it. She would've loved the ring." A small laugh left her lips. "The stone was worth millions and millions but my father was prepared to give it to my mother because she loved it so much. They were like that, you know. People before things, before money."

And, because she was such a scaredy-cat when it came to men and relationships, she would never have what her parents experienced. She'd never know what a soul-deep connection felt like. Maybe this baby would make her better, stronger, more courageous. Maybe, in a year or two or ten, she'd manage to move past her fears, stop equating love with loss and take a chance.

It wouldn't be with Tyce; loving him wasn't an option. Despite their mind-blowing sexual connection, he'd never settle down, not the way that she imagined she'd need him to. Like Connor, a relationship was way down his list of priorities.

"Does the general public know about the stone or should I write a promise in blood that I will never reveal its existence?" Tyce asked, his eyes glinting with amusement.

"Get a sharp knife and a piece of paper." Of everything she had to worry about, Tyce talking out of turn wasn't a concern. She trusted him. He wasn't the type to blab.

"I used another red diamond for the Ballantyne photo shoot, explaining that it was my mom's favorite stone but not explaining why. I didn't want to use the ring because it would've generated a tsunami of publicity. I just wanted to remember it—think about it—as a stone my mom loved, part of a ring my dad had made for her, a symbol of the family he adored."

Tyce's thumb stroked her jaw. "I can understand that. Your parents sound like they were good people, Sage."

She nodded as he thumbed away a tear that sneaked out of the corner of her eye. "They really were, Tyce. So was Connor. I know that Connor got your mom pregnant but if he'd known about Lachlyn he would've…"

Tyce placed a kiss against her temple. "Ssh, sweetheart. It's okay, Sage."

It wasn't, but here, half lying against Tyce's chest, she felt like it could be. She felt like nothing could hurt her, that there was a strong wall between her and life's next hard slap. Yeah, she definitely felt safe, Sage thought, her eyes drooping closed.

Dammit. That wasn't good.

She should push away, should push *him* away, make him go, but she didn't have the strength or the inclination. She just wanted to lie here, soaking in Tyce's heat and strength and allow herself to drift off to sleep.

Eight

Three days later, Sage sat on the corner of her sofa, her feet on an ottoman. Tyce was still with her and he was clearing up after dinner. He was a fabulous cook, far better than she was. She glanced down at the papers on her lap and wrinkled her nose. Depending on the answers to the surveys she held in her hand, Tyce might even be a better parent than her...

When they had started to talk about the baby, they both, swiftly, realized that the real work started once the baby was born and that they had no idea what they were doing. They both knew how to change a diaper and make a bottle; Sage had looked after her nephews often enough for the mechanics to sink in and Tyce remembered changing and feeding Lachlyn when he was little more than a kid himself. They'd agreed that, because the baby would be raised in two separate homes, they needed a consensus on how the logistics would work, on what mattered and what didn't, what lines couldn't be crossed.

Not knowing how to start, they'd turned to the net.

Sage felt Tyce's breath on her cheek and she looked up to see him leaning down, his mouth close to her ear. "Do you think these parenting surveys are a good idea?"

Sage looked into his eyes and she shrugged. "I don't know. But I think they would give us an idea of our different parenting styles. I think I'll be more of an operate-from-instinct type of parent and I suspect that you will be the disciplined one."

"What makes you say that?"

"Oh, the fact that you do Tai Chi at the crack of dawn, you go to the dojo four times a week and that you run six miles a day."

"Eight," Tyce corrected her and Sage saw the flash of the dimple in his cheek as the corners of his mouth lifted. Then she noticed that he was holding a bag of frozen peas, which he dropped into her lap.

"Slap it against your tailbone and that bruise," he told her, holding a glass of red wine in his other hand.

Sage tried to twist her waist so that the bag of peas hit the right spot but winced when she turned. While she wasn't in as much pain as she had been the evening of the accident, she was still damned sore. Tyce whipped the bag from her hand.

"Can you lean forward a bit?" he asked her, his big hand on her shoulder.

Sage leaned forward so that he could slide the bag down her back. She winced again as the cold seeped through the fabric of her yoga pants. With her injuries, yoga pants, a snug sports top and hoodie was all Tyce had seen her in. Super casual wasn't her best look. "Damn, I'm not sure what's worse, the cold or the bruise."

Tyce sat down next to her, his muscled thigh pressing

into hers, and her body started to tingle. "Trust me, the bruise is worse," Tyce said.

"That bad?" she asked. After all, she couldn't see it herself.

"Size of a football and a deep, angry blue," Tyce told her. "You hit the ground at speed."

He snagged a copy of the survey from her lap and squinted at the paper. "Okay, let's do this. Question one... Is diaper changing a job for the mom, the dad or both of you?" His lips twitched. "That's easy. If it's loaded, it's your job."

"And if I'm not with you?" Sage asked, feeling the heat from his body, his fresh, citrus-masculine-Tyce smell drifting up her nose. Her sensitive nipples tightened and her blood slowly heated.

"The kid will have to hold it," Tyce replied before flashing her one of his sexy, oh-so-rare grins. "I'm kidding. I'll do my share but, fair warning, I'll try and charm you into doing it if I can. If I can't charm you, I might resort to begging."

He'd probably succeed too, Sage thought as drops of water from the frozen packet of peas ran down her butt and she twisted her arm, wanting to pull the bag away.

Tyce placed his hand on hers and shook his head. "Five more minutes. Please?"

Sage pulled her hand out from under his and gave him a reluctant nod. Tyce's hand moved up to her shoulder so she partially spun around so that the back of her head rested on his chest. She looked down at her sheet of paper.

"The two most important qualities I want my child to possess? Mmm, that's hard."

Tyce didn't hesitate. "Resilience and determination."

Sage nodded, immediately understanding that his

childhood would've been even more difficult if he hadn't been blessed with enormous doses of those traits.

"You?" Tyce asked.

Sage bit the inside of her lip. "I'd like our child to be bold and courageous. To have confidence."

"Just like her, or his, mama."

Sage tipped her head back, saw the warmth in his eyes and wanted to explain that she wasn't bold, or brave. She was scared to live life to the fullest, scared of what life had in store for her, scared to love, to open herself up and feel. She wanted to tell Tyce that her default habit was to run from people and situations that made her feel uncomfortable, that every day she spent with him was a curious combination of terror and exhilaration. He made her feel alive, like she was plugged into an unseen source of energy that replenished and renewed. She also had a knot in her stomach because she knew that this couldn't last, her bruises would fade and Tyce would move back to the periphery of her life, leaving her feeling empty and alone.

Sage saw Tyce swallow, noticed that he clutched the paper a little tighter, felt the tension radiating off him. He cleared his throat and when he spoke his voice was a low growl. "Next question... I know my partner is going to be a wonderful parent because...*hell.*"

Sage faced him and she caught the fear in his eyes, the flicker of insecurity that crossed his face. She frowned. "Wait... Do you not think that you will be a good parent?"

Tyce's expression changed to inscrutability and, because she did it herself, Sage knew that it was his way of retreating, silently telling her that he didn't want to continue this discussion. She took the piece of paper from his hand, dropped it, and the bag of peas, to the floor. She turned to face him and placed her hand on his heart and felt the thud-thud-thud of his heart beneath her palm. "Why on earth would you think that?"

Tyce took a long time to answer. "Because I had a crappy upbringing? Because I never had chance to be a child so I have no idea how to relate to one? How am I going to deal with a child when I can barely tolerate people?"

"You seem to be able to tolerate me," Sage pointed out.

Tyce raked his hand through his hair. "Yeah, well, you…you're the exception to the rule."

It would be easy to make a joke in order to lighten the mood, to push away the cloud of emotion hanging over their heads. But Sage didn't want to, not this time, this *one* time. Sage lifted her hand to run her fingers along his jaw. "Tyce, you're a man who steps up to the plate, who accepts his responsibilities, who does the right thing. Sure, you're not the most voluble person in the world but, when you speak, you always have something valuable to say. You're intelligent and talented—" her fingers drifted over his mouth and she handed him a small smile "—and you're hot. Our baby will be just fine and you will be too."

Tyce felt her words wash over him, as restorative as soft, soaking summer rain. Funny how, with a few words, Sage could make him miss something he'd never had. He'd read so many positive reviews, was the recipient of numerous awards, a million kudos about his art, but he'd never been complimented for the man he was. It made his stomach flip, his heart pound, his soul sigh.

It definitely lowered his resistance to her, made him want to throw caution to the wind and take what he constantly craved. Tyce allowed his thumb to drift across her chin and slide across her full bottom lip but if he

kissed her now he wouldn't be able to stop. He'd pull
her clothes off her spectacular body and he'd kiss every
patch of her skin, starting with her mouth and ending
with her toes. He'd wait until she was writhing with
need, unable to remember her own name, wait until she
was screaming his before sliding into her and pitching
them into oblivion.

He wanted her with an intensity that rocked him to
his core.

Sage leaned forward, curled her fingers around his
neck and rested her forehead on his cheekbone. Sparks
skittered through him. "Make love to me, Tyce. Just once
more."

She'd echoed his thoughts, subconsciously picking up
on his burning desire. Tyce groaned and shook his head.
"It's not a good idea, Sage. You're still bruised and it'll
make the situation, us, so much more complicated."

"I need not to think, I need to step out of my head,"
Sage murmured. "You can do that for me because you're
the only one who can."

"You're hurt—"

"I'm fine and I want you. I want to remember how
good we were together and I want to forget all the complications, just for a little while. You're the best medicine
for what ails me, Tyce."

He shouldn't; this wasn't a good idea. They had a
child to raise together, a life to navigate as co-parents
and friends, hearts to protect.

"Making love to you always made me feel centered,
stronger, better. Make me feel like that again, Tyce."

He was just a man and not half as strong as he thought
he was. Hell, around Sage, he wasn't strong at all. She
made him *feel*, made him ache, made him step out from
behind his walls. He shouldn't do this; it wasn't smart

but, like her, he was throbbing with need, desperate to have her and taste her, to lose himself in her.

Just once.

Tyce watched caution fly away on the wind as his mouth touched hers. Her lips immediately opened and he swept his tongue inside, and then he was riding the storm. Yeah, this, *Sage*, her hand against his chest, the fingers of her other hand raking through his hair, was what he couldn't resist. Her mouth was pure sugar-spice and he could kiss her until time fizzled away.

He needed to take this slow, Tyce reminded himself as he unzipped the front of her hoodie. He eased the sides apart and left her lips long enough to pull his head back so that he could look at her. Her nipples were pushing through the fabric of her sports top and he had to taste one bud. He pulled the stretchy fabric down and sucked her nipple into his mouth, laving her with his tongue before taking her in even deeper. She felt so amazing, familiar yet different.

Sage was making those little breathy moans that turned him steel hard. Tyce pushed her hoodie off and lifted her top up and over her head. He tossed both to the floor, gently pushing her back so that she lay flat on the couch.

Putting his hands on either side of her head, he looked down into her lovely face. "Are you okay? Sure you want to do this?"

"Yes and I'm fine."

She wasn't; he could see a little pain under her passion. "Tell me if you want to stop."

Sage's low laugh danced over his skin. "Not a chance." She tapped his chest. "You have too many clothes on, Latimore."

Tyce sat back, pulled his T-shirt over his head and

sucked in his breath when Sage's hand ran over a pec, across a nipple and over his stomach. She tugged at the band of his jeans. "Off."

"You first." Tyce slid his hands along her back, across her hips, his thumbs hooking the band of her yoga pants and pulling them down. He looked at the tiny triangle of fabric covering her secret, feminine places and couldn't help his eyes moving up, to her stomach. He hauled in a breath and placed a hot, openmouthed kiss on her tiny baby bump, before placing his ear on her stomach.

Sage's hand touched his hair and he knew that she was also thinking of their baby, the fact that they'd made another person doing what they did best, and that was loving each other... Giving each other pleasure.

Talking about pleasure, Tyce pulled up and back. He'd heard Sage's hiss of pain when she lifted her butt to take off her pants and he had no intention of hurting her again. He'd have to be creative making love to her and that was okay; creativity was one of his strongest traits.

Tyce slipped his fingers under the thin bands of her thong and twisted, snapping first one side of her panties and then the other. His heart beating a million miles per minute, he pulled the fabric from between her legs and then Sage was naked, looking as beautiful as he'd ever seen her.

He just looked and then looked some more, his concentration breaking when Sage's hand danced across her stomach and headed lower. Oh, hell, no, giving her pleasure was his job.

Tyce quickly shucked his pants, his mind swirling with possibilities. Missionary sex was out, as was her kneeling on top of him. Hell, he doubted that he'd even get inside her but that was okay. Giving Sage pleasure, rocketing her to an orgasm, was more important than him getting off.

Naked now, Tyce slid his fingers between her folds, dazed by her wet warmth. It was such a turn-on to know she wanted him as much as he wanted her. They'd messed up so often but this truly was what they did best.

Sage's fingers pressed his onto her most sensitive spot. "I need you, Tyce. I need this."

Her low, slow and sexy words sent more blood, if that was possible, to his already throbbing erection. Sage's hand moved to her side and she encircled him and Tyce was quite certain that if she kept up that squeezing, stroking action, he'd lose it.

But, judging by her trembling limbs and her flushed body, her desperate eyes, Sage was hovering on the edge, as well. Tyce moved so that he was looming over her, his arms holding his weight off her. Positioning himself, he rubbed her, his shaft sliding over that bundle of nerves. Sage moaned her approval and he repeated the action, loving her heat and the friction and hell, just being close to her. Being inside her would be better but this was almost as good. Tyce lifted one hand and pushed her hair out of her eyes, wanting to watch her climb. Her eyes met his and he stepped into the deep, now-foggy blue. She lifted her hips and he shook his head. "Let me do the work, sweetheart."

"Then get on with it," Sage hissed.

God, he'd forgotten how demanding she could be when she was on the brink and he wasn't giving her what she wanted. In the past he'd loved to tease her, taking her, and her temper, higher until she shattered in his arms.

She was on the brink now, so close. And so was he. Unable to resist, Tyce pushed himself between her legs, sliding into her hot tight channel, keeping her legs together so that she didn't put any more pressure on her coccyx and bruises than necessary. She was hot and tight and he couldn't move the way he wanted to but he'd deal. He was inside Sage and he'd stepped into heaven.

Sage moaned and he gently thrust against her, short shallow strokes that were more erotic than he believed possible. Tyce rested his elbows on cushions next to her head. He cradled her face and kissed her, his tongue matching the rhythm of his hips.

He felt Sage's breath quicken, felt her tremble and then felt the gush of warmth against him, the tightening of her internal walls. That was all he needed and he tensed as pleasure rocketed through him. He groaned into Sage's mouth and then again, holding her tight as tremors passed from her body to his, his to hers.

While his brain and body patched itself back together, he stroked Sage's glorious frame and dropped gentle kisses on her mouth, her cheekbone, her jaw. His hand stopped when it reached her stomach and his big hand covered most of her slight bump.

His. The thought came from his heart and skittered through his body. The baby was his and so was she. Somehow, in whatever form they took, and on some level they would always be his.

The next morning, Sage stood in her shower and lifted her face up to receive a blast of hot water. She ached in places she didn't know she had, good places, places that had been long neglected. Her body felt like she'd spent the day at a spa, loose and relaxed.

Her mind felt like a turtle trying to walk through peanut butter.

Sage placed her hands on the wall of the shower cubicle and watched the water swirl around the drain. What were the implications of making love with Tyce? Was it a once-off thing? What did any of it, all of it, mean?

Sage closed her eyes in frustration and slapped her hand against the white tiles. What had happened to her ordered, calm life? Three months ago she felt calm and in charge and one night—one night!—with Latimore flipped everything around.

Tyce was an amazing lover, but he was also a good man. Good seemed like a bland word but Sage thought it was underused and misunderstood. Good didn't mean rich or good-looking; it meant that someone was prepared to do the right thing, the honorable thing, to take the path less traveled, even if it flew in the face of convention. Good, to her, meant that he was responsible, honorable and honest.

She liked him…

Sage sighed. She'd forgotten how much she enjoyed his company out of the bedroom. She spoke more than he did but, over these past few days, Tyce held up his end of the conversation. They'd discussed movies and politics, books and, of course, art. Actually, they'd argued about art… Tyce, surprisingly, had a fondness for the Dutch Golden Age of painting, artists like Hals and van Baburen, and Sage preferred art from the twentieth century.

But whether they were talking art or music, spending time with Tyce was…fun. Stimulating and relaxing at the same time. She felt she could say anything to him and he wouldn't judge her. Connor was like that and Sage was reminded of how much alike they were. Strong, alpha, honorable men. Honest men…about everything. Including their antipathy toward relationships and commitment.

Like before, Tyce tempted her to open up, to give him more, to delve beneath the surface of her armor. That was still a very dangerous path to walk down and she couldn't allow herself to take it. She could not drop her shields and let him into her heart. That way lay hurt, disappointment and madness. Tyce had the power, like nobody she'd ever encountered before, to turn her life upside down. Loving and then losing him would devastate her and having to interact with him as they raised a child together would be like trying to dodge asteroid strikes while walking through the last level of hell.

Frankly, that scenario was best to be avoided. If she was smart she'd say thanks for the fun time and push him out of her apartment and her life. She'd done it with other men, not many, and she could do it with Tyce. But she didn't want to. She wanted more sex, more conversations and yes, she thought as her stomach growled, more of his fabulous cooking.

Maybe she could have a fling with him. She could enjoy his body and his mind and when they ran out of steam, which they would, she'd revert back to being friends and co-parents because she'd been sensible and kept her heart out of their interactions.

She could do that, she decided. Connor told her she could do anything she wanted to…

Okay, maybe he hadn't been thinking of her in terms of her having a no strings fling when he imparted those words of wisdom. But she was a smart, modern woman and like millions of smart, modern women she knew that the act of sex was not a declaration of love, commitment or anything other than the giving and receiving of pleasure.

She could keep her heart out of the equation and stay emotionally protected.

Couldn't she?

Nine

Tyce looked around as Sage finally made an appearance the next morning. She looked better than she had last night, but her walk down the cast-iron staircase suggested that she was still feeling a little stiff. Standing at her sloping windows, he watched her as she headed straight for the coffee machine, her eyes foggy from sleep. They'd only been together a few weeks so long ago but some things hadn't changed: the great sex, obviously, the fact that she squeezed toothpaste from the middle of the tube and that her brain didn't start to work properly until after nine and three cups of coffee, now decaffeinated because of the baby.

Tyce looked at his watch. It was bang on nine and he'd been up since five, had gone to his warehouse to pick up clothes and returned here before six. He'd then pushed back her furniture and done an hour of Tai Chi before heading outside for a run. Sage was barely functional.

Tyce walked across the room, his bare feet making no sound on the wooden floors. "Morning," he said, stopping a foot from Sage's turned back.

Sage yelped, squealed and groaned. She turned around quickly and, hand on her heart, scowled at him. "Holy crap, Latimore! Scare me to death, why don't you?"

"Sorry."

Stepping around her, Tyce reached for a cup from the cupboard above the coffee machine and placed it beneath the spout of the machine. He hit a button and the air between them filled with the rich scents of very expensive coffee. For the last few years he'd been living on a budget, curtailing his expenses, but good coffee was one of the few luxuries he'd been unable to deny himself.

Sex with Sage, as he'd decided last night when she lay across his chest, damp and boneless, was another of the necessities of life he couldn't do without. Speaking of, it had been too long since he'd last kissed her...

Tyce was just about to place his hands on her hips, lower his mouth to hers, when she spoke.

"So, I supposed we'd better talk about what happened last night."

Ugh. He really didn't want to. Tyce succumbed to his urge to touch and hooked his hand around her neck, using his thumb to tip her face upward. "I always prefer action to discussion."

Sage half smiled. "I know you do but I think that, three years ago, one of our faults was that we spent too much time making love and not nearly enough time talking."

Tyce mock frowned at her. "FYI, a man can never spend enough time in bed."

"Duly noted." Sage placed her hands on his chest and pushed away. "But, sorry for you, I do have something to say."

Dammit, Tyce thought, stepping back. *Here it comes... I don't think this is a good idea; we shouldn't complicate the situation; I've got a lot on my plate.* He was expecting at least one excuse for them not to continue sleeping together, possibly all three.

"Are you interested in having more sex with me?"

Hot damn. Was that even a serious question? Judging by the traces of insecurity he saw in her eyes and the tremor in her voice, it sure sounded like one. Hell, yes, he wanted to sleep with her again. As many times as was humanly possible. "Uh... Yes?"

"You don't sound too sure," Sage replied.

"Trust me, I'm damn sure," Tyce growled. "What's this about, Sage?"

Sage placed her hand over the rim of her cup and rolled the cup on the counter. "Well, we can do that, if you want."

Holy crap. "Is that something you want too, Sage?"

He knew it was but he suddenly needed the words. "Yes. But..."

Yes. It was a small-sounding word but it had huge consequences. He was going to have her again, and soon. As soon as she gave him the green light he'd kiss her and then he'd pull that thin cashmere jersey off her slim frame and he'd flip open the button to her jeans. They'd be naked and on the way to heaven.

"But it can't be more than sex, Tyce," Sage said, rushing her words. "It's what we're good at. The rest of the stuff, we aren't good at that." She crossed her arms and rocked on her heels. "I don't want to be hurt again, Tyce. I don't want to hurt you."

"I hear you, Sage. I don't want to hurt you either. But we don't have to label this, define this. We don't have to put on restrictions, shove what we have into a box. No expectations, no pressure," Tyce told her. "We're just two people who think the other is hot, who are having a baby together and who are now sleeping together."

Tyce couldn't help but notice the relief in her eyes but sighed at the worry one layer down. Sage was still so damn vulnerable, and he'd have to be careful with her and for her. He'd have to be the one who kept an eye on how far and fast this went because there was, no matter what he said, always the possibility of this situation blowing up in their faces. They had a baby to raise together and they couldn't do that effectively if they ended up hating or resenting each other.

It was important that he looked at this situation clearly. He'd been alone for so damn long, hell, he'd spent his life alone and he didn't know how to make the emotional connections that people needed. Only now, as an adult, did he realize how tired and drained he was when he was younger from constantly living in a state of fight-or-flight. Yeah, he'd take Sage's offer of sex—what man wouldn't?—but he'd put himself in a situation of feeling out of control and desperate.

But, for now, he'd enjoy her, take what she was so generously offering because making love with Sage was earth-shattering.

Tyce lifted his hand to touch her, to connect, but she shook her head and stepped out of his reach. Damn, she wasn't done talking…

"I know that we are equally responsible for me being pregnant but I have this crazy urge to apologize, to say sorry for messing up your life with a baby."

God. That was what she was thinking? That her being pregnant was something he regretted? Man, she couldn't be more wrong. He regretted many things, particularly his inability to be the type of man she needed, but he had no regrets about their still-baking baby.

Maybe that was because he was starting to see their child as a bridge back to some sort of normality, a way to modify his ideas about families and what they meant. He was being given a second chance, as an adult, to create a unit that had all the people in all the right roles. He and Sage wouldn't live together but his child would have a mother and a father and they would be the adults and their child would have the freedom to be a child.

And yes, maybe he was looking at this baby as the one soul with whom he could reconnect emotionally; a safe place to try that. His kid would be *his* kid, would be a big part of his life for the next eighteen years at least, right?

Tyce placed his hands on either side of Sage's face, thinking that her skin was so soft, that she smelled like a field of gently scented roses. Her blue eyes locked on his and he took a step so that her breasts just touched his chest. He needed to get closer, needed to feel her in his arms, needed... God, he needed her. His head started to swim but he knew he couldn't afford to be distracted; his answer was too important to mess up. "We've made a muddle of a lot of things, Sage, but you having my baby? That's not one of them."

"Are you sure? He, or she, is going to flip our world."

"That's not always a bad thing and I'm strapped in for the ride." He kissed her nose before pulling her closer, hugging her tight. "The baby is a gift that I haven't said thank you for so...thank you. I have many regrets, Sage, but this baby will never be one of them."

Tyce felt a little of her tension seep out of her body so he lowered his head and slowly, gently kissed the corner of her mouth, leaving his lips there, inhaling her unique scent. This time he allowed his head to swim, and placed a hand in the middle of her back and pulled her up against his body, his erection pushing into her stomach, her breasts against his chest. Sage sighed and once again he slowly, gently traced the seam of her mouth, the edges of her lips. He wanted to plunge and plunder, to allow their crazy passion to spiral but he knew that if he let passion reign, he'd lose her.

This was a kiss of promise, of tenderness, something different than what they'd ever shared before. This wasn't the time, he reminded his junk, to do what came naturally. That time would come later and he could wait. This moment was too important to mess up.

Tyce pulled back and then stepped away from her, running his hands through his hair. He risked looking at Sage. She held her fingers to her lips, her eyes wide and dreamy. Tyce started to move toward her, caught himself and muttered a silent curse.

His sensible side surfaced. If he didn't corral his emotional side he would create that which would be forever difficult to tame. Later, he could love her when emotion wasn't running quite so high, when his heart wasn't trying to punch its way out of his chest. Yeah, it was better if they calmed down a little.

Or a lot.

Sage had run out of excuses to delay meeting Lachlyn. She'd deliberately missed a dinner at The Den to introduce Lachlyn to the clan and she'd postponed meeting her for coffee. Twice. Her excuses were so thin they had holes in them. Giving in to verbal pressure from her brothers, and subtle, silent pressure from Tyce, Sage finally asked Tyce's sister to meet her at The Den. Linc and Tate and their kids were out of town so she had her childhood home to herself and she thought it was the right place for their first meeting.

Sage stepped into the hallway of the famous brownstone and started to unwrap her scarf. "Maybe we should've met at a coffee shop."

Tyce, who'd offered to accompany her to The Den and stay to introduce them before leaving them to talk, didn't reply. He just stood in the double-volume hallway, his eyes darting around the magnificent space. Tyce was another reason why she couldn't delay meeting Lachlyn any longer. The newest member of the clan was his sister and she couldn't keep avoiding her baby's aunt.

Despite her excuses not to meet Lachlyn, Sage could admit to feeling a tad braver, a little stronger about the changing circumstances. Also, being around Tyce made her feel like she should step up a bit more. He was consistently strong and she was not talking about that most very excellent body she adored. He was mentally tough and if they were going to co-parent together, be in each other's lives, she had to be, as well.

She wanted to be the best version of herself, for her baby, obviously, but also for Tyce.

"Are you okay, Sage?"

Sage darted a look at him and shrugged. Was she? This was a little similar to an adopted child meeting her biological mother for the first time. "I'm nervous, jittery, excited, nauseous."

Tyce's smile touched his sexy mouth. "She's feeling the same."

"You should be with her, Tyce. This is a big deal for her," Sage said, feeling guilty.

"Lach is an excited nervous but you're a terrified nervous," Tyce replied. "Lachlyn isn't going to run like a rabbit but you might."

True. *Will she like me?* Sage placed a hand on her stomach. *Will I like her? Will she get my jokes?* God, she really hoped Lachlyn had a sense of humor. *Would she ask to borrow money or clothes or, God, jewels? No, of course she wouldn't, this was Tyce's sister, for goodness' sake, and Tyce wouldn't have raised her to think like that.*

Will she like me? Will I like her?

Now she was repeating her thoughts and totally losing it. Sage glanced at her watch, a minute to go, if Lachlyn was the prompt type.

"Take a breath, Sage."

"Why am I doing this?"

"I'm presuming that's a rhetorical question?" Tyce asked, his hands in the pockets of his leather jacket.

"Lachlyn might fly into my life, hang around and then disappear again."

Tyce walked over to her and rubbed his hands up and down her arms. "Why would you think that?"

"Because that's what people do!" She frowned. "What if we bonded, if we came to love each other and she died? Of cancer or in a helicopter crash?"

"Dramatic much, Sage? She's an archivist—she deals with documents. She might die from falling off a ladder or after being buried by falling boxes but she won't die from a helicopter crash."

Sage frowned at her lover. "You're mocking me."

"Just a little."

He didn't understand and he probably never would. Sure, she sounded like a drama queen but she'd had her life wrenched apart; she'd experienced death and desolation. She knew that bad things happened when they were least expected to.

She couldn't do this, she thought. She couldn't let Lachlyn in. Sage picked up her coat from where she'd tossed it onto the chaise lounge to the left of the door. She shoved her arm into a sleeve. If she hurried, she could leave before Lachlyn arrived.

The heavy chimes of the doorbell rang through the hallway and, looking through the glass inserts, Sage saw a tiny blonde standing outside, her chin pushed into the folds of a pink scarf.

Lachlyn was here, actually here. Suddenly Sage didn't know what to do or what to say. Her eyes flew to Tyce's face and she lifted up her hands. "Will you stay?"

"Are you sure that's what you want?"

"Please?"

"Hang on a sec, Lach," Tyce called out. He stepped up to Sage and cupped the back of her head with his large hand, pulling her forehead to his chest. His head dropped and Sage heard his rumbling, sexy voice close to her ear.

"She's just as scared as you are. Like you, she just wants to be liked. She also just wants to know about her dad, this family. She's the interloper here, Sage. This is your house, your family. There's no reason for you to be scared."

"I don't like letting people in, Tyce." It was a massive admission and Sage wondered if he'd understand that she wasn't talking about this house or her family but about letting people into her life.

"Me neither, honey. But neither can we stay the same. We have to learn and we have to grow. And we can only do that by allowing new people and new experiences into our lives." Tyce dropped a kiss into her hair. "She's a nice person, Sage. You could come to love her."

And that was the problem, Sage thought. Loving someone was fine—she could do that. She just didn't want to deal with the fallout when they stopped loving her and disappeared from her life in whatever form that took.

"Open the door, honey," Tyce said, stepping away and giving her an encouraging smile. "You've got this."

Sage shook her head. She really didn't feel like she did.

Thank God, the first official, welcome-to-the-family-Lachlyn dinner was over and Sage could finally go home.

She looked around the crowded hallway of The Den, thinking of so many other dinners they'd ended here in a flurry of goodbyes. Connor always stood to the left of the imposing front door, the last person they saw before leaving the house.

Changes, Sage thought, yanking her coat belt tighter. God, she hated them.

"If you pull that any tighter you're going to cut off your air supply," Tyce told her, putting his hand on hers.

Sage, irritated, swatted his hand away. "I've been tying my coat for a while now."

"What is your problem?" Tyce asked, keeping his voice low. "You've been scratchy all evening."

Where to start? Instead of answering him, she looked around the hallway and swallowed the compressed ball of emotion in her throat. She'd barely had time to recover, to digest her meeting with Lachlyn this afternoon when Linc had sprung this family dinner on her, blithely explaining that he'd already sent Tyce an invitation and thereby taking the decision about inviting him to accompany her out of her hands.

Would she have asked him? Probably not. After the meeting with Lachlyn, which had been emotional and difficult, she'd realized how easy it was to rely on Tyce's steady presence and his strength. Counting on Tyce was a dangerous habit to slide into. He was her lover, sure, but she refused to fall in love with him and relying on him for anything other than help to raise their child was foolish. She was setting herself up for an almighty fall and that had to stop immediately.

Having Tyce with her, in The Den, made her feel like they were imposters, acting a role. They were sleeping together; they were not in a relationship and she didn't like all the side-eye she'd received from her family whenever Tyce put his arm around her shoulder and his hand on her knee. They were not a couple and he had no right to give her family the impression that they were.

Sage looked around at the faces she loved best. Beck had his arms around Cady's waist, his chin resting on her shoulder. Jaeger was holding Ty and Piper was tucked into his side. Tate's hand was on Shaw's head and Ellie was asleep, her beautiful face on Tate's shoulder. Love streamed out of Tate's eyes every time she looked at Linc.

Oh, damn, every time she spent time with her brothers and their wives, she started to think that she might want the love they'd found. And that was the real source of her irritation. She started thinking about how it would feel to walk out of this house with her hand in Tyce's, heading back to their place, content in the idea that they were creating a family within a family.

Even if she was prepared to take a chance on love—she wasn't but this was all hypothetical—Tyce wasn't the man to give it to her.

He didn't want to immerse himself in a relationship like her brothers had; he didn't want the day-to-day interactions, the ups and the downs. He wanted to be their baby's father and, for as long as it worked between them, for them to sleep together. When that stopped, when the passion faded away, he would too.

But the more time she spent with him, the more she was at risk of feeling more for him than she should, the more she wanted what her sisters-in-law had: a strong, sexy man standing at her side, ready to go to war for and with her.

Too many *more*s, she thought.

She had to readjust her thinking. Pronto.

Sage looked at Lachlyn and saw that Linc had his arm around her shoulders. Her big brother was scooping another lost Ballantyne chick under his arm. It was what he did so why was her throat closing, why did she feel like she was being pushed out of her own family?

Oh, God, how old was she? Thirteen?

"I need to go home," she muttered, walking toward the front door.

"Sage, wait!" Linc said and Sage heard the note of excitement in his voice. Wondering what he was about to slap her with now, Sage briefly rested her forehead on the door before turning around. Linc stood on the first step of the staircase and Lachlyn, tiny and blonde, stood next to him.

The hallway fell silent and Sage looked around at the faces she loved best. Sage darted a glance at Tyce and saw that his obsidian eyes were looking at her with a small frown. He seemed to be trying to look into her soul and she didn't like it. He had no right to do that; his having access to her body didn't mean that he was allowed to walk around her mind.

She didn't like any of it. Her world wasn't just changing, it was morphing into something different right before her eyes and she had no control over what was happening.

"So, as a welcome-to-the-family gift, Lachlyn," Linc said, "we thought that you might like Connor's favorite ring."

We? What *we*? She hadn't been consulted about giving anything of Connor's to Lachlyn! And his favorite ring? The one Sage and Connor had spent hours together designing and making since the bands of amber, pieces of an ancient meteorite and platinum, had required careful workmanship?

What the hell?

"He said that it was his all-time favorite ring," Linc continued. "He designed and made it and wore it every day."

Excuse me? She'd spent as many hours on that ring as Connor had. Maybe more. Sage watched as Linc handed Lachlyn the ring and blinked back tears.

So this was sharing, she thought. Her home, her brothers, the memories of her father. Frankly, it sucked.

God, what a day. She'd had enough.

Sage yanked open the door and stepped into the dark, tossing a cool, general good-night over her shoulder. She'd barely made it to the wrought iron gate when she felt Tyce take her hand. She immediately jerked her hand away and shoved it into her coat pocket.

"I didn't give her the ring, Sage."

"You brought her into our life," Sage whipped back. Direct hit, she realized, but she took no pleasure in the color draining from his face, the danger sparking in his eyes.

Tyce swallowed and looked away, and Sage knew that he was trying to control his temper. "I realize that this has been a tough day for you. It's not easy having someone come into your life, your family, and turn it upside down."

"This is all your fault," Sage said, her temper roiling and boiling. "You sought me out years ago as a way to connect with my family—"

"I explained that," Tyce said in a tight voice.

"Then you slept with me and bought millions of Ballantyne shares."

"You slept with me too."

Sage ignored him and dived deeper into her anger, knowing that she was lobbing accusations at his head when she most wanted to yell at him for not being able to give her what her brothers gave their wives.

Not that she could accept his love…

Sage knew that she was being irrational and that he was a handy target. It wasn't fair or right but if she didn't vent, she'd explode.

"Then you got me pregnant!" Sage shouted, her chest heaving.

"You forgot to blame me for poverty, climate change and the price of oil," Tyce said, gripping her biceps. He pulled in a slug of cold air and when he spoke his voice was calm. "Connor conceived Lachlyn so blame him. We are equally responsible for the pregnancy. This is all new, Sage, and you're scared. I get it. We're all picking our way through a minefield right now but yelling at each other isn't going to help.

"We've got to find a way to deal with this, with us, with the situation," Tyce added.

Sage desperately wanted to allow her tears to fall, to place her head against his chest and weep, taking strength from his arms. She wanted to kiss him, allow him to sweep her away from the here and now, to take her someplace where she didn't have to think of the baby, about the fact that she'd never have the emotional security that being in a committed relationship gave a person who was strong and brave enough to take that chance. She wasn't strong and she wasn't brave and she probably never would be.

"Just give Lachlyn a chance. Give this situation a chance. Let life unfold and trust that we'll all find our way."

Feeling sick and sad and still so very pissed off—anger was so much easier to deal with than fear—Sage lifted her chin and nailed Tyce with a sardonic look. "Get out of my head, Tyce. I never gave you permission to walk around in there. And keep your opinions about my family to yourself! You don't know us and you don't know what makes us tick. You don't know jack about what having a real family means!"

Tyce jerked his head back, clearly shocked. She couldn't blame him; she sounded like a bitch on steroids. Her words had been designed to hurt and so unnecessary. Sage closed her eyes and held up her hand. Before she could apologize, Tyce turned around and started walking away.

Crap. Sage reached out and grabbed his elbow and he stopped.

"Tyce—"

Tyce's granite like expression killed the words in her throat. "I understand that you've had a rough day, Sage, but that doesn't mean that I get to be your verbal punch bag. I lived with a mother who was far better at that than you are but, as an adult, I no longer have to take the hits."

Dammit, she'd really angered him but, worse, she knew that she'd also hurt him. God, she felt ugly.

Tyce started to walk down the street, to the corner. "Where are you going?" Sage asked him.

"I'll hail a cab on the corner." He gestured to the cab that had pulled up next to them a few minutes before. "You take this one." Tyce nodded to her arm. "Your arm is fine and you don't need me hanging around all the time. We could probably both do with some space."

Tyce opened the cab door and gestured her inside. "Go home, Sage. We'll talk." He pushed his hand into his hair, his face expressionless.

"When?"

Tyce's smile held absolutely no warmth. "Oh, sometime between now and the baby's birth. Because, you know, I'm just the guy who knows nothing about anything, especially family."

Tyce slammed the door closed and Sage looked at him through the wet window. He turned his back on her and walked away, his broad back ramrod straight.

Sage felt a tear slide down her cheek and rested her temple on the glass of the window as the cab pulled away.

Her anger had nothing to do with Tyce and everything to do with her issues and her insecurities. She'd lashed out at him, projecting all her unhappiness in his direction. Had it been another subconscious attempt to push him away?

Probably, Sage admitted. But, because she'd been ugly and vicious and unfair, she'd hurt him. Sage felt humiliation and remorse roll through her.

And more than a little self-disgust.

Ten

Heavy rock blasting through the bottom floor of the warehouse, Tyce pushed up his welding helmet and frowned at the flicker of lights that was his version of a doorbell. It was past ten on a cold March night and, since few people knew of this address or that he lived here, he had no idea who was leaning on his doorbell. Dropping his welding rod and whipping off his helmet, he shoved his hands through his hair and walked across the cold concrete floor toward the small side door that stood adjacent to the huge roller doors.

Whipping the door open, he frowned at the small bundle of clothes stamping her feet on the sidewalk outside.

All he could see was big eyes and a pink nose. "Sage? What the hell?"

He opened the door wider and she hurried into the warehouse. She pulled her hands out of her pockets and started to unwind her scarf but he shook his head. "Upstairs. It's a hell of a lot warmer up there than it is down here."

Sage took the hand he held out and he pulled her toward the steel staircase that led to the second floor, which he'd converted into an apartment. Once inside, he started to unwind her scarf and helped her shrug out of her coat. Sage kept her eyes on his face and he wondered if she'd hoofed it across the Brooklyn Bridge to continue fighting with him. God, he hoped not. He didn't have the mental energy an argument required.

Tyce tossed her coat and scarf onto the chair next to the door and watched as Sage walked over to his fireplace and put her hands out to the fake flames. She sighed, slim shoulders lifting and falling. She turned around slowly, her eyes miserable when they met his.

Tyce tensed, waiting for the next blow to fall.

"I'm sorry. I was ugly and irrational and you have every right to be angry with me."

Tyce rubbed his lower jaw, stunned. An apology was the one statement he hadn't expected.

"Change scares me. Losing control terrifies me. Meeting Lachlyn was difficult and then we had the dinner—"

"You're a gorgeous, successful woman. Why would meeting Lachlyn, who is as normal as can be, freak you out?"

"I keep people at a distance and if I feel like there is a chance of them getting closer than I feel comfortable with, I get anxious. And stressed. And then, as you saw, I freak out."

So that explained a thing or two. "Did you pick a fight in an attempt to push me away too?"

Sage nodded. "Yeah, probably. It's what I do best."

For the first time, Tyce saw her as she truly was, stripped down. She wasn't Sage, the Ballantyne princess or Sage, the wealthy, successful jewelry designer. She was just Sage, a woman who was facing incredible changes, whose life had been flipped upside down and inside out. Yeah, she'd been a bitch of epic proportions earlier but her insecurity, her churning emotion and her fears made her seem more real, more authentic.

Humbled by her apology, touched by her honesty, Tyce ducked his head and slapped his mouth across hers. He heard her intake of breath, felt her fighting the instinct to pull back and to step away from him but when he gently suckled on her bottom lip she fell toward him. Tyce wrapped his arms around her and hauled her in. Through the silk and cotton of their T-shirts, he could feel her hard nipples digging into his pecs and air rushed from his chest. Needing to feel her skin while he explored her mouth, he pushed his hand beneath the band of her leggings and his knees nearly buckled when he held her round but firm bottom in his hand.

He was kissing Sage and she was kissing him back, her tongue sliding into his mouth, tangling with his. Despite them making love frequently over the past two weeks, he still couldn't quite believe that she was back in his bed and his life. Tyce pulled her into him, his fingers sliding into the space between her legs and he could feel the moist heat from her core flowing over his skin.

She wanted him just as much as he wanted her and the thought made him feel as weak as a newborn and as strong as an ox. She was both his salvation and his destruction, his pleasure and his pain.

And he wanted her with all the ferocity of a winter's storm.

But that didn't mean that they should tumble into bed. They had a mountain to climb, a million words that they needed to exchange, issues to iron out. Their earlier fight was behind them and, now that he understood what fueled her anger, he found her humble and sincere apology easy to accept.

But he still had something to say. Tyce pulled back and stepped away from her, knowing that there was no way he'd get this out if he was touching her.

"Look, we're going to be in each other's lives for a long time—" he wanted to think forever and in every way possible but that wasn't likely "—and we need to be each other's best friends. That means being honest, about everything. If you feel sick or pissed off or overwhelmed, I want to know about it. And I'll be as open as I can…" Tyce took a deep breath. "That being said, there is something I should tell you."

"Okay. What?"

"This warehouse, it's all I have. I don't have that much money in the bank."

Sage, genuinely, didn't look like she cared. "Can I ask why?" she eventually asked. "You're, like, the highest paid artist in the world."

"Those Ballantyne shares are expensive, Sage. I haven't had much cash for the last couple of years. I've been living a lie. The Chelsea apartment? It's owned by one of my biggest clients who allowed me to crash there."

"That explains the lack of art, the lack of anything personal," Sage stated, looking remarkably sanguine. "I never liked that place. It wasn't you."

Tyce almost smiled at that; she'd hit the nail on the head. It really wasn't him. The real him was this place, redbrick and steel, a punch bag and a mat in the corner, welding machines and chain saws. It was comfortable couches and worn rugs. It was industrial Brooklyn, hard, masculine, gritty.

Tyce thought of Sage's girly loft. She was expensive

gems and delicate designs. She was cream couches and soft beds, the wrought iron frame surrounding the bed dotted with tulle and fairy lights. She was expensive; he was functional.

"I'm working on a couple of pieces that I'll be able to sell in a month or two. I want to pay for the baby, your medical expenses to have the baby, for whatever you or the baby needs." He held up his hand. Tyce knew that he could never compete with her wealth. It was stupid to try but he wanted to be able to, at the very least, provide the best for her and his baby. "I know that you can pay for it without my help but... I just want to, okay?"

Sage nodded, her expression inscrutable. "Okay, we'll work it out." Sage sent him an uncertain smile. "So... are we good?"

They were, very good indeed. In fact, he was starting to feel more than good, he felt fan-friggin-tastic. Tyce felt like they'd ripped down a couple of barriers between them, that their fights had flattened some obstacles between them. Or he could be feeling light-headed because he couldn't stop looking at her, drinking her in. Demanding, a little crazy, warm, generous, funny, she was everything he'd ever wanted.

Tyce battled to get his brain to function properly. He knew that he should say something. She was trying, very earnestly, to make amends but all he wanted to do was to blurt out that he thought that they'd turned a corner, they might, maybe, have a shot at...something. Something bigger and brighter than this, whatever this was.

Tyce felt the burn below his rib cage as that thought lodged in his brain. Terror, his childhood companion, drifted into his head, accompanied by doubt, another old ally.

Would he ever be able to fight off both long enough

to be with her, to be the man she needed? Deepening his relationship with Sage meant losing his freedom but, at the same time, he couldn't imagine a life without her in it.

He felt dizzy, confused, utterly at sea.

Too much, too soon, Tyce told himself. *You're tired and played out. Think about commitment and monogamy and forever and what you want from her when you aren't punch-drunk with tiredness and overwhelmed by emotion. In the morning you might decide otherwise. This might be an overreaction, a figment of your imagination.*

Take a breath and calm the hell down.

Tyce pushed his hands into the front pockets of his jeans and found his voice. "Want some coffee? I have decaf."

Sage nodded and followed him to the small galley kitchen that ran along the back wall of the apartment. There was also a sitting and dining area and two en suite bedrooms tucked into this corner of the warehouse. A steel-and-wood gangway running above his workshop and home gym linked the apartment to his painting studio. Tyce knew that Sage, who was intensely interested in art, would ask for a tour but his studio, with all the sketches and portraits of her, would be firmly off-limits.

If she saw the many sketches of her she'd definitely think he was a psycho and go running for the hills.

Sage looked up at the pipes running across the ceiling and the massive wooden beams that contrasted with the redbrick walls. Her eyes focused on a massive wooden propeller he'd hung on the far wall and her lips quirked. "I love this... This is you. This is your space. Masculine and minimalistic."

And so very different from her light-filled, pink-tinged, feminine space. If they ever ended up living together, how would they...

Whoa there, cowboy, cool your jets. You decided not to go there, remember? You were going to wait until your brain was functioning properly before you made any life-changing, crazy-ass decisions.

Take a breath, dude. And another...

He focused on making coffee, decaf, of course, then realized he needed something a lot stronger than coffee. He poured a mug for Sage, then reached for a bottle of whiskey and dropped a healthy amount into a glass. Sipping, he felt the burn in his throat, the warmth in his stomach, and his heart slowed down, his lungs opening to allow more air to flow inside. Yeah, that was more like it.

Sage looked around, her eyebrows raised. "So, where's your studio? Where do you paint?"

He'd known she'd ask and instead of blowing her off, as he'd intended to do, he gestured to the door in the corner of the loft. "It's on the other side of the building. Through that door is a catwalk that takes you there."

Sage's eyes lit up. "Can I see it?"

He wanted to say no but he'd just told her that they needed to be honest with each other. Nodding, he walked across the room to open the door onto the gangway. Taking Sage's mug from her, he held her coffee and his whiskey and gestured for her to step out. Sage stepped onto the narrow walkway and looked down at his workbenches and equipment below. He'd just started a new sculpture and pieces of half-bent steel and wood lay scattered across the concrete floor. "What's that going to be?"

Tyce shrugged. "Not sure yet. I'm still waiting for it to make sense."

Sage nodded. Because she was an artist herself, he didn't need to explain the creative process to her, that he was following his instincts, trusting that it would all work out in the end.

"God, it's cold up here," Sage said, wrapping her arms around herself.

"The warehouse is a bitch to heat but I'm normally doing some sort of physical activity down there, either working on a sculpture or working out, so I don't notice it much. The studio is heated."

They'd reached the door that led to his most private space and Tyce took a deep breath as Sage opened the door. "The light switch is on the left."

Sage flipped the switch and light filled the messy room. Tyce handed Sage her mug, took a sip of his whiskey and wondered what she—the first person to step into this space—thought. He looked around, trying to see the familiar setting through new eyes. The windows were incredible, leaded panes letting in every bit of light and shelves held paints and brushes and trowels. Blank canvases were stacked against one wall and there was a half-finished, shades-of-blue abstract taking up the space opposite. Sage looked at the oil for a long time, sipping her coffee before glancing down at the stack of canvases facing the wall. Ah, crap. Well, what had he thought would happen?

"May I?"

Tyce nodded and she immediately sank to the floor, placing the mug by her knee and flipping the first canvas around. He squinted at the charcoal-and-ink sketch and let out a sigh of relief; it was a portrait of Lachlyn, her nose buried in a book. Sage said nothing and turned another canvas around and Tyce sucked in his breath. His mother was lying on the floor next to her bed, her knees pulled up, her eyes vacant.

"She looks a little like Lachlyn… Is this your mom?" Sage asked, glancing up.

Tyce nodded. "Yeah, as I mentioned, she suffered from chronic depression. She'd stay like that for days."

Sage thankfully didn't comment. She just flipped through the portraits, wrinkling her nose when she came across the one of her working at her bench. She looked at the date and lifted her eyes to his, her eyebrows raised. Tyce felt his cheeks warm. "I saw a photo of you in a magazine. I decided to copy it."

Still no comment. Tyce felt ants crawling up his skin as she flipped through the portraits, many of which were of her. After examining the last one, she rested her forearms on her knees.

He saw the anger in her eyes when all that blue slammed into his. "Why the hell have you never exhibited these? They are so good, Tyce, possibly even better than your sculptures and your oils. They are emotional and, sometimes, hard to look at but so damn real!"

Tyce ran a finger along the edge of his ragged sweatshirt, trying to keep up. "I can't do it," he admitted.

"Why on earth not?" Sage cried. "They are fantastic. The emotion jumps off the canvas."

His feelings about her, about them, were a tangled mess but she was still the mother of his child and she deserved to know the truth. The entire truth. Tyce paced the area in front of the oil painting, his fingers holding the glass tumbler in a tight grip. "I discovered that I could sell my portraits when I was thirteen or so. I'd take my sketch pad to Central Park and sketch people who passed by. I'd shove the drawing under their nose and they'd pay me... I still don't know if they paid because they thought the work was good or because they felt sorry for the too-thin kid in old clothes."

Sage quietly sipped of her coffee, her silence encouraging him to continue.

"I did that for a few years. I finished high school and was offered a scholarship to art school but I had to work and the only job I could find was in construction. To make some extra cash, I agreed to pose naked for an art class comprised mostly of women wanting to dabble in art."

Sage just lifted one arched eyebrow higher, looking unaffected. Her shoulders lifted in a tiny *So?*

"I used to draw portraits of the women, which they'd buy. Then they'd take me home and they'd pose naked, telling me that the portrait was for their husband or their lover."

"And you'd end up sleeping with them," Sage said, her tone utterly prosaic.

Tyce rubbed the back of his neck. "I sold many portraits and I slept with quite a few women."

Sage tipped her head to the side and just looked at him. "So?" When he sent her a puzzled look, she continued. "I'm sorry but I'm trying to find the link between you sleeping with someone and why you won't sell your portraits."

Tyce couldn't understand why she was being obtuse. "I slept with them, Sage!"

"You were nineteen and you would've slept with a gorilla if it wore lipstick," Sage replied, impatient. Then the confusion cleared from her eyes. "Oh…wait, I get it. You don't know whether they used the sketches as an excuse to pay you for sex."

Nailed it, Tyce thought morosely, turning away from her.

Tyce heard Sage stand up, heard the sound of her mug hitting the surface of his desk and then felt her hand on his back. He waited for her words, his heart bouncing off his rib cage. "You don't actually know how good you are, do you? That's why you don't attend your own exhibitions, why you don't do interviews... You don't think that you are worth the accolades, the money."

Tyce whirled around and pointed at the oil. "I did that oil in half a day, Sage! I slapped some paint on a canvas, I didn't even think about it and idiots will pay me a quarter mil for it, maybe a whole lot more. The sculptures take more work but nothing that's worth the price tags the galleries put on my pieces. My portraits, they mean something, but yeah, every time I think of selling one, exhibiting one, I feel that I am that confused kid again, trying to keep his head above water, not sure whether he was being pitied or paid for being a stud."

He sucked in a breath and continued. "Art...art was where I retreated to when my mom wouldn't talk, wouldn't move for days on end. It was the place I could hide out in, pretend everything was okay. I used to lose time sketching and drawing. It was the place where I fell into that creative zone where nothing could touch me."

"Are you not going there anymore?" Sage gestured to the oil. "Because this tells me that you are..."

"It's just so damn easy, Sage."

Sage placed her hands on his chest and tipped her lovely face back to look at him, her eyes full of warmth... Love? Affection? "Tyce, you've had a hard life. You've looked after your mother, your sister and you sacrificed so damn much for them, your scholarship, your wealth to buy the Ballantyne shares, your youth. Aren't you allowed to have one thing in your life that's easy? Could this not be life giving you a break?"

Tyce dropped his forehead so that it met hers, hauling in big breaths of much-needed air. Could she be right? Could he finally accept that not everything had to be a fight, a battle to be won?

"You're so talented, Tyce, the most amazing artist I know."

"You're biased." Tyce rumbled the words, so badly wanting to believe her.

Sage stepped back and looked at him. "Do you remember when you painted the *Tired Ballerina*?"

The painting in her loft. God, he didn't but it was early on in his career.

"It was nine years ago and I've always been obsessed about ballet and wished I had the talent to be a professional dancer. I saw that painting and I fell in love with it. I was nineteen, twenty? I begged Connor to buy it for me but he wouldn't. When I turned twenty-one Connor released some money into my trust fund and I tracked down the owner and I paid him three times what he originally paid. I hadn't met you yet but I wanted that painting more than I wanted to breathe."

Touched, Tyce opened his mouth to speak but she held up her hand to stop him from saying anything. "I persuaded my siblings to buy Jaeger one of your sculptures for a birthday present, and Connor, at my insistence, bought another three of your paintings for his private collection. One is on the main wall of the reception area of Ballantyne International. Connor said that, while he'd never liked the *Tired Ballerina*, he loved your new work. He said that you were going to be one of the best and one of the most influential artists of the twenty-first century and… Guess what? You are. You are worth every cent you are paid. If you don't believe one word I've ever said, please, please, believe that."

Tyce closed his eyes, not wanting her to see the emotion there and he dug his fingers into her skin, hoping that she wouldn't feel the trembling in his hands. He felt both tired and rejuvenated, wiped out and energized.

And God, free. Sage's words made him feel empowered, unrestricted. She made him feel like he could take on the world single-handed and win. He wanted to tell her how much what she'd said meant to him, how life-changing it was, but the words stuck in his throat. He ducked his head and hoped that he could convey what he was trying to say with his mouth, his hands, by worshipping her body.

But Sage was way ahead of him. She stood on her toes and placed her lips on his, her tongue tracing the seam of his lips, demanding that he open up. He whispered a *Hell, yeah* and she slid her tongue into his and she dialed up the temperature, demanding his response. Tyce yanked her to him, his hands looking for bare skin. He was still pulling her shirt out of her jeans when Sage's hand slid under his sweatshirt and her fingers tap-danced their way across his abs, her thumb swiping the space between his belly button and the low band of his jeans. His stomach muscles contracted and she groaned her approval and her kisses turned wild.

Then Sage's hands attacked the button on his jeans. Who was this woman taking control, whose hand was sliding underneath his underwear to encircle him? She'd been timid, sometimes shy about telling him what turned her on but today she knew exactly what she wanted. Tyce felt blood pump into his erection and he turned rock hard in her hand.

Sage gave another throaty murmur of approval and she wrenched her mouth from his and stepped back to pull his shirt up and over his head. As soon as his chest was bare she slapped her open mouth against his sternum, her tongue tracing a fiery path down his body.

Holy crap, she couldn't possibly be thinking of...

He'd pleasured her like this before but he knew that

she wasn't comfortable, yet, to reciprocate. He'd spent many, many nights imagining Sage doing exactly this but his imagination, which was powerful, had nothing on this. Her tongue flicked over his abs and he groaned and reached back to grab the edge of a shelf, convinced that his knees were about to buckle.

Sage pushed his jeans down his legs and worked her fingers under the band of his underwear. Cool air touched his straining erection and her fiery mouth on his skin was a complete contrast. He didn't know if he could handle this: his fantasies had fallen well short of how she made him feel. In his dreams, his heart never felt like it was about to beat through his chest, like he didn't have a single spark of brainpower left, that the whole world was reduced to her mouth on him.

He couldn't do it… It was too much. Then Sage took him inside her mouth, and his brain, that teeny tiny organ, shut down completely.

Tyce gripped the counter and tipped his head back, thinking that if he watched her, he'd lose it completely. His chest heaved and beads of sweat popped on his skin. This, Sage, being loved by her, was all his fantasies and wishes and hopes and dreams coming true.

Oh, it wasn't just about the sex—which was terrifyingly fantastic—but all of this. She was in his studio and she'd said everything he most needed to hear about his art, had placed his past actions into perspective, had opened up a new world to him. He wanted this, all of it. He wanted her in his life, to be a big part of hers, he wanted to raise their baby together. That much he knew… There would be no thinking about this in the morning.

He needed her. He always had.

Tyce gripped her shoulders, pulled her up and slapped his mouth on hers. In between hot and heavy kisses, they managed to pull their clothes off, scattering them across his paint-splattered floor. When they were both naked, Tyce locked his arms beneath her bottom and lifted her up, sighing when her slim legs encircled his waist. Unable to wait, he pushed her down and he slid into her, wet and warm and wonderful.

Sage gasped and Tyce saw stars behind his eyes. Not convinced that his knees weren't about to buckle, he rested her against his oil painting, and Sage's head fell back. Tyce stopped and looked at her, eyes closed, long hairs falling through the still-wet paint of his creation, her milky shoulders against the various shades of blue.

Knowing that he couldn't hold on for much longer, Tyce commanded Sage to open her eyes. When she did, he sighed and fell a little deeper in love. "I want to watch your eyes as you come. But do it soon, please?"

Sage pressed down, her butt sliding down the canvas, and he sunk even farther into her. She gasped, yelled and contracted around him and he was lost.

Then he spun away into a vortex of a million shades of blue.

The next morning, Tyce walked Sage to the taxi and she noticed the amusement in his eyes as he pulled a cap over her head.

"What?" she mock demanded, thinking that he looked, if it was possible, ten times sexier than he had last night. He had rings around his eyes, so did she since they hadn't spent much time sleeping, but the shadows in his eyes were gone.

"I was just thinking about the streaks of French ultramarine on your butt," he told her, laughter rolling through his expression.

Sage frowned at him. "I'm more upset that you destroyed your painting than I am about some oil paint on my ass."

Last night, when they came up for air and were marginally functional, Sage felt the wet paint on her bottom and had whirled around to look at the painting, which now sported a perfect imprint of her butt cheeks. Instead of being upset about his ruined painting, Tyce had cried with laughter.

"I'll do something with it," Tyce told her, lifting his hands to cradle her face. "Maybe. Or I might just keep it as a reminder of the best sex of my life. And the best conversation."

Sage smiled and curled her gloved hands around his strong wrists. "Just remember that I think you are fabulous."

Tyce lifted one arrogant eyebrow but she saw the hint of uncertainty in his eyes. "A fabulous artist?"

"Just all round fabulous."

Tyce smiled, lowered his mouth to hers and gently kissed it. His mouth held a hint of passion but it went deeper than that; she could taste his promises, the suggestion of a future together. The hope that this time they could make it work, that they could be better and braver.

"What's your plan of action for the day?" Tyce asked her when he lifted his mouth from hers.

"Um... I have a client meeting at Ballantyne's and then I'm heading home as I have to finish the Saudi princess's ring." Sage glanced at the taxi driver. He wasn't looking impatient yet so she had a minute or two. "And your plans?"

"When you fell asleep, I started to think about all the work I'm dying to do so I might hole up here and just... work. Fall into that zone."

Sage smiled, immediately understanding what he was

trying to say. "So, if you don't answer my calls or respond to my texts I mustn't panic?"

"That okay with you?"

Sage smiled and nodded. "Very okay. Let me know when you come up for air. But it had better be before Thursday morning as we have a ten o'clock appointment with Dr. Charles, the obstetrician."

"Day after tomorrow at ten. No problem," Tyce told her. "I'm pretty sure that my need to have you again will bring me back to the land of the living way before then."

Sage stood on her toes to slant her mouth over his in a hot, openmouthed kiss. "Can't wait. Have fun."

Tyce opened the passenger door to the taxi and when she was seated, he bent down to kiss her again. His fabulous eyes were full of mischief when he pulled back. "Oh, and maybe I should tell you that you have blue streaks running through the back of your hair."

He slammed the door shut but Sage could still hear his laughter. She pushed her hat off her head and pulled a hank of hair in front of her face. Lifting her eyes upward, she immediately noticed the strands of French ultramarine.

Dammit! She spun around to look out through the window at Tyce and saw that he was looking down, his eyes on the screen of his phone.

Ten seconds later her phone buzzed with an incoming text.

Want to come back? I'm have this idea of tossing paint onto a canvas and rolling around in it with you. It would be a piece for my very private collection.

Sage smiled, shuddered with longing and flipped another look over her shoulder but Tyce had gone back into his building.

So tempted, Sage typed back, But I doubt the Saudi princess, or my boss brother, would understand me blowing off a meeting with one of our biggest clients to play with paint. Rain check?

Eleven

"Do you want to get some coffee?" Tyce asked Lachlyn as they left the small, warm studio and stepped into the icy wind barreling down the street. Lachlyn had asked him to meet her at a new gallery she'd discovered, thinking that he'd enjoy the eclectic pieces sourced from all over the world. He had.

"Sure." Lachlyn looked around. "There's a coffee shop at the end of the block."

"Sage's apartment is around the corner. She's at a meeting at Ballantyne HQ but her coffee is fantastic."

Lachlyn nodded her agreement and they started walking in the direction of Sage's apartment. "How is Sage?" she asked.

"Fine. Why do you ask?"

"Oh, because when you told me you were moving in with her after her accident, you said it would just be for a couple of days. It's been a couple of weeks and you're still there. Did she crack her spine or is her arm paralyzed?"

Tyce narrowed her eyes at his sister. "Smart-ass."

But it was fair question. Why was he still living with Sage? Every day he made the trek to Brooklyn, worked in his studio and at night he made his way back to SoHo. It was because making love with Sage was like a Class A drug and he was hooked. He couldn't imagine a day without her in it, not waking up next to her, exploring her body every night. God, that sounded like he was...

No, don't say it, don't think it. His need to be with her had nothing to do with the L-word, or a future they could spend together, a life they could make. He was still the reserved, taciturn, need-to-be-alone artist he always was.

Except that his actions, every damned day, contradicted his words. *Crap.*

"So, what did you think of The Den?" he asked in a deliberate attempt to change the subject. They hadn't had any time to talk about her meeting the Ballantynes and how she felt about her new family. Talking about The Den, and Lachlyn's extensive tour of the house with Jo, Linc's mother, was his way of easing into that conversation.

"Oh, Tyce...it's definitely the most amazing house I've ever seen." Lachlyn shoved her gloved hand into the crook of his elbow and snuggled in. "There is a Picasso hanging in a small sitting room, Lalique glassware everywhere and, I swear, what I thought might be a Fabergé egg."

Remotely possible but not likely, Tyce thought.

"You only saw the one lounge and the formal dining room but Linc and Tate mostly use a massive room that's as normal as any I've seen. There were toys on the floor, drawings on the fridge. Okay, admittedly, most people don't have purple crayons squished into Persian carpets but I liked that room. I could see that Tate and Linc *lived* there."

Lachlyn continued her description of the iconic brownstone occupied by generations of Ballantynes and he let her ramble because he was interested in the house Sage grew up in. His ears pricked up at the mention of Linc's state-of-the-art gym and climate-controlled wine cellar in the basement.

"And Sage?" Tyce asked, his heart picking up speed. "What did you think of her?"

Sage and Lachlyn were the two women who were going to be in his life for a long, long time. It was important that they liked each other. And they were also now part of the same family. That was important too.

"She's a little prickly." His sister frowned. "Maybe that's not the right word... Scared? Vulnerable?"

"But do you *like* her?" Tyce persisted.

"Yes, I suppose I do." Lachlyn frowned again. "We were supposed to have dinner this week but she postponed. I've sent her a couple of texts trying to reschedule but she's booked up at the moment."

Tyce frowned at the note of hurt he heard in Lachlyn's voice. Trying to reassure her, he put his arm around her shoulder and hugged her close. "I have heard many mutterings of a picky Saudi princess who can't make up her damn mind."

They turned the corner onto Sage's block and, like a homing beacon, Tyce's eyes were drawn to a slim figure at the end of the street, wearing black pants tucked into black boots, and a scarlet coat. Sage was looking down at her phone and wasn't paying attention to her surroundings.

Tyce nudged Lachlyn. "Sage is home early—her meeting must have been rescheduled. Let's catch up with her."

Lachlyn looked anxious. "Let me give her a heads-up, tell her that I'm here."

"Nah, let's just go," Tyce insisted. "It's too cold to hang around."

Lachlyn shook her head and pulled out her phone, pressing buttons. Tyce looked down, saw that her phone was dialing Sage's number and looked across the road. He watched Sage look down at her phone and when she grimaced, he knew that she had read the caller ID. Instead of answering Lachlyn's call, she shoved her phone back into her coat pocket.

His temper bubbled and when he clocked Lachlyn's miserable expression, it burned a hole in his stomach. His sister blinked away her tears and tried to smile. "Yeah, so I guess it's me and not work that's the problem."

"Lach—" Tyce said, at a loss for what to say. He looked down into her bewildered face and, in that moment, his baby sister was wearing the exact expression that was a feature of her childhood spent with their mother.

I love you—what's wrong with me that you can't love me back? Do I make you sad? Am I the problem?

Lachlyn reached up to kiss his cheek. "It's okay, Tyce. Maybe she's not ready for me." Lachlyn patted his arm. "I'll talk to you later, okay?"

Tyce watched Lachlyn walk away, anger and disappointment rolling through him. He looked across the street, all his anger directed at Sage, who was walking, head down, toward the front door of her place. Tyce took his own phone and dialed her number...

Sage looked down at her phone and saw Tyce's name flash on her screen. Lifting the phone to her ear, she stopped and turned toward the side of the building, putting her back to the wind. "Hi."

"Hey." Tyce's voice sounded funny but Sage thought that it could just be the wind playing tricks with her ears.

"I'm with Lachlyn and I thought that we could come to the apartment for coffee. Are you going to be home soon?"

Yeah, he definitely sounded weird. Almost angry, Sage thought. Sage rubbed the back of her neck, trying to massage the tension away. Her princess had arrived ten minutes late for their meeting and stormed out in a huff after another five, declaring that Sage's designs were all rubbish and plebeian and that she hated every one.

She felt battered and tired and all she wanted was to climb into a hot bath and to go to bed early. She didn't want to talk to anyone, not even Tyce, tonight. She felt like she hadn't had a moment alone for the month and all she wanted was an empty apartment and some quiet.

"Sage? Are you there?"

"I'm still at work." The lie ran smoothly off her tongue even as it burned a hole in her stomach. But if she told him the truth, then he'd demand to know why she needed time alone, what was bugging her, why she was avoiding him and his sister. She just didn't have the energy to deal with any of it.

"I'm going to be working late so—" she hesitated "— maybe you should stay at your place tonight?"

"Okay then."

Sage looked down at her dead phone and winced. God, she hated lying and wished she hadn't. She should've just told him that she needed some time alone; of everyone she knew, Tyce was the person most likely to understand that. And he was a big boy; if he asked what was wrong and she said that she didn't feel like talking, he'd understand.

There was no need to lie…yet she'd done it. Sage felt acid coat her throat, feeling thoroughly ashamed of herself.

She'd have to confess the lie and that wasn't going to be fun.

But she was a big girl and she'd done the crime, so she'd take the consequences.

Sage looked down at her screen and saw the "missed" call she'd ignored from Lachlyn and remorse swamped her. And she felt guilty for blowing their plans, for using work as an excuse to avoid her.

Sage sucked in some cold air thinking that it was bad timing, that she did need to get on top of work; she didn't really have the time to start a new relationship. With Tyce living with her and taking up her time at night and the tiredness from the pregnancy hormones, and the horrible weather…

And the famine in the Sudan and the bomb blast in Pakistan and the phase of the moon…

God, she was just one crazy, twisted knot of excuses.

The truth was that she was scared. No, terrified. Scared of what she felt for Tyce, scared of what she could feel for Lachlyn. Scared of being hurt, left alone, lost.

But, most of all, she was scared to live. To love.

Sage wrapped her arms around her waist as she walked the last yards to her building. A series of pictures flashed into her head and they were of the last vacation she'd spent with her parents. They'd flown to Hawaii and she remembered they'd all taken surfing lessons. Her brothers had picked up the skill immediately but she and her dad had struggled to find their balance. On the cinema screen in her head, her mom, who was a Californian girl, was skimming down what looked like, to her, a monstrous wave. Her dark hair was flying, she was whooping like a maniac and she had the most enormous smile on her face.

Her dad had looked at her and grinned. "That's your mom, Sagie. Wild and free, so in love with life."

Sage wiped a tear off her face and thought that she might look like her mom but she wasn't anything like her. She was cautious and closed off and a slave to her fears. Yes, she'd experienced incredible personal loss but she'd survived it and if it happened again, she would survive that too. Hearts might get dinged and broken but they didn't actually kill you.

She could, Sage realized, spend the rest of her life in a cage where it was safe and, yeah, boring, or she could break out of jail and start to explore her world. She was young, rich and reasonably smart; she could have a wonderful life if she found a little bit of her mom's courage, her bold spirit.

Someday, not today, she would have to try. She owed that to the memory of her parents, to Connor...

"So, working late, huh?"

Sage let out a low scream as Tyce appeared beside her, a yard from the steps leading up to the front door. Sage slapped her hand against her heart as she caught her breath. "Dammit, Tyce! I hate it when you do that!"

"Yeah?" Tyce's eyes were as hard and cold as frozen coal. "Coincidentally, I hate it when you lie to me."

Oh, crap, she was so busted. Sage scratched her forehead, looking for the right words. Tyce didn't give her a chance. "So, who were you blowing off? Me? Lachlyn? Both of us?"

Sage shoved her shaking hands into the pockets of her coat. Before she could reply, her phone rang and she pulled it out. Blessing Linc for the interruption since it gave her a little time to construct a decent apology, she answered his call. Linc was hoping for a date night with Tate and was wondering if she could babysit Shaw and Ellie.

"Sorry, Linc, not tonight. I'm exhausted and I have a headache and all I want to do is climb into a hot bath and go to bed early." Sage forced herself to look at Tyce, sighing at his hard expression. This is what she should've said to him instead of that stupid lie. "I just need some time alone."

"No worries, I'll ask Beck and Cady. Later."

Sage disconnected the call and before she could speak, Tyce did. "So, you need some space, huh? No problem." Tyce started to walk away but Sage caught his sleeve and tugged, her actions asking him to stay. Suddenly she didn't want to be alone. She just wanted to step into his arms, allow his strength and solidity to suck the tension from her. In his arms, she realized, was the place she felt safest.

"Tyce—"

Tyce's snapped-out swear was the perfect accompaniment to his pissed-off scowl. "I am so mad at you, Sage. You lied to me and that's a pretty big deal to me. I don't deal in lies. But worse than that, you hurt my sister. I'm not sure what games you are playing, but she wants to get to know you, to be your friend, that's all she's asking." Tyce pointed to a spot down and across the street. "We saw you walking. Lachlyn called you and you pulled a face when you saw her name on your phone. That was strike one. You let her call ring out and Lachlyn watched you do it. Strike two."

Sage felt like he'd stabbed her in the heart. Ah, no, damn, no.

"She walked away from me, crying. Then you freaking lied to me? Strike three, Sage."

"You set me up!" Sage retorted. "You wanted to see what I would do, say."

"That's your defense?" Tyce gripped her arms in his big hands, bending down so that his face was level with hers. "Bad move, Ballantyne. Lachlyn and I spent our childhoods with a mother who didn't love us enough to want to get better, who didn't want us around and gave us no attention. She certainly had no interest in getting to know us, on any level. It was far more fun being a chronic depressive. My point is, we know when we're not wanted."

His voice, so calm and so controlled, cut through her. Sage felt hot tears running down her cheeks. "Tyce, I'm sorry. I didn't mean to make either of you feel like that."

Tyce dropped his hands, held them up and stepped away. "As I said… You want space? Take as much as you need."

Sage held her fist to her mouth as she watched Tyce stride away. She called out to him in the vain hope that he would turn around and come back. Tyce just broke into a jog, leaving her standing in the icy wind.

Ashamed and annoyed at herself, and so very embarrassed, Sage looked up at her building and considered going up. She could take that bath and try for an early night but she knew that the chances of her sleeping were minimal at best. She was exhausted but sleep would be elusive unless she found Tyce and apologized. Sage thought about using her cell phone to call him but that would be too easy, the cowardly way out. She needed to look him in the eye and take her medicine like the big girl she now was.

Where would he have gone on a cold winter's night? To the apartment in Chelsea or the studio in Brooklyn? He'd go to where his art was, Sage decided. If he was half as frustrated as she was, then he'd try to lose himself in his work, to fall into that space where pesky problems and annoying people faded away.

But before she went to Tyce, she had to mend a blown-up fence. Sage pulled out her phone. She held her breath, knowing that the chance of her call being answered was slim to none.

"Hello?"

"Lach?" Sage heard her voice break as she used Tyce's pet name for his sister. "I've really messed up. Firstly, I'm sorry that I ignored your call—I'm not very good at letting people in and I got scared. I'm really, really sorry."

"Okay," Lachlyn replied, her tone cautious.

"You are so like Connor, Lachlyn. It's taking some time to get used to."

"I can't help that," Lachlyn said, her voice cool.

"I know," Sage replied. "Just give me some time, please? I'm feeling a little overwhelmed."

"So am I, Sage."

God, she'd never considered the situation from Lachlyn's point of view, she'd never thought about how hard it had to be to step into a family and wonder if they'd like her, even love her. Sage had been so selfish, so caught up in her own drama.

These Latimores certainly had a way of making her see herself clearly.

"I can forgive you for hurting me, Sage, but I will never forgive you if you hurt Tyce. If you ask me to pick a side between you and your brothers, or Tyce, I will, always, always pick Tyce. Do not doubt that."

Sage appreciated the sentiment and she respected Lachlyn's loyalty to her brother.

"I'm going to head to his studio to apologize."

"That's not a good idea and he won't appreciate it.

Give him some time and space to deal with his anger," Lachlyn suggested.

"Okay." Sage rubbed the back of her neck. "I am sorry for earlier, Lachlyn. And I need you to know that it's not my intention to hurt Tyce."

"Really?" Lachlyn sounded skeptical. "For someone who is acting unintentionally, you're doing a damn fine job of doing just that."

The next evening, Sage stood in the doorway of the sitting room of The Den holding Ellie. She looked across the space to the Ballantyne women. Piper and Cady sat on the Persian carpet on either side of Amy, and Tate sat on the big leather couch close to them. Each of them held a book containing fabric swatches but only Amy was flipping through hers and cursing like a sailor. There were four books of open fabric samples on the carpet in front of her and another five on the coffee table. From her position in the doorway, Sage could only see minuscule differences in the shades of cream.

Sage rubbed her cheek against Ellie's curls and cuddled the little girl closer. Linc had bundled her into her arms as soon as she stepped into The Den, telling her that Shaw had accidentally emptied an entire bottle of bath bubbles into his bath.

Accidentally-on-purpose, Sage was sure.

"What are you doing?" Sage asked the women.

Four heads swiveled around and Tate crossed the room to her, giving her, and Ellie, a warm hug. Ellie deserted Sage by tumbling into her mom's arms.

Sage greeted everyone and gestured to the books. "What are you trying to decide? Can I help?"

"The exact shade of cream for the reception tablecloths."

Behind Amy, Cady rolled her eyes, and Sage hid her smile. There had been murmurs of Amy turning into Bridezilla but only when they were very, very sure that Amy wasn't around. Amy, as Linc and Beck's PA, was the power behind the Ballantyne throne.

"Jules told me that I am driving her mad with the wedding arrangements and she's threatening to kidnap me and take me to Vegas." Amy pushed out her bottom lip. "I just want it to be perfect."

Sage bent down and gave her a hug. "You're overthinking it, honey. Choose one—they are all pretty much the same."

Amy glared at the books. "I will. After I look through the books on the floor once more. How are you?"

Sage shrugged, thinking that there was no point in lying. "Horrible." Sage plopped down into the corner of the couch and rubbed the back of her neck. "I really messed up. Again."

Four sets of sympathetic eyes rested on her face and, for the first time ever, the words tumbled out of her as she explained what a complete idiot she'd been and how she'd hurt Lachlyn. And Tyce.

"I apologized to Lachlyn and I've tried to call Tyce, repeatedly, but he's ignoring me," Sage said.

She shoved her hands into her hair and saw the sympathetic faces. She lifted up her hand. "Don't feel too sorry for me, guys—this was all my fault. I knew that if I allowed myself to get close that I'd get hurt."

Sage stared at the books of fabric swatches, her eyes wet with tears. "I love him. I do. I think I always have but as soon as he gets too close, I push him away."

Tate sank to the floor next to her legs and rested her temple against Sage's knee. "Oh, honey. What are you going to do?"

Sage shrugged. Since this was the first time she'd frankly and openly admitted that she loved Tyce, to herself as well as to her family, she hadn't given the next step much thought. "I don't know. I know I need to apologize but I can't do that unless I speak to him. And I don't know if I can do the whole sleeping-together-without-love thing anymore. I want to tell him that I love him but I think that he might run. Fast and hard." Sage placed a hand on her stomach. "And, man, that will hurt like a bitch and you guys know how hard I work to avoid being hurt."

"So you love him?" Tate asked.

Sage nodded. "Yes, I love him." Of that much she was sure. "I always have."

"So do it," Tate said, her voice firm.

Sage frowned. "Sorry, what?"

"So you're scared, so he might run. Do it anyway," Tate said, resting her hand on Sage's thigh. "We think that we have to get rid of the fear first when, actually, what we have to do is act first. Only then does the fear go away."

Cady nodded. "The only way to stop being afraid of loving someone is to love them."

Sage stared at her flat biker boots. "But what if he leaves?" she quietly asked. "Or dies?"

"Then he leaves or dies," Piper said. She climbed to her feet and, moving behind her, leaned over and wrapped her arms around Sage's waist, her chin on her shoulder. "We can't be responsible for, or try to control, what other people do, baby. We only have control over our actions. We can only worry about what we can control."

Sage hugged Piper's arms to her, her eyes filling with tears. This was what a support base felt like, what belonging to a tribe of strong women felt like. These were the Ballantyne women—Sage had always thought that Amy should change her name to Ballantyne and be done with it—and they were a unit. And, her blurry eyes focused on her niece, who was sitting in Tate's lap, they were raising another generation of strong Ballantyne women.

Their wise counsel made sense and she was grateful for it. She wasn't sure if she'd take their advice but she'd certainly think about it. She'd think about it a lot.

"Wine!" Amy said, standing up. "I know that Linc recently bought a case of Domaine de la Romanée-Conti. He won't miss a bottle, or three."

Tate groaned. "He'll kill us, Ames. It's one of the most expensive wines in the world."

"Pfft." Amy waved her concerns away.

"Touch my wine and you're fired," Linc said, striding into the room. He walked into the center of the carpet, dropped a kiss on his wife's head and grinned when his daughter held up her arms, her face splitting into a huge smile at the sight of her dad.

Sage fought tears and tried not to think of her baby looking at Tyce like that. She owed it to their child, she owed it to herself, to tell Tyce how she felt, to express what she wanted. If she didn't, she'd regret it for the rest of her life.

She needed to be brave because if she wasn't, how would she teach her child to be courageous, to take a chance?

Yes, it was scary; yes, terror was congealing her blood but Tyce was worth a little fear.

Sage just stared at the carpet—Was that a purple crayon buried in the threads?—as determination pushed fear into a corner, holding it at bay. She could do this. She would do this.

Sage stood up, smiled and headed for the door. The last thing she heard as she bolted out was Tate's cheerful statement. "That's our girl. Ames, the case of wine is still in the hallway—neither Linc or I have had a minute to take it down to the cellar. Go grab a bottle. Or three."

Twelve

We really need to talk.

Tyce looked at his phone and sighed. Yeah, they did. *Where are you?*

Tyce waited for her reply message to appear on his screen. Sage was at The Den. Of course she was; when her world fell apart she had a place, people to run to. He didn't. Neither did Lachlyn.

I can come to you. Are you at your studio?

Tyce shook his head, a futile gesture since Sage couldn't see it.

Just finished dinner with my agent. I'll come to you.
Okay. I'll wait.

Tyce stepped off the pavement and raised his arm to

hail a taxi, cursing when the cab cruised past him. He jammed his bare hands into the pockets of his leather bomber jacket.

Another yellow cab turned down the street and Tyce held up his hand, thinking he'd lose it if the cab didn't stop. It did and he yanked the door open and climbed inside, tossing the address to the driver. He dropped his temple to the cool window and, staring at the rain-soaked city, he became aware of the headache pounding his temples.

Too much talking, he thought. His argument with Sage left a sour taste in his mouth and a stain on his soul. Every time he felt like they were moving forward, Sage pushed them backward.

Tyce felt the hard knot of tension in his stomach, knowing it was there because he was sure that she was going to call it off, to put them firmly in the friends and co-parent category.

He couldn't blame her because how could they keep taking five steps forward and six backward?

They'd been together for nearly a month and their expiration date was closing in on them. Sage had to be feeling antsy and, like before, she wanted out.

Tyce ordered his heart to pick itself up from the floor. Breaking up wasn't a bad move, Tyce rationalized, because he knew that being alone was so much easier. When he was alone he didn't feel drained. Lonely? Sure. Emotionally exhausted? No.

He hadn't been so at sea since before his mom died, and he'd forgotten what it felt like to *feel*. It wasn't fun. Tyce felt like he was walking along the edge of a precipice, one slip and he'd crash and break. Yeah, he could move on from this fight but there would always be another, and another…

He'd escaped a life of emotional drama; he'd run from relationships because he hated feeling like he was a vessel constantly being emptied and never refilled.

These fights, dealing with Sage's issues, sucked him dry. His thoughts were a million miles from his art, from his livelihood and he couldn't afford to be distracted. He had a bank account to replenish and he'd need every ounce of energy he had to deal with becoming a dad, being the best father he could.

So when Sage called it quits, he'd kiss her on the cheek and walk away because, dammit, *he was better off alone*. He knew how to be alone. Loneliness didn't scare him; emotion did. When he lived his life alone, he had control, he was in his comfort zone.

Sage, this up-and-down relationship, took him way out of his comfort zone. He'd started to rely on her when he'd only ever relied on himself.

That scared the living hell out of him. What had he been thinking?

Enough of that, Tyce suddenly decided. He couldn't, wouldn't do that anymore.

If she, he, they, called it quits today—and that was going to happen—then they'd have four or five months on their own to get used to the idea of not sleeping together—of not sharing a life together. They'd be able to act like mature adults as they figured out a way to raise their child together.

But he'd always want her...

Don't think about that, dingbat. Don't go there... You have to do this or else you are going to be miserable for the rest of your life.

Okay, more miserable, he clarified.

His decision made—God, it might be the right one but it still sucked—Tyce moved on to problem number two.

Before the week was out, their lives—all their lives, his, Sage's, Lachlyn's and the rest of the Ballantynes'—would be turned on their heads. Turned on their heads? Tyce snorted at his choice of words. There was a crap storm coming and there was no hiding from it.

Earlier Lachlyn called and told him that she'd been accosted by a reporter on her way to work and had been subjected to a barrage of questions. Was she Connor's daughter? Did the Ballantynes know? Was she owner of Lach-Ty, the company that'd made bulk purchases of Ballantyne shares? Lachlyn sounded like she was on the verge of tears and Tyce could hear the relentless yapping of the reporter in the background. He'd rapidly changed directions to go to Lachlyn, to see who was harassing her and to try to ascertain how much the reporter actually knew.

The guy knew a lot more than Tyce was comfortable with. When he arrived on Lachlyn's doorstep, Tyce got into his face, demanding to know where he'd stumbled across this information. The young reporter, at least a foot shorter than Tyce but ridiculously confident, refused to divulge his sources. Tyce endured fifteen minutes batting off his pointed questions, hoping for a hint of the source, but he earned nothing more than a headache.

After the reporter left, he spent another hour with Lachlyn, watching her pace her living room and listening to her rambling commentary about the Ballantynes and whether she wanted to become a member of the famous family or not. Of course she did; she liked all of them. She was just rattled by the reporter's verbal attack.

Whether she wanted to or not, Tyce knew that she no longer had a choice. The story was going to break sooner rather than later and all they could do was manage the process. Maybe they should just announce

Sage's pregnancy at the same time; it might get lost in the bigger news of a brand-new Ballantyne. If they announced it at a later stage, it would just give this story legs. Damned press, why couldn't they just leave them the hell alone to walk through the chaos of their lives on their own?

Realizing that the taxi had pulled up outside The Den, Tyce paid the cab driver and walked through the gate and up those imposing steps.

This would be the last time, for a while at least, that he'd stand in front of this door, the last time he'd see Sage.

They had to do this, he reminded himself, placing his hand on the door. Because a little hurt now would avoid open heart surgery later.

He didn't need her; he didn't anyone. He never had.

Sage, sitting on a stair halfway up to the next floor, saw Linc open the front door to The Den and looked through the slats down into the hallway and watched Tyce step into her childhood home.

This is it, she thought, do or die.

She knew that if she didn't ask for what she wanted, she had no chance of getting it, that if she didn't step forward she'd always be in the same place.

It was an easy concept to think about but putting those words into action was going to be an act of epic proportions.

Oh, God…she was about to risk her heart, her pride, her damned safety when she told Tyce that she wanted more, needed more… What the hell was she doing? Was she mad?

Do it anyway, a little voice said inside her. *Whether it's mad or not, safe or not, do it anyway.*

Sage stood up and Tyce immediately looked up, frustration and something that might be fear in his eyes. Sage walked down the staircase, her hand resting on her belly, noticing the purple stripes under Tyce's eyes.

Yeah, she hadn't slept much either.

"Hey," Sage said, stopping on the last step, her hand gripping the banister.

"Hey."

"Thanks for coming over."

Tyce jammed his hands into the front pockets of his jeans and shrugged. "Sure."

Sage heard footsteps and looked past Tyce's shoulder. Oh, God, the crew from downstairs were now all in the hall, their faces alight with curiosity. Did they really expect her to spill her soul in front of them? It was a strong possibility.

"We're all heading out," Amy said, holding a book of fabric swatches under her arm.

"Give us five seconds to grab our coats and we'll get out of your way," Piper said, her eyes darting between her face and Tyce.

Tyce waved them into the room. "Hell, come on in," he said. "When have Sage and I ever had a conversation that you lot haven't, in some way, been a part of?"

He sounded blasé but Sage could see the tension in his body, the anger in his eyes.

"That's not fair!" Sage hurled the words at him. She reined in her temper and concentrated on her breathing. If they started a fight now, if they waited for the crew to leave, she'd never say what she needed to.

Ignoring her family, Sage focused on Tyce, moving up to him and placing her hand on his heart. "I'm sorry. I was so completely out of line and I'm asking for your forgiveness."

Tyce pushed an agitated hand through his hair and

stepped back, breaking the contact between them. When she didn't speak again, Tyce lifted an eyebrow.

"That it?" he asked and gestured to the door. "If yes, then I'm going to head out because I'm pretty beat."

Sage heard, and ignored, the gasp from her audience. "No, that's not it," Sage said, forcing steel into her spine. Putting her hands behind her back, she twisted her fingers together.

"I can't do this anymore." Sage picked out her words, careful with each one.

Tyce handed her a quick, jerky nod. "Yeah, me neither. Let's just call it quits before this blows up in our faces."

Oh, God, oh, Jesus. Sage placed her hand on her stomach as his words smacked into her. He was breaking up with her?

What the hell?

Sage fought the instinct to back away, to agree with him. It would be so easy to smile, to nod, to agree with his assessment of the situation. To allow him to walk away. But that wasn't what she wanted. She wanted a lover, a partner, someone to live her life with, to share the momentous occasions and the ordinary.

She wanted him in her life on an everyday basis.

Sage shook her head. "I'm sorry you feel that way but that wasn't what I was going to say."

Tyce frowned. "Sorry?"

"I don't want to break up, in fact I'd like us to be together. Permanently."

Tyce just stared at her, shock on his face. Sage didn't know what else to say, how to express her heart, how to ask for what she wanted. Didn't he understand that she was willing to risk her stable, constant life for one filled with a lot of passion, a little uncertainty, risk? Didn't he understand how hard it was for her to be in this position, to love someone so much and be scared of being rejected? Words, pleading, desperate words bubbled in her throat and as they rose they burst apart and all that remained was a bitter taste on her tongue.

But she knew that if she didn't speak them, if she let them die, if she let him walk out that door without expressing them, she'd lose the moment forever.

Tyce took a step back and, operating on instinct, Sage grabbed the open sides of his leather bomber jacket to hold him in place. He started to pry her hands off but she tightened her grip and shook her head.

"All I'm asking you to do is to stand here and listen to me, just for a minute, maybe two. I know you are angry but you need to hear this. You need to hear *me*."

"You've got two minutes and that's it," Tyce growled.

"Okay, I'll keep it short."

Sage pulled in a deep breath and looked for her courage. This was too vital to mess up but her tongue was battling to form the words. Voice croaky, she got the first sentence out. "I love you. I think I fell in love with you the first time I saw you and I've loved nobody else, ever. I want you, I want us. You, me, our baby, a family."

Tyce didn't react and just stood statue still.

"Be my family, Tyce, within this family. Yeah, my brothers are annoying but you can handle them."

Still no response. Sage blew out a breath, dropped her hands and stared down at the floor. "If my love isn't enough, then walk out that door and we'll communicate about the baby through lawyers."

It was an ultimatum but she had to know, she couldn't live with maybes or possibilities. He either loved her or he didn't, he either wanted a life with her or didn't. It was actually a fairly simple choice.

Tyce shook his head. His words, when he finally

spoke, felt like splashes of acid on her soul. "It won't work, Sage. I'm sorry."

"Now it's your turn to push me away."

Tyce nodded. "It's easier to be alone... We both know this." Out of the corner of her eye, she saw Tate's hand shoot out to grab Linc's arm as he stepped forward. Really? Did Linc think that he could force Tyce to stay? Feeling shocked and saddened, Sage watched as Tyce opened the front door with a vicious yank. In the open doorway, he stopped abruptly and Sage couldn't help the surge of relief, the rush of hope.

Maybe he'd changed his mind; maybe he was prepared to give them a chance.

Instead of moving toward her, Tyce looked at Linc instead. "You should know that, somehow, certain members of the press have information about Lachlyn, about Lach-Ty and about her connection to Connor. Handle it any way you see fit."

"Tyce—" Linc stepped forward and Tyce shook his head and stepped into the cold, dark night.

Sage stared at the door for a long time before turning back to her family. She tried to smile but she could feel her chin wobbling, the tears sliding down her cheeks. "So," she said, trying for jaunty but failing miserably, "anyone have any idea what I can do about this gaping, bloody hole where my heart used to reside?"

Tyce, standing in his studio, released a violent curse and threw his custom-made palette knife across the room so that it bounced off a wall. Annoyed and frustrated, he punched his fist through the big blue abstract canvas before shoving his hands into his hair.

He had to get out of his studio, get out of the warehouse. He couldn't think in here, couldn't create, couldn't paint. The portraits of Sage were all facing the wall but he knew that they were there and he was constantly tempted to turn them around, to waste minutes and hours looking at her glorious face, remembering how they loved each other.

Your choice, moron.

It had been two weeks since he'd seen her and he'd spent every minute of each day missing her. The news was out that Lachlyn was a Ballantyne and the press had gone nuts, as he'd expected. Surprisingly, Sage's pregnancy wasn't reported on and, for big mercies, he was grateful.

He'd called Lachlyn to find out if she was okay, if she needed his help to deal with the press, but she'd moved into The Den and he heard that Linc had hired a bodyguard to accompany her wherever she went until the furor died down. The press had camped outside his warehouse for half a day but wet, snow-tinged rain had sent them scurrying back into their holes.

He had to get out of this place, get some fresh air. Tyce walked out of his studio and onto the catwalk and heard voices below him.

"You guys do know that this is breaking and entering, don't you? We could be arrested for this." Tyce immediately recognized Beckett's voice so he rested his forearms on the catwalk and waited to see what they were doing.

A voice he'd never heard before replied in a laconic drawl. "*I'll* be arrested and my PI license will be revoked since I picked the lock."

Linc walked further into the warehouse, followed by Jaeger and Beckett and lastly, a guy he didn't recognize. Unlike Sage's brothers, Mr. Ex-Military's eyes were darting around the warehouse looking for threats. His eyes shot upward and immediately clocked Tyce standing on the catwalk.

Super soldier—because the guy was a fighter, anyone could see that—gave him a quick nod.

"Whose stupid-ass idea was this anyway?" Jaeger muttered.

"Mine," Linc said, his voice rock hard. "I'm done with the situation and we're going to sort it out. I don't care if he has six black belts and a lightsaber, the imbecile is going to listen to us. If that takes one of us getting the crap kicked out of us, then so be it."

Tyce lifted his eyebrows at the desperation he heard in Linc's voice but he still remained quiet.

"Speak for yourself," Jaeger said.

"Reame can handle him," Beck said.

"You never told me that he had a couple of black belts," Reame said, looking amused. He looked up at Tyce. "Do you?"

Tyce almost smiled when three heads shot up to look at him. "A couple. In Tae Kwon Do and Krav Maga."

Reame swore and held up his hands. "He's all yours," he told the Ballantyne brothers, but Tyce knew whose side he'd be on if blows were traded. It wasn't his. As always, he was alone.

"What the hell do you want?" he demanded. "And what's so important that you broke into my place to tell me?"

"No breaking, only entering. I'm Reame Jepson, by the way."

He'd heard of Linc's oldest friend, the man the Ballantyne siblings had known since they were children. Not only were they great friends but the ex-soldier's company also handled the security for Ballantyne International and, from what he understood, many other Fortune 500 companies. Tyce gave Reame a brief nod but kept his eyes on Linc. "Say what you have to say, then get the hell out of my warehouse."

Linc nodded. "Okay. So this is what you need to know... Sage loves you."

She'd said that and maybe she believed it to be true but it wasn't enough. Love, sex, attraction wasn't enough. It was easier, better, safer to be on his own. "So?"

"We're here because my sister is miserable and looks like a corpse."

"Again, so? What do you want me to do?"

"I thought you said he was intelligent," Reame said to Jaeger, still sounding amused.

"I was wrong," Jaeger replied. "He's as dumb as a post."

Linc tossed him a curse and threw up his hands. "Can you all please concentrate?" He gripped the bridge of his nose with his fingers. Back in control, he looked up at Tyce again. "What I, we, want you to do is to tell her that you love her and then tell the world that you are thrilled to be the father of her child. I want to be able to tell the world that our family is expanding and we're excited that you and Lachlyn are part of our family. But really, I—we—just want Sage to be happy."

Tyce felt like he'd been hit by a piece of Canadian maple. He just stared at Linc, trying to assimilate his words. He knew that Linc was happy to have Lachlyn as part of the family but he never thought that Sage's brothers might feel the same about him.

Jaeger cleared his throat and Tyce's eyes bounced from his to Sage's second-eldest brother. "Did you ever consider that maybe your quest for Lachlyn to be part of a family was something you, subconsciously, needed? Maybe you were projecting your need for a family onto her."

"That's deep," Reame mocked, his mouth quirking.

"Shut up, half-wit," Jaeger muttered.

Tyce ignored their insults, thinking about Jaeger's comment. Was there any truth in his statement, any at all? Tyce gripped the banister as he considered his question and faced the obvious truth. Yes, he'd also wanted to be part of a family, wanted people he could lean on, people who would stand in his corner, who would fight for and with him.

He was used to walking alone, fighting his own battles. It was what he knew, what he felt comfortable doing and when Sage offered him something bigger, something he didn't know how to handle, he shot her down in flames. He thought he'd, one day, be okay with it. After all, he knew how to be an army of one.

He wasn't okay with it and walking away from her had frickin' ripped his heart and soul in two. Not to be melodramatic or anything.

"Do you know how much courage it took for Sage to open herself up to you, to ask for something more?" Linc demanded.

"She pushes people away!" Tyce protested, trying to grasp a straw that wasn't there.

"Sure, until she asked you to step in the ring with her. And you still haven't realized that when Sage pushes the hardest is when she most wants someone to push her back and not take no for an answer."

Jaeger sent him a cocky smile. "She might be our sister but she's a hell of a catch, Latimore. And you walked away from her? Moron."

Linc's fist slammed into Jaeger's biceps. "You are not helping!"

Tyce was barely aware of the hissed argument going on below him. He felt like Linc had handed him a new

pair of glasses and a fuzzy world had just become clear.
Linc's words resonated deep inside him and he knew
them to be pure truth.

Sage had stepped way out of her comfort zone to ask
him to love her and, God, he now, finally, could appreciate it. With this new knowledge, the last pieces of the
puzzle that made up the full picture of his lover, his only
love, fell into place.

She was his *it*, that indefinable, amazing, better part
of his soul. He needed to go to her, to sort this out, but...

Hell. There was a damn good chance that he'd blown
his opportunity with her, that she'd refuse to allow him
back into her life. Tyce pushed his shoulders back, determination coursing through him. To hell with that. He
did love her and Sage did need someone to push her
back, to not take no for an answer. And he was the man
to do it. He'd bucked the system all his life but, at the
most important time, he'd walked away from the most
vital thing in his life.

Jaeger, this one time, was right. Tyce was a moron.

He walked across the catwalk and jogged down the
stairs to the concrete floor below. He looked at Linc. "I
hear you."

"Hearing is one thing but are you going to do something about it?"

Tyce nodded. "I am."

Beck cleared his throat and sent him a smile that shriv-
eled his sack. "Good to know. Now, there's just one more
thing we need to do."

"What's that?"

Jaeger cocked his head. "You made Sage cry," he said,
sounding like he was ordering a cup of coffee.

Oh, crap. They said they'd rip him apart if he made
Sage cry and judging by their hard expressions, she'd

been crying a lot. Well, he was a fighter; he could tolerate three punches. Once it was done, they could all move on.

"Jesus," he muttered as he stood in front of the three Ballantyne brothers, bracing himself for what was to come. "Okay, take your hit."

Jaeger and Beck exchanged looks and Reame just grinned. Jaeger lifted a dark eyebrow, his eyes dark and cold. "You're going to make it right with Sage?"

Tyce nodded. "I already said that, didn't I? Yeah, I'm going to make it right." Damn, waiting for a punch was worse than the punch itself.

"If you hurt her again, we'll set Reame on you and he's a sneaky son of a bitch with mad skills. He'd do some damage," Beck told him, echoing Jaeger's icy demeanor.

"Understood." Tyce nodded. He looked at Linc, relieved that he'd avoided being hit by Sage's hotheaded brothers. They were more gracious than he might have been if some guy messed Lachlyn around. Linc looked like he always did, calm and controlled.

Okay then, dodged a bullet. Phew.

Tyce pulled in a breath, started to take his hands out of his pockets, thinking that he'd invite them upstairs. The big fist came out of nowhere, slammed into his jaw and he dropped backward, his butt connecting with the cold and very hard concrete. Crap, that hurt. Tyce looked up at Linc, who had a self-satisfied smile on his face.

Right, he hadn't seen that coming, Tyce thought, holding his jaw. "God, it hurts like a mother," he moaned.

"Good." Linc held out his hand to Tyce to pull him up. "You got coffee? We still have business to discuss before you go groveling back to Sage. And you will grovel."

"I will grovel," Tyce agreed, allowing Linc to pull him up. Holding his jaw, he lifted his eyebrows. "What business?"

Linc gestured to an amused Jaeger and Beck. "We're going to repay you the money you spent buying Lach-Ty shares. We inherited Connor's money so we'll spend it to reimburse you for Lachlyn's share of the company. We'll also add her as a co-owner of the assets we own jointly, like the art collection, the properties and the gem collection."

Holy crap, now he was really seeing stars. Tyce wiggled his jaw and started to lead them to the stairs. As his foot hit the bottom stair, an idea popped into his head. "If I ask you to, do you think you could get Sage somewhere for me?"

"Possibly," Linc replied.

"And instead of reimbursing me for what I paid for the shares, could we do a swap?"

"What swap?" Jaeger asked, his eyes still amused. Yeah, it would be a while before he lived that punch down.

"There's a red diamond ring in your family collection that Sage loves. I'd rather have the stone than the money because I'd like to put it on your sister's finger."

Linc looked at him, then looked at his brothers. Some sort of silent communication happened between them and Linc finally nodded. "I think we can work that out."

Reame was the last one up the stairs and Tyce heard his chuckle. "I have to say that life is never boring with you Ballantynes."

Now there was a statement Tyce fully agreed with.

Thirteen

Sage didn't want to go to an art exhibition and she deeply resented her bossy future sisters-in-law—sadly, her brothers were rubbing off on them—turning up at her apartment and bundling her into the shower. Amy had always been bossy so that wasn't anything new. Art exhibition, cocktails and clubbing, they told her. Just the five of them setting Manhattan alight.

Ugh. The last thing in the world she felt like doing was having a girls' night out: the point of which was to drink copious amounts of alcohol to make you forget about your lousy man and to give you the courage to dance with, possibly kiss, some random guy. She was pregnant and the thought of kissing anyone else but Tyce made her want to throw up. What she most wanted to do was to go over to Tyce's warehouse to beg him, again, to reconsider her offer, to plead with him to love her.

Stupid heart, wanting what it couldn't have. So, not

having an excuse to stay in—being pregnant and miserable wasn't a good enough excuse for the women in her life—she was out and about and wearing this silly dress with her bigger-than-normal boobs on display. It was a baby doll dress in a multicolored print and it effectively hid her blossoming baby bump.

"Take me home," Sage begged as they piled out of a taxi in front of the gallery where she and Tyce met again several months ago. She frowned at Piper. "Why are we here? They don't have an exhibition scheduled. And why are all the lights off?"

"It's an exhibition by a Norwegian installation artist, something to do with bioluminescence," Piper replied, tucking her hand into Sage's arm. "It's got to be dark to see the effect of the art."

"Don't want to go," Sage said, digging her heels in and looking at the cab. "I'm tired and my ankles are swollen and I have a backache."

Okay, she was whining but she couldn't do art, any type of art, right now. Was she asking too much to be allowed to nurse her weeping, bleeding heart in peace? Her mind was too full of Tyce as it was; memories of what they did and said to each other replayed on the megascreen of her mind, and coming back to this place, the place where they met, was simply too much for her.

She missed him so much she felt like she was walking around with a fraction of her heart.

"You're not far along enough to be complaining about a backache and swollen ankles," Cady told her, placing a hand in the middle of her back and pushing her toward the door.

"And you're not carrying twin boys so I have no sympathy for you," Piper added.

Tate rubbed Piper's big bump and smiled. "Fifteen

minutes, Sage, and then we will take you wherever you want to go."

Sage perked up at that suggestion. "Home?"

"If that's what you want," Tate replied as they walked up the flight of stairs to the front door. Tate pulled the door open and ushered her into the dark gallery. Sage rolled her eyes at the complete darkness. Honestly some of these exhibitions were just ridiculous and in trying to do something weird and wonderful they forgot to be practical. How was she supposed to see the art if she couldn't see two inches in front of her face? Anyone could trip, she could bump into people...

Speaking of, why didn't she hear any chatter, why was the gallery so very silent?

Light flooded into the room and Sage blinked, her eyes needing a moment to refocus. Well, that was going to ruin the impact of the bioluminescence.

Sage immediately, instinctively, looked right to the spot where she first met Tyce and frowned at the massive blue abstract oil hanging on the wall. It held the outline of what looked like a woman's back and bottom and to the right of where her head should be; she could clearly see a fist-size hole in the canvas.

Sage gasped, recognizing the painting as being the one Tyce pushed her against when he made love to her that night in his studio. Barely breathing, she slowly looked around the gallery and when she saw what was on the walls, the room started to spin.

All his portraits were hanging on the walls, a good portion of which were of her. There were some of his mom, some of Lachlyn, many of random New Yorkers—from street people to buskers and servers—and they were all fantastic. Only the big blue abstract painting and the portraits of her, and of Lachlyn and his mom, had not-for-sale stickers on them.

Sage held her face, in awe of his talent. It was a small exhibition, roughly and quickly tossed together but it was that much more powerful for it. This wasn't slick and smooth, it was rough and tender and…open. This was Tyce allowing the world to look inside.

That type of vulnerability took courage and heart. So much heart. Pity that she had no claim on it.

Sage heard heavy footsteps behind her and slowly turned to watch Tyce walk across the room toward her, hands in the pockets of a pair of black dress slacks, his white dress shirt tucked in. God, he was so beautiful, Sage thought, in the most masculine way. Tough and tall, with his enigmatic eyes and strong face.

Sage's first instinct was to throw herself into his arms, to gush over his art, to demand to know why he was holding this portrait exhibition. Why now? Why here, at this place from their past? Then she remembered that this was the man who'd tossed her love away, who'd rejected her heart. She didn't know why she was here—her sisters-in-law were in big, big trouble.

Overwhelmed, Sage turned around and headed toward the door, tears burning her eyes.

"Please don't cry. And please don't go," Tyce quietly said and she heard the longing and uncertainty in his voice. She stopped but kept her back to him, furiously brushing tears away with her fingertips.

Sage felt Tyce's big hands on her shoulders before his hands moved down her arms and encircled her waist, holding her against him. "Please don't go," he whispered, his mouth against her temple.

"Why should I stay?"

"You should stay—" Tyce's voice rumbled in her ear

"—because I am the world's biggest idiot for letting you go, then and now. You should stay because you make my world brighter, my thinking clearer, my world turn. You should stay because we have a baby to raise and I'd like us to do that together."

Sage felt the first sparks of hope and ruthlessly smothered them. She pushed against his arm and he immediately released her. He looked tired, she thought, drawn, his face whiter than normal. His eyes glinted with uncertainty and worry and an emotion that went deeper than that, that might be, dare she think it, love?

"I'm sorry I wasn't brave, before." Tyce cradled her face in his hands and kissed her softly, his lips giving hers a quick caress. She wanted more and judging by his tense body, so did he but he drew back and lifted his mouth from hers. "I want us to stop hoping and dreaming and be more."

Sage stared at him, uncomprehending.

"I want you in my bed and in my life, being the first person I see every morning and the last person I see at night. I want that for the rest of my life. I want our kid, or kids, to fly into our bedroom and jump on the bed, on us. I want us, Sage. You and me. I need you."

God, she felt so humbled, so in awe of his courage to do this again, to open himself up to her again.

"I know that your instinct is to push me away, Sage, but I'm asking you not to. And I'm telling you that if you do, every time you do, I'm going to hold you tighter, love you more." Tyce pushed her hair off her forehead and rested his head on hers. "One more time, Sage, please. Be brave, for us. Take a chance on me."

"Tyce." Sage gripped his arms, feeling dizzy.

"Is that another no?" Tyce asked, worry in his eyes. No, not worry, soul-deep fear.

"No, it's not a no. I mean... God, yes. Please." Sage knew that she was messing up her words and cursed her thick tongue.

"You're going to have to be clearer than that, honey."

Yes, she realized that. Holding his arms for balance, she looked up into his exotic, sexy face, the one she'd missed so much. "I'll be brave—I'm not going to push you away, I promise."

"And you don't break your promises," Tyce murmured as a spark returned to his eyes.

"I promise to love you, whether we have six weeks or sixty years."

"I'm planning on sixty years," Tyce told her.

Sage lifted her arms and wound them around Tyce's neck.

Tyce kissed her temple, her cheek, the corner of her mouth as she murmured the words she so needed to say, that he needed to hear. "I love you. I miss you. I'm so, so sorry I hurt you."

Their kisses were softer, gentler, simply tasting their new beginning, testing out how love felt in sunlight instead of shadows. Passion rumbled but they both pushed it away; passion was for later. This was something new, something that needed a little attention, a bit of nurturing.

Five, ten or twenty minutes could have passed when Tyce pulled his mouth and hands off her but was keeping her plastered against his long frame. Sage rested her cheek against his chest and nodded. This was where she belonged.

Tyce's hand stroked her hair. "We still need to talk, sweetheart."

Sage wrinkled her nose. "Do we have to? I'm kind of liking this."

Tyce smiled, pure sunshine in his eyes. Yeah, those shadows were gone and it was about time.

"I am too but we have a bunch of people in the back room and they are getting anxious."

"What? Who? Carol and her assistants?" Sage asked, thinking of the gallery owner and her staff. She gestured to his art. "And is this a real exhibition? Are you going to sell your portraits?"

Tyce looked around. "Yeah, I think so. Should I keep it low-key like this or give it to a high-end gallery?"

"I like this," Sage replied, walking into the middle of the room but keeping her hand in his. "I think the portraits need a smaller, more intimate space. I think you should keep it as it is but—" she pointed to the ruined abstract in that prominent position "—that goes." She sent him an amused look. "I thought we had an agreement about you not exhibiting anything that had any connection to our love life."

Tyce wrapped his arm around her waist. "It stays. It makes me laugh."

"It's awful, Tyce," Sage protested.

"Yeah, but everyone will wonder why it's there and will concoct all sorts of crazy ideas about it and only you and I will know the truth."

For him to leave that awful painting hanging on the wall was his way of telling her, and the world, that he was finally secure about his talent as an artist, his place in the world. "But why does it have a hole in it?" Sage asked.

"I was standing in front of it, thinking about you, and I was so pissed off that I punched it."

"Talking about punches, why do you have a bruise on your jaw?" Sage asked, her eyes narrowing.

"Oh, that's courtesy of your brother," Tyce replied, his tone blasé.

"Jaeger punched you?" Sage shrieked.

"Linc, and it happened five minutes before he told me that you Ballantynes are repaying me for Lachlyn's shares. Was that your idea?"

Sage wrinkled her nose. "If Connor had known about Lachlyn then that's what would have happened. The money should be with you in a month or two—did Linc explain that?"

Tyce's hand caressed her back. "Some of the money will be in my back account. Not much but more than I had before."

Sage stepped away from him and put her hands on her hips. "What do you mean by that? I know that we all signed papers to transfer our share of the assets, to liquidate the cash."

Tyce's hands slid into the pockets of his pants. "Yep, but I'm diverting some of that money back into the Ballantyne coffers. Well, Linc and I are still arguing about this. He says that the object in question belongs to you, that it's right for you to own it, but I'd still like to pay for it."

Object? What object? What on earth was he talking about? Tyce opened his hand and Sage looked at a small square of white tissue paper resting in his palm.

"Trying to buy a ring for a jewelry designer is a bitch so I thought that I'd try something else."

"A ring?" Sage asked, knowing that she sounded stupid but not quite believing what she was hearing.

Tyce flipped open the tissue paper to reveal the brilliance of the red diamond flower ring. "Like this stone, you are rare and precious and you take my breath away. Will you please, please marry me?"

Sage stared at the ring, tears burning her eyes. "My mom's ring. Oh my God, Tyce, that's my mom's red diamond!" Sage reached out to pick up the ring but Tyce snapped his fist closed. Sage jerked her head up and saw the mischief in his eyes.

"You Ballantynes… You see gemstones and everything instantly goes out your head." Tyce waved his closed fist in front of her face. "Say yes and you can have the ring."

"Are you bribing me?" Sage demanded, smiling, her hand holding his fist.

"Apparently so," Tyce said. "So, are you going to marry me for your mom's ring?"

Sage reached up to hold his face. "I am going to marry you because I am stupidly in love with you and I intend to stay that way for the rest of my life. Because I can't imagine myself being with anyone else but you." She smiled, teasing him. "But I can't lie, the ring is a factor."

Tyce kissed her, his lips curving against her mouth. "I'll take it. Love you, babe."

"And it's about damn time!"

Sage whipped around to see her brothers, their wives, Amy, Reame and Lachlyn walking from the storeroom at the back, the men carrying bottles of champagne and the women carrying glasses.

After kissing Lachlyn—she had another sister, yay!— Sage narrowed her eyes and looked at Tyce. "Why are they here?"

"I needed their help to set this all up, to get you here," Tyce said, shrugging. "Apparently they have their uses."

Sage heard the affection under his sarcasm and thought that he and her brothers would be just fine. She, however, was not. Sage walked up to Linc and poked her finger in his chest. "What the hell were you thinking, punching Tyce? Seriously, what is wrong with you?"

Linc brushed her hand away. "He deserved it." Linc

kissed her cheek and gave her a quick hug. Sage hugged him back and felt him stiffen in her arms. She pulled away and found him looking at the destroyed canvas. "What the hell is that?" he demanded.

Jaeger also tipped his head to the side and sent Tyce a look of pure confusion. "I don't get it, Latimore. They pay you for this garbage?"

Tyce and Sage exchanged a long look filled with everything they were going to spend the rest of their lives saying. *I love you. You're gorgeous. Can't wait to get you naked.*

Tyce laughed and shrugged. "Yep. Strange but true."

"What's it called?" Jaeger asked, moving closer to the wall.

Sage's eyes didn't waver from Tyce's face. "It's called *Love, Lost and Found.*"

Tyce's eyes warmed and softened at her answer and he wore his love and devotion for her like a coat of armor. She'd finally found her warrior and damn, it felt amazing.

"You Ballantynes are so weird," Reame said, popping the cork on a bottle of champagne. He looked at Lachlyn and raised his brows. "Their madness is contagious. Run... Run now."

Tyce grinned at Reame. "It's not madness—it's love." He looked from Reame to Lachlyn and smiled. "You two should try it—it's not so bad."

Reame and Lachlyn looked equally horrified and Sage smiled at their expression. Actually, come to think of it, her new sister and the man Sage considered her fourth brother looked really good together...

* * * * *

*If you liked Sage's story,
pick up these other*
BALLANTYNE BILLIONAIRES *books from
Joss Wood!*

*HIS EX'S WELL-KEPT SECRET
REUNITED... AND PREGNANT
THE CEO'S NANNY AFFAIR*

as well as reader favorite
MARRIED TO THE MAVERICK MILLIONAIRE

Available now from Mills & Boon Desire!

MILLS & BOON®

PASSIONATE AND DRAMATIC LOVE STORIES

LET'S TALK
Romance

For exclusive extracts, competitions
and special offers, find us online:

f facebook.com/millsandboon

⊚ @millsandboonuk

🐦 @millsandboon

Or get in touch on 0844 844 1351*

For all the latest titles coming soon, visit
millsandboon.co.uk/nextmonth

Want even more
ROMANCE?

Join our bookclub today!

'Mills & Boon books, the perfect way to escape for an hour or so.'

Miss W. Dyer

'Excellent service, promptly delivered and very good subscription choices.'

Miss A. Pearson

'You get fantastic special offer and the chance to get books before they hit the shops'

Mrs V Hall

**Visit millsandbook.co.uk/Bookclub
and save on brand new books.**

MILLS & BOON